FOR T

“Exhilarati
readers hoo

—*Publishers Weekly*

“The propulsively paced plot has a definite Lifetime Movie Channel vibe, but Jackson effectively juices things up with plenty of sexy suspense and a generous amount of high-octane thrills.”

—*Booklist*

PARANOID

“Jackson gradually builds up the layers of this tangled psychological thriller, leading to a stunning finale. Jackson knows how to keep readers guessing and glued to the page.”

—*Publishers Weekly*

LIAR, LIAR

“The author’s managing of the past and present separately is an effective method of clue dangling to keep readers in the dark until the huge OMG reveal. Fans of Lisa Gardner, Paula Hawkins, and J.T. Ellison will devour this one-sitting nail-biter.”

—*Library Journal* (starred review)

YOU WILL PAY

“This suspenseful thriller is packed with jaw-dropping twists.”

—*In Touch Weekly*

NEVER DIE ALONE

“Jackson definitely knows how to keep readers riveted.”

—*Mystery Scene*

TELL ME

“Absolutely tension filled . . . Jackson is on top of her game.”

—*Suspense Magazine*

Books by Lisa Jackson

Stand-Alones

SEE HOW SHE DIES
FINAL SCREAM
RUNNING SCARED
WHISPERS
TWICE KISSED
UNSPOKEN
DEEP FREEZE
FATAL BURN
MOST LIKELY TO DIE
WICKED GAME
WICKED LIES
SOMETHING WICKED
WICKED WAYS
WICKED DREAMS
SINISTER
WITHOUT MERCY
YOU DON'T WANT TO KNOW
CLOSE TO HOME
AFTER SHE'S GONE
REVENGE
YOU WILL PAY
OMINOUS
BACKLASH
RUTHLESS
ONE LAST BREATH
LIAR, LIAR
PARANOID
ENVIOUS
LAST GIRL STANDING
DISTRUST
ALL I WANT FROM SANTA
AFRAID
THE GIRL WHO SURVIVED
GETTING EVEN

Cahill Family Novels

IF SHE ONLY KNEW
ALMOST DEAD
YOU BETRAYED ME

Rick Bentz/Reuben Montoya Novels

HOT BLOODED
COLD BLOODED
SHIVER
ABSOLUTE FEAR
LOST SOULS
MALICE
DEVIOUS
NEVER DIE ALONE

Pierce Reed/ Nikki Gillette Novels

THE NIGHT BEFORE
THE MORNING AFTER
TELL ME
THE THIRD GRAVE

Selena Alvarez/ Regan Pescoli Novels

LEFT TO DIE
CHOSEN TO DIE
BORN TO DIE
AFRAID TO DIE
READY TO DIE
DESERVES TO DIE
EXPECTING TO DIE
WILLING TO DIE

Published by Kensington Publishing Corp.

GETTING EVEN

LISA JACKSON

ZEBRA BOOKS
KENSINGTON PUBLISHING CORP.
www.kensingtonbooks.com

ZEBRA BOOKS are published by

Kensington Publishing Corp.
119 West 40th Street
New York, NY 10018

This book is a work of fiction. Names, characters, businesses, organizations, places, events, and incidents either are the product of the author's imagination or are used fictitiously. Any resemblance to actual persons, living or dead, events, or locales is entirely coincidental.

To the extent that the image or images on the cover of this book depict a person or persons, such person or persons are merely models, and are not intended to portray any character or characters featured in the book.

If you purchased this book without a cover you should be aware that this book is stolen property. It was reported as "unsold and destroyed" to the Publisher and neither the Author nor the Publisher has received any payment for this "stripped book."

All Kensington titles, imprints, and distributed lines are available at special quantity discounts for bulk purchases for sales promotion, premiums, fund-raising, and educational or institutional use.

Special book excerpts or customized printings can also be created to fit specific needs. For details, write or phone the office of the Kensington Sales Manager: Kensington Publishing Corp., 119 West 40th Street, New York, NY 10018. Attn. Sales Department. Phone: 1-800-221-2647.

ZEBRA BOOKS and the Z logo Reg. U.S. Pat. & TM Off.

First Printing: March 2023
Yesterday's Lies was published previously by Harlequin in *Proof of Innocence* by Lisa Jackson in 2014.
Zachary's Law was published previously by Silhouette in 1986.

ISBN-13: 978-1-4201-5554-9
ISBN-13: 978-1-4201-5555-6 (eBook)

10 9 8 7 6 5 4 3 2 1

Printed in the United States of America

Contents

Yesterday's Lies

Chapter One

THE SWEATING HORSE snorted as if in premonition and his dark ears pricked forward before flattening to his head. Tory, who was examining the bay's swollen hoof, felt his weight shift suddenly. "Steady boy," she whispered. "I know it hurts. . . ."

The sound of boots crunching on the gravel near the paddock forced Tory's eyes away from the tender hoof and toward the noise. Keith was striding purposefully toward her, his lanky rawboned frame tense, the line of his mouth set.

"Trask McFadden is back."

The words seemed to thunder across the windswept high plateau and echo in Tory's ears. Her back stiffened at her brother's statement, and she felt as if her entire world was about to dissolve, but she tried to act as if she was unaffected. Her fingers continued their gentle probing of the bay stallion's foreleg and her eyes searched inside the swollen hoof for any sign of infection.

"Tory, for God's sake," Keith called a little more loudly as he leaned over the top rail of the fence around the enclosed paddock, "did you hear what I said?"

Tory stood, patted the nervous stallion affectionately and took in a steadying breath before opening the gate. It groaned on its ancient hinges. She slipped through the dusty rails and faced her younger brother. His anxious expression said it all.

So Trask was back. After all these years. Just as he said he would be. She suddenly felt cold inside. Shifting her gaze from the nervous bay stallion limping within the enclosed paddock to the worried contours of Keith's young face, Tory frowned and shook her head. The late-afternoon sun caught in her auburn hair, streaking it with fiery highlights of red and gold.

"I guess we should have expected this, sooner or later," she said evenly, though her heart was pounding a sharp double time. Nervously wiping her hands on her jeans, she tried to turn her thoughts back to the injured Quarter Horse, but the craggy slopes of the distant Cascade Mountains caught her attention. Snow-covered peaks jutted brazenly upward against the clear June sky. Tory had always considered the mountains a symbolic barrier between herself and Trask. The Willamette Valley and most of the population of the state of Oregon resided on the western side—the other side—of the Cascade Mountains. The voting public were much more accessible in the cities and towns of the valley. The unconventional Senator McFadden rarely had to cross the mountains when he returned to his native state. Everything he needed was on the other side of the Cascades.

Now he was back. Just as he had promised. Tory's stomach knotted painfully at the thought. *Damn him and his black betraying heart.*

Keith studied his older sister intently. Her shoulders slumped slightly, and she brushed a loose strand of hair away from her face and back into the ponytail she always wore while working on the Lazy W. She leaned over the split rail, her fists balled beneath her jutted chin and her jaw tense. Keith witnessed the whitening of the skin over her cheekbones and thought for a moment that she might faint; but when her gray-green eyes turned back to him they seemed calm, hiding any emotions that might be raging within her heart.

Trask. Back. After all these years and all the lies. Tory shook her head as if to deny any feelings she might still harbor for him.

"You act as if you don't care," Keith prodded, though he had noticed the hardening of her elegant features. He leaned backward; his broad shoulders supported by the rails of the fence. His arms were crossed over his chest, his dusty straw Stetson was pushed back on his head and dark sweat-dampened hair protruded unevenly from beneath the brim as he surveyed his temperamental sister.

"I can't let it bother me one way or the other," she said with a dismissive shrug. "Now, about the stallion . . ." She pointed to the bay. "His near foreleg—I think it's laminitis. He's probably been putting too much weight on the leg because of his injury to the other foreleg." When Keith didn't respond, she clarified. "Governor's foot is swollen with founder, acute laminitis. His temperature's up, he's sweating and blowing and he won't bear any weight on the leg. We're lucky so far, there's no sign of infection—"

Keith made a disgusted sound and held up his palm in frustration with his older sister. *What the hell was the matter with her? Hadn't she heard him? Didn't she care?* "Tory, for Christ's sake, listen to me and forget about the horse for a minute! McFadden always said he'd come back; *for you.*"

Tory winced slightly. Her gray-green eyes narrowed against a slew of painful memories that made goose bumps rise on her bare arms. "That was a long time ago," she whispered, once again facing her brother.

"Before the trial."

Closing her eyes against the agony of the past, Tory leaned heavily against the split cedar rails and forced her thoughts to the present. Though her heart was thudding wildly within her chest, she managed to remain outwardly calm. "I don't think McFadden will bother us" she said.

"I'm not so sure. . . ."

She forced a half smile she didn't feel. "Come on, Keith, buck up. Let's not borrow trouble. We've got enough as it is, don't you think?" Once again she cast a glance at the bay stallion. He was still sweating and blowing. She had examined him carefully and was thankful that there was no evidence of infection in the swollen tissues of his foot.

Keith managed to return his sister's encouraging grin but it was short-lived. "Yeah, I suppose we don't need any more trouble. Not now," he acknowledged before his ruddy complexion darkened and his gray eyes lost their sparkle. "We've had our share and we know who to thank for it," he said, removing his hat and pushing his sweaty hair off his brow. Dusty streaks lined his forehead. "All the problems began with McFadden, you know."

Tory couldn't deny the truth in her younger brother's words. "Maybe—"

"No maybe about it, Tory. If it hadn't been for McFadden, Dad might still be alive." Keith's gray eyes clouded with hatred and he forced his hat onto his head with renewed vengeance.

"You can't be sure of that," Tory replied, wondering why she was defending a man she had sworn to hate.

"Oh no?" he threw back at her. "Well, I can be sure of one thing! Dad wouldn't have spent the last couple of years of his life rotting in some stinking jail cell if McFadden's testimony hadn't put him there."

Tory's heart twisted with a painful spasm of guilt. "That was my fault," she whispered quietly.

"The hell it was," Keith exploded. "McFadden was the guy who sent Dad up the river on a bum rap."

"You don't have to remind me of that."

"I guess not," he allowed. "The bastard used you, too." Keith adjusted his Stetson and rammed his fists into his pockets. "Whatever you do, Sis," he warned, "don't stick up for him. At least not to me. The bottom line is that Dad is dead."

Tory smiled bitterly at the irony of it all and smoothed a wisp of hair out of her face. She had made the mistake of defending Trask McFadden once. It would never happen again. "I won't."

She lifted her shoulders and let out a tortured breath of air. *How many times had she thought about the day that Trask would return? How many times had she fantasized about him? In one scenario she was throwing him off her property, telling him just what kind of a bastard he was; in another she was making passionate love with him near the pond. . . .* She cleared her throat and said, "Just because he's back in town doesn't mean that Trask is going to stir up any trouble."

Keith wasn't convinced. "Trouble follows him around."

"Well, it won't follow him here."

"How can you be so sure?"

"Because he's not welcome." Determination was evident in her eyes and the thrust of her small proud chin. She avoided Keith's narrowed eyes by watching a small whirlwind kick up the dust and dry pine needles in the corral. Governor snorted impatiently and his tail switched at the ever-present flies.

Keith studied his sister dubiously. Though Tory was six years his senior, sometimes she seemed like a little kid to him. Especially when it came to Trask McFadden. "Does *he* know that you don't want him here?"

Tory propped her boot on the bottom rail. "I think I made it pretty clear the last time I saw him."

"But that was over five years ago."

Tory turned her serious gray-green eyes on her brother. "Nothing's changed since then."

"Except that he's back and he's making noise about seeing you again."

Tory's head snapped upward and she leveled her gaze at her brother. "What kind of noise?"

"The kind that runs through the town gossip mill like fire."

"I don't believe it. The man's not stupid, Keith. He knows how I—we feel about him. He's probably back in town visiting Neva. He has before."

"And all those times he never once mentioned that he'd come for you. Until now. He means business. The only reason he came back here was for you!"

"I don't think—"

"Damn it, Tory," Keith interjected. "For once in your life, just listen to me. I was in town last night, at the Branding Iron."

Tory cast Keith a concerned glance. He scowled and continued, "Neva's spread it around town. She said Trask was back. For you!"

Tory's heart nearly stopped beating. Neva McFadden was Trask's sister-in-law, the widow of his brother, Jason. It had been Jason's mysterious death that had started all the trouble with her father. Tory still ached for the grief that Neva McFadden and her small son had borne, but she knew in her heart that her father had had no part in Jason McFadden's death. Calvin

Wilson had been sent to prison an innocent victim of an elaborate conspiracy, all because of Trask McFadden's testimony and the way Tory had let him use her. Silent white-hot rage surged through Tory's blood.

Keith was still trying desperately to convince her of Trask's intentions. "Neva wouldn't lie about something like this, Tory. McFadden will come looking for you."

"Great," she muttered, before slapping the fence. "Look, I want you to tell Rex and any of the other hands that Trask McFadden has no business on this property. If he shows up, we'll throw him off."

"Just like that?"

"Just like that." She snapped her fingers and her carefully disguised anger flickered in her eyes.

Keith rubbed his jaw. "How do you propose to do that? Threaten him with a rifle aimed at his head?"

"If that's what it takes."

Keith raised a skeptical brow. "You're serious?"

Tory laughed nervously. "Of course not. We'll just explain that if he doesn't remove himself, we'll call the sheriff."

"A lot of good that will do. We call the sheriff's office and what do you suppose will happen? Nothing! Paul Barnett's hands are tied. He owes his career—and maybe his whole political future—to McFadden. Who do you think backed Paul in the last election? McFadden." Keith spit out Trask's name as if it were a bitter poison. "Even if he wanted to, how in the hell would Paul throw a United States senator out on his ear?" Keith added with disgust in his voice, "Paul Barnett is in McFadden's back pocket."

"You make it sound as if Trask owns the whole town."

"Near enough; everyone in Sinclair thinks he's a god,

y'know. Except for you—and sometimes I'm not so sure about that."

Tory couldn't help but laugh at the bleak scene Keith was painting. "Lighten up," she advised, her white teeth flashing against her tanned skin. "This isn't a bad western movie where the sheriff and the townspeople are all against a poor defenseless woman trying to save her ranch—"

"Sometimes I wonder."

"Give me a break, Keith. If Trask McFadden trespasses—"

"We're all in big trouble. Especially you."

Tory's fingers drummed nervously on the fence. She tried to change the course of the conversation. "Like I said I think you're borrowing trouble," she muttered. "What Trask McFadden says and what he does are two different things. He's a politician. Remember?"

Keith's mouth twisted into a bitter grin and his eyes narrowed at the irony. "Yeah, I remember; and I know that the only reason that bastard got elected was because of his testimony against Dad and the others. He put innocent men in jail and ended up with a cushy job in Washington. What a great guy."

Tory's teeth clenched together and a headache began to throb in her temples. "I'm sure that central Oregon will soon bore our prestigious senator," she said, her uncertainty carefully veiled. "He'll get tired of rubbing elbows with the constituents in Sinclair and return to D.C. where he belongs, and that's the last we'll hear of him."

Keith laughed bitterly. "You don't believe that any more than I do. If Trask McFadden's back it's for a reason and one reason only: you, Tory." He slouched against the fence, propped up by one elbow. "So, what are you going to do about it?"

"Nothing."

"Nothing?"

Her gray-green eyes glittered dangerously. "Let's just wait and see. If Trask has the guts to show up, I'll deal with him then."

Keith's lower lip protruded and he squinted against the glare of the lowering sun. "I think you should leave. . . ."

"What!"

"Take a vacation, get out of this place. You deserve one, anyway; you've been working your tail off for the past five years. And, if McFadden comes here and finds out that you're gone for a few weeks, he'll get the idea and shove off."

"That's running, Keith," Tory snapped. "This is my home. I'm not running off like a frightened rabbit, for crying out loud. Not for Trask McFadden, not for any man." Determination underscored her words. Pride, fierce and painful, blazed in her eyes and was evident in the strong set of her jaw.

"He's a powerful man," Keith warned.

"And I'm not afraid of him."

"He hurt you once before."

Tory squared her shoulders. "That was a long time ago." She managed a tight smile and slapped her brother affectionately on his shoulder. "I'm not the same woman I used to be. I've grown up a lot since then."

"I don't know," Keith muttered, remembering his once carefree sister and the grin she used to wear so easily. "History has a way of repeating itself."

Tory shook her head and forced a smile, hoping to disarm her younger brother. She couldn't spend the rest of her life worrying about Trask and what he would or wouldn't do. She had already spent more hours than she would admit thinking about him and the shambles he'd attempted to make of her life. Just because he was back in Sinclair . . . "Let's forget about McFadden for a while, okay? Tell Rex I want to try ice-cold poultices on our friend here." She nodded in the direction of the bay stallion. "And I don't want him ridden until we determine if he needs a special shoe." She paused and her eyes rested on the sweating bay. "But he should be walked at least twice a day. More if possible."

"As if I have the time—"

Tory cut him off. "Someone around here must have the time," she snapped, thinking about the payroll of the ranch and how difficult it was to write the checks each month. The Lazy W was drowning in red ink. It had been since Calvin Wilson had been sent to prison five years before. *By Trask McFadden.* "Have someone, maybe Eldon, if you don't have the time, walk Governor," she said, her full lips pursing.

Keith knew that he was being dismissed. He frowned, cast his sister one final searching look, pushed his hat lower on his head and started ambling off toward the barn on the other side of the dusty paddock. He had delivered his message about Trask McFadden. The rest was up to Tory.

TRASK PACED IN the small living room feeling like a caged animal. His long strides took him to the window where he would pause, study the distant snow-laden mountains through the paned glass and then return to the other side of the room to stop before the stone fireplace where Neva was sitting in a worn rocking chair. The rooms in the house were as neat and tidy as the woman who owned them and just being in the house—Jason's house—made Trask restless. His business in Sinclair wasn't pleasant and he had been putting it off for more than twelve hours. Now it was time to act.

"What good will come of this?" Neva asked, shaking her head with concern: Her small, beautiful face was set in a frown and her full lips were pursed together in frustration.

"It's something I've got to do." Trask leaned against the mantel, ran his fingers under the collar of his shirt and pressed his thumb thoughtfully to his lips as he resumed pacing.

"Sit down, will you?" Neva demanded, her voice uncharacteristically sharp. He stopped midstride and she smiled, feeling suddenly foolish. "I'm sorry," she whispered, "I just hate to see you like this, all screwed up inside."

"I've always been this way."

"Hmph." She didn't believe it for a minute and she suspected that Trask didn't either. Trask McFadden was one of the few men she had met in her twenty-five years who knew his own mind and usually acted accordingly. Recently, just the opposite had been true and Neva would have had to have been a blind woman not to see that Trask's discomfiture was because of Tory Wilson. "And you think seeing Tory again will change all that?" She didn't bother to hide her skepticism.

"I don't know."

"But you're willing to gamble and find out?"

He nodded, the lines near the corners of his blue eyes crinkling.

"No matter what the price?"

"What's that supposed to mean?"

Neva stared at the only man she cared for. Trask had helped her, been at her side in those dark lonely nights after Jason's death. He had single-handedly instigated an investigation into the "accident," which had turned out to be the premeditated murder of her husband. Though Trask had been Jason's brother, his concern for Neva had gone beyond the usual bounds and she knew she would never forget his kindness or stop loving him.

Neva owed Trask plenty, but she couldn't seem to get through to him. A shiver of dread raced down her spine. Trask looked tired, she thought with concern, incredibly tired, as if he were on some new crusade. His hair had darkened from the winter in Washington, D.C., and the laugh lines near his mouth and eyes seemed to have grown into grooves of disenchantment. His whole attitude seemed jaded these days, she mused. Maybe that's what happened when an honest man became a senator. . . .

At that moment, Nicholas raced into the room and breathlessly made a beeline for his mother. "Mom?" He slid to a stop, dusty tennis shoes catching on the polished wood floor.

"What, honey?" Neva stopped rocking and rumpled Nicholas's dark hair as he scrambled into her lap.

"Can I go over to Tim's? We're going to build a tree house out in the back by the barn. His mom says it's okay with her. . . ."

Neva lifted her eyes and smiled at the taller boy scurrying after Nick. He was red-haired and gangly, with a gaping hole where his two front teeth should have been. "If you're sure it's all right with Betty."

"Yeah, sure," Tim said. "Mom likes it when Nick comes over. She says it keeps me out of her hair."

"Does she?" Neva laughed and turned her eyes back to Nicholas. At six, he was the spitting image of his father. Wavy brown hair, intense blue eyes glimmering with hope—so much like Jason. "Only a little while, okay? Dinner will be ready in less than an hour."

"Great!" Nicholas jumped off her lap and hurried out of the living room. The two boys left as quickly as they had appeared. Scurrying footsteps echoed down the short entry hall.

"Remember to shut the door," Neva called, but she heard the front door squeak open and bang against the wall.

"I'll get it." Trask, glad for the slightest opportunity to escape the confining room, followed the boys, shut the door and returned. Facing Neva was more difficult than he had imagined, and he wondered for the hundredth time if he were doing the right thing. Neva didn't seem to think so.

She turned her brown eyes up to Trask's clouded gaze when he reentered the room. "That," she said, pointing in the direction that Nicholas had exited, "is the price you'll pay."

"Nick?"

"His innocence. Right now, Nicholas doesn't remember what happened five years ago," Neva said with a frown. "But if you go searching out Tory Wilson, all that will change. The gossip will start all over again; questions will be asked. Nick will have to come to terms with the fact that his father was murdered by a group of men whose relatives still live around Sinclair."

"He will someday anyway."

Neva's eyes pleaded with Trask as she rose from the chair. "But not yet, Trask. He's too young. Kids can be cruel. . . . I just want to give him a few more years of innocence. He's only six."

"This has nothing to do with Nick."

"*The hell it doesn't!* It has everything to do with him. His father was killed because he knew too much about that Quarter Horse swindle." Neva wrapped her arms around her waist as if warding off a sudden chill, walked to one of the windows and stared outside. She stared at the Hamiltons' place across the street, where Nicholas was busily creating a tree house, blissfully unaware of the brutal circumstances surrounding his father's death. She trembled. "I don't want to go through it all again," Neva whispered, turning away from the window.

Trask shifted from one foot to the other as his conscience twinged. His thick brows drew together into a pensive scowl and he pushed impatient fingers through the coarse strands of his brown hair. "What if I told you that one of Jason's murderers might have escaped justice?"

Neva had been approaching him. She stopped dead in her tracks. "What do you mean?"

"Maybe there were four people involved in the conspiracy—not just three."

"I—I don't understand."

Trask tossed his head back and stared up at the exposed beams of the cedar ceiling. The last thing he wanted to do was hurt Neva. She and the boy had been through too much already, he thought. "What I'm saying is that I have reason to believe that one of the conspirators might never have been named. In fact, it's a good guess that he got away scot-free."

Neva turned narrowed eyes up to her husband's brother. "Who?"

"I don't know."

"This isn't some kind of a morbid joke—"

"Neva," he reproached, and she had only to look into his serious blue eyes to realize that he would never joke about anything as painful and vile as Jason's unnecessary death.

"You thought there were only three men involved. So what happened to change your mind?"

Knowing that he was probably making the biggest blunder of his short career in politics, Trask reached into his back pocket and withdrew the slightly wrinkled photocopy of the anonymous letter he had received in Washington just a week earlier. The letter had been his reason for returning—or so he had tried to convince himself for the past six days.

Neva took the grayish document and read the few sentences before shaking her head and letting her short blond curls fall around her face in neglected disarray. "This is a lie," she said aloud. The letter quivered in her small hand. "All the men connected with Jason's death were tried and convicted. Judge Linn Benton and George Henderson are in the pen serving time and Calvin Wilson is dead."

"So who does that leave?" he demanded.

"No one."

"That's what I thought."

"But now you're not so sure?"

"Not until I talk to Victoria Wilson." *Tory.* Just the thought of seeing her again did dangerous things to his mind. "She's the only person I know who might have the answers. The swindle took place on some property her father owned on Devil's Ridge."

Neva's lower lip trembled and her dark eyes accused him of crimes better left unspoken. Trask had used Victoria Wilson to convict her father; Neva doubted that Tory would be foolish enough to trust him again. "And you think that talking with Tory will clear this up?" She waved the letter in her hand as if to emphasize her words. "This is a prank, Trask. Nothing more. Leave it alone." She fell back into the rocker still clenching the letter and tucked her feet beneath her.

Trask silently damned himself for all the old wounds he was about to reopen. He reached forward, as if to stroke Neva's bent head, but his fingers curled into a fist of frustration. "I wish I could, Neva," he replied as he gently removed the letter from her hand and reached for the suede jacket he'd carelessly thrown over the back of the couch several hours earlier. He hooked one finger under the collar and tossed the jacket over his shoulder. "God, I wish I could."

"You and your damned ideals," she muttered. "Nothing will bring Jason back. But this . . . vendetta you're on . . . could hurt my son."

"Even if what I find out is the truth?"

Neva closed her eyes. She raised her hand and waved him off. She knew there was no way to talk sense to him when he had his mind made up. "Do what you have to do, Trask," she said wearily. "You will anyway. Just remember that Nicholas is the one who'll suffer." Her voice was low; a warning. "You and I—we'll survive. We always do. But what about Nick? He's in school now and this is a small town, a very small town. People talk."

Too much, Trask thought, silently agreeing. *People talk too damned much.* With an angry frown, he turned toward the door.

Neva heard his retreating footsteps echoing down the hall, the door slamming shut and finally the sound of an engine sparking to life then rumbling and fading into the distance.

Chapter Two

AS DUSK SETTLED over the ranch, Tory was alone. And that's the way she wanted it.

She sat on the front porch of the two-story farmhouse that she had called home for most of her twenty-seven years. Rough cedar boards, painted a weathered gray, were highlighted by windows trimmed in a deep wine color. The porch ran the length of the house and had a sloping shake roof supported by hand-hewn posts. The house hadn't changed much since her father was forced to leave. Tory had attempted to keep the house and grounds in good repair . . . to please him when he was released. Only that wouldn't happen. Calvin Wilson had been dead for nearly two years, after suffering a painful and lonely death in the penitentiary for a crime he didn't commit. All because she had trusted Trask McFadden.

Tory's jaw tightened, her fingers clenched over the arm of the wooden porch swing that had been her father's favorite. Guilt took a stranglehold of her throat. If only she hadn't believed in Trask and his incredible blue eyes—eyes Tory would never have suspected of anything less than the truth. He had used her shamelessly and she had been blind to his true motives, in love enough to let him take advantage of her. *Never again,* she swore to herself. *Trusting Trask McFadden was one mistake that she wouldn't make twice!*

With her hands cradling her head, Tory sat on the varnished slats of the porch swing and stared across the open fields toward the mountains. Purple thunderclouds rolled near the shadowy peaks as night fell across the plateau.

Telling herself that she wasn't waiting for Trask, Tory slowly rocked and remembered the last time she had seen him. It had been in the courtroom during her father's trial. The old bitterness filled her mind as she considered how easily Trask had betrayed her . . .

THE TRIAL HAD already taken over a week and in that time Tory felt as if her entire world were falling apart at the seams. The charges against her father were ludicrous. No one could possibly believe that Calvin Wilson was guilty of fraud, conspiracy or *murder*, for God's sake, and yet there he was, seated with his agitated attorney in the hot courtroom, listening stoically as the evidence against him mounted.

When it had been his turn to sit on the witness stand, he had sat ramrod stiff in the wooden chair, refusing to testify in his behalf.

"Dad, please, save yourself," Tory had begged on the final day of the trial. She was standing in the courtroom, clutching her father's sleeve, unaware of the reporters scribbling rapidly in their notepads. Unshed tears of frustration and fear pooled in her large eyes.

"I know what I'm doin', Missy," Calvin had assured her, fondly patting her head. "It's all for the best. Trust me . . ."

Trust me.

The same words that Trask had said only a few days before the trial. And then he had betrayed her completely. Tory paled and watched in disbelief and horror as Trask took the stand.

He was the perfect witness for the prosecution. Tall, good-looking, with a proud lift of his shoulders and piercing blue eyes, he cut an impressive figure on the witness stand, and his reputation as a trustworthy lawyer added to his appeal. His suit was neatly pressed, but his thick gold-streaked hair remained windblown, adding to the intense, but honest, country-boy image he had perfected. The fact that he was the brother of the murdered man only added sympathy from the jury for the prosecution. That he had gained his information by engaging in a love affair with the accused's daughter didn't seem to tarnish his testimony in the least. If anything it made his side of the story appear more poignantly authentic and the district attorney played it to the hilt.

"And you were with Miss Wilson on the night of your brother's death," the rotund district attorney suggested, leaning familiarly on the polished rail of the witness stand. He stared at Trask over rimless glasses, lifting his bushy brown eyebrows in encouragement to his star witness.

"Yes." Trask's eyes held Tory's. She was sitting behind her father and the defense attorney, unable to believe that the man she loved was slowly, publicly shredding her life apart. Keith, who was sitting next to her, put a steadying arm around her shoulder, but she didn't feel it. She continued to stare at Trask with round tortured eyes.

"And what did Miss Wilson confide to you?" the D.A. asked, his knowing eyes moving from Trask to the jury in confidence.

"That some things had been going on at the Lazy W . . . things she didn't understand."

"Could you be more specific?"

Tory leaned forward and her hands clutched the railing separating her from her father in a death-grip.

The corner of Trask's jaw worked. "She—"

"You mean Victoria Wilson?"

"Yeah," Trask replied with a frown. "Tory claimed that her father had been in a bad mood for the better part of a week. She . . . Tory was worried about him. She said that Calvin had been moody and seemed distracted."

"Anything else?"

Trask hesitated only slightly. His blue eyes darkened and delved into hers. "Tory had seen her father leave the ranch late at night, on horseback."

"When?"

"July 7th."

"Of this year—the night your brother died?"

The lines around Trask's mouth tightened and his skin stretched tautly over his cheekbones. "Yes."

"And what worried Miss Wilson?"

"Objection," the defense attorney yelled, raising his hand and screwing up his face in consternation as he shot up from his chair.

"Sustained." Judge Miller glared imperiously at the district attorney, who visibly regrouped his thoughts and line of questioning.

The district attorney flashed the jury a consoling smile. "What did Miss Wilson say to you that led you to believe that her father was part of the horse swindle?"

Trask settled back in his chair and chewed on his lower lip as he thought. "Tory said that Judge Linn Benton had been visiting the ranch several times in the past few days. The last time Benton was over at the ranch—"

"The Lazy W?"

Trask frowned at the D.A. "Yes. There was a loud argument between Calvin and the judge in Calvin's den. The door was closed, of course, but Tory was in the house and she overheard portions of the discussion."

"Objection," the defense attorney called again. "Your honor, this is only hearsay. Mr. McFadden can't possibly know what Miss Wilson overheard or thought she overheard."

"Sustained," the judge said wearily, wiping the sweat from his receding brow. "Mr. Delany . . ."

The district attorney took his cue and his lips pursed together thoughtfully as he turned back to Trask and said, "Tell me what you saw that convinced you that Calvin Wilson was involved in the alleged horse switching."

"I'd done some checking on my own," Trask admitted, seeing Tory's horrified expression from the corner of his eye. "I knew that my brother, Jason, was investigating an elaborate horse swapping swindle."

"Jason told you as much?"

"Yes. He worked for an insurance company, Edward's Life. Several registered Quarter Horses had died from accidents in the past couple of years. That in itself wasn't out of the ordinary, only two of the horses were owned by the same ranch. What was suspicious was the fact that the horses had been insured so heavily. The company didn't mind at the time the policy was taken out, but wasn't too thrilled when the horse died and the claim had to be paid.

"Still, like I said, nothing appeared out of the ordinary until a company adjuster, on a whim, talked with a few other rival companies who insured horses as well. When the computer records were cross-checked, the adjuster discovered a much higher than average mortality rate for highly insured Quarter Horses in the area surrounding Sinclair, Oregon. Jason, as a claims investigator for Edward's Life, was instructed to check it out the next time a claim came in. You know, for fraud. What he discovered was that the dead horse wasn't even a purebred Quarter Horse. The mare was nothing more than a mustang, a range horse, insured to the teeth."

"How was that possible?"

"It wasn't. The horse was switched. The purebred horse was still alive, kept on an obscure piece of land in the foothills of the Cascade Mountains. The way Jason figured it, the purebred horse would either be sold for a tidy sum, or used for breeding purposes. Either way, the owner would make out with at least twice the value of the horse."

"I see," the D.A. said thoughtfully. "And who owned this piece of land?"

Trask paused, the corners of his mouth tightening. "Calvin Wilson."

A muffled whisper of shock ran through the courtroom and the D.A., while pretending surprise, smiled a bit. Tory thought she was going to be sick. Her face paled and she had to swallow back the acrid taste of deception rising in her throat.

"How do you know who owned the property?"

"Jason had records from the county tax assessor's office. He told me. I couldn't believe it so I asked his daughter, Victoria Wilson."

Tory had to force herself not to gasp aloud at the vicious insinuations in Trask's lies. She closed her eyes and all the life seemed to drain out of her.

"And what did Miss Wilson say?"

"That she didn't know about the land. When I pressed her she admitted that she was worried about her father and the ranch; she said that the Lazy W had been in serious financial trouble for some time."

The district attorney seemed satisfied and rubbed his fleshy fingers together over his protruding stomach. Tory felt as if she were dying inside. The inquisition continued and Trask recounted the events of the summer. How he had seen Judge Linn Benton with Calvin Wilson on various occasions; how his brother, Jason, had almost concluded his investigation of the swindle; and how Calvin Wilson's name became linked to the other two men by his damning ownership of the property.

"You mean to tell me that your brother, Jason, told you that Calvin Wilson was involved?"

"Jason said he thought there might be a connection because of the land where the horses were kept."

"A connection?" the district attorney repeated, patting his stomach and looking incredulously at the jury. "I'd say that was more than 'a connection.' Wouldn't you?"

"I don't know." Trask shifted uneasily in his chair and his blue eyes narrowed on the D.A. "There is a chance that Calvin Wilson didn't know exactly what was happening on the land as it is several miles from the Lazy W."

"But what about the mare that was switched?" the D.A. prodded. "Wasn't she registered?"

"Yes."

"And the owner?"

"Calvin Wilson."

"So your brother, Jason McFadden, the insurance investigator for Edward's Life, thought that there might be a connection?" the D.A. concluded smugly.

"Jason was still working on it when the accident occurred." Trask's eyes hardened at the injustice of his brother's death. It was just the reaction the district attorney had been counting on.

"The accident which took his life. Right?"

"Yes."

"The accident that was caused by someone deliberately tampering with the gas line of the car," the D.A. persisted.

"Objection!"

"Your honor, it's been proven that the engine of Jason McFadden's car had been rigged with an explosive device that detonated at a certain speed, causing sparks to fly into the gas line and explode in the gas tank. What I'm attempting to prove is how that happened and who was to blame."

The gray-haired judge scowled, settled back in his chair and stared at the defense attorney with eyes filled with the cynicism of too many years on the bench. "Overruled."

The D.A. turned to face Trask.

"Let's go back to the night that Victoria Wilson saw her father leave the ranch. On that night, the night of July 7th, what did you do?"

Trask wiped a tired hand around his neck. "After I left Tory, I waited until Calvin had returned and then I confronted him with what Jason had figured out about the horse swapping scam and what I suspected about his involvement in it."

"But why did you do that? It might have backfired in your face and ruined your brother's reputation as an insurance investigator."

Trask paused for a minute. The courtroom was absolutely silent except for the soft hum of the motor of the paddle fan. "I was afraid."

"Of what?"

Trask's fingers tightened imperceptibly on the polished railing. "I was afraid for Jason's life. I thought he was in over his head."

"Why?"

"Jason had already received an anonymous phone call threatening him, as well as his family." Trask's eyes grew dark with indignation and fury and his jaw thrust forward menacingly. "But he wouldn't go to the police. It was important to him to handle it himself."

"And so you went to see Calvin Wilson, hoping that he might help you save your brother's life."

"Yes." Trask glared at the table behind which Tory's father was sitting.

"And what did Calvin Wilson say when you confronted him?"

Hatred flared in Trask's eyes. "That all the problems were solved."

At that point Neva McFadden, Jason's widow, broke down. Her small shoulders began to shake with the hysterical sobs racking her body and she buried her face in her hands, as if in so doing she could hide from the truth. Calvin Wilson didn't move a muscle, but Tory felt as if she were slowly bleeding to death. Keith's face turned ashen when Neva was helped from the courtroom and his arm over Tory's shoulders tightened.

"So," the D.A. persisted, turning everyone's attention back to the witness stand and Trask, "you thought that because of your close relationship with Calvin Wilson's daughter, that you might be able to reason with the man before anything tragic occurred."

"Yes," Trask whispered, his blue eyes filled with resignation as he looked from the empty chair in which Neva had been sitting, to Calvin Wilson and finally to Tory. "But it didn't work out that way . . ."

* * *

TORY CONTINUED TO rock in the porch swing. A gentle breeze rustled the leaves of the aspen trees and whispered through the pines . . . just as it had on the first night she'd met him. All her memories of Trask were so vivid. Passionate images filled with love and hate teased her weary mind. Falling in love with him had been too easy . . . but then, of course, he had planned it that way, and she had been trapped easily by his deceit. Thank God she was alone tonight, she thought, so that she had time to think things out before she had to face him again.

It had taken a lot of convincing to get Keith to leave the ranch, but in the end he had gone into town with some of the single men who worked on the Lazy W. It was a muggy Saturday night in early summer, and Keith had decided that he would, against his better judgment, spend a few hours drinking beer and playing pool at the Branding Iron. It was his usual custom on Saturday evenings and Tory persuaded him that she wanted to be left alone. Which she did. If what Keith had been saying were true, then she wanted to meet Trask on her own terms, without unwanted ears to hear what promised to be a heated conversation.

The scent of freshly mown hay drifted on the sultry breeze that lifted the loose strands of hair away from her face. The gentle lowing of restless cattle as they roamed the far-off fields reached her ears. She squinted her eyes against the gathering night. Twilight had begun to color the landscape in shadowy hues of lavender. Clumps of sagebrush dappled the ground beneath the towering ponderosa pines. Even the proud Cascades loomed darkly, silently in the distance, a cold barrier to the rest of the world. *Except that the world was intruding into her life all over again.* The rugged mountains hadn't protected her at all. She had been a fool to think that she was safe and that the past was over and done.

The faint rumble of an engine caught Tory's attention. *Trask.*

Tory's heart began to pound in anticipation. She felt the faint stirrings of dread as the sound came nearer. He'd come back. Just as he'd promised and Keith had warned. A thin sheen of sweat broke out on her back and between her breasts. She clenched her teeth in renewed determination and her fingers clenched the arm of the swing in a death grip.

The twin beams of headlights illuminated the stand of aspen near the drive and a dusty blue pickup stopped in front of her house. Tory took in a needed breath of air and trained her eyes on the man unfolding himself from the cab. An unwelcome lump formed in her throat.

Trask was just as she had remembered him. Tall and lean, with long well-muscled thighs, tight buttocks, slim waist and broad chest, he looked just as arrogantly athletic as he always had. His light brown hair caught in the hot breeze and fell over his forehead in casual disarray.

So much for the stuffy United States senator image, Tory thought cynically. His shirt was pressed and clean, but open-throated, and the sleeves were pushed over his forearms. The jeans, which hugged his hips, looked as if they had seen years of use. *Just one of the boys . . .* Tory knew better. She couldn't trust him this night any more than she had on the day her father was sentenced to prison.

Trask strode over to the porch with a purposeful step and his eyes delved into hers.

What he encountered in Tory's cynical gaze was hostility—as hot and fresh as it had been on the day that

Calvin Wilson had been found guilty for his part in Jason's death.

"What're you doing here?" Tory demanded. Her voice was surprisingly calm, probably from going over the scene a thousand times in her mind, she thought.

Trask climbed the two weathered steps to the porch, placed his hands on the railing and balanced his hips against the smooth wood. His booted feet were crossed in front of him. He attempted to look relaxed, but Tory noticed the inner tension tightening the muscles of his neck and shoulders.

"I think you know." His voice was low and familiar. It caused a prickling sensation to spread down the back of her neck. Looking into his vibrant blue eyes made it difficult for her not to think about the past that they had shared so fleetingly.

"Keith said you were spreading it around Sinclair that you wanted to see me."

"That's right."

"Why?"

His eyes slid away from her and he studied the starless sky. The air was heavy with the scent of rain. "I thought it was time to clear up a few things between us."

The memory of the trial burned into her mind. "Impossible."

"Tory—"

"Look, Trask," she said, her voice trembling only slightly, "you're not welcome here." She managed a sarcastic smile and gestured toward the pickup. "And I think you'd better leave before I tell you just what a bastard I think you are."

"It won't be the first time," he drawled, leaning against the post supporting the roof and staring down at her. His eyes slid lazily down her body, noting the elegant curve of her neck, the burnished wisps falling free of the loose knot of auburn hair at the base of her neck, the proud carriage of her body and the fire in her eyes. She was, without a doubt, the most beautiful and intelligent woman he had ever known. Try as he had to forget her, he had failed. Distance and time hadn't abated his desire; if anything, the feelings stirring within burned more torridly than he remembered.

He had the audacity to slant a lazy grin at her and Tory's simmering anger began to ignite. Her voice seemed to catch in her throat. "Leave."

"Not yet."

Righteous indignation flared in her eyes. "Leave, damn you . . ."

"Not until we get—"

"Now!" Her palm slapped against the varnished wooden arm of the swing and she pushed herself upward. "I don't want you ever to set foot on this ranch again. I thought I made that clear before, but either you have an incredibly short memory, or you just conveniently ignored out last conversation."

"Just for the record; I haven't forgotten anything. And that was no conversation," he speculated. "A war zone maybe, a helluva battle perhaps, but not idle chitchat."

"And neither is this. I don't know why you're here, Trask, and I don't really give a damn."

"You did once," he said softly, his dark eyes softening.

The tone of his voice pierced into her heart and her self-righteous fury threatened to escape. "That was before you used me, senator," she said, her voice a raspy whisper. One slim finger pointed at his chest. "Before you took everything I told you, turned it around and testified against my father!"

"And you still think he was innocent," Trask said, shaking his head in wonder.

"I know he was." Her chin raised a fraction and she impaled him with her flashing gray-green eyes. "How does it feel to look in the mirror every morning and know that you sent the wrong man to prison?" Hot tears touched the back of her eyes. "My father sat alone, slowly dying, the last few years of his life spent behind bars, all because of your lies."

"I never perjured myself, Tory."

Her lips pursed together in her anger. "Of course not. You were a lawyer. You knew just how to answer the questions; how exactly to insinuate to the jury that my father was part of the conspiracy; how to react to make the jury think that he was there the night that Jason found out about the swindle, how he inadvertently took part in your brother's death. Not only did you blacken my father's name, Trask, as far as I'm concerned, you took his life just as certainly as if you had thrust a knife into his heart." She took a step backward and placed her hand on the doorknob. Her fingers curled over the cold metal and her voice was edged in steel. "Now, get off this place and don't ever come back. You may be a senator now, maybe even respected by people who are only privy to your public image, but as far as I'm concerned you're nothing better than an egocentric opportunist who used the publicity surrounding his brother's death to get him elected!"

Trask's eyes flashed in the darkness. He took a step closer to her, but the hatred in her gaze stopped him dead in his tracks. "I only told the truth."

Rage stormed through her veins, thundered in her mind. Five long years of anger and bewilderment poured out of her. "You sensationalized this story, used it as a springboard to get you in the public eye, crushed everyone you had to so that you would get elected." The unshed tears glistened in her eyes. "Well, congratulations, senator. You got what you wanted."

With her final remarks, she opened the door and slipped through it, but Trask's hand came sharply upward and caught the smooth wood as she tried to slam the door in his face. "You've got it all figured out—"

"Easy to do. Now please, get off my land and out of my life. You destroyed it once, isn't that enough?"

Something akin to despair crossed his rugged features, but the emotion was quickly disguised by determination. "No."

"No?" she repeated incredulously. *Oh, God, Trask, don't put me through this again . . . not again.* "Well once was enough for me," she murmured.

"I don't think so."

"Then you don't know me very well. I'm not the glutton for punishment I used to be." She pushed harder on the door, intent on physically forcing him out of her life.

"I wouldn't be so sure about that."

"What!"

"Look at you—you're still punishing yourself, blaming yourself for your father's conviction and death."

The audacity of the man! She felt her body begin to shake. "No, Trask. As incredible as you might find all this, I blame you. After all, you were the one who testified against my father . . ."

"And you've been hating yourself ever since."

"*I* can look in the mirror in the morning. *I* can live with myself."

"Can you?" His skepticism echoed in the still night air.

"I don't see any reason for discussing any of this. I've told you that I want you out of my life."

"And I don't believe it."

Once again she tried to slam the door, but his broad shoulder caught the hard wood. "You've got one incredible ego, senator," she said, wishing there was some way to put some distance between her body and his.

"You were waiting for me," he accused, his eyes sliding from her face down her neck, past the open collar of her blouse to linger at the hollow of her throat.

"Of course I was."

"Alone."

She was gripping the edge of the door so tightly that her fingers began to ache. "I didn't want the gossip to start all over again. Keith told me that you were looking for me, so I decided to wait. I prefer to keep my conversations with you private. You know, without a judge, jury or the press looking over my shoulder, ready to use every word against me."

His eyes slid downward, noticing the denim skirt and soft apricot-colored blouse. "So why did you get dressed up?"

"Don't flatter yourself, senator. I usually take a shower after working with the horses all day. The way I dress has nothing to do with you." Her eyes narrowed slightly. "So why don't you just take yourself and that tremendous ego of yours out of here? If you need a wheelbarrow to carry it there's one in the barn."

He shoved his body into the doorway, wedging himself between the door and the jamb. Tory was strong, she put all of her weight against the door, but she was no match for the powerful thrust of his shoulders as he pushed his way into the darkened hallway. "You're going to hear what I have to say whether you like it or not."

"No!"

"You don't have much of a choice."

"Get out, Trask." Her words sounded firm, but inwardly she wavered; the desperation she had noticed earlier flickered in his midnight-blue eyes. As much as she hated him, she still felt a physical attraction to him. *God, she was a fool.*

"In a minute."

She stepped backward and placed her hands on her hips. Her breath was expelled in a sigh of frustration. "Since I can't convince you otherwise, why don't you just say what you think is so all-fired important and then leave."

He eyed her suspiciously and walked into the den.

"Wait a minute—"

"I need your help."

Tory's heart nearly stopped beating. There was a thread of hopelessness in his voice that touched a precarious part of her mind and she had to remind herself that he was the enemy. He always had been. Though Trask seemed sincere she couldn't, wouldn't let herself believe him. "No way."

"I think you might change your mind."

"You've got to be kidding," Tory whispered.

She followed him into the den, her father's den, and swallowed back her anger and surprise. Trask had placed a hand on the lava rock fireplace and his head was lowered between his shoulders. How familiar it seemed to have him back in the warm den her father had used as an office. Knotty pine walls, worn comfortable furniture, watercolors of the Old West, Indian weavings in orange and brown, and now Trask, leaning dejectedly against the fireplace, looking for all the world as if he truly needed her help, made her throat constrict with fond memories. *God, how she had loved this man.* Her fist curled into balls of defeat.

"I'm not kidding, Tory." He glanced up at her and she read the torment in his eyes.

"No way."

"Just listen to me. That's all I ask."

Anger overcame awe. "I can't help you. I won't."

His pleas turned to threats. "You'd better."

"Why? What can you do to me now? Destroy my reputation? Ruin my family. Kill my father? You've already done all that, there's nothing left. You can damned well threaten until you're blue in the face and it won't affect me . . . or this ranch."

In the darkness his eyes searched her face, possessively reading the sculpted angle of her jaw, the proud lift of her chin, the tempting mystique of her intelligent gray-green eyes. "Nothing's left?" he whispered, his voice lowering. One finger reached upward and traced the soft slope of her neck.

Tory's heart hammered in her chest. "Nothing," she repeated, clenching her teeth and stepping away from his warm touch and treacherous blue eyes.

He grimaced. "This has to do with your father."

She whirled around to face him. "My father is dead." Shaking with rage she pointed an imperious finger at his chest. "Because of you."

His jaw tightened and he paced the length of the room in an obvious effort to control himself. "You'd like to believe that I was responsible for your father's death, wouldn't you?"

All of the anguish of five long years poured out of her. "You were. He could have had the proper medical treatment if he hadn't been in prison—"

"It makes it easier to think that I was the bad guy and that your father was some kind of a saint."

"All I know is that my father would never have been a part of anything like murder, Trask." She was visibly shaking. All the old emotions, love, hate, fear, awe and despair, churned inside her. Tears stung her eyelids and she fought a losing battle with the urge to weep.

"Your father was a desperate man," he said quietly.

"What's that supposed to mean?"

"Desperate men make mistakes; do things they wouldn't normally do." The look on his face was pensive and worried. She noticed neither revenge nor anger in his eyes. *Trask actually believed that her father had been nothing better than a common horse thief.*

"You're grasping at straws. My father was perfectly fine."

Trask crossed the room, leaned an arm on the mantel and rubbed his chin. All the while his dusky blue eyes held hers. "The Lazy W was losing money hand over fist." She was about to protest but he continued. "You know it as well as anyone. When you took over, you were forced to go to the bank for additional capital to keep it running."

"Because of all the bad publicity. People were afraid to buy Quarter Horses from the Lazy W because of the scandal."

"Right. The scandal. A simple scam to make money by claiming that the purebred Quarter Horses had died and offering as proof bodies of horses who resembled the blue bloods but weren't worth nearly as much. No one around here questioned Judge Benton's integrity, especially when his claims were backed up by the local veterinarian, George Henderson. It was a simple plan to dupe and defraud the insurance companies of thousands of dollars and it would never have come off if your father hadn't provided the perfect hiding spot for the purebreds who hadn't really met their maker. It all boiled down to one helluva scandal."

"I can't believe that Dad was involved in that."

"The horses were found on his property, Tory." Trask frowned at her stubborn pride. "You're finding it hard to believe a lot of things these days, aren't you?" he accused, silently damning himself for the torture he was putting her through. "Why didn't your father defend himself when he had the chance, on the witness stand? If he was innocent, pleading the fifth amendment made him look more guilty than he was."

A solitary tear slid down her cheek. "I don't want to hear any more of this . . ."

"But you're going to, lady. You're going to hear every piece of incriminating evidence I have."

"Why, Trask?" she demanded. "Why now? Dad's dead—"

"And so is Jason. My brother was murdered, Tory. Murdered!" He fell into a chair near the desk. "I have reason to believe that one of the persons involved with the horse swindle and Jason's death was never brought to justice."

Her eyes widened in horror. "What do you mean?"

"I think there were more than three conspirators. Four, maybe five . . . who knows? Half the damned county might have been involved." Trask looked more haggard and defeated than she had ever thought possible. The U.S. senator from Sinclair, Oregon, had lost his luster and become jaded in the past few years. Cynical lines bracketed his mouth and his blue eyes seemed suddenly lifeless.

Tory's breath caught in her throat. "You're not serious."

"Dead serious. And I intend to find out who it was."

"But Judge Benton, he would have taken everyone

down with him—no one would have been allowed to go free."

"Unless he struck a deal, or the other person had something over on our friend the judge. Who knows? Maybe this guy is extremely powerful . . ."

Tory shook her head, as if in so doing she could deny everything Trask was suggesting. "I don't believe any of this," she said, pacing around the room, her thoughts spinning crazily. *Why was Trask dredging all this up again. Why now? Just when life at the Lazy W had gotten back to normal* . . . "And I don't want to. Nothing you can do or say will change the past." She lifted her hands over her head in a gesture of utter defeat. "For God's sake, Trask, why are you here?"

"You're the only one who can help me unravel this, Tory."

"And I don't want to."

"Maybe this will change your mind." He extracted a piece of paper from his wallet and handed it to her. It was one of the photocopies of the letter he'd received.

Tory read the condemning words and her finely arched brows pulled together in a scowl of concentration. "Who sent you this?" she demanded.

"I don't know."

"It came anonymously?"

"Yes. To my office in Washington."

"It's probably just a prank."

"The postmark was Sinclair, Oregon. If it's a prank, Tory, it's a malicious one. And one of your neighbors is involved."

Tory read the condemning words again:

One of your brother's murderers is still free.
He was part of the Quarter Horse swindle

involving Linn Benton, Calvin Wilson and George Henderson.

"But who would want to dig it all up again?"

Trask shook his head and pushed his fingers through his hair. "Someone with a guilty conscience? Someone who overheard a conversation and finally feels that it's time to come clean? A nosy journalist interested in a story? I don't know. But whoever he is, he wants me involved."

Tory sank into the nearest chair. "And you couldn't leave it alone."

"Could you?"

She smiled bitterly and studied the letter in her hand. "I suppose not. Not if there was a chance to prove that my father was innocent."

"Damn it, Tory!" Trask exclaimed. "Calvin had the opportunity to do that on the witness stand. He chose to hide behind the fifth amendment."

Tory swallowed as she remembered her father sitting in the crowded courtroom. His thick white hair was neatly in place, his gray eyes stared straight ahead. Each time the district attorney would fire a question at him Calvin would stoically respond that he refused to answer the question on the basis that it might incriminate him. Calvin's attorney had been fit to be tied in the stifling courtroom. The other defendants, Linn Benton, a prominent circuit court judge and ringleader of the swindle and George Henderson, a veterinarian and local rancher whose spread bordered the Lazy W to the north, cooperated with the district attorney. They had plea bargained for shorter sentences. But, for reasons he wouldn't name to his frantic daughter, Calvin Wilson accepted his guilt without a trace of regret.

"Face it, Tory," Trask was saying. "Your father was involved for all the right reasons. He was dying of cancer, the ranch was in trouble financially, and he wouldn't be able to take care of either you or your brother. He got involved with the horse swindle for the money . . . for you. He just didn't expect that Jason would find out about it and come snooping around." He walked to the other side of the room and stared out the window at the night. "I never wanted to think that your father was involved in the murder, Tory. I'd like to believe that he had no idea that Jason was onto him and the others. But I was there, I confronted the man and he looked through me as if whatever I said was of no significance." Trask walked across the room and grabbed Tory's shoulders. His face was twisted in disbelief. "*No significance! My brother's life, for God's sake, and Calvin stood there like a goddamn wooden Indian!*"

Tory tried to step away. "Not murder, Trask. My father wouldn't have been involved in Jason's death. He . . ." Her voice broke. ". . . couldn't."

"You don't know how much I want to believe you."

"But certainly—"

"I don't think your father instigated it," he interjected. "As a matter of fact, it's my guess that Benton planned Jason's 'accident' and had one of his henchmen tamper with the car."

"And Dad had to pay."

"Because he wouldn't defend himself."

She shook her head. "Against your lies." His fingers tightened over the soft fabric of her blouse. Tension charged the hot night air and Tory felt droplets of nervous perspiration break out between her shoulders.

"I only said what I thought was the truth."

The corners of her mouth turned bitterly downward

and her eyes grew glacial cold. "The truth that you got from me."

His shoulders stiffened under his cotton shirt, and his eyes drilled into hers. "I never meant to hurt you, Tory, you know that."

For a fleeting moment she was tempted to believe him, but all the pain came rushing back to her in a violent storm of emotion. She felt her body shake with restraint. "I trusted you."

He winced slightly.

"I trusted you and you used me." The paper crumpled in her hand. "Take this letter and leave before I say things that I'll regret later."

"Tory . . ." He attempted to draw her close, but she pulled back, away from his lying eyes and familiar touch.

"I don't want to hear it, Trask. And I don't want to see you again. Now leave me alone—"

A loud knock resounded in the room and the hinges on the front door groaned as Rex Engels let himself into the house.

"Tory?" the foreman called. His steps slowed in the hallway, as if he was hesitant to intrude.

"In here." Tory was relieved at the intrusion. She stepped away from Trask and walked toward the door. When Rex entered he stopped and stared for a moment at Trask McFadden. His lips thinned as he took off his dusty Stetson and ran his fingers over the silver stubble on his chin. At five foot eight, he was several inches shorter than Trask, but his body was whip-lean from the physical labor he imposed on himself. Rugged and dependable, Rex Engels had been with the Lazy W for as long as Tory could remember.

The foreman was obviously uncomfortable; he shifted

from one foot to the other and his eyes darted from Tory to Trask and back again.

"What happened?" Tory asked, knowing immediately that something was wrong and fearing that Keith was in the hospital or worse . . .

"I got a call from Len Ross about an hour ago," Rex stated, his mouth hardening into a frown. Tory nodded, encouraging him to continue. Ross was a neighboring rancher. "One of Ross's boys was mending fence this afternoon and he noticed a dead calf on the Lazy W." Tory's shoulders slumped a little. It was always difficult losing livestock, especially the young ones. But it wasn't unexpected; it happened more often than she would like to admit, and it certainly didn't warrant Rex driving over to the main house after dark. There had to be something more. Something he didn't want to discuss in front of Trask. "And?"

Rex rubbed his hand over his neck. He looked meaningfully at Trask. "The calf was shot."

"What?" Tory stiffened.

"From the looks of it, I'd guess it was done by a twenty-two."

"Then you saw the calf?" Trask cut in, his entire body tensing as he leaned one shoulder against the arch between den and entryway.

"Yep."

"And you don't think it was an accident?" Tory guessed.

"It's not hunting season," the foreman pointed out, moving his gaze to Trask in silent accusation. "And there were three bullet holes in the carcass."

Tory swallowed against the sickening feeling overtaking her. First Trask with his anonymous letter and the threat of dredging up the past again and now evidence that someone was deliberately threatening her livestock. "Why?" she wondered aloud.

"Maybe kids . . ." Rex offered, shifting his gaze uneasily between Tory and Trask. "It's happened before."

"Hardly seems like a prank," Trask interjected. There were too many unfortunate coincidences to suit him. Trask wasn't a man who believed in coincidence or luck.

Rex shrugged, unwilling to discuss the situation with the man who had sent Calvin Wilson to prison. He didn't trust Trask McFadden and his brown eyes made it clear.

Once the initial shock had worn off, Tory became furious that someone would deliberately kill the livestock. "I'll call Paul Barnett's office when we get back," she said.

"Get back?"

"I want to see the calf." Her gray-green eyes gleamed in determination; she knew that Rex would try to protect her from the ugly sight.

"There's not much to see," Rex protested. "It's dark."

"And this is my ranch. If someone has been deliberately molesting the livestock, I want to know what I'm up against. Let's go."

Rex knew there was no deterring her once she had set her mind on a plan of action. In more ways than one, Victoria was Calvin's daughter. He looked inquiringly at Trask and without words asked, what about him?

"Trask was just leaving."

"Not yet," Trask argued. "I'll come with you."

"Forget it."

"Listen to me. I think that this might have something to do with what we were discussing."

The anonymous letter? Her father's imprisonment? The horse swindle of five years ago? "I don't see how—" she protested.

"It won't hurt for me to take a look."

He was so damned logical. Seeing no reasonable argument, and not wanting to make a scene in front of Rex, Tory reluctantly agreed. "I don't like this," she mumbled, reaching for her jacket that hung on a wooden peg near the door and bracing herself for the unpleasant scene in the fields near the Ross property.

"Neither do I."

The tone of Trask's voice sent a shiver of dread down Tory's spine.

Rex cast her a worried glance, forced his gray Stetson onto his head and started for the door. As Tory grabbed the keys to her pickup she wondered what was happening to her life. Everything seemed to be turning upside down. All because of Trask McFadden.

Chapter Three

TRASK SAT ON the passenger side of the pickup, his eyes looking steadily forward, his pensive gaze was following the disappearing taillights of Rex's truck.

Tory's eyebrows were drawn together in concentration as she attempted to follow Rex. Her fingers curled around the steering wheel as she tried to maneuver the bouncing pickup down the rutted dirt road that ran the length of the Lazy W toward the mountains.

The tension within the darkened interior of the pickup was thick enough to cut with a knife. Silence stretched tautly between Tory and Trask and she had to bite her tongue to keep from screaming at him that she didn't want him forcing himself back into her life.

She downshifted and slowed to a stop near the property line separating the Lazy W from Len Ross's spread.

"Over here," Rex announced when she shut off the engine, grabbed a flashlight out of the glove box and jumped from the cab of the truck. Trask held apart the strands of barbed wire, which surrounded the pastures, as she wrapped her skirt around her thighs, climbed through the fence and followed the beam of Rex's flashlight. Trask slid through the fence after her. Though he said nothing, she was conscious of his presence, his long legs taking one stride to every two of her smaller steps.

The first large drops of rain began to fall just as Tory approached the crumpled heap near a solitary pine tree. The beam of Rex's flashlight was trained on the lifeless white face of the calf. Dull eyes looked unseeingly skyward and a large pink tongue lolled out of the side of the heifer's mouth.

"Dear God," Tory whispered, bending over and touching the inert form. Her stomach lurched uncomfortably as she brushed the flies from the curly red coat of the lifeless animal. Living on the ranch as she had for most of her twenty-seven years, Tory was used to death. But she had never been able to accept the unnecessary wanton destruction of life that had taken the small Hereford. It was all so pointless. Her throat tightened as she patted the rough hide and then let her hands fall to her sides.

Rex ran his flashlight over the calf's body and Tory noticed the three darkened splotches on the heifer's abdomen. Dried blood had clotted over the red and white hairs. Tory closed her eyes for a second. Whoever had killed the calf hadn't even had the decency to make it a clean kill. The poor creature had probably suffered for several hours before dying beneath the solitary ponderosa pine tree.

"What about the cow—the mother of the calf?"

"I took care of her," Rex stated. "She's with the rest of the herd in the south pasture."

Tory nodded thoughtfully and cocked her head toward the dead calf. "Let's cover her up," she whispered. "I've got a tarp in the back of the truck."

"Why?" Rex asked, but Trask was already returning to the pickup for the tarp.

"I want someone from the sheriff's office to see the calf and I don't want to take a chance that some scavenger finds her. A coyote could clean the carcass by morning," Tory replied, as she stood and dusted off her skirt. In the darkness, her eyes glinted with determination. "Someone did this—" she pointed to the calf "—deliberately. I want that person found."

Rex sucked in his breath and shook his head. "Might not be that easy," he thought aloud.

"Well, we've got to do something. We can't just sit by and let it happen again."

Rex shook his head. "You're right, Tory. I can't argue with that. Whoever did this should have to pay, but I doubt if having someone from the sheriff's office come out will do any good."

"Maybe not, but at least we'll find out if any of the other ranchers have had similar problems."

Rex forced his hands into the pockets of his lightweight jacket and pulled his shoulders closer to his neck as the rain began to shower in earnest. "I'll check all the fields tomorrow, just to make sure that there are no other surprises."

"Good."

Rex glanced uneasily toward the trucks, where Trask was fetching the tarp. "There's something else you should know," the foreman said. His voice was low, as if he didn't want to be overheard.

Tory followed Rex's gaze. "What?"

"The fence . . . someone snipped it. Whoever did this—" he motioned toward the dead calf "—didn't bother to climb through the fence or use the gate. No, sir. They clipped all four wires clean open."

Tory's heart froze. Whoever had killed the calf had done it blatantly, almost tauntingly. She felt her stomach quiver with premonition. Things had gone from bad to worse in the span of a few short hours.

"I patched it up as best I could," Rex was saying

with a frown. "I'll need a couple of the hands out here tomorrow to do a decent job of it."

"You don't think this is the work of kids out for a few kicks," Tory guessed.

Rex shrugged and even in the darkness Tory could see him scowl distractedly. "I don't rightly know, but I doubt it."

"Great."

"You don't have anyone who bears you a grudge, do you?" Rex asked uncomfortably.

"Not that I know of."

"How about someone who still has it in for your pop? Now that he's gone, you'd be the most likely target." He thought for a minute, as if he was hesitant to bring up a sore subject. "Maybe someone who's out to make trouble because of the horse swindle?"

"I don't think so," Tory murmured. "It's been a long time . . . over five years."

"But McFadden is back. Stirring up trouble . . ." If Rex meant to say anything more, he didn't. Trask reappeared with the heavy tarp slung over his shoulder. Without a word the two men covered the small calf and lashed the tarp down with rope and metal stakes that Trask had brought from the truck.

"That about does it," Rex said, wiping the accumulation of rain from the back of his neck once the unpleasant job had been completed. "It would take a grizzly to rip that open." He stretched his shoulders before adding, "Like I said, I'll check all the fences and the livestock myself, in the morning. I'll let you know if anything looks suspicious." Rex's concerned gaze studied Trask for a tense second and Tory saw the muscles in Trask's face tighten a bit.

"I'll talk to you in the morning," Tory replied.

“’Night,” Rex mumbled as he turned toward his truck.

“Thanks for checking it out, Rex.”

“No problem.” Rex pushed his hat squarely over his head. “All part of the job.”

“Above and beyond the call of duty at ten o’clock at night.”

“All in a day’s work,” Rex called over his shoulder.

Tory stood beside Trask and watched the beam of Rex’s flashlight as the foreman strode briskly back to the truck.

“Come on,” Trask said, placing his arm familiarly around her shoulders. “You’re getting soaked. Let’s go.”

Casting a final despairing look at the covered carcass, Tory walked back to the pickup with Trask and didn’t object to the weight of his arm stretched over her shoulders. This night, when her whole world was falling apart, she felt the need of his strength. She supposed her contradictory feelings for him bordered on irony, but she really didn’t care. She was too tired and emotionally drained to consider the consequences of her renewed acquaintance with him.

“I’ll drive,” Trask said.

“I can—”

“I’ll drive,” he stated again, more forcefully, and she reached into her pocket and handed him the keys, too weary to argue over anything so pointless. He knew the back roads of the Lazy W as well as anyone. He had driven them often during the short months of their passionate but traitorous love affair. How long ago that happy carefree time in her life seemed now as they jostled along the furrowed road.

Trask drove slowly back to the house. The old engine of the truck rumbled through the dark night, the wipers pushed aside the heavy raindrops on the windshield, and the tinny sound of static-filled country music from an all-night radio station drifted out of the speakers.

"Who do you think did it?" Trask asked as he stopped the truck near the front porch.

"I don't have any idea," Tory admitted with a worried frown. "I don't really understand what's going on. Yesterday everything was normal: the worst problem I had to deal with was a broken combine and a horse with laminitis. But now—" she raised her hands helplessly before reaching for the door handle of the pickup "—it seems that all hell has broken loose." She looked toward him and found his eyes searching the contours of her face.

"Tory—" He reached for her, and the seductive light in his eyes made her heartbeat quicken. His fingers brushed against the rain-dampened strands of her hair and his lips curved into a wistful smile. "I remember another time," he said, "when you and I were alone in this very pickup."

A passionate image scorched Tory's mind. Just by staring into Trask's intense gaze she could recall the feel of his hands against her breasts, the way her skin would quiver at his touch, the taste of his mouth over hers. "I think we'd better not talk or even think about that," she whispered.

His fingers lingered against her exposed neck, warming the wet skin near the base of her throat. "Can't we be together without fighting?" he asked, his voice low with undercurrents of restrained desire.

After all these years, Trask still wanted her; or at least he wanted her to think that he still cared for her—just a little. Maybe he did. "I . . . I don't know."

"Let's try."

"I don't think I want to," she admitted, but it was too late. She watched with mingled fascination and dread as his head lowered and his mouth closed over hers, just as his hand pressed against her shoulder, pulling her against his chest. She was caught up in the scent of him; the familiar odor of his skin was dampened with the rain and all of her senses reawakened with his touch.

The warmth of his arms enveloped her and started the trickle of desire running in her blood. Warm lips, filled with the smoldering lust of five long years, touched hers and the tip of his tongue pressed urgently against her teeth.

I can't let this happen, she thought wildly, pressing her palms against his shoulders and trying to pull out of his intimate embrace. When he lifted his head from hers, she let her forehead fall against his chin. Her hands remained against his shoulders and only her shallow breathing gave her conflicting emotions away. "We can't start all over, you know," she said at length, raising her head and gazing into his eyes. "It's not as if either of us can forget what happened and start over again."

"But we don't have to let what happened force us apart."

"Oh, Trask, come on. Think about it," Tory said snappishly, although a vital but irrational part of her mind wanted desperately to believe him.

"I have. For five years."

"There's no other way, Trask. You and I both know it." Before he could contradict her or the illogical side of her nature could argue with her, she opened the door of the truck and dashed through the rain and across the gravel drive to the house.

She was already in the den when Trask entered the room. He leaned insolently against the archway. The rain had darkened his hair to a deep brown and the shoulders of his wet shirt clung to his muscles. Standing against the pine wall, his arms crossed insolently over his chest, his brilliant eyes delving into hers, he looked more masculine than she ever would have imagined. Or wanted. "What are you running from?" he asked.

"You . . . me . . . us." She lifted her hands into the air helplessly before realizing how undignified her emotions appeared. Then, willing her pride back into place, she wrapped her arms around herself and settled into the chair behind her father's desk. She hoped that the large oak table would put distance between her body and his—give her time to get her conflicting emotions back into perspective.

Trask looked bone-weary as he sauntered around the den and, uninvited, poured himself a healthy drink from the mirrored bar near the fireplace. He lifted the bottle in silent offering, but Tory shook her head, preferring to keep her wits about her. Her reaction to Trask was overwhelming, unwelcome and had to be controlled. She couldn't let herself be duped again. What was it they always said? Once burned, twice shy? That's the way it had to be with Trask, she tried to convince herself. He'd used her once. Never again.

He strode over to the window, propping one booted foot against a small stool, sipping his drink and staring out at the starless night. Raindrops slid in twisted paths down the panes.

"This ever happened before?" Trask asked. He turned and leaned against the windowsill, one broad hand supporting most of his weight.

"What?"

"Some of your livestock being used for target practice."

Her eyes narrowed at the cruel analogy. "No."

Swirling the amber liquor in his glass, he stared at her. "Don't you think it's odd?"

"Of course."

Trask shook his head. "More than that, Tory. Not just odd. What I meant is that it seems like more than a coincidence. First this letter—" he pointed to the anonymous note still lying face up crumpled on a small table "—and now the calf."

Tory felt the prickling sensation of dread climb up her spine. "What are you getting at?"

"I think the dead calf is a warning, Tory."

"What!"

"Someone knows I'm here looking for the person that was unconvicted in the original trial for Jason's murder. I've made no bones about the fact that I intended to visit you. The calf was a message to stay away from me."

Tory laughed nervously. "You're not serious. . . ."

"Dead serious."

Tory felt the first stirrings of fear. "I think you've been in Washington too long, senator," she replied. "Too many subcommittees on underworld crime have got you jumping at shadows. This is Sinclair, Oregon, not New York City."

"I'm not kidding, Tory." His eyes glittered dangerously and he finished his drink with a scowl. "Someone's trying to scare you off."

"It was probably just a prank, like Rex said."

"Rex didn't believe that and neither do you."

"You know how kids are: they get an idea in their heads and just for kicks—"

"They slaughter a calf?" he finished ungraciously. Anger flashed in his eyes and was evident in the set of his shoulders. "Real funny: a heifer with three gunshot wounds. Some sense of humor."

"I didn't say it was meant to be funny."

His fist crashed violently into the windowsill. "Damn

it, Tory, haven't you been listening to a word I've said? It's obvious to me that someone is trying to scare you off!"

"Then why not send me a letter . . . or phone me? Why something as obscure as a dead calf? If you ask me, you're grasping at straws, trying to tie one event to the other just so that I'll help you in this . . . this wild-goose chase!" Realizing that he only intended to continue the argument, she reached for the phone on the corner of the desk.

Trask's eyes were blazing and the cords in his neck protruded. He was about to say something more, but Tory shook her head, motioning for him to be silent as she dialed the sheriff's office and cradled the receiver between her shoulder and her ear. "No, Trask, what you're suggesting doesn't make any sense. None whatsoever."

"Like hell! If you weren't so damned stubborn—"

"Deputy Smith?" Tory said aloud as a curt voice answered the phone. "This is Tory Wilson at the Lazy W." Tory held up her hand to silence the protests forming on Trask's tongue. As quickly as possible, she explained everything that had occurred from the time that Len Ross's hands had noticed the dead animal.

"We'll have someone out in the morning," the deputy promised after telling her that no other rancher had reported any disturbances in the past few weeks. Tory replaced the phone with shaking hands. Her brows drew together thoughtfully.

"You're beginning to believe me," Trask deduced. He was still angry, but his rage was once again controlled.

"No—"

"You'd better think about it. Has anything else unusual happened around here?"

"No . . . wait a minute. There was the combine that broke down unexpectedly and I do have a stallion with laminitis, but they couldn't be connected . . . never mind." *What was she thinking about? Governor's condition and the broken machinery were all explainable problems of running the Lazy W. The malicious incident involving the calf—that was something else again.* She forced a fragile smile. "Look, Trask, I think you'd better leave."

"What about the letter?" he demanded, picking up the small piece of paper and waving it in her face. "Are you going to ignore it, too?"

"I wouldn't take it too seriously," she allowed, lifting her shoulders.

"No?"

"For God's sake, Trask, it isn't even signed. That doesn't make much sense to me. Why wouldn't the person who wrote it want to be identified, that is if he has a logical authentic complaint? If the man who wrote this note wanted you to do something, why didn't he bother to sign the damned thing?"

"Maybe because he or she is afraid. Maybe the person who was involved with the swindle and avoided justice got away because he's extremely powerful—"

"And maybe he just doesn't exist." She eyed the grayish sheet of paper disdainfully. "That could be a letter from anyone, and it doesn't necessarily mean it's true."

"Tory—" His eyes darkened at her obstinacy.

"As I said before, I think it's time you left."

He took a step nearer to her, but she held up her hand before motioning toward the letter. "I can't help you with this. I have enough tangible problems here on the ranch. I don't have time to deal with fantasies."

Trask watched as she forced the curtain of callous disinterest over her beautiful features. The emerald-green eyes, which had once been so innocent and loving, turned cold with determination. "Oh, God, Tory, is this what I did to you?" he asked in bewilderment. "Did what happened between us take away all your trust? All your willingness to help? Your concern for others as well as yourself?" He was slowly advancing upon her, his footsteps muffled by the braided rug.

Tory's heart pounded betrayingly at his approach. It pulsed rapidly in the hollow of her throat and Trask's intense gaze rested on the revealing cleft.

"I've missed you," he whispered.

"No—"

"I didn't mean for everything between us to end the way it did."

"But it did. Nothing can change that. You sent my father to prison."

"But I only told the truth." He paused at the desk and hooked a leg over the corner as he stared down at her.

"Let's not go over this again. It's been too long, Trask. Too many wounds are still fresh." She swallowed with difficulty but managed to meet his stare boldly. "I've hated you a long time," she said, feeling her tongue trip over the lie she had held true for five unforgiving years.

"I don't believe it."

"You ruined me single-handedly."

"Your father did that." He leaned forward. He was close enough to touch her, but he stopped just short and stared down into her eyes. Eyes that had trusted him with her life five years earlier. "What did you expect me to do? Lie on the witness stand? Would you have preferred not knowing about your father?"

She couldn't stand it anymore; couldn't return his self-righteous stare. "He was innocent, damn it!" Her fists curled into knots of fury and she pushed herself up from the chair.

"Then why didn't he save himself, tell his side of the story?"

"I don't know." Her voice trembled slightly. "Don't you think I've asked myself just that question over and over again?" She felt his arms fold around her, draw her close, hold her body against his as he straightened from the desk. She heard the steady beating of his heart, felt the warmth of his breath caress her hair and she knew in a blinding flash of truth that she had never stopped loving him.

"If there were another man involved in the horse swindle, don't you want to see him accused of the crime?"

"So he could be put behind bars like my father."

"Oh, Tory," he said, releasing a sigh as his arms tightened around her. "How can you be so damned one-sided? You used to care what happened to people . . ."

"I still do."

"But not to the extent that you're willing to help me find out who was involved in my brother's murder and the Quarter Horse swindle."

She felt herself sag against him. *It would be so nice just to forget about what happened. Pretend that everything was just as it had been on the night she'd met Trask McFadden before her life had become irrevocably twisted with his.* "I just don't know if it will do any good. For all you know that letter could be phony, the work of someone who gets his jollies by stirring up trouble."

"Like the dead calf?"

Tory ran her fingers through her hair. "You don't know that the two incidents are related."

"But we won't find out unless we try." He held her closer and his breath whispered through her hair. "Just give it a chance, Tory. Trust me."

The same old words. Lies and deceit. Rolling as easily off his tongue as they had in the past. All the kindness in her heart withered and died.

She extracted herself from his embrace and impaled him with her indignant green-eyed stare. "I can't help you, Trask," she whispered. "You're on your own this time." She reached for the copy of the note and slowly wadded it into a tight ball before tossing the damning piece of paper into the blackened fireplace.

Trask watched her actions and his lips tightened menacingly. "I'm going to find out if there was any truth to that letter," he stated emphatically. "And I'm going to do it with or without your help."

Though her heart was pounding erratically, she looked him squarely in the eye. "Then I guess you're going to do it alone, aren't you, senator?"

Looking as if he had something further to say, Trask turned on his heel and walked out of the room. The front door slammed behind him and the engine of his pickup roared to life before fading in the distance.

"You bastard," Tory whispered, sagging against the windowsill. "Why can't I stop loving you?"

Chapter Four

FOR SEVERAL HOURS after Trask had left the ranch, Tory sat on the window seat in her bedroom. Her chin rested on her knees as she stared into the dark night. Raindrops pelted against the panes, drizzling against the glass and blurring Tory's view of the lightning that sizzled across the sky to illuminate the countryside in its garish white light. To the west, thunder rolled ominously over thc mountains.

So Trask had come back after all. Tory frowned to herself and squinted into the darkness. *But he hadn't come back for her,* as he had vowed he would five years past. This time he had returned to Sinclair and the Lazy W because he needed her help to prove that another man was part of the Quarter Horse swindle as well as involved in Jason McFadden's premeditated death.

With tense fingers she pushed the hair out of her eyes. Seeing Trask again had brought back too many dangerous memories. Memories of a younger, more carefree and reckless period of her life. Memories of a love destined to die.

As she looked through the window into the black sky, Tory was reminded of a summer filled with hot sultry nights, the sweet scent of pine needles and the familiar feel of Trask's body pressed urgently against hers.

She had to rub her hands over her arms as she remembered the feel of Trask's hard muscles against her skin, the weight of his body pinning hers, the taste of his mouth . . .

"Stop it," she muttered aloud, pulling herself out of her wanton reverie. "He's the man that sent Dad to prison, for God's sake. Don't be a fool—not twice."

She walked over to the bed and tossed back the quilted coverlet before lying on the sheets and staring at the shadowed ceiling. Her feelings of love for Trask had been her Achilles' heel. She had trusted him with every breath of life in her body and he had used her. Worse than that he had probably planned the whole affair; staging it perfectly. And she'd been fool enough to fall for his act, hook, line and sinker. But not again.

With a disconsolate sigh, she rolled onto her side and stared at the nightstand. In the darkness she could barely make out the picture of her father.

"Oh, Dad," Tory moaned, twisting away from the picture. "I wish you were here." Calvin Wilson had been an incredibly strong man who had been able to stand up to any adversity. He had been able to deal with the loan officers of the local banks when the ranch was in obvious financial trouble. His calm gray eyes and soft-spoken manner had inspired the local bankers' confidence when the general ledgers of the Lazy W couldn't.

He had stood stoically at the grave site of his wife of fifteen years without so much as shedding a tear. While holding his children close he had mourned silently for the only woman he had truly loved, offering strength to his daughter and young son.

When he had faced sentencing for a crime he hadn't committed he hadn't blinked an eye. Nor had he so much as flinched when the sentence of thirty years in prison had been handed down. He had taken it all without the slightest trace of fear. When he'd found out that he was terminally ill with a malignant tumor, Calvin Wilson had been able to look death straight in the eye. Throughout his sixty-three years, he had been a strong man and a loving father. Tory knew in her heart that he couldn't have been involved in Jason McFadden's murder.

Then why didn't he stand up for himself at the trial?

If he had spoken out, told his side of the story, let the court hear the truth, even Trask's damning testimony would have been refuted and maybe Calvin Wilson would be alive now. And Trask wouldn't be back in Sinclair, digging up the past, searching for some elusive, maybe even phantom, conspirator in Jason's death.

And now Trask had returned, actually believing that someone else was involved in his brother's death.

So it all came back to Trask and the fact that Tory hadn't stopped loving him. She knew her feelings for him were crazy, considering everything they had been through. She loved him one minute, hated him the next and knew that she should never have seen him again. He could take his wild half-baked theories, anonymous letters and seductive smile straight back to Washington where they all belonged. Surely he had better things to do than bother her.

"Just leave me alone, Trask," Tory said with a sigh. "Go back to Washington and leave me alone . . . I don't want to love you anymore . . . I can't . . ."

THE NEXT MORNING, after a restless night, Tory was making breakfast when Keith, more than slightly hung over, entered the kitchen. Without a word he walked to the refrigerator, poured himself a healthy glass of orange juice and drank it in one swallow. He then slumped into a chair at the kitchen table and glared up at Tory with red-rimmed eyes.

"Don't tell me you're dehydrated," Tory said with a teasing lilt in her voice.

"Okay, I won't. Then you won't have to lecture me."

"Fair enough." From the looks of it Keith's hangover was punishment enough for his binge, Tory thought, and she had been the one who had insisted that he go into town last night. If he were suffering, which he obviously was, it was partially because of her insistence that he leave the ranch. She flipped the pancakes over and decided not to mention that Keith hadn't gotten home until after three. He was over twenty-one now, and she didn't have to mother him, though it was a hard habit to break considering that the past five years she had been father, mother and sister all rolled into one.

"How about some breakfast?" she suggested, stacking the pancakes on a plate near a pile of crisp bacon and placing the filled platter on the table.

"After a few answers."

"Okay." Tory slid into the chair facing him and poured syrup over her stack of hotcakes. "Shoot."

"What have you decided to do about McFadden?" Keith asked, forking a generous helping of bacon onto his plate.

"I don't know," Tory admitted. She took a bite from a strip of bacon. "Maybe there's nothing I can do."

"Like hell. You could leave."

"Not a chance, we went over this yesterday." She reached for the coffeepot and poured each of them a cup of coffee.

"McFadden will come here."

"He already has."

"What!" Keith's face lost all of its color. "When?"

"Last night. While you were in town."

Keith rubbed his palm over the reddish stubble on his chin. "Damn, I knew something like this would happen."

"It wasn't that big of a deal. We just talked."

Keith looked at his older sister as if she had lost her mind. "You did what?" he shouted, rising from the breakfast table.

"I said I talked with him. How else was I supposed to find out what he wanted?"

Keith's worried eyes studied her face. "So what happened to the woman who, just yesterday afternoon, was going to bodily throw Trask McFadden off her land if he set foot on it. You know, the lady with the ready rifle and deadly aim?"

"Now, wait a minute—" Tory's face lost all of its color and her eyes narrowed.

"Weren't you the one who suggested that we point a rifle at his head and tell him to get lost?"

"I was only joking . . ."

"Like hell!" Keith sputtered before truly seeing his sister for the first time that morning. A sinking realization hit him like a ton of bricks. "Tory, you're still in love with him, aren't you? I can't believe it! After what he did to you?" Keith stared at his sister incredulously before stalking over to the refrigerator and pouring himself a large glass of milk. "This isn't happening," he said, as if to console himself. "This is all just a bad dream . . ."

"I'm not in love with him, Keith," Tory said, tossing her hair over her shoulder and turning her face upward in order to meet Keith's disbelieving gaze.

"But you were once."

"Before he testified against Dad."

"Goddamn," Keith muttered as he sucked in his breath and got hold of himself. His large fist curled in frustration. "I knew he'd show up the minute I left the ranch. What did he want?"

"My help."

"Your what? I can't believe it. After what he put you through? The nerve of that bastard!" He took a long swig from his glass with one hand, then motioned to his sister. "Well go on, go on, this is getting better by the minute."

"He thinks that there may have been someone else involved in Jason's murder and the horse swindle."

"Are you kiddin'?" Keith placed his empty glass on the counter and shook his head in disbelief. "After all this time? No way!"

"That's what I told him."

"But he didn't buy it?"

"I'd say not."

"Great! The dumb bastard will probably drag all of it up again. It'll be in the papers and everything." Keith paced between the table and the back door. He squinted against the bright morning sunshine streaming through the dusty windowpanes and looked toward the barn. "Dad's name is sure to come up."

"Sit down and eat your breakfast," Tory said, eyeing Keith's neglected plate.

Keith ignored her. "This is the last thing we need right now, you know. What with all the problems we're having with the bank . . ." He swore violently, balled one fist and smashed it into his other palm. "I should never have left you last night, I knew it, damn it, I knew it!" His temper threatened to explode completely for a minute before he finally managed to contain his fury.

Slowly uncurling his fist, he regained his composure and added with false optimism, "Oh, well, maybe McFadden got whatever it was he wanted off his chest and now it's over."

Tory hated to burst Keith's bubble, but she had always been straight with her brother, telling him about the problems with the ranch when they occurred. There was no reason to change now. "I don't know that it's over."

"What's that supposed to mean?"

"I don't think Trask is going to let up on this. He seemed pretty determined to me." Tory had lost all interest in her breakfast and pushed her plate aside. Unconsciously she brushed the crumbs from the polished maple surface of the table.

"But why? What's got him all riled up after five years?" Keith wondered aloud. "His term as a senator isn't up for another couple of years, so he isn't looking for publicity . . ."

"He got a letter."

Keith froze. He turned incredulous gray eyes on his sister. "Wait a minute. The man must get a ton of mail. What kind of a letter got under his skin?"

"An anonymous one."

"So what?"

No time like the present to drop the bomb, she supposed. With a feeling of utter frustration she stood, picked up her plate and set it near the sink. "If you want to read it, there's a copy in the den, in the fireplace."

"In the fireplace! Wonderful," Keith muttered sarcastically as he headed through the archway that opened to the short hallway separating the living room, kitchen, dining room and den.

"Hey, what about this breakfast?" Tory called after him.

“I’m not hungry,” Keith replied, from somewhere in the vicinity of the den.

“Great,” Tory muttered under her breath as she put the uneaten pancakes and bacon on another plate. “Tomorrow morning it’s cold cereal for you, brother dear.” With a frown at the untouched food, she opened the door to the back porch and set the plate on the floorboards. Alex, the ranch’s ancient Border collie, stood on slightly arthritic legs and wagged his tail before helping himself to Keith’s breakfast.

“Serves him right,” Tory told the old dog as she petted him fondly and scratched Alex’s black ears. “I’m glad someone appreciates my cooking.”

Tory heard Keith return to the kitchen. With a final pat to Alex’s head, she straightened and walked into the house.

Keith was standing in the middle of the kitchen looking for all the world as if he would drop through the floor. He was holding the crumpled and now slightly blackened piece of paper in his hands and his face had paled beneath his tan. He set the paper on the table and smoothed out the creases in the letter. “Holy shit.”

“My sentiments exactly.”

“So how does he think you could help him?” Keith asked, his eyes narrowing in suspicion.

“I don’t know. We never got that far.”

“And this—” he pointed down at the paper “—is why he wanted to see you?”

“That’s what he said.”

Keith closed his eyes for a minute, trying to concentrate. “That’s a relief, I guess.”

Tory raised an inquisitive brow. “Meaning?”

Keith smiled sadly and shook his head. “That I don’t want to see you hurt again.”

"Don't worry, brother dear," she assured him with a slightly cynical smile, "I don't intend to be. But thanks anyway, for the concern."

"I don't want to be thanked, Tory. I just want you to avoid McFadden. He's trouble."

Tory couldn't arguc the point. She turned on the tap and started hot water running into the sink. As the sink filled, she began washing the dishes before she hit Keith with the other bad news. "Something else happened last night."

"I'm not sure I want to know what it is," Keith said, picking up his coffee cup and drinking some of the lukewarm liquid. With a scowl, he reached for the pot and added some hot coffee to the tepid fluid in his cup.

"You probably don't."

He poured more coffee into Tory's empty cup and set it on the wooden counter, near the sink. "So what happened?"

"There was some other nasty business yesterday," Tory said, ignoring the dishes for the moment and wiping her hands on a dish towel. As she picked up her cup she leaned her hips against the edge of the wooden counter and met Keith's worried gaze.

"What now?" he asked as he settled into the cane chair near the table and propped his boots on the seat of another chair.

"Someone clipped the barbed wire on the northwest side of the ranch, came in and shot one of the calves. Three times in the abdomen. A heifer. About four months old."

Keith's hand hesitated over the sugar bowl and his head snapped up. "You think it was done deliberately?"

"Had to be. I called the sheriff's office. They're sending a man out this morning. Rex is spending the morning going over all of the fence bordering the ranch and checking it for any other signs of destruction."

"Just what we need," Keith said, cynicism tightening the corners of his mouth. "Another crisis on the Lazy W. How'd you find out about it?"

"One of Len Ross's men noticed it yesterday evening. Len called Rex and he checked it out."

"What about the rest of the livestock?"

"As far as I know all present and accounted for."

"Son of a bitch!" Keith forgot about the sugar and took a swallow of his black coffee.

"Trask thinks it might be related to that." She pointed to the blackened letter.

"Trask thinks?" Keith repeated, his eyes narrowing. "How does he know about it?"

"He was here when Rex came over to tell me about it."

Keith looked physically pained. "Lord, Tory, I don't know how much more of your cheery morning news I can stand."

"That's the last of the surprises."

"Thank God," Keith said, pushing himself up from the table and glaring pointedly at his older sister. "You're on notice, Tory."

She had to chuckle. "For what?"

"From now on when I decide to stay on the ranch rather than checking out the action at the Branding Iron, I'm not going to let you talk me out of it."

"Is that so? And how would you have handled Trask when he showed up on the porch?"

"I would have taken your suggestion yesterday and met him with a rifle in my hands."

"This isn't 1840, you know."

"Doesn't matter."

"You can't threaten a United States senator, Keith."

"Just you watch," Keith said, reaching for his Stetson

on the peg near the back door. "The next time McFadden trespasses, I'll be ready for him." With those final chilling words, he was out the back door of the house and heading for the barn. Tory watched him with worried eyes. Keith's temper had never had much of a fuse and Trask's presence seemed to have shortened it considerably.

It was her fault, she supposed. She should never have let Keith see the books. It didn't take a genius to see that the Lazy W was in pitiful financial shape, and dredging up the old scandal would only make it worse. But Keith had asked to see the balance sheets, and Tory had let him review everything, inwardly pleased that he had grown up enough to care.

DEPUTY WOODWARD ARRIVED shortly after ten. Tory had been in the den writing checks for the month-end bills when she had heard the sound of a vehicle approaching and had looked out the window to see the youngest of Paul Barnett's deputies getting out of his car. Slim, with a thin mustache, he had been hired in the past year and was one of the few deputies she had never met. Once, while in town, Keith had pointed the young man out to her.

When the chimes sounded, Tory put the checkbook into the top drawer of the desk and answered the door.

"'Mornin'," Woodward said with a smile. "I'm looking for Victoria Wilson."

"You found her."

"Good. I'm Greg Woodward from the sheriff's office. From what I understand, you think someone's been taking potshots at your livestock."

Tory nodded. "Someone has. I've got a dead calf to prove it."

"Just one?"

"So far," Tory replied. "I thought maybe some of the other ranchers might have experienced some sort of vandalism like this on their ranches."

The young deputy shook his head. "Is that what you think it was? Vandalism?"

Tory thought about the dead calf and the clipped fence. "No, not really. I guess I was just hoping that the Lazy W hadn't been singled out."

Woodward offered an understanding grin. "Let's take a look at what happened."

Tory sat in the passenger seat of the deputy's car as he drove down the rutted road she had traveled with Trask less than twelve hours earlier. The grooves in the dirt road were muddy and slick from the rain, but Deputy Woodward's vehicle made it to the site of the clipped fence without any problem.

Rex was already working on restringing the barbed wire. He looked up when he saw Tory, frowned slightly and then straightened, adjusting the brim of his felt Stetson.

As Deputy Woodward studied the cut wire and corpse of the calf, he asked Tory to tell him what had happened. She, with Rex's help, explained about Len Ross's call and how she and Rex had subsequently discovered the damage to the fence and the calf's dead body.

"But no other livestock were affected?" Woodward asked, writing furiously on his report.

"No," Rex replied, "at least none that we know about."

"You've checked already?"

"I've got several men out looking right now," Rex said.

"What about other fences, the buildings, or the equipment for the farm?"

"We have a combine that broke down last week, but it was just a matter of age," Tory said.

Woodward seemed satisfied. He took one last look at the calf and scowled. "I'll file this report and check with some of the neighboring ranchers to see if anything like this has happened to anyone else." He looked meaningfully at Tory. "And you'll call, if you find anything else?"

"Of course," Tory said.

"Does anyone else know what happened here?" the young man asked, as he finished his report.

"Only two people other than the ranch hands," Tory replied. "Len Ross and Trask McFadden."

The young man's head jerked up. "Senator McFadden?"

Tory nodded and offered a confident smile she didn't feel. Greg Woodward was a local man. Though he had probably still been in high school at the time, he would have heard of Jason McFadden's murder and the conspiracy of the horse swindlers who had been convicted. "Trask was visiting last night when Rex got the news from Len and came up to the house to tell me what had happened."

"Did he make any comments—being as he was here and all—or did he think it was vandalism?"

Tory's mind strayed to her conversation with Trask and his insistence that the animal's death was somehow related to the anonymous letter he had received. "I don't know," she hedged. "I suppose you'll have to ask him—"

"No reason to bother the senator," Rex interjected, his eyes traveling to Tory with an unspoken message. "He doesn't know any more than either of us."

Deputy Woodward caught the meaningful glance between rancher and foreman but didn't comment. He had enough sense to know that something wasn't right at the Lazy W and that Senator McFadden was more than a casual friend. On the drive back with Tory, Woodward silently speculated on the past scandal and what this recently divulged information could mean.

When the deputy deposited Tory back at the house, she felt uneasy. Something in the young man's attitude had changed when she had mentioned that Trask had been on the ranch. *It's starting all over again,* she thought to herself. *Trask has only been in town two days and the trouble's starting all over again. As if she and everyone connected with the Lazy W hadn't suffered enough from the scandal of five years past.*

TORY PARKED THE pickup on the street in front of the feed store in Sinclair. So far the entire day had been a waste. Deputy Woodward hadn't been able to ease her mind about the dead calf; in fact, if anything, the young man's reaction to the news that Trask knew of the incident only added to Tory's unease.

After Deputy Woodward had gone, Tory had attempted to do something, anything to keep her mind off Trask. But try as she might, she hadn't been able to concentrate on anything other than Trask and his ridiculous idea—no, make that conviction—that another person was involved in the Quarter Horse swindle as well as his brother's death.

He's jumping at shadows, she told herself as she stepped out of the pickup and into the dusty street, but she couldn't shake the image of Trask, his shoulders erect in controlled, but deadly determination as he had stood in her father's den the night before. She had witnessed the outrage in his blue eyes. *He won't let up on this until he has an answer,* she told herself with a frown.

She pushed her way into the feed store and made short work of ordering supplies for the Lazy W. The clerk, Alma Ray, had lived in Sinclair all her life and had worked at Rasmussen Feed for as long as Tory could remember. She was a woman in her middle to late fifties and wore her soft red hair piled on her head. She had always offered Tory a pleasant smile and thoughtful advice in the past, but this afternoon Alma's brown eyes were cold, her smile forced.

"Don't get paranoid," Tory cautioned herself in a whisper as she stepped out of the feed store and onto the sidewalk. "It's not as if this town is against you, for God's sake. Alma's just having a bad day—"

"Tory."

At the sound of her name, Tory turned to face Neva McFadden, Jason's widow. Neva was hurrying up the sidewalk in Tory's direction and Tory's heart sank. She saw the strain in Neva's even features, the worry in her doe-brown eyes. Images of the courtroom and Neva's proud face twisted in agony filled Tory's mind.

"Do you have a minute?" Neva asked, clutching a bag of groceries to her chest.

It was the first time Neva McFadden had spoken to Tory since the trial.

"Sure," Tory replied. She forced a smile, though the first traces of dread began to crawl up her spine. It couldn't be a coincidence that Neva wanted to talk to her the day after Trask had returned to the Lazy W. "Why don't we sit down?" She nodded in the direction of the local café, which was just across the street from the feed store.

"Great," Neva said with a faltering smile.

Once they were seated in a booth and had been

served identical glasses of iced tea Tory decided to take the offensive. "So, what's up?"

Neva stopped twirling the lemon in her glass. "I wanted to talk to you about Trask."

"I thought so. What about him?"

"I know that he went to see you last night and I have a good idea of what it was about," Neva stated. She hesitated slightly and frowned into her glass as if struggling with a weighty decision. "I don't see any reason to beat around the bush, Tory. I know about the letter Trask received. He showed me a copy of it."

"He showed it to me, too," Tory admitted, hiding her surprise. She had assumed that Trask hadn't spoken to anyone but her. It wouldn't take long for the gossip to start all over again.

"And what do you think about it?" Neva asked.

Tory lifted her shoulders. "I honestly don't know."

Neva let out a sigh and ignored her untouched drink. "Well, I do. It was a prank," Neva said firmly. "Just someone who wants to stir up the trouble all over again."

"Why would anyone want to do that?"

"I wish I knew," Neva admitted, shaking her head. The rays of the afternoon sun streamed through the window and reflected in the golden strands of her hair. Except for the lines of worry surrounding her eyes, Neva McFadden was an extremely attractive woman. "I wish to God I knew what was going on."

"So do I."

Neva's fingers touched Tory's forearm. She bit at her lower lip, as if the next words were awkward. "I know that you cared for Trask, Tory, and I know that you think he . . ."

"Used me?"

"Yes."

"It was more than that, Neva," Tory said, suddenly

wanting this woman who had borne so much pain to understand. "Trask betrayed me and my family."

Neva stiffened and she withdrew her hand. "By taking care of his own."

"He lied, Neva."

Neva shook her head. "That's not the way it was. He just wanted justice for Jason's death."

"Justice or revenge?" Tory asked, and could have kicked herself when she saw the anger flare in Neva's eyes.

"Does it matter?"

Tory shrugged and frowned. "I suppose not. It was a horrible thing that happened to Jason and you. And . . . and I'm sorry for . . . everything . . . I know it's been hard for you; harder than it's been for me." Her mouth suddenly dry, Tory took a long drink of the cold tea and still felt parched.

"It's over," Neva said. "Or it was until Trask came back with some wild ideas about another person being involved in Jason's death."

"So you think the letter was a prank."

"Of course it was."

"How can you be sure?"

Neva avoided Tory's direct gaze. "It's been five years, Tory. Five years without a husband or father to my son."

All the feelings of remorse Tory had felt during the trial overcame her as she watched the young woman battle against tears. "Neva, I'm sorry if my family had any part in the pain you and Nicholas have felt."

"Your father was involved with Linn Benton and George Henderson. I know you never believed that he was guilty, Tory, but the man didn't even stand up for himself at the trial."

Tory felt as if a knife, five years old and dull, had

been thrust into her heart. “I don’t see any reason to talk about this, Neva. I’ve already apologized.” Tory pushed herself up from the table. “I think I should go.”

“Don’t! Sit down, Tory,” Neva pleaded. “Look, I didn’t mean to start trouble. God knows that’s the last thing I want. The reason I wanted to talk to you is because of Trask.”

Tory felt her heart begin to pound. She took a seat on the edge of the booth, her back stiff. “So you said.”

“Don’t get involved with him again, Tory. Don’t start believing that there was more to what happened than came out in the trial.”

“I know there was more” Tory stated, feeling a need to defend her father.

“I don’t think so. And even if there was, what would be the point of dredging it all up again? It won’t bring Jason back to life, or your father. All it will do is bring the whole sordid scandal back into the public eye.”

Tory leaned back and studied the blond woman. There was more to what Neva was suggesting than the woman had admitted. Tory could feel it. “But what if the letter Trask received contains part of the truth? Don’t you want to find out?”

“No.” Neva shook her head vehemently.

“I don’t understand—”

“That’s because you don’t have a child, Tory. You don’t have a six-year-old son who needs all the protection I can give him. It’s bad enough that he doesn’t have a father, but does he have to be reminded, taunted, teased about the fact that his dad was murdered by men in this town that he trusted?”

“Oh, Neva—”

“Think about it. Think long and hard about who is going to win if Trask continues his wild-goose chase;

no one. Not you, Tory. Not me. And especially not Nicholas. He's the loser!"

Tory chose her words carefully. "Don't you think your son deserves the truth?"

"Not if it costs him his peace of mind." Neva lifted her chin and her brown eyes grew cold. "I know that you don't want another scandal any more than I do. And as for Trask, well—" she lifted her palms upward and then dropped her hands "—I hope that, for both your sakes, you don't get involved with him again. Not just because of the letter. I don't think he could handle another love affair with you, Tory. The last time almost killed him." With her final remarks, Neva reached for her purse and sack of groceries and left the small café.

"So much for mending fences," Tory muttered as she paid the small tab and walked out of the restaurant. After crossing the street, she climbed into her pickup and headed back to the Lazy W. Though she had never been close to Neva, not even before Jason's death, Tory had hoped that someday the old wounds would heal and the scars become less visible. Now, with the threat of Trask opening up another investigation into his brother's death, that seemed impossible.

As Tory drove down the straight highway toward the ranch, her thoughts turned to the past. Maybe Neva was right. Maybe listening to Trask would only prove disastrous.

Five years before, after her father's conviction, Tory had been forced to give up her dream of graduate school to stay at the Lazy W and hold the ranch together. Not only had the ranch suffered financially, but her brother, Keith, who was only sixteen at the time, needed her support and supervision. Her goal of becoming a veterinarian as well as her hopes of becoming Trask McFadden's wife had been shattered as easily as crystal against stone.

When Calvin had been sent to prison, Tory had stayed at the ranch and tried to raise a strong-willed younger brother as well as bring the Lazy W out of the pool of red ink. In the following five years Keith had grown up and become responsible, but the ranch was still losing money, though a little less each year.

Keith, at twenty-one, could, perhaps, run the ranch on his own. But it was too late for Tory. She could no more go back to school and become a veterinarian than she could become Trask McFadden's wife.

Chapter Five

THE BUILDINGS OF the Lazy W, made mostly of roughhewn cedar and fir, stood proudly on the flat land comprising the ranch and were visible from the main highway. Tory wheeled the pickup onto the gravel lane that was lined with stately pines and aspen and led up to the house.

Purebred horses grazed in the fields surrounding the stables, whole spindly legged foals romped in the afternoon sunlight.

Tory's heart swelled with pride for the Lazy W. Three hundred acres of high plateau held together by barbed wire and red metal posts had been Tory's home for all of her twenty-seven years and suddenly it seemed that everyone wanted to take it away from her. Trask, with his damned investigation of the horse swindle of five years ago, was about to ruin her credibility as a Quarter Horse breeder by reminding the public of the shady dealings associated with the Lazy W.

Tall grass in the meadow ruffled in the summer breeze that blew across the mountains. White clouds clung to the jagged peaks of the Cascades, shadowing the grassland. This was the land she loved and Tory would fight tooth and nail to save it—even if it meant fighting Trask every step of the way. He couldn't just come marching back into her life and destroy everything she had worked for in the past five years!

Tory squinted against the late-afternoon sun as she drove the pickup into the parking lot near the barn and killed the engine. The warm westerly wind had removed any trace of the rainstorm that had occurred the night before and waves of summer heat shimmered in the distance, distorting the view of the craggy snow-covered mountains.

She pushed her keys into the pocket of her jeans and walked to the paddock where Governor was still separated from the rest of the horses. Eldon, one of the ranch hands, was dutifully walking the bay stallion.

"How's our patient?" Tory asked as she patted Governor on the withers and lifted his hoof. Governor snorted and flattened his ears against his head. "Steady, boy," Tory murmured softly.

"Still sore, I'd guess," the fortyish man said with a frown. His weathered face was knotted in concern.

"I'd say so," Tory agreed. "Has he been favoring it?"

"Some."

"What about his temperature?" Tory asked as she looked at the sensitive tissue within the hoof.

"Up a little."

She looked up and watched Governor's ribs, to determine if his breathing was accelerated, but it wasn't.

"I'll call the vet. Maybe Anna should have a look at it."

"Wouldn't hurt."

She released Governor's hoof and dusted her hands on her jeans. "I'll see if she can come by tomorrow; until then we'll just keep doing what we have been for the past two days."

"You got it."

Tory, with the intention of pouring a large glass of

lemonade once she was inside the house, walked across the gravel parking area and then followed a worn path to the back porch. Alex was lying in the shady comfort of a juniper bush. He wagged his tail as she approached and Tory reached down to scratch the collie behind his ears before she opened the door to the kitchen.

"Tory? Is that you?" Keith yelled from the vicinity of the den when the screen door banged shut behind her.

"Who else?" she called back just as she heard his footsteps and Keith entered the homey kitchen from the hall. His young face was troubled and dusty. Sweat dampened his hair, darkening the strands that were plastered to his forehead. "You were expecting someone?" she teased while reaching into the refrigerator for a bag of lemons.

"Of course not. I was just waiting for you to get back."

"That sounds ominous," she said, slicing the lemons and squeezing them on the glass juicer. "I'm making lemonade, you want some?"

Keith seemed distracted. "Yeah. Sure," he replied before his gray eyes darkened. "What took you so long in town?"

Tory looked up sharply. Keith hadn't acted like himself since Trask was back in Oregon. "What is this, an inquisition?"

"Hardly." Keith ran a hand over his forehead, forcing his hair away from his face. "Rex and I were just talking . . . about what happened last night."

"You mean the calf?" she asked.

"Partially." Keith had taken the wooden salt shaker off the table and was pretending interest in it.

Tory felt her back stiffen slightly as she poured sugar and the lemon juice into a glass pitcher. "And the rest of your discussion with Rex centered on Trask, is that it?"

"Right."

At that moment Rex walked into the room. He fidgeted, removed his hat and worked the brim in his gnarled fingers.

"How about a glass of lemonade?" Tory asked, as much to change the direction of the conversation as to be hospitable.

"Sure," the foreman responded. A nervous smile hovered near the corners of his mouth but quickly faded as he passed a hand over his chin. "I thought you'd like to know that all of the horses and cattle are alive and accounted for."

Relief seeped through Tory's body. So the calf was an isolated incident—so much for Trask's conspiracy theories about vague and disturbing warnings in the form of dead livestock. "Good. What about any other signs of trouble?"

Rex shook his head thoughtfully. "None that I could see. None of the animals escaped through that hole in the fence, and we couldn't find any other places where the fence was cut or tampered with."

Tory was beginning to feel better by the minute. The dark cloud of fear that had begun to settle over her the evening before was slowly beginning to dissipate. "And the fence that was damaged has been repaired?"

"Yep. Right after you brought the deputy out to look at the calf. Did it myself."

"Thanks, Rex."

"All part of the job," he muttered, avoiding her grateful glance.

"Well, then I guess the fact that the rest of the livestock is okay is good news," Tory said, wincing a little as she remembered the unfortunate heifer. Neither man responded. "Now, I think we should take some precautions to see that this doesn't happen again."

Rex smiled slightly. "I'm open to suggestion."

"Wait a minute, Tory," Keith cut in abruptly as Tory turned back to the pitcher of lemonade and began adding ice water to the cloudy liquid. "Why are you avoiding the subject of McFadden?"

"Maybe I'm just tired of it," Tory said wearily. She had hoped to steer clear of another confrontation about Trask but knew the argument with her brother was inevitable. She poured the pale liquid into three glasses filled with ice and offered a glass to each of the men.

"McFadden's not going to just walk away from this, you know," Keith said.

"I know."

"Then for Pete's sake, Tory, we've got to come up with a plan to fight him."

"A plan?" Tory repeated incredulously. She had to laugh as she took a sip of her drink. "You're beginning to sound paranoid, Keith. A plan! People who make up plans are either suffering from overactive imaginations or are trying to hide something. Which are you?"

"Neither. I'm just trying to avoid another scandal, that's all," Keith responded, his eyes darkening. "And maybe save this ranch in the process. The last scandal nearly destroyed the Lazy W as well as killed Dad, or don't you remember?"

"I remember," Tory said, some of the old bitterness returning.

"Look, Sis," Keith pleaded, his voice softening a little. "I've studied the books and worked out some figures. The way I see it, the Lazy W has about six months to survive. Then the note with the bank is due, right?"

"Right," Tory said on a weary sigh.

"The only way the bank will renew it is if we can prove that we can run this place at a profit. Now you're close, Tory, damned close, but all it takes is for all the old rumors to start flying again. Once people are reminded of what Dad was supposedly involved in, we'll lose buyers as quickly as you can turn around, and there go the profits."

"You don't know that—"

"I sure as hell do."

Tory shifted and avoided Keith's direct stare. She knew what he was going to say before the words were out.

"The only way the Lazy W can stay in business is to sell those Quarter Horses you've been breeding. You know it as well as I do. And no one is going to touch those horses with a ten-foot pole if they think for one minute that the horses might be part of a fraud. The reputation of this ranch is . . . well, shady or at least it was, all because of the Quarter Horse scam five years ago. If all the publicity is thrown into the public eye again, your potential buyers are going to dry up quicker than Devil's Creek in a hot summer."

"And you think that's what will happen if Trask is allowed to investigate his anonymous letter?"

"You can count on it."

Tory's eyes moved from the stern set of Keith's jaw to Rex. "You've been awfully quiet. What do you think?"

"I think what I always have," Rex said, rubbing his chin. "McFadden is trouble. Plain and simple."

"There's no doubt about that," Tory thought aloud, "but I don't know what any of us can do about it."

"Maybe you can talk him out of dredging everything up again," Keith suggested. "However, I'd like it better if you had nothing to do with the son of a bitch."

Tory glared at her younger brother. "Let's leave reference to Trask's parentage and any other ridiculous insults out of this, okay? Now how do you know he'll be back?"

"Oh, he'll be back all right. He's like a bad check; he just comes bouncing back. As sure as the sun comes up in the morning, McFadden will be back."

Tory shook her head and frowned into her glass. She swirled the liquid and stared at the melting ice. "So if he returns to the Lazy W, you want me to try and persuade him to ignore the letter and all this nonsense about another man being involved in the Quarter Horse swindle and Jason's death. Have I got it right?"

"Essentially," Keith said.

"Not exactly an intricate plan."

"But the only one we've got."

Tory set her glass on the counter and her eyes narrowed. "What if the letter is true, Keith? What if another person was involved in Jason's death, a man who could, perhaps, clear Dad's name?"

Keith smiled sadly, suddenly old beyond his years. "What's the chance of that happening?"

"'Bout one in a million, I'd guess," Rex said.

"Less than that," Keith said decisively, "considering that McFadden wouldn't be trying to clear Dad's name. He's the guy who put Dad in the prison in the first place, remember? I just can't believe that you're falling for his line again, Sis."

Tory paled slightly. "I'm not."

"Give me a break. You're softening to McFadden and you've only seen him once."

"Maybe I'm just tired of everyone trying to manipulate me," Tory said hotly. She stalked across the room and settled into one of the chairs near the table. “This whole thing is starting to reek of a conspiracy or at the very least a cover-up!”

“What do you mean?” Keith seemed thoroughly perplexed. Rex avoided Tory’s gaze and stared out the window toward the road.

“I mean that I ran into Neva McFadden at the feed store. She wanted to talk to me, for crying out loud! Good Lord, the woman hasn’t breathed a word to me since the trial and today she wanted to talk things over. Can you believe it?”

“ ‘Things’ being Trask?” Keith guessed.

“Right.” Tory smiled grimly at the irony of it all. Neva McFadden was the last person Tory would have expected to beg her to stay away from Trask and his wild theories.

“You know that she’s in love with him, don’t you?” Keith said, and noticed the paling of Tory’s tanned skin. Whether his sister denied it or not, Tory was still holding a torch for McFadden. That thought alone made Keith’s blood boil.

“She didn’t say so.”

“I doubt if she would: at least not to you.”

“Maybe not,” Tory whispered.

“So anyway, what did she want to talk about?”

“About the same thing you’re preaching right now. That Trasks’ anonymous letter was just a prank, that we should leave the past alone, that her son would suffer if the scandal was brought to the public’s attention again. She thought it would be wise if I didn’t see Trask again.”

“Too late for that,” Rex said, removing his hat and running his fingers through his sweaty silver hair as he stared through the window. His thick shoulders slumped and his amiable smile fell from his face. "He's coming down the drive right now."

"Great," Keith muttered.

Tory's heart began to pound with dread. "Maybe we should tell him everything we discussed just now."

"That would be suicide, Tory. Our best bet is to convince him that his letter was nothing more than a phony—"

A loud rap on the door announced Trask's arrival. Keith let out a long breath of air. "Okay, Sis, you're on."

Tory's lips twisted cynically. "If you're looking for an Oscar-winning performance, you're going to be disappointed."

"What's that supposed to mean?" Keith asked warily.

"Haven't you ever heard the expression 'You catch more flies with honey than with vinegar'?" Without further explanation, she walked down the short corridor, ignored the round of swearing she heard in the kitchen and opened the front door.

Trask was about to knock again. His fist was lifted to his shoulder and his jaw was set angrily. At the sight of Tory, her gray-green eyes sparkling with a private joke, he was forced to smile and his angular features softened irresistibly. When Senator McFadden decided to turn on the charm, the effect was devastating to Tory's senses, even though she knew she couldn't trust him.

"I thought maybe you were trying to give me a not-so-subtle hint," Trask said.

Tory shook her head and laughed. "Not me, senator. I'm not afraid to speak my mind and tell you you're not welcome."

"I already knew that."

"But you're back." She leaned against the door, not bothering to invite him inside, and studied the male contours of his face. Yes, sir, the senator was definitely a handsome man, she thought. Five years hadn't done him any harm—if anything, the added maturity was a plus to his appearance.

"I hoped that maybe you'd reconsidered your position and thought about what I had to say."

"Oh, I've thought about it a lot," Tory replied. "No one around here will let me forget it."

"And what have you decided?" Cobalt-blue eyes searched her face, as if seeing it for the first time. Tory's heart nearly missed a beat.

"Why don't you come inside and we'll talk about it?" Tory stepped away from the door allowing him to pass. Keith and Rex were already in the den and when Trask walked through the archway, the tension in the room was nearly visible.

"It takes a lot of guts for you to come back here," Keith said. He walked over to the bar and poured himself a stiff drink.

"I said I would," Trask responded. A confident grin contrasted with the fierce intensity of his gaze.

"But I can't believe that you honestly expect Tory or anyone at the Lazy W to help you on . . . this wild-goose chase of yours."

"I just want to look into it."

"Why?" Keith demanded, replacing the bottle and lifting the full glass to his lips.

Trask crossed his arms over his chest. "I want to know the truth about my brother's death."

Keith shook his head. "So all of a sudden the testimony at the trial wasn't enough. The scandal wasn't enough. Sending an innocent man to jail wasn't enough. You want more."

"Only the truth."

Keith's jaw jutted forward. "It's a little too late, don't ya think, McFadden? You should have been more interested in the truth before taking that witness stand and testifying against Calvin Wilson."

"If your father would have told his side of the story, maybe I wouldn't be here right now."

"Too late for second-guessing, McFadden," Keith said, his voice slightly uneven. "The man's dead."

An uncomfortable silence filled the room. Rex shifted restlessly and pushed his Stetson over his eyes. "I've got to get home," he said. "Belinda will be looking for me." He headed toward the door and paused near the outer hallway. "I'll see ya in the morning."

"Good night, Rex," Tory said just as the sound of the front door slamming shut rattled through the building.

"I think maybe you should leave, too," Keith said, taking a drink of his Scotch and leaning insolently against the rocks of the fireplace. He glared angrily at Trask and didn't bother to hide his contempt. "We're not interested in hearing what you have to say. You said plenty five years ago."

"I didn't perjure myself, if that's what you're insinuating."

"I'm not insinuating anything, McFadden. I believe in telling it straight out."

"So do I."

"Then you'll understand when I ask you to leave and tell you that we don't want any part of your plans to drag up all the scandal about the horse swindle again. It won't do anyone a bit of good, least of all the people on this ranch. You'll have to find another way to get elected this time, senator."

Trask leaned a hip against the back of a couch and turned his attention away from Keith to Tory. His blue eyes pierced hers. "Is that how you feel?" he demanded.

Tory looked at Trask's ruggedly handsome face and tried to convince herself that Trask had used her, betrayed her, destroyed everything she had ever loved, but she couldn't hide from the honesty in his cold blue stare. He was dangerous. As dangerous as he had ever been, and still Tory's heart raced at the sight of him. She knew her fascination for the man bordered on lunacy. "I agree with Keith," she said at last. "I can't see that opening up this whole can of worms will accomplish anything."

"Except make sure that a guilty party is punished."

"So you're still looking for retribution," she whispered, shaking her head. "It's been five years. Nothing is going to change what happened. Neva's right. Nothing you can do or say will bring Jason back."

"Neva?" Trask repeated. "You've been talking to her?" His features froze and the intensity of his stare cut Tory to the bone.

"Today, she ran into me on the street."

"And the conversation just happened to turn to me." The corners of his mouth pulled down.

Tory's head snapped upward and her chin angled forward defiantly. "She's worried about you, senator, as well as about her son. She thinks you're on a personal vendetta that will do nothing more than open up all the old wounds again, cause more pain, stir up more trouble."

Trask winced slightly and let out a disgusted sound. "I'm going to follow this through, Tory. I think you can understand. It's my duty to my brother. He was murdered, for God's sake! Murdered! And one of the men responsible might still be free!

"The way I see it, you have two options: you can be with me or against me, but I'd strongly suggest that you think about all of the alternatives. If your father was innocent, as you so self-righteously claim, you've just gotten the opportunity to prove it."

"You would help me?" she asked skeptically.

"Don't believe him, Tory," Keith insisted, walking between Tory and Trask and sending his sister pleading glances. "You trusted him once before and all he did was spit on you."

Trask's eyes narrowed as he focused on Tory's younger brother. "Maybe you'd better just stay out of this one, Keith," he suggested calmly. "This is between your sister and me."

"I don't think—"

"I can handle it," Tory stated, her gaze shifting from Trask to Keith and back again. Her shoulders were squared, her lips pressed together in determination. Fire sparked in her eyes.

Keith understood the unspoken message. Tory would handle Trask in her own way. "All right. I've said everything I needed to say anyway." He pointed a long finger at Trask. "But as far as I'm concerned, McFadden, you have no business here." Keith strode out of the room, grabbed his hat off the wooden peg in the entry hall, jerked open the front door and slammed it shut behind him.

Trask watched Keith leave with more than a little concern. "He's got more of a temper than you did at that age."

"He hates you," Tory said simply.

Trask smiled wryly and pushed his fingers through his hair. "Can't say as I blame him."

"I hate you, too," Tory lied.

"No, no you don't." He saw that she was about to protest and waved off her arguments before they could be voiced. "Oh, you hate what I did all right. And, maybe a few years back, you did hate me, or thought that you did. But now you know better."

"I don't know anything of the kind."

"Sure you do. You know that I haven't come back

here to hurt you and you know that I only did what I did five years ago because I couldn't lie on the witness stand. The last thing I wanted to do was send your dad to prison—"

Tory desperately held up a palm. "Stop!" she demanded, unable to listen to his lies any longer. "I—I don't want to hear any more of your excuses or rationalizations—"

"It's easier to hate me, is that it?"

"No—yes! God, yes. I can't have you come in here and confuse me and I don't want to be a part of this . . . investigation or whatever you want to call it. I don't care about anonymous letters."

"Or dead calves?"

"One has nothing to do with the other," she said firmly, though she had to fight to keep her voice from trembling.

Trask studied his hands before lifting his eyes to meet her angry gaze. "I think you're wrong, Tory. Doesn't it strike you odd that everyone you know wants you to avoid me?"

She shook her head and looked at the ceiling. "Not after the hell you put me through five years ago," she whispered.

"You mean that it hasn't crossed your mind that someone is deliberately trying to keep you out of this investigation for a reason?"

"Such as?"

"Such as hiding the guilty person's identity."

"I can't be involved in this," Tory said, as if to convince herself. She had to get away from Trask and his damned logic. When she was around him, he turned her mind around. She began walking toward the door but stopped dead in her tracks when he spoke.

"Are you afraid of the truth?"

"Of course not!" She turned and faced him.

He pushed himself away from the couch. "Then maybe it's me."

"Don't be ridiculous," she said, but as he advanced upon her, she saw the steadfastness of his gaze. It dropped from her eyes to her mouth and settled on the rising swell of her breasts. "I'm not afraid of you, Trask. I never have been. Not even after what you did to me."

He stopped when he was near her and his eyes silently accused her of attempting to deceive him. When he reached forward to brush a wayward strand of hair away from her face, his fingertip touched her cheek, but she didn't flinch. "Then maybe you're afraid of yourself."

"That's nonsense."

"I don't think so." His fingers wrapped around her nape and tilted her head upward as he lowered his head and captured her lips with his. His mouth was warm and gentle, his tongue quick to invade her parted lips. Memories of hot summer nights, star-studded skies and bodies glistening with the sheen of perfect afterglow filled her mind. How easily she could slip backward . . .

The groan from deep in his throat brought her crashing back to a reality as barren as the desert. He didn't love her, had never loved her, but was attempting once again to use her. As common sense overtook her, Tory tried to step backward but the arms surrounding her tightened, forcing her body close.

"Let go of me," she said, her eyes challenging.

"I don't think so. Letting you go was the biggest mistake I've ever made and believe me, I've made my share. I'm not about to make the same mistake twice."

"You may have made a lot of mistakes, Trask, but you didn't have a choice where I was concerned. I swore that I'd never let you hurt me again, and it's a promise to myself that I intend to keep."

The warm hands at the base of her spine refused to release her. Instead they began to slowly massage her, and through the thin fabric of her cotton blouse, she could feel Trask's heat. It seeped through the cloth and warmed her skin, just as it had in the past.

His lips caressed her face, touching the sensitive skin of her eyelids and cheeks.

"I can't let this happen," she whispered, knowing that she was unable to stop herself.

Her skin began to flush and the yearnings she had vowed dead reawakened as his mouth slid down her throat and his hands came around to unbutton her blouse. As the fabric parted Tory could feel his lips touching the hollow of her throat and the swell of her breasts.

"Trask, please . . . don't," she said, swallowing against the desire running wildly in her blood.

His tongue circled the delicate ring of bones at the base of her throat while his hands opened her blouse and pushed it gently off her shoulders. "I've always loved you, Tory," he said as he watched her white breasts rise and fall with the tempo of her breathing.

Her rosy nipples peeked seductively through the sheer pink lace of her bra and the swelling in his loins made him say things he would have preferred to remain secret. "Love me," he pleaded, lifting his gaze to her green eyes.

"I . . . I did, Trask," she replied, trying to think rationally. She reached for the blouse that had fallen to the floor, but his hand took hold of her wrist. "I loved you more than any woman should love a man and . . . and I paid for that love. I will never, never make that mistake again!"

The fingers over her wrist tightened and he jerked her close to his taut body. With his free hand he tilted her face upward so that she was forced to stare into his intense blue eyes. "You can come up with all the reasons and excuses you want, lady, but they're all a pack of lies."

"You should know, senator. You wrote the book on deceit."

His jaw whitened and his lips twisted cynically. "Why don't you look in the mirror, Tory, and see the kind of woman you've become: a woman who's afraid of the truth. You won't face the truth about your father and you won't admit that you still care for me."

"There's a big difference between love and lust."

"Is there?" He cocked a thick brow dubiously and ran his finger down her throat, along her breastbone to the front clasp of her bra. "What we felt for each other five years ago, what would you call that?"

"All those emotions were tangled in a web of lies, Trask. Each one a little bigger than the last. That's how I've come to think of what we shared: yesterday's lies." He released her slowly and didn't protest when she reached for her blouse and slipped it on.

"Then maybe it's time to start searching for the truth."

"By reopening the investigation into your brother's death?"

"Yes. Maybe if we set the past to rest, we could think about the future."

Tory let out a disgusted sound. "No way, senator. You know what they say, 'You can never go back.' Well, I believe it. Don't bother to tease me with vague promises about a future together, because I don't buy it. Not anymore. I've learned my lesson where you're concerned. I'm not as gullible as I used to be, thank God." She stepped away from him and finished buttoning her blouse.

His lips tightened and he pinched the bridge of his nose with his fingers, as if trying to thwart a potential headache. "Okay, Tory, so you aren't interested in a relationship with me—the least you can do is help me a little. If you really believe your father's name can be cleared, I'm offering you the means to do it."

"How?"

"I want to go up to Devil's Ridge tomorrow."

The request made her heart stop beating. Devil's Ridge was a piece of land not far from the Lazy W. It had once been owned by her father, and Calvin had willed the forty-acre tract in the foothills of the Cascades to Keith. Devil's Ridge was the parcel of land where the Quarter Horses were switched during the swindle; the piece of land that had proved Calvin Wilson's involvement in the scam.

"Tory, did you hear me?"

"Yes."

"Will you come with me?"

No! I can't face all of the scandal again. "If you promise that no one else will know about it." Tory saw the questions in his eyes and hastened to explain. "I don't want any publicity about this, until you're sure of your facts, senator."

"Fair enough." He studied her face for a minute. "Are you with me on this, Tory?"

"No, but I won't hinder you either," she said, tired of arguing with Trask, Keith, Neva and the whole damned world. "If you want permission to wander around Devil's Ridge, you've got it. And I'll go with you."

"Why?"

"Because I want to keep my eye on you, senator."

"You still don't trust me, do you?" he asked.

"I can't let myself." *It's my way of protecting myself against you.*

A cloud of anguish darkened his eyes but was quickly dispersed. "Then I'll be here around noon tomorrow."

"I'll be waiting."

He had started toward the door, but turned at the bittersweet words. "If only I could believe that," he said before opening the door and disappearing through it. Tory watched his retreating figure through the glass.

The late-afternoon sun was already casting lengthening shadows over the plains of the Lazy W as Trask strode to his pickup and, without looking backward, drove away.

"WHAT BUSINESS is it of yours?" Trask demanded of his sister-in-law. She was putting the finishing touches on a birthday cake for Nicholas, swirling the white frosting over the cake as if her brother-in-law's tirade was of little, if any, concern. "Why did you confront Tory?"

"It is my business," Neva threw back coolly as she surveyed her artwork and placed the knife in the empty bowl. When she turned to face Trask, her small chin was jutted in determination. "We're talking about the death of my husband, for God's sake. And you're the one who brought me into it when you started waving that god-awful note around here yesterday afternoon."

"But why did you try to convince Tory to stay out of it? She could help me."

Neva turned world-weary brown eyes on her brother-in-law. "Because I thought she might be able to get through to you. You don't listen to many people, Trask.

Not me. Not your advisors in Washington. No one. I thought maybe there was a chance that Tory might beat some common sense into that thick skull of yours."

"She tried," Trask admitted.

"But failed, I assume."

"This is something I have to do, Neva." Trask placed his large hands on Neva's slim shoulders, as if by touching he could make her understand.

With difficulty, Neva ignored the warmth of Trask's fingers. "And damn the consequences, right? Your integrity come hell or high water." She wrestled free of his grip.

"You're blowing this way out of proportion."

"Me?" she screamed. "What about you? You get one crank letter and you're ready to tear this town apart, dig up five-year-old dirt and start battling a new crusade." She smiled sadly at the tense man before her. "Only this time I'm afraid you'll get hurt, Don Quixote; the windmills might fight back and hurt you as well as your Dulcinea."

"Whom?"

"Dulcinea del Tobaso, the country girl whom Don Quixote selects as the lady of his knightly devotion. In this case, Victoria Wilson."

"You read too much," he said.

"Impossible."

Trask laughed despite the seriousness of Neva's stare. "Then you worry too much."

"It comes with the territory of being a mother," she said, picking up a frosting-laden beater and offering it to him. "Someone needs to worry about you."

He declined the beater. "I get by."

She studied the furrows of his brow. "I don't know, Trask. I just don't know."

"Just trust me, Neva."

The smile left her face and all of the emotions she had been battling for five long years tore at her heart. "I'd trust you with my life, Trask. You know that."

"Neva—" He took a step closer to her but she walked past him to the kitchen window. Outside she could watch Nicholas romp with the puppy Trask had given him for his birthday.

"But I can't trust you with Nicholas's life," she whispered, knotting her fingers in the corner of her apron. "I just can't do that and you have no right to ask me." Tears began to gather in her large eyes, and she brushed them aside angrily.

Trask let out a heavy sigh. "I'm going up to Devil's Ridge tomorrow."

"Oh, God, no." Neva closed her eyes. "Trask, don't—"

"This is something I have to do," he repeated.

"Then maybe you'd better leave," she said, her voice nearly failing her. Trask was as close to a father to Nicholas as he could be, considering the separation of more than half a continent. If she threw Trask out, Nicholas would never forgive her. "Do what you have to do."

"What I have to do is stay here for Nicholas's birthday party."

Neva smiled through her tears. "You're a bastard, you know, McFadden, but a charming one nonetheless."

"This is all going to work out."

"God, I hope so," she whispered, once again sneaking a glance at her dark-haired son and the fluff of tan fur with the beguiling black eyes. "Nicholas worships the ground you walk on, you know."

Trask laughed mirthlessly. "Well, if he does, he's the only one in town. There's no doubt about it, I wouldn't win any popularity contests in Sinclair right now."

"Oh, I don't know, you seem to have been able to worm your way back into Tory's heart."

"I don't think so."

"We'll see, senator," Neva mused. "I think Victoria Wilson has never gotten you out of her system."

Chapter Six

ANNA HUTTON LIFTED Governor's hoof and examined it carefully. Her expert fingers gently touched the swollen tissues, and the bay stallion, glistening with nervous sweat, snorted impatiently. "Steady, there," she murmured to the horse before lifting her eyes to meet Tory's worried gaze. "I'd say your diagnosis was right on the money, Tory," Anna remarked, as she slowly let the horse's foot return to the floor of his stall. "Our boy here has a case of acute laminitis. You know, girl, you should have been a vet." She offered Tory a small grin as she reached for her leather bag and once again lifted Governor's hoof and started cleaning the affected area.

"I guess I got sidetracked," Tory said. "So I'll have to rely on your expertise."

Anna smiled knowingly at her friend before continuing to work with Governor's hoof. The two women had once planned to go to graduate school together, but that was before Tory became involved with Trask McFadden and all of the bad press about Calvin Wilson and the Lazy W had come to light.

Tory's eyes were trained on Anna's hands, but her thoughts were far away, in a time when she had been filled with the anticipation of becoming Trask's wife. How willingly she had given up her career for him . . .

Glancing up, Anna noticed Tory's clouded expression and tactfully turned the conversation back to the horse as she finished cleaning the affected area. Governor flattened his dark ears to his head and shifted away from the young woman with the short blue-black hair and probing fingers. "You might want to put him in a special shoe, either a bar shoe or a saucer; and keep walking him. Have you applied any hot or cold poultices or put his hoof in ice water?"

"Yes, cold."

"Good, keep doing that," Anna suggested, her eyes narrowing as she studied the stallion. "I want to wait another day and see how he's doing tomorrow, before I consider giving him adrenaline or antihistamines."

"A woman from the old school, huh?"

"You know me, I believe the less drugs the better." She patted the horse on the shoulder. "He's a good-looking stallion, Tory."

"The best," Tory replied, glancing affectionately at the bay. "We're counting on him."

"As a stud?"

"Uh-huh. His first foals were born this spring."

"And you're happy with them?"

Tory nodded and smiled as she held open the stall gate for her friend. "I've always loved working with the horses, especially the foals."

Anna chuckled and shook her head in amazement as the two women walked out of the stallion barn and into the glare of the brilliant morning sun. "So you decided to breed Quarter Horses again, even after what happened with your father. You're a braver woman than I am, Victoria Wilson."

"Or a fool."

"That, I doubt."

"Keith thought raising horses again was a big mistake."

"So what does he know?"

"I'll tell him you said that."

"Go ahead. I think it takes guts to start over after the trial and all the bad publicity . . ."

"That was all a horrible mistake."

Anna placed her hand on Tory's arm. "I know, but I just thought that you wouldn't want to do anything that might . . . you know, encourage all the old rumors to start up again. I wouldn't."

"You can't run away from your past."

"Especially when our illustrious Senator McFadden comes charging back to town, stirring it all up again."

Tory felt her back stiffen but she managed a tight smile as they walked slowly across the gravel parking lot. "Everyone has to do what they have to do. Trask seems to think it's his duty to dig it all up again . . . because of Jason."

One of Anna's dark brows rose slightly. "So now you're defending him?"

"Of course not!" Tory said too quickly and then laughed at her own reaction. "It's just that Trask's been here a couple of times already," she admitted, "and, well, just about everyone I know seems to think that I shouldn't even talk to him."

"Maybe that's because you've led everyone to believe that you never wanted to see him again. After all, he did—"

"Betray me?"

"Whatever you want to call it." Anna hesitated a moment, biting her lips as if contemplating the worth of her words. "Look, Tory. After the trial, you were pretty messed up, bitter. It's no wonder people want to protect you from that kind of hurt again."

"I'm a grown woman."

"And now you've changed your mind about Trask?"

Tory shook her head and deep lines of worry were etched across her brow. "It's just that—"

"You just can't resist the guy."

"Anna!"

"Oh, don't look so shocked, Tory. In my business it's best to say the truth straight out. You know that I always liked Trask, but that was before he nearly destroyed my best friend."

"I wasn't destroyed."

"Close enough. And now, just when it looks like you're back on your feet again, he comes waltzing back to Sinclair, stirring up the proverbial hornet's nest, digging up dead corpses and not giving a damn about who gets hurt, including you and Neva. It tends to make my blood boil a bit."

"So you don't think I should see him."

Anna smiled cynically. She stopped to lean against the fence and gaze at the network of paddocks comprising the central core of the Lazy W. "Unfortunately what I think isn't worth a damn, unless it's about your livestock. I'm not exactly the best person to give advice about relationships, considering the fact that I've been divorced for almost a year myself." She hit the top rail of the fence with new resolve. "Anyway, you didn't ask me here to talk about Trask, and I've got work to do."

"Can't you stay for a cup of coffee?" Anna was one of Tory's closest friends; one of the few people in Sinclair who had stood by Tory and her father during Calvin's trial.

Anna squinted at the sun and cocked her wrist to check her watch. "I wish I could, but I'm late as it is." She started walking to her van before turning and facing

Tory. Concern darkened her brown eyes. "What's this I hear about a calf being shot out here?"

"So that's going around town, too."

Anna nodded and shrugged. "Face it, girl. Right now, with McFadden back in town, you're big news in Sinclair."

"Great," Tory replied sarcastically.

"So, what happened with the calf?"

"I wish I knew. One of Len Ross's hands saw the hole in the fence and discovered the calf. We don't know why it was shot or who did it."

"Kids, maybe?"

Tory lifted her shoulders. "Maybe," she said without conviction. "I called the sheriff and a deputy came out. He was going to see if any of the other ranchers had a similar problem."

"I hope not," Anna said, her dark eyes hardening. "I don't have much use for people who go around destroying animals."

"Neither do I."

Anna shook off her worried thoughts and climbed into the van. The window was rolled down and she cast Tory one last smile. "You take care of yourself, okay?"

"I will."

"I'll be back tomorrow to see how old Governor's doing."

"And maybe then you'll have time for a cup of coffee."

"And serious conversation," Anna said with mock gravity. "Plan on it."

"I will!"

With a final wave to Tory, Anna put the van in gear and drove out of the parking lot toward the main road.

* * *

AN HOUR LATER Tory sat in the center of the porch swing, slowly rocking on the worn slats, letting the warm summer breeze push her hair away from her face and bracing herself for the next few hours in which she would be alone with a man she alternately hated and loved.

Trask arrived promptly at noon. Fortunately, neither Keith nor Rex were at the house when Trask's Blazer ground to a halt near the front porch. Though Tory felt a slight twinge of conscience about sneaking around behind her brother's back, she didn't let it bother her. The only way to prove her father's innocence, as well as to satisfy Trask, was to go along with him. And Keith would never agree to work with Trask rather than against him.

What Tory hadn't expected or prepared herself for was the way her pulse jumped at the sight of Trask as he climbed out of the Blazer. No amount of mental chastising seemed to have had any effect on the feeling of anticipation racing through her blood when she watched him hop lithely to the ground and walk briskly in her direction. His strides were long and determined and his corduroy pants stretched over the muscles of his thighs and buttocks as he approached. A simple shirt with sleeves rolled over tanned forearms and a Stetson pushed back on his head completed his attire. *Nothing to write home about,* she thought, but when she gazed into his intense blue eyes she felt trapped and her heart refused to slow its uneven tempo.

"I thought maybe you would have changed your mind," Trask said. He mounted the steps and leaned against the rail of the porch, his long legs stretched out before him.

"Not me, senator. My word is as good as gold," she replied, but a defensive note had entered her voice;

she heard it herself, as did Trask. His thick brows lifted a bit.

"Is it? Good as gold that is?" He smiled slightly at the sight of her. Her skin was tanned and a slight dusting of freckles bridged her nose. The reckless auburn curls had been restrained in a ponytail, and she was dressed as if ready for a long ride.

"Always has been." She rose from the swing and her intelligent eyes searched his face. "If you're ready—" She motioned to the Blazer.

"No time like the present, I suppose." Without further comment, he walked with her to his vehicle, opened the door of the Blazer and helped her climb inside.

"What happened to Neva's pickup?" Tory asked just as Trask put the Blazer in gear.

"I only used it yesterday because this was in the shop."

"And Neva let you borrow her truck?"

"Let's say I persuaded her. She wasn't too keen on the idea."

"I'll bet not." She tapped her fingers on the dash and a tense silence settled between them.

The road to Devil's Ridge was little more than twin ruts of red soil separated by dry blades of grass that scraped against the underside of the Blazer. Several times Trask's vehicle lurched as a wheel hit a pothole or large rock hidden by the sagebrush that was slowly encroaching along the road.

"I don't know what you hope to accomplish by coming up here," Tory finally said, breaking the smothering silence as she looked through the dusty windshield. She was forced to squint against the noonday glare of the sun that pierced through the tall long-needled ponderosa pines.

"It's a start. That's all." Trask frowned and downshifted as they approached a sharp turn in the road.

"What do you think you'll find?" Tory prodded.

"I don't know."

"But you're looking for something."

"I won't know what it is until I find it."

"There's no reason to be cryptic, y'know," she pointed out, disturbed by his lack of communication.

"I wasn't trying to be."

Tory pursed her lips and folded her arms across her chest as she looked at him. "You just think that you're going to find some five-year-old clue that will prove your theories."

"I hope so."

"It won't happen, senator. The insurance investigators and the police sifted through this place for weeks. And that was right after the indictments . . ." Her voice drifted off as she thought about those hellish days and nights after her father bad been arrested. All the old feelings of love and hate, anger and betrayal began to haunt her anew. Though it was warm within the interior of the Blazer, Tory shivered.

"It doesn't hurt to look around," Trask insisted. He stepped on the throttle and urged the truck up the last half mile to the crest of the hill.

"So this is where it all started," Tory whispered, her eyes moving over the wooded land. She hadn't set step on Devil's Ridge since the scandal. Parched dry grass, dusty rocks and sagebrush covered the ground beneath the pine trees. The land appeared arid, dryer than it should have for late June.

"Or where it all ended, depending upon your point of view," Trask muttered. He parked the truck near a small group of dilapidated buildings, and pulled the key from the ignition. The Blazer rumbled quietly before dying. "If Jason hadn't come up here that night five years ago, he might not have been killed." The words were softly spoken but they cut through Tory's heart as easily as if they had been thin razors.

She had been reaching for the handle of the door but stopped. Her hand was poised over the handle and she couldn't hold back a weary sigh. "I'm sorry about your brother, Trask. You know that. And though I don't believe for a minute that Dad was responsible for your brother's death, I want to apologize for anything my father might have done that might have endangered Jason's life."

Trask's eyes softened. "I know, love," he said, before clearing his throat and looking away from her as if embarrassed at how easily an endearment was coaxed from his throat. "Come on, let's look around."

Tory stepped out of the Blazer and looked past the few graying buildings with broken windows and rotting timbers. Her gaze wandered past the small group of paddocks that had been used to hold the purebred Quarter Horses as well as their not-so-blue-blooded counterparts. Five years before, this small parcel of land had been the center of a horse swindle and insurance scam so large and intricate that it had become a statewide scandal. Now it was nothing more than a neglected, rather rocky, useless few acres of pine and sagebrush with a remarkable view. In the distance to the east, barely discernible to the naked eye were the outbuildings and main house of the Lazy W. From her viewpoint on the ridge, Tory could make out the gray house, the barn, toolshed and stables. Closer to the mountains she saw the spring-fed lake on the northwestern corner of the Lazy W. The green and gold grassland near the lake was dotted with grazing cattle.

"Hard to believe, isn't it?" Trask said.

Tory jerked her head around and found that he was

staring at her. The vibrant intensity of his gaze made her heartbeat quicken. "What?"

"This." He gestured to the buildings and paddocks of the ridge with one hand before pushing his hat off his head and wiping an accumulation of sweat off his brow.

"It gives me the creeps," she admitted, hugging her arms around her breasts and frowning.

"Too many ghosts live here?"

"Something like that."

Trask smiled irreverently. His brown hair ruffled in the wind. "I'll let you in on a secret," he said with a mysterious glint in his eyes.

"Oh?"

"This place gives me the creeps, too."

Tory laughed in spite of herself. If nothing else, Trask still knew how to charm her out of her fears. "You'd better be careful, senator," she teased. "Admitting something like that could ruin your public image."

Trask's smile widened into an affable slightly off-center grin that softened the square angle of his jaw. "I've done a lot of things that could ruin my public image." His gaze slid suggestively down her throat to the swell of her breasts. "And I imagine that I'll do a few more."

Oh, Trask, if only I could trust you, she thought as she caught the seductive glint in his eyes and her pulse continued to throb traitorously. She forced her eyes away from him and back to the ranch.

"I wish we could just forget all this, you know," she said, still staring at the cattle moving around the clear blue lake.

"Maybe we can."

"How?"

"If it turns out to be a prank."

"And how will you know?" she asked, turning to face him again.

He shook his head. "I've just got to play it by ear, Tory; try my best and then . . ."

"And then, what? If you don't find anything here today, which you won't, what will you do? Go to the sheriff?"

"Maybe."

"But?"

"Maybe I'll wait and see what happens."

That sounded encouraging, but she felt a small stab of disappointment touch her heart. "In Washington?"

"Probably."

She didn't reply. Though she knew he was studying her reaction, she tried to hide her feelings. That she wanted him to stay in Sinclair was more than foolish, it was downright stupid, she thought angrily. The man had sent her father to jail, for God's sake. And now that Calvin was dead, Trask was back looking for another innocent victim. As she walked toward the largest of the buildings Tory told herself over and over again that she hated Trask McFadden; that she had only accompanied him up here to get rid of him once and for all, and that she would never think of him again once he had returned to Washington, D.C. Unfortunately, she knew that all of her excuses were lies to herself. She still loved Trask as passionately and as blindly as she had on the bleak night he had left her to chase down, confront and condemn her father.

"It would help me if I knew what I was looking for," she said.

"Anything that you think looks out of place. We can start over here," he suggested, pointing to the largest of the three buildings. "This was used as the stables." Digging his boots into the dry ground, he pushed with his shoulder against the door and it creaked open on rusty hinges.

Tory walked inside the musty structure. Cobwebs hung from the exposed rafters and everything was covered with a thick layer of dust. Shovels, rakes, an ax and pick were pushed into one corner on the dirt floor. Other tools and extra fence posts leaned against the walls. The two windows were covered with dust and the dried carcasses of dead insects, letting only feeble light into the building. Tory's skin prickled with dread. Something about the abandoned barn didn't feel right and she had the uneasy sensation that she was trespassing. Maybe Trask was right; all the ghosts of the past seemed to reside on the hilly slopes of the ridge.

Trask walked over to the corner between the two windows and lifted an old bridle off the wall. The leather reins were stiff in his fingers and the bit had rusted. For the first time since receiving the anonymous letter he considered ignoring it. The brittle leather in his hands seemed to make it clear that all he was doing was bringing back to life a scandal that should remain dead and buried.

He saw the accusations in Tory's wide eyes. God, he hadn't been able to make conversation with her at all; they'd both been too tense and at each other's throats. Confronting the sins of the past had been harder than he'd imagined; but that was probably because of the woman involved. He couldn't seem to get Victoria Wilson out of his system, no matter how hard he tried, and though he'd told himself she was trouble, even an adversary, he kept coming back for more.

In the past five years Trask's need of her hadn't diminished; if anything it had become more passionate and persistent than before. Silently calling himself the worst kind of fool, he looked away from Tory's face and continued his inspection of the barn.

Once his inspection of the stable area had been accomplished, he surveyed a small shed, which, he surmised, must have been used for feed and supplies. Nothing.

The last building was little more than a lean-to of two small, dirty rooms. One room had served as an observation post; from the single window there was a view of the road and the Lazy W far below. The other slightly larger room was for general use. An old army cot was still folded in the corner. Newspapers, now yellowed, littered the floor, the pipe for the wood stove had broken near the roof line and the few scraps of paper that were still in the building were old wrappers from processed food.

Tory watched as Trask went over the floor of the cabin inch by inch. She looked in every nook and cranny and found nothing of interest. Finally, tired and feeling as if the entire afternoon had been a total waste of time, she walked outside to the small porch near the single door of the shanty.

Leaning against one of the rough cedar posts, she stared down the hills, through the pines to the buildings of the Lazy W. Her home. Trask had single-handedly destroyed it once before—was she up here helping do the very same thing all over again? *History has a way of repeating itself,* she thought to herself and smiled cynically at her own stupidity for still caring about a man who would as soon use her as love her.

Trask's boots scraped against the floorboards and he came out to the porch. She didn't turn around but knew that he was standing directly behind her. The warmth of his breath fanned her hair. For one breathless instant she thought that his strong arms might encircle her waist.

"So what did you find, senator?" she asked, breaking the tense silence.

"Nothing," he replied.

The "I told you so" she wanted to flaunt in his face died within her. When she turned to face him, Tory noticed that Trask suddenly looked older than his thirty-six years. The brackets near the corners of his mouth had become deep grooves.

"Go ahead, say it," he said, as if reading her mind.

She let out a disgusted breath of air. "I think we're both too old for those kinds of games, don't you?"

He leaned against the building and crossed his arms over his chest. "So the little girl has grown up."

"I wasn't a little girl," she protested. "I was twenty-two . . ."

"Going on fifteen."

"That's not nice, senator."

"Face it, Tory," he said softly. "You'd been to college sure, and you'd worked on the ranch, but in a lot of ways—" he touched her lightly on the nape of her neck with one long familiar finger, her skin quivered beneath his touch "—you were an innocent."

She angled her head up defiantly. "Just because I hadn't known a lot of men," she began to argue.

"That wasn't it, and you know it," Trask said, his fingers stopping the teasing motion near her collar. "I was talking about the way you looked up to your father, the fact that you couldn't make a decision without him, your dependency on him."

"I respected my father, if that's what you mean."

"It went much further than that."

"Of course it did. I loved him." She took one step backward and folded her arms over her chest. "Maybe you don't understand that emotion very well, but I do. Simple no-holds-barred love."

"It went beyond simple love. You worshipped him, Tory; put the man on such a high pedestal that he was bound to fall; and when you discovered that he was human, that he did make mistakes, you couldn't face it. You still can't." His blue eyes delved into hers, forcing her to return their intense stare.

"I don't want to hear any of this, Trask. Not now."

"Not ever. You just can't face the truth, can you?"

A quiet anger had begun to invade her mind. It started to throb and pound behind her eyes. "I faced the truth a long time ago, senator," she said bitterly. "Only the man that I worshipped, the one that I placed on the pedestal and who eventually fell wasn't my father."

Trask's jaw tightened and his eyes darkened to a smoldering blue. "I did what I had to do, Tory."

"And damn the consequences?"

"And damn the truth."

There was a moment of tense silence while Tory glared at him. Even now, despite her anger, she was attracted to him. "I think we'd better go," she said. "I'm tired of arguing with you and getting nowhere. I promised to bring you up here so you could snoop around and I've kept my end of the bargain."

"That you have," he said, rubbing his hands together to shake off some of the dust. "Okay, so we found nothing in the buildings—I'd like to walk around the corral and along the road."

"I don't see why—"

"Humor me," he insisted. "Since we've already wasted most of the afternoon, I'd like to make sure that I don't miss anything." He saw the argument forming in her mind. "This way we won't have to come back."

And I won't have to make excuses to Keith or Rex,

Tory thought. “All right, senator,” she agreed. “You lead, I’ll follow.”

They spent the next few hours walking the perimeter of the land, studying the soil, the trails through the woods, the fence lines where it was still intact. Nothing seemed out of the ordinary to Tory and if Trask found anything of interest, he kept it to himself.

“I guess Neva was right,” Trask said with a grimace.

“About what?”

“A lot of things, I suppose. But she thought coming up here would turn out to be nothing more than a wild-goose chase.”

“So now you’re willing to concede that your anonymous letter was nothing more than a prank?”

Trask pushed his hat back on his head and squinted thoughtfully up at the mountains. “I don’t know. Maybe. But I can’t imagine why.”

“So you’re not going to give it up,” Tory guessed. “The diligent hardworking earnest Senator McFadden won’t give up.”

“Enough already,” Trask said, chuckling at the sarcasm in Tory’s voice. “Why don’t we forget about the past for a while, what d’ya say?”

“Hard to do, considering the surroundings.”

“Come on,” Trask said, his anger having melted at the prospect of spending time alone with Tory now that what he had set out to do was accomplished. “I’ve got a picnic hamper that Neva packed; she’ll kill me if we don’t eat it.”

“Neva put together the basket?” Tory asked, remembering Keith’s comment to the effect that Neva was in love with Trask.

“Grudgingly,” he admitted.

“I’ll bet.”

“Nicholas and I teamed up on her though.”

"And she couldn't resist the charms of the McFadden men."

Trask laughed deep in his throat. "Something like that."

"This is probably a big mistake."

"But you'll indulge me?"

"Sure," she said easily. "Why not?" *A million reasons why not,* and she ignored all of them. The sun had just set behind the mountains and dusk had begun to shadow the foothills. An evening breeze carrying the heady scent of pine rustled through the trees.

After taking the cooler and a worn plaid blanket out of the back of the Blazer, Trask walked away from the buildings to a clearing in the trees near the edge of the ridge. From there, he and Tory were able to look down on the fields of the ranch. Cattle dotted the landscape and the lake had darkened to the mysterious purple hue of the sky.

"Bird's-eye view," she remarked, taking a seat near the edge of the blanket and helping Trask remove items from the cooler and arrange them on the blanket.

Trask sat next to her, leaning his back against a tree and stretching his legs in front of him. "Why did your father buy this piece of land?" he asked, while handing Tory a plate.

Tory shrugged. "I don't know. I think he intended to build a cabin for Mother . . ." Her voice caught when she thought of her parents and the love they had shared. As much to avoid Trask's probing stare as anything, she began putting food onto her plate. "But that was a long time ago when they were both young, before Mom was sick."

"And he could never force himself to sell it?"

"No, I suppose not. He and Mom had planned to

retire here, where they still could see the ranch and be involved a little when Keith took over."

"Keith? What about you?"

She smiled sadly and pretended interest in her meal. "Oh, you know, senator. I was supposed to get married and have a dozen wonderful grandchildren for them to spoil . . ." Tory heard the desperation in her voice and cleared her throat before boldly meeting his gaze. "Well, things don't always turn out the way you plan, do they?"

Trask's jaw tightened and his eyes saddened a little. "No, I guess not. Not always."

Trask was silent as he leaned against the tree and ate the meal that Neva had prepared. The home-baked bread, fried chicken, fresh melon salad and peach pie were a credit to any woman and Trask wondered why it was that he couldn't leave Tory alone and take the love that Neva so willingly offered him. Maybe it was because she had been his brother's wife, or, more honestly, maybe it was because no other woman affected him the way Tory Wilson could with one subtle glance. To distract himself from his uncomfortable thoughts, he reached into the cooler.

"Damn!"

"What?"

Trask frowned as he pulled out a thermos of iced tea. "I told Neva to pack a bottle of wine."

Tory looked at the platters of food. "Maybe next time you should pack your own lunch. It looks like she did more than her share, especially considering how she feels about what you're doing." After taking the thermos from his hands, she poured them each a glass of tea.

Trask didn't seem consoled and ignored his drink.

"We don't need the wine," Tory pointed out. "Maybe

Neva knew that it would be best if we kept our wits about us."

"Maybe." Trask eyed Tory speculatively, his gaze centering on the disturbing pout of her lips. "She thinks I've given you enough grief as it is."

"You have."

Trask took off his hat and studied the brim. "You're not about to let down a bit, are you?"

"What do you mean?"

"Just that you're going to keep the old barriers up, all the time."

"You're the one intent on digging up the past; I'm just trying to keep it in perspective."

"And have you?"

Tory's muscles went tense. She took a swallow of her tea before answering. "I'm trying, Trask. I'm trying damned hard. Everyone I know thinks I'm crazy to go along with your plans, and I'm inclined to believe them. But I thought that if you came up here, poked around, did your duty, so to speak, that you'd drop it and the fires of gossip in Sinclair would die before another scandal engulfed us. I knew that you wouldn't just let go of the idea that another person was involved in your brother's death, and I also realized that if I fought you, it would just drag everything out much longer and fuel the gossip fires."

He set his food aside and wrapped his arms around his knees while studying the intriguing angles of Tory's face. "And that's the only reason you came up here with me?"

"No."

He lifted his thick brows, encouraging her to continue.

After setting her now empty plate on the top of the basket, she leaned back on her arms and stared at the countryside far below the ridge. "If by the slim chance you did find something, some clue to what had happened, I thought it might prove Dad's innocence."

"Oh, Tory . . ." He leaned toward her and touched her cheek. "I know you don't believe this, but if there were a way to show that Calvin had no part in the Quarter Horse swindle, or Jason's death, don't you think I'd be the first to do it?"

He sounded sincere and his deep blue eyes seemed to look through hers to search for her soul. God, but she wanted to believe him and trust in him again. He had been everything to her and the hand on her cheek was warm and encouraging. It conjured vivid images from a long-ago love. She had trouble finding her voice. The wind rustled restlessly through the branches overhead and Tory couldn't seem to concentrate on anything but the feel of Trask's fingers against her skin. "I . . . I don't know." She finished the cold tea and set her glass on the ground.

"My intention wasn't to crucify your father, only to tell my side of the story, in order that Jason's murderers were found out and brought to justice. If Calvin wasn't guilty, he should have stood up for himself—"

"But he didn't; and your testimony sent him to prison." She swallowed back the hot lump forming in her throat.

"Would it help you to know that I never, never meant to hurt you?" he asked, lowering his head and tenderly brushing his lips over hers.

"Trask—" The protest forming in her throat was cut off when his arms wrapped around her and he drew her close, the length of his body pressed urgently to hers.

"I've missed you, Tory," he admitted, his voice rough with emotions he would rather have denied.

"And I've missed you."

"But you still can't forgive me?"

She shook her head and for a moment she thought he would release her. He hesitated and stared into her pain-filled eyes. "Oh, hell," he muttered, once again pulling her close to him and claiming her lips with his.

His hands were warm against her back and through the fabric of her blouse she felt the heat of his fingers against her skin. Her legs were entwined with his and his hips pressed urgently to hers, pinning her to the ground as one of his hands moved slowly upward and removed the leather thong restraining her hair.

"God, you're beautiful," he whispered against her ear as he twined his fingers in her hair, watching the auburn-tinged curls frame her face in wild disarray. Slumberous green eyes rimmed with dark curling lashes stared up at him longingly. "I want you, Tory," he said, his breathing ragged, his heart thudding in his chest and the heat in his loins destroying rational thought. "I've wanted you for a long time."

"I don't know that wanting is enough, Trask," she whispered, thinking about the agonizing hours she had spent in the past five years wanting a man she couldn't have; wishing for a father who was already dead; desiring the life she had once had before fate had so cruelly ripped it from her.

"Just let me love you, Tory."

The words had barely been said when she felt Trask stiffen. He turned to look over his shoulder just as a shot from a rifle cracked through the still mountain air.

Tory's blood ran cold with fear and a scream died in her throat. Trask flattened himself over her body, protectively covering her as the shot ricocheted through the trees and echoed down the hillside. *Dear God, what was happening? The sound was so close!*

With the speed and agility of an athlete, Trask scrambled to his feet while jerking her arm and pulling her to relative safety behind a large boulder.

Tory's heart was hammering erratically as adrenaline pumped through her veins. She pushed her hair out of her eyes and discovered that her hands were shaking. "Oh, God," she whispered in desperate prayer.

"Are you okay?" His eyes scanned her face and body.

Her voice failed her but she managed to nod her head.

"You're sure?"

"Yes!"

"Who knows we're here?" Trask demanded, his hushed voice harsh, his eyes darting through the trees.

"No one—I didn't tell anyone," she replied.

"Well someone sure as hell knows we were here!"

"But—"

"Shh!" He clamped his hand over her mouth and raised a finger to his lips as he strained to hear any noise that might indicate the whereabouts of the assailant. Far down the hillside, the sound of hurried footsteps crackled through the brush. Tory's skin prickled with fear and her eyes widened until she realized that the footsteps were retreating, the sound of snapping branches becoming more distant.

Trask moved away from the protection of the boulder as if intent on tracking the assailant.

"Trask! No!" Tory screamed, clutching at his arm. "Leave it alone."

He tried to shake her off and turned to face her.

"Someone's taking shots at us and I'm going to find out who."

"No wait! He has a rifle, you . . . you can't go. You don't have any way of protecting yourself!"

"Tory!"

"Damn it, Trask, I'm scared!" she admitted, holding his gaze as well as his arm. Her lower lip trembled and she had to fight the tears forming in her eyes. "You can't die, too," she whispered. "I won't let you!" He stood frozen to the spot. "I love you, Trask," Tory admitted. "Please, please, don't get yourself killed. It's not worth it. Nothing is!" Tory felt near hysteria as she clutched at his arm.

Trask stood stock still, Tory's words restraining him. "You love me?" he repeated.

"Yes!" Her voice broke. "Oh, God, yes."

"But you've been denying—"

"I know, I know. It's just that I don't want to love you."

"Because of the past."

"Yes."

"Then we have to find out the truth," he decided.

"It's not worth getting killed."

Trask's eyes followed the sound of the retreating footsteps and the skin whitened over his cheekbones as he squinted into the encroaching night. His one chance at finding the accomplice in Jason's murder had just slipped through his fingers. When silence once again settled on the ridge, he turned his furious gaze on Tory. His grip on her shoulders, once gentle, was now fierce.

"Who did you tell that we were here?" he demanded.

"No one!"

"But your brother and that foreman, Rex Engels, they knew we would be here this afternoon."

Tory shook her head and her green eyes blazed indignantly. She jerked away from his fingers and scooted backward on the ground. "I didn't tell anyone, Trask. Not even Keith or Rex; they . . . neither one of them would have approved. As far as I know the only person who knew we were coming here today was Neva!"

The corners of Trask's mouth tightened and he glared murderously at Tory. "Someone set us up."

"And you think it was me?"

"Of course not. But it sure as hell wasn't Neva!"

"Why not? She didn't want you coming up here, did she? She doesn't want you to look into Jason's death, does she? Why wouldn't she do something to sabotage you?"

He walked away a few steps and rubbed the back of his neck. "That just doesn't make any sense."

"Well nothing else does either. The anonymous note, the dead calf and now this—" She raised her hands over her head. "Nothing is making any sense, Trask. Ever since you came back to the Lazy W, there's been nothing but trouble!"

"That's exactly the point, isn't it?" he said quietly, his mouth compressing into an angry line. "Someone's trying to scare you; warn you to stay away from me."

"If that's his intention, whoever he is, he's succeeded! I'm scared right out of my mind," she admitted while letting her head fall into her palm.

"What about the rest, Tory? That shot a few minutes ago was a warning to you to stay away from me!" He looked over his shoulder one last time.

"If that's what it was—"

"That's exactly what it was," he interjected. "Let's go, before someone decides to take another potshot at us."

"You think that's what they were trying to do?"

"I'm certain of it."

"But maybe someone saw a rattlesnake, or was hunting."

"It's not deer season."

"Maybe rabbits—" She saw the look of disbelief on his face. "Or maybe the guy was a poacher . . . or someone out for target practice."

"It's nearly dark, Tory. I don't know about you, but I don't like being the bull's-eye."

From the look on Trask's rugged features, Tory could tell that he didn't believe her excuses any more than she did. He walked over to her and placed his hands upon her shoulders, drawing her close, holding her as he started walking back to the Blazer. "I'd like to believe all those pitiful reasons, too," he admitted.

"But you can't."

"Nope." He opened the door of the Blazer for her, helped her inside and climbed into the driver's seat. "No, Tory," he said, his voice cold. "Someone's trying to keep us apart, by scaring us with dead cattle and rifle shots."

"And that means there must be some truth to the letter," she finished for him.

"Exactly." He smiled a little remembering Tory's confession of love, started the Blazer, circled around the parking lot and started driving down the rutted lane back to the Lazy W.

Chapter Seven

"SO WHERE IS everyone?" Trask asked as he parked the truck near the barn.

"I don't know," Tory admitted uneasily. She got out of the Blazer and started walking toward the back of the dark house. The only illumination came from a pale moon and the security lamps surrounding the buildings of the ranch.

Trask was on Tory's heels, his footsteps quickening so that he could catch up with her. "What about your brother, where is he?"

If only I knew. "He and Rex were working on the broken combine this afternoon," she thought aloud, trying to understand why the ranch was deserted. "They probably went into town for a part, got held up and decided to stay for dinner . . ."

"Or he was up on the ridge with a rifle?" Trask suggested.

Tory turned quickly and couldn't disguise the flush of anger on her cheeks. "Don't start in about Keith, okay? He would never do anything that might jeopardize my life."

"You're sure about that?"

"As sure as I am about anything." Tory turned toward the house, dashed up the steps to the porch and unlocked the back door. She had trouble keeping her fingers steady as she worked with the lock. What was it Keith had said just yesterday? His words came back to her in chilling clarity.

"I would have met McFadden with a rifle in my hands . . . the next time McFadden trespasses, I'll be ready for him."

Tory's stomach knotted with dread and disgust. Trask had her thoughts so twisted that now she was doubting her own brother; the boy she had helped rear since their mother's death. Ignoring the hideous doubts crowding her mind, she flipped on the light and walked into the kitchen.

"What about the foreman?"

"Rex?"

"Yeah."

Tory almost laughed at the absurdity of Trask's insinuation. "You've got to be kidding! I've known Rex since I was a little girl—he'd do anything for the ranch. It's been his life. Dad hired him when Rex was down and out, when no other rancher in this state would touch him. Besides, neither Rex nor Keith knew where I was this afternoon."

Trask leaned against the cupboards, supporting his weight with his hands while Tory made a pot of coffee. Deep furrows etched his brow. "Why wouldn't anyone hire Rex?"

"You want to see all of the skeletons in the closet, don't you?"

"Only if it helps me understand what's going on."

"Well, forget it. Rex was in trouble once, when he was younger—before I was born. Dad hired him."

"What kind of trouble?" Trask persisted.

Tory frowned as she tried to remember. "I don't really know. Dad never talked about it. But once, when I was about eleven and I was supposed to be studying,

I overheard Dad talking to Rex. It was something to do with Rex's past. It had to do with his ex-wife, I can't remember her name, it was something like Marlene or . . . Marianne, maybe. Something like that. Anyway, there was some sort of trouble between them, talk of him drinking and becoming abusive. She left Rex and no one would hire him."

"Except your dad."

"Right. And Rex has been with the Lazy W ever since."

"Without any trouble."

"Right."

Trask bit at his lower lip pensively. "I thought he was married."

"He is. He married Belinda about seven years ago."

"So he's above suspicion."

"Of course he is. He was the one who showed us the dead calf in the first place, remember?" She tapped her fingers on the counter impatiently. "Look, I don't like the thoughts that are going through your head. You're more than willing to start pointing fingers at anyone associated with the ranch, but no one here knew where we were going."

"We could have been followed," he said, rubbing the back of his neck and watching her movements.

She was about to pull some mugs down from the shelf, but hesitated and her slim shoulders slumped. "God, you're as bad as Keith," she muttered.

"What's that supposed to mean?"

"Just that the both of you have overactive, extremely fertile imaginations when it comes to each other. If you'd just sit down and try to straighten all of this out like adults instead of going for each other's throat, we'd all be a lot better off."

"I agree."

Trask grabbed a chair from the table, placed it on the

floor and straddled it. He folded his arms over the back of the chair and rested his chin on his arms as he studied Tory.

"You agree?" she repeated incredulously.

"Of course. It just makes sense that if we all work together we can accomplish much more in a shorter space of time."

"And then you could finish this business and fly back to Washington," she thought aloud. Suddenly the future seemed incredibly bleak.

"Don't you want me to go?" he asked.

Swallowing a lump in her throat, she pushed her burnished hair from her face. "It doesn't really matter what I want," she whispered. "You've got an important job in Washington, people depend on you. There was a time when I would have begged you to stay . . ."

"And now?"

She winced, but decided to put her cards on the table. As the coffee finished perking and filled the room with its warm scent, she leaned one hip against the counter and stared into his deep blue eyes. "And now I think we're all better off if you go back to the capital, senator. I fell in love with you once and I won't let it happen again. Ever."

"What about what you said on the ridge?" he asked softly.

"I was scared; nothing more. I didn't want you to do anything foolish!"

"Tory—" He stood, but she cut off his next words.

"I don't want to hear it, Trask. Here—" She quickly poured them each a cup of coffee and tried to think of a way, any way, to change the course of the conversation. "Take your coffee and we'll drink it in the den."

"You can't ignore or deny what's happening between us."

"What's happening is that I'm trying to help you figure out if that note you received is a phony. That's all." She turned away from him and walked down the hall, hoping that her hands and voice would remain steady.

Once in the den she snapped on two lamps and walked over to the window. *Where was Keith?* She needed him now. Being alone with Trask was more than foolhardy, it was downright dangerous and seductive. She stood in front of the window and sipped her coffee as she looked across the parking lot to the shadowy barns.

Trask entered the room. She heard rather than saw him and felt the weight of his stare. His eyes never left her as he crossed the room and propped one booted foot on the hearth. "What are you afraid of, Tory?"

"I already told you, I'm not afraid . . . just confused. Everything in my life seems upside-down right now."

"Because of me?"

She let out a long sigh. "Yes."

"It will be over soon," he said. "Then your life will be back to normal—if that's what you want."

My life will never be the same again, Trask. "Good. I . . . I just want all this . . . nonsense to be over." She took a long sip of her coffee and set the empty mug on the windowsill. Her fingers had stopped shaking. "It's late. I think maybe you should leave."

"Maybe," he agreed, cocking a dark brow. "But I think it's time we settled some things between us." He reached over and snapped off the lamp on an end table. With only the light from the small brass lamp on the desk, the corners of the room became shadowed, more intimate.

Bracing herself, she turned and faced him. "Such as?"

He leaned back against the rocks of the fireplace and all of his muscles seemed to slacken. Defeat darkened his eyes. "Such as the fact that I've never gotten over you—"

"I told you, I don't want to hear this," she said, walking away from the window and shaking her head. "The past is over and done—it can't be changed or repeated. What happened between us is over. You took care of that."

"I love you, Tory," he said slowly, his voice low.

Tory stopped dead in her tracks. How long had she waited, ached, to hear just those words? "You don't understand the first thing about love, Trask. You never have."

"And you're always quick to misjudge me."

"You can't expect me to trust you, Trask, not after what happened to my father. It was all because of you."

Trask's face hardened and a muscle in the back of his jaw tightened. "Calvin is dead; I can't change that." He pushed away from the fireplace and crossed the room to stand before her. "Don't you think I wish he were alive? Don't you realize how many times I've punished myself, knowing that he died in prison, primarily because of my testimony?" His troubled eyes searched her face and he reached forward to grip her shoulders. "Damn it, woman, I'd have given my right arm to hear his side of the story—only the man wouldn't tell it. It was as if he'd taken this vow of silence as some sort of penance for his crimes!" Trask's voice was low and threatening. "I've been through hell and back because of that trial!"

The grip on her arms was punishing, the conviction on Trask's face enough to cut her to the bone. "God, Trask, I wish I could believe you," she admitted, her voice trembling.

"But you can't."

"You betrayed me!"

He gave her a shake. Her hair fell over her eyes. "I told the truth on the witness stand. Nothing less. Nothing more." His voice was rising with his anger. "And your father didn't do a damned thing to save himself! Don't you think I've lain awake at night wondering what really happened on the night Jason was killed?" His face contorted with his rage and agony.

"I . . . I don't know . . ."

"Damn it, Tory! Believe it or not, I'm human. If you cut me, I bleed." He released her arms and let out a disgusted breath of air. Blue eyes seared through hers. "And, lady, you've cut me to ribbons . . ."

She let her face fall into her hands. Her entire body was shaking and the tears she would rather have forced back filled her eyes to spill through her fingers. "God, I wanted to trust you, Trask. I . . . I spent more than my share of sleepless nights wondering why did you use me? Why did you tell me you loved me? Why was I such a fool to believe all your lies . . . all your goddamned lies!" She began to sob and she felt the warmth of his arms surround her. "Let go of me," she pleaded.

"Never again." With one hand he snapped off the light on the desk. The room was suddenly shrouded in darkness. Only the pale light from a half-moon spilled through the windows. "Oh, love, I never used you. Never—"

"No . . . Trask . . ." His lips touched her hair, and his arms held her close. The heat of his body seemed to reach through her flesh and melt the ice in her heart. "I . . . I just loved you too much."

"Impossible."

"I know it's stupid," she conceded, letting the barriers that had held them apart slowly fall, "but I want to trust you again. God, I've wanted to be able to talk to you for so long; you don't know how many times I just wished that you were here, that I could talk to you."

"You should have called."

"I couldn't! Don't you see? You were my whole world once and you destroyed everything I'd ever loved. My father, my career, this ranch, and our love—everything."

"All because I told the truth."

"Your perception of the truth!"

"Tory, listen to me, you have to understand one thing: throughout it all I always loved you. I still do."

She felt the cold hatred within her begin to thaw and her knees went weak as she leaned against him, felt the strength of his arms, the comfort of his kiss. How many times had she dreamed and fantasized about being in Trask's arms again? "You love me, Trask," she sniffed, slowly pulling out of his embrace and drying her eyes with her fingers, "when it's convenient for you. It was convenient for you five years ago when you were trying to help your brother with the horse swindle and it's convenient now, when you need my help." She stepped back and held his gaze. "I won't be used again, you know. Not by you."

"I wouldn't." His blue eyes were honest; the jut of his jaw firm with conviction. It was impossible not to believe him.

Tory cleared her throat. "Then what about Neva?"

"What about her?"

"Are you staying with her?" she asked, knowing the question was none of her business, but unable to help herself.

Trask's skin tightened over his cheekbones and his muscles tensed, but he didn't look away. "I did the first night. Since then, I've opened up the cabin on the Metolius River. It wasn't ready when I got into Sinclair," he began to explain and then let out an angry oath. "Hell, Tory, does it matter?" he demanded.

Her eyes turned cold. "Not really, I guess. I just like to know what or whom I'm up against. With you and that damned anonymous letter of yours, sometimes it's hard to tell."

"I'm not having an affair with my brother's widow, if that's what you want to know."

"It's none of my business."

"Like hell! Haven't you listened to a word I've said?" When she didn't respond, he curled a fist and slammed it into the wall near the desk, rattling a picture of an Indian war party. "Hell, woman, I'd be a liar to say that I've spent that past five years celibate, but I'm not involved with anyone right now except for you!" Once again his fingers captured her, winding comfortably behind her neck.

"We're not involved!"

With her indignation, his anger dissipated into the intimate corners of the room. Trask's smile was lazy and confident. "That's where you're wrong. We've been involved since the first time I laid eyes on you. Where was it? Rafting on the Deschutes River!"

"That was a long time ago," she murmured, recalling the wild ride down the white water. Though she had gone with another man, Trask's eyes hadn't left her throughout the day. Even then she'd seen the spark of seduction in his incredible blue gaze. Sitting on the raft, his tanned skin tight over lean corded muscles, his wet hair shining brown-gold in the summer sun, he didn't bother to hide his interest in her. And she fell. Lord, she fell harder than any sane person had a right to fall. She had met him later that night and within two weeks they'd become lovers. The irony of it all was that she had thought she would spend the rest of her life with him. *Only it didn't work out that way.*

"Let's not talk about the past."

He let go of her, holding her only with his eyes. "We have to sort this out."

"What's the point? Nothing will come of it." She felt the urge to back away but stood her ground. "I'll admit that I loved you once, but it's over. It's been over for a long time."

"Liar." He reached for her, drawing her body close to his. When his lips touched hers, and she tasted him, her resistance fled. Familiar yearnings awoke within the most feminine part of her, causing a bittersweet ache that only he could salve. Instead of pushing him away, she was leaning closer to him, her body reacting to the sensual feel of his hands on her skin, her blood pulsing with need as it rushed through her veins. "You want me," he whispered against her ear.

"No . . ."

"Let me love you."

Desire was heating her blood, thundering in her head, and the touch of his lips on her face and neck only made the throbbing need within her more painful. "I don't think—" she tried to say, but his lips cut off the rest of her objection.

She felt the warm invasion of his tongue and returned his kiss without restraint. When his lips moved downward to touch her neck and then slid still lower, she could do nothing but wait in anticipation. His tongue rimmed the hollow of her throat and she was forced to swallow against the want of him.

Suddenly, Trask released her, and Tory wanted to cry out against the bereft feeling she was left with. She watched as he strode to the den door and locked it, then moved toward her quickly banishing the cold feeling.

Warm hands outlined her ribs before reaching upward to mold a swollen breast. She felt her nipple tighten against the feel of his fingers and she let out a low moan of desire.

Slowly he removed her blouse, slipping each button through its hole and letting the fabric part to display her rounded breasts, swollen and bound only by the sheer white lace of her bra. His fingers teased the hardened nipple, and Tory leaned closer to him, the ache within her spreading throughout her body.

A primal groan escaped from his lips as he lowered himself to his knees and licked first one rose-tipped breast before suckling the other. The lace of the bra became moist and Trask's warm breath fanned the sheer fabric to send sharp electric currents through Tory's body. She closed her eyes and was blind to everything but the hunger for him. Her fingers twined in his hair.

The warmth of his hands pressed against the small of her back, bringing her closer to him, pressing more of her breast into his mouth. He groaned with the savage urgency of his lust, sucking hungrily from the white mound.

Scorching feelings of desire once awakened in Tory were impossible to smother. With each touch of his hand, Tory lost ground to the urges of her flesh. With each stroke of his tongue, the ache within her throbbed more painfully. With the heated pressure of his body against hers, she felt the urge to arch against him, demanding more of his sensual touch.

Five years she had waited for the feel of him, denying her most secret dreams and now the pain of those long empty nights alone was about to be rewarded. The scent of him was strong in her nostrils and the sound of his breathing filled her ears.

Her fingers curled in his hair as he removed her bra

and took her naked breast in his mouth. She cradled his head to her body, holding on to him for dear life knowing that her love for this man would never be returned and not caring about the consequences. This night, for a few short hours, he was hers—alone.

She moaned his name when his fingers sought the front opening of her jeans and touched the sensitive skin of her abdomen.

"Trask, please," she whispered hoarsely as his tongue traced the delicate swirl of her navel and he pulled her jeans and underwear off her body. Slowly she was pressed to the floor by the weight of his body. The braided carpet felt coarse against her bare skin, but she didn't care.

She helped him remove his clothes and her fingers caressed the fluid muscles of his shoulders and chest. His body tensed beneath the tantalizing warmth of her touch.

Sweat dotted his brow; his restraint was obvious in the coil of his muscles. When Tory reached for the waistband of his pants, his abdominal muscles tightened. With all of the willpower he could muster, he stopped her by taking hold of her wrist and forced her chin upward with his other hand. His eyes searched hers. "I love you, Tory," he said, his voice rough. "I always have. But I want you to be sure about this . . . stop me now, if you have to, while it's still possible."

Closing her eyes against the flood of tears that threatened to spill, she tried to speak, to tell him how much she wanted him. Her lips quivered, but all the words she thought she should say wouldn't come.

Trask kissed her softly and wound his fingers in the thick auburn strands of her tousled hair. "If only I could make you happy," he murmured before capturing her lips in his and shifting his weight so that his body covered hers in a protective embrace.

As his flesh touched hers, his body heated until it glistened in a film of sweat. Her arms wound around his back and she clung to him as he became one with her, moving gently at first and then more quickly as her body responded to the familiarity of his touch. His hands massaged her breasts in the rhythm of his love-making.

"Oh, God," he whispered against her ear as the heat within her seemed to burst and he, too, surrendered. "Tory," he called, his voice raspy. "Just love me again." And then he fell against her, his weight a welcome burden.

The tears that had been welling beneath her lids began to stream down her cheeks. "Shh," he whispered, "everything will be okay."

Slowly Trask rolled to his side and held her close to him. He kissed her and tasted the salt of her tears. For several minutes, they clung to each other in silence and Tory, her head pressed against his chest, listened to the steady beating of Trask's heart. Surrounded by his strength, she was lost in her feelings of love and despair for this man.

"Regrets?" he asked, once his breathing had slowed. Tenderly he brushed a tear from the corner of her eye.

"No . . ."

"But?"

Her voice trembled slightly. "I'm not sure that getting involved again is the smartest thing to do. But then I've made a lot of questionable decisions lately."

He propped himself on one elbow and stared down at her. His face was shadowed but even in the darkness Tory could see the seductive slash of his smile.

"Why not . . . get involved, that is?"

"I only agreed to see you because of the letter . . . and, well, having an affair with you now will only complicate things."

His grin slowly faded, and his hands caressed her bare shoulders. "I think you'd better say what you mean and quit beating around the bush."

Tory gathered her courage. The next words were difficult, but necessary. She couldn't continue to live in a crystal dreamworld that could shatter so easily. "All right, senator. What I'm trying to say is that I'm not comfortable with short-term affairs. You and I both know that when all of this . . . note business is cleared up, you'll be returning to Washington."

"You don't like dead-end relationships?"

"Exactly."

"You could come to Washington with me," he suggested. His arms tightened around her, holding her close to the contours of his body.

Tory almost laughed. She reached for her jeans. "And what would you do if I took you up on your offer?" she said. "I'm no more ready for the Washington social scene than you are to explain a mistress from Oregon."

"I was talking about a wife, not a mistress."

Tory's heart missed a beat and pain darkened her eyes. "Oh, Trask. Don't—"

"I asked you to marry me five years ago—remember?"

"That was before the trial."

"Forget the trial!" He jerked her roughly to him and she was forced to gaze into the intensity of his eyes.

"How can I? You're here, looking for another conspirator in your brother's death, for crying out loud!" She jerked on her jeans and reached for her blouse as all of the old bitterness returned to her heart. "And don't think that just because we made love you have to dangle a wedding ring in front of my nose. I fell for that trick once before—"

Trask's patience snapped. He took hold of her upper arms and refused to let go. "You're so damned self-righteous. I don't know how to make it any clearer to you that I love you. Asking you to marry me isn't a smoke screen for some dark ulterior motive. It's a proposal, plain and simple. I want you to be my wife and I was hoping that you could rise above the past and come to terms with your feelings as a mature adult woman!"

"I can."

He let go of her arms. "And?"

The lump in her throat swelled uncomfortably. "I love you even though I've been denying it, even to myself," she whispered. "I love you very much, but . . . but I'm not sure that I *like* you sometimes. As for marriage—we're a long way from making a decision like that."

Trask's back teeth ground together. "Have you been seeing someone else?"

Tory let out a disgusted sigh. "No. Not seriously."

"I heard that you were going to be married a couple of years back to some schoolteacher."

Tory smiled sadly with her confession. "It didn't work out." She turned away from him and began dressing. He watched as she slid her arms through the sleeves of her blouse.

"Why?"

Wasn't it obvious? "Because of you. As crazy as it sounds, senator, you're a hard act to follow." She smiled sadly at her own admission. How many times had she tried to deny, even to herself, that she still loved him?

"That's some consolation," he said, relief evident on his face. He had pulled on his cords, and pushed his arms through his shirt, but it was still gaping open, displaying in erotic detail, the muscles of his chest and abdomen. "I want you to consider my proposal."

"I think it's five years too late."

One dark brow quirked. “Better late than never, isn’t that what they say?”

“‘They’ aren’t always right.”

Trask smiled cynically as he helped her to her feet. “Marry me, Tory. I need you.”

“Not now, don’t ask—”

“We put it off too long once before.”

“I can’t make a decision like this; not now, anyway. We’ve got too many things hanging over our heads. I . . . I need time, and so do you.”

“You think that I’m caught up in the moment.”

Her head snapped up. “I wouldn’t be surprised.”

“What would it take to convince you?”

“Time—enough time to put all of what happened behind us.”

“Five years isn’t enough?”

Tory smiled sadly. “Not when one party is interested in dredging it all up again.”

He leaned forward, pushing his forehead against hers and locking his hands behind her shoulders. “I love you and I’m worried about you.”

“I’m fine,” she tried to assure him.

“Yeah, I can tell.” He patted her gently on the buttocks. “So who would want to fill that gorgeous skin of yours full of buckshot?” he asked.

“No one was shooting at me.”

His face became stern. “Whoever shot the calf wasn’t playing around.”

“I’m okay,” she insisted but he didn’t seem convinced. *“Really.”*

“I think you should come and stay with me at the cabin. You’d be safer.”

“I can’t.”

He rubbed his chin in frustration. “Look, Tory, I

dragged you into this mess and now it seems to be getting dangerous. I feel responsible."

"You don't have to. I can look after myself."

"If another person was involved in the Quarter Horse swindle, he's also involved in murder, Tory. Jason's murder. There's no telling to what lengths he might go to protect himself. The dead calf and the potshot taken at us today are serious."

"Don't try to scare me; I'm already scared."

"Then?"

"I told you, I can handle it."

Impatiently Trask raked his fingers through his hair. "I want to keep an eye on you, but I have to go to Salem, to the penitentiary, tomorrow."

"To talk to George Henderson?"

"And Linn Benton."

Tory felt her throat constrict at the mention of her father's two "partners" in the horse swindle. "Do you think that's smart?"

Trask's eyes narrowed and in the darkness Tory could see the hardening of his jaw. "If someone else was involved, they'd know about it."

"And what makes you so sure they'd talk to you?"

"I already set up the meeting through the warden. Henderson and Benton are both up for parole in the next couple of years—your dad took most of the blame, you know. While he was handed down thirty years, they plea bargained for shorter sentences."

"It was never fair," she whispered.

"Because Calvin didn't even try to defend himself!" When she blanched he touched her lovingly on the chin. "Look, knowing the likes of Benton and Henderson, they won't want to stir up any trouble that might foul up their chances for parole."

"And you intend to throw your weight around, now that you're a senator and all."

"That's about the size of it."

"Isn't that unethical?"

"But effective."

She couldn't argue with his logic, though she didn't like the idea of involving Henderson and Benton. A small feeling of dread skittered down her spine. "When will you be back?"

"Tomorrow night. I'll come by here and let you know what happened."

"Good."

"Are you sure you won't come with me to the cabin?" he asked, pushing a wisp of hair out of her eyes. "It might be safer." Once again his eyes had darkened seductively.

"That depends upon what you call safe, senator," she said teasingly, trying to push aside her fears. "Besides, the Lazy W is home. I feel safer on this ranch than I do anywhere in the world. I've managed to make it by myself for five years. I think I'll be okay for the next twenty-four hours." She winked conspiratorially at him and he couldn't resist kissing her provocative pout.

Trask realized that there was no point in arguing further with Tory. Short of bodily carrying her to the Blazer and taking her hostage, there was no way of getting her to leave the ranch. "Just remember that I love you and that I expect you to take care of yourself."

She couldn't hide the catch in her voice. "I will."

He reached for his hat and forced it onto his head before kissing her once more and striding out of the house. Tory watched him from the window and smiled when she saw him tuck his shirttails into his cords. Then he climbed into the Blazer and roared down the lane.

"It's too easy to love you," she whispered as she mounted the stairs and headed to her bed . . . alone.

TRASK DROVE LIKE a madman. His fingers were clenched around the steering wheel of the Blazer and the stream of oaths that came from his mouth were aimed at his own stupidity.

He skidded to a stop at the main intersection in town and slammed his fist into the steering wheel. He was furious with himself. Inadvertently, because of his own damned impatience, he had placed Tory in danger.

"Damn it all to hell," he muttered, stripping the gears of the Blazer as he pushed the throttle and maneuvered through town. He drove without conscious thought to Neva's house. After parking the Blazer in the driveway, Trask strode to the front door and let himself in with his own key.

"Trask?" Neva called anxiously from her room. She tossed on her robe and hurried into the hallway. Trask was standing in the living room, looking as if he'd like to break someone's neck. "What are you doing here at this time of night?"

"I need to use your phone. There isn't one at the cabin."

"Go ahead." She pushed the blond hair away from her face and stared at the disheveled state of Trask's clothes and the stern set of his jaw. "You nearly scared me to death, you know."

"Sorry," he said without regret and paced between the living room and hallway. "I should have called."

"It's okay." She sighed and looked upward to the loft where her son was sleeping. "At least you didn't wake Nicholas . . . yet." She folded her arms over her chest and studied Trask's worried expression. "Are you going to tell me what's wrong or do I have to guess?"

"I'm really not sure."

"Don't tell me, Tory didn't go along with your plan."

"That wasn't it, no thanks to you." He frowned. In the past he'd been able to confide everything to Neva, but now things had changed; he sensed it. "Look, let me use the phone in the den and then we can talk."

"Okay. How about a cup of coffee?"

"How about a beer?"

Neva's brows shot upward. "That bad?"

"I don't know, Neva." He shook his head and the lines of worry near the corners of his eyes were more evident than they had been. "I just don't know." He walked through the kitchen to the small office where his brother had once planned to expose the biggest horse swindle in the Pacific Northwest.

Trask closed the door to the den and stared at the memorabilia that Neva had never managed to put away. A picture of Jason holding a newborn Nicholas was propped up on the desk. Jason's favorite softball glove and a ball autographed by Pete Rose sat on a bookcase next to all of the paperback thrillers Jason had intended, but never had time, to read. A plaque on the wall complemented the trophies in the bookcase; mementos of a life cut off much too early.

The desk chair groaned as Trask sat down, picked up the phone and punched out the number of the sheriff's department. After two rings the call was answered and Trask was told that Paul Barnett wasn't in the office, but would return in the morning.

"Great," Trask muttered. Rather than leave his name with the dispatcher, Trask hung up and drummed his fingers on the desk as he considered his alternatives. *You've been a fool,* he thought as he leaned back in the chair and put his fingers together tent style. *How could you have been so stupid?*

It was one thing to come back to Sinclair and start a quiet investigation; quite another to come back and flaunt the reasons for his return. Although he hadn't told anyone other than Neva and Tory about the anonymous letter, he hadn't hidden the fact that he was back in Sinclair for the express purpose of seeing Tory again. By now, half the town knew his intentions. The guilty persons could certainly put two and two together.

And so Tory was in danger, because of him. Trask took off his hat and threw it onto the worn leather couch. His mouth felt dry for the need of a drink.

The trouble was, Trask wasn't cut out for this cloak-and-dagger business. Never had been. Even the back-scratching and closed-door deals in Washington rubbed him the wrong way. As a junior senator, he'd already ruffled more than his share of congressional feathers.

With a grimace he pulled a copy of the anonymous letter out of his wallet and laid it on the desk while he dialed Paul Barnett's home number and waited. It took several rings, but a groggy-voiced Barnett finally answered.

The conversation was short and one-sided as Trask explained why he was in Sinclair and what had happened.

"I'll need to see the original note," Barnett said, once Trask had finished his story. All the sleep was out of the sheriff's voice. "I already sent one of my men out to check out the dead calf. As far as we can tell, it was an isolated incident."

"A warning," Trask corrected.

"Possibly."

"The same as the rifle shot this evening."

"I'll check into it, do what I can."

"Good. Tory's not going to like the fact that I called you. She wanted to keep things under wraps until we'd found what we were looking for."

"That's foolish of course, but I can't say as I blame her, considering what happened to her pa and the reputation of that ranch."

"What happened to Calvin and the ranch aren't important. Right now she needs protection. Whether she knows it or not," he added grimly.

"I don't have the manpower to have someone cover the Lazy W day and night, you know."

"I'll take care of that end. John Davis, a private investigator in Bend, owes me a favor—a big one."

"And you've called him?"

"I will."

"Good. And the note?"

"I'll bring it over within the hour."

"I'll be waiting."

Just as Trask hung up the phone, Neva knocked quietly on the door and entered the den. She offered Trask a mug filled with coffee. "We were out of beer," she lied.

Trask grinned at the obvious deception. "I don't need a mother, you know."

Neva leaned against the doorjamb and eyed him sadly. "Sometimes I wonder."

"I do all right."

"I read the papers, Trask. What do they call you? 'The young rogue senator from Oregon'?"

"Sometimes." He took a sip from the cup and let the warm liquid salve his nerves. "When are you going to take all this stuff—" he motioned to Jason's softball trophies and plaques "—down and put it away?"

"Maybe never."

Trask frowned and shook his head. "You're a young beautiful woman, Neva—"

"With a six-year-old son who needs to know about his father."

"Maybe he needs a new one."

Neva looked shocked. "He's a McFadden, Trask. Your brother's son. You want some stranger to raise him?"

"He'll always be a McFadden; but he could use some male influence."

"He has you," she said softly.

"I live in Washington."

"Until you don't get reelected."

Trask nearly choked on his coffee. "That's what I like to hear: confidence." Trask's eyes darted around the room and his smile faded. "You can't live in the past, Neva."

"I was going to say exactly the same thing to you."

Trask caught her meaningful glance and frowned into his cup before finishing his coffee in one swallow and setting the empty mug on the desk. "I've got to go."

"You could stay," she suggested, her cheeks coloring slightly. "Nicholas would be thrilled."

Trask shook his head, stood up, grabbed his hat and kissed Neva on the forehead. "Can't do it. I've got things to do tonight."

"And tomorrow?"

"I'll be in Salem."

Neva paled and sank into the nearest chair. Her fingers nervously gripped her cup. "I knew it," she said with a sigh. "You're going to see Linn Benton and George Henderson in the pen, aren't you?"

"Yes."

"Oh, Trask, why?" Doe-soft eyes beseeched him.

"It's important." He saw the tears of frustration fill

her large eyes and he felt the urge to comfort her. "Look, Neva—"

She sniffed the tears aside and met his gaze. "It's all right, Trask. I'll manage. And when Nicholas wonders why all of his friends are pointing fingers at him and whispering behind his back, I'll tell him." Using the sleeve of her robe to dry her cheeks, she forced a frail smile. "Do what you have to do, senator. Don't worry about how it affects a six-year-old boy who worships the ground you walk on."

"You're not making this easy—"

"Damn it, Trask, I'm not trying to! I'd do anything I could to talk you out of this . . . madness."

Trask's eyes became incredibly cold. "How far would you go to protect your child?"

"As far as I had to."

"Regardless?"

"Nicholas's health, safety and well-being are my first concerns."

"And what about your health and safety?"

Neva smiled cynically. "I can't wait until you have a child, Trask. Then I'll ask you the same question."

"I just think you should put yourself first occasionally."

"Pearls of wisdom, senator. I'll think about them."

Trask paused at the door. "By the way, thanks for the picnic lunch today."

"You're welcome, I guess. Did you bring the cooler in?"

A picture of the empty cooler, scattered dishes and rumpled blanket filled his mind. In the urgency of the moment after the rifle shot had pierced the air, he had forgotten to retrieve anything. "No, uh, Tory wanted to clean it. I'll pick it up tomorrow and bring it back."

A spark of interest flickered in Neva's dark eyes. "So the picnic went well?"

For a reason he didn't understand, Trask lied to his sister-in-law for the first time in his life. No need to worry her, he thought, but he knew there was more to his evasive answer than he would acknowledge. "It was fine."

"And what did you find on Devil's Ridge?"

"Absolutely nothing." *Except a potential assassin.*

"But you're still going to Salem tomorrow," she said with a sigh. "You just can't let it drop, can you?"

"Not this time."

"Well go on." She waved him off with a limp hand. "You've got things to do, remember? Just be careful. Linn Benton, whether he's in prison or not, is still very powerful. He may have been stripped of his judicial robes, but he's still a wealthy and influential man with more than his share of friends, all of whom haven't forgotten that your testimony was instrumental in sending him to prison."

"Good night, Neva," Trask said, without waiting for a reply. There was none. He walked out the front door.

As he stepped off the porch and headed for the Blazer, he heard a noise and turned. Before he could see his assailant, Trask felt the thud of a heavy object strike the back of his head. Blinding lights flashed behind his eyes just as a knee caught him in the stomach and he fell forward onto the dry ground. Before he lost consciousness he heard a male voice that was vaguely familiar.

"Leave it alone, McFadden," it warned gruffly. Trask tried to stand, but was rewarded with another sharp kick in the abdomen. "You're out of your league, senator."

Chapter Eight

THE FIRST THING Trask remembered were hands, incredibly soft hands, holding his head. A woman's voice, filled with anguish and fear, was calling to him from a distance and there was pain, a pain so intense it felt as if it was splintering his head into a thousand fragments.

"Trask . . . Oh, dear God . . ." the woman cried out, nearly screaming with terror as she looked down on him. Moonlight caught in her silver hair, but the features of her face were blurred and indistinct. *"Trask!"*

His mouth felt cotton-dry and when he tried to speak the voice that he heard didn't sound like his own. "Neva?" He reached forward and his fingers touched her hair before his hand dropped to the ground. A blinding stab of pain shot through his brain when he tried to lift his head.

"Oh, God, Trask . . . are you all right?" Her fingers were exploring the lump on the back of his head and tears gathered in her large eyes. "I was afraid something like this might happen, but I just couldn't believe . . ."

He opened his eyes and tried to focus. It was dark, but the woman's face was definitely that of his sister-in-law. Propping himself on one elbow he tried to push his body upright to stand, but the jarring pain in his ribs and abdomen made him suck in his breath and remain on the hard ground.

"What happened?" Neva demanded, looking at the beaten man with pitying eyes.

As if she could have prevented what happened, Trask thought dizzily and then discarded his annoying thought. Neva's head moved quickly from side to side, her eyes darting from one shadowed tree to another as if she half expected to discover the man who had attacked him lurking in the still night.

"Someone jumped me—" Trask began to explain.

"I knew it!" Her attention swung back to the injured man. "I knew that something like this would happen!" She let out a breath of despair and her shoulders slumped in resignation. As if finding an answer to an inner struggle, Neva clenched her fist in determination. "I'm going to call the police and then I'll get an ambulance for you."

"Hold on a minute," Trask ground out, again leveling himself up on one elbow. Sweat had broken out on his forehead and chest and several buttons were missing from his shirt. "I don't need an ambulance or the police . . ."

"You've been beaten, for God's sake!" she shrieked.

"Neva, get hold of yourself," he insisted as his groggy mind began to clear. *Tory! If anything had happened to her . . .*

With one hand he reached forward and held on to Neva's arm. "I've got to get into the house—to a phone," he stated. Disjointed but brutally clear images of Tory and what might have happened to her began to haunt him.

"You need a doctor."

"You're a nurse. Can't you just fix me up?"

She eyed him severely. "No. You need X-rays. And an examination by a doctor. You might have a concussion, maybe cracked ribs and God only knows what else." Gingerly she touched the deep cut along his jaw where his chin had crashed into the ground.

"I'll be fine," Trask said angrily, mentally cursing himself for not being more careful with Tory's safety. "Just help me up and get me into the house. Whoever did this to me may have gone after Tory."

"Tory?" Neva repeated, freezing.

"I don't have time to talk, damn it!" A dozen hideous scenarios with Tory as the unwitting victim filled his mind.

"Yes, sir," Neva snapped back at him, offering her body as support as he rose unsteadily. With her arm around his torso to brace him, Neva forced Trask to lean on her as they walked up the steps to the front door. "Before you do anything else, I expect you to tell me exactly what happened."

"Later."

Once inside the house, she examined his head and offered him an ice pack. "Lucky for you you've got a thick skull," she murmured tenderly. "Now, what else?"

He motioned to his side. She took off his shirt and frowned at the purple bruise already discoloring his ribs. "Someone doesn't like you poking around," she decided.

"No one likes me poking around," he said with what was an attempt at a smile. "Not even you."

"Maybe you should take this warning seriously," she suggested.

"Can't do it, Neva."

"Oh, Trask, why not?"

"I'll explain once I make a few calls—"

"Mom?" Nicholas was standing on the landing of the stairs to the loft. His blue eyes rounded at the disheveled and battered sight of Trask sprawled over the couch in the living room.

"Nick, I thought you were asleep." Neva's eyes flickered with fear before darting from Trask to her son and back again. Her gaze silently implored Trask to keep the truth from Nicholas.

The young boy ignored his mother and his eyes clouded with worry. "What happened, Uncle Trask?"

"Would you believe a barroom brawl?" Trask asked, forcing a painful grin.

"Naw." Nicholas stuck out his lower lip pensively and looked at his mother. "Is that really what happened?"

Neva shrugged.

"Sort of," Trask intervened, sensing Neva's discomfiture. "We good guys always have to be on the lookout, you know."

Nicholas came down the last few steps. The boy's eyes were round with excitement and hero worship for his uncle. "Mom? Did Uncle Trask get into a fight?"

"I don't really know," Neva said nervously.

"So where's the other guy?"

"He took off," Trask said, attempting levity. "He'd had enough I guess."

"Because you beat him?" Nicholas sat on the edge of the couch.

Trask had to laugh and the pain in his ribs seared through his body. "Unfortunately the other guy got the better of me."

Nicholas frowned petulantly while stepping closer to the couch and surveying his uncle. "But the good guys are always supposed to win."

"Only on television," Trask replied, ruffling the boy's coarse hair. "Or if they get help from their friends."

Trask's eyes moved from Nicholas to Neva. She paled slightly and tried to avoid his gaze.

"Come on, Nick. You can have a piece of pie and a glass of milk. Then you've got to go back to bed. Uncle Trask has to make some phone calls." She placed the telephone on the coffee table and carefully stepped over the cord. "Here, take these," she said to Trask, offering him aspirin and a glass of water.

"Thanks."

"But I want to stay up." Nicholas turned pleading eyes on his uncle.

"You'd better do what your mom says," Trask suggested.

"But it's not fair!"

"Nothing ever is," Neva replied softly, thinking of Jason's early death and the men who were responsible for his murder as she guided Nicholas into the kitchen and waited while he ate his pie.

When Nicholas had finished eating, over his loud protests, Neva put him back into bed. She watched the boy until his breathing became regular and he fell asleep with one arm tossed around the neck of the puppy Trask had given him for his birthday. Her throat tightened at the sight of her tousle-headed son sleeping so blissfully unaware of any of the suffering or malice in the world. How desperately she wanted to protect him.

As Nicholas started to snore, Neva could hear Trask talking on the phone in the living room though most of the one-sided conversation was muffled.

"Damn!" Trask muttered as he slammed the receiver of the telephone back into the cradle. He had tried calling Tory twice, but no one at the Lazy W had bothered to answer the phone. Fortunately his other calls had gotten through. He ran his fingers through his hair and swung his feet over the edge of the couch.

"This has gone on long enough," Neva said tightly as she came down the stairs and took a seat in her favorite rocker. "The next time someone attacks you, it might be your life, senator . . . or maybe someone else's." Her voice cracked and her hands worked nervously in her lap. "I think you should call the sheriff. Let Paul Barnett do his job and wash your hands of this accomplice to the conspiracy theory right now."

"I already have," he said slowly as he watched her. For the first time since he had returned to Sinclair, Trask had an inkling of Neva's true fears and he finally understood her odd behavior.

With a groan, he stood. Neva started. "You should be lying down—in the guest room."

Trask walked over to her and, placing both hands on either arm of the wooden rocker, he imprisoned her in the chair. "Why don't you tell me what's really going on, Neva, what you're really afraid of?" he suggested, his voice cold. "Come on, level with me." His blue eyes pierced into hers.

"I'm afraid for you," she whispered.

"Not good enough."

"And for Nicholas." She rubbed her chin nervously and tried to avoid his stare. It was impossible as his face was only inches from hers.

"That's better."

Tears started to pool in her eyes. "The kids at school—"

"Are not what you're afraid of, are they? Someone's been threatening you and Nicholas."

"No . . . oh, God, no," she cried, desperation and fear contorting her face.

He placed one hand over hers. "Neva?"

There was silence, tense unbearable silence. Only the sound of the clock ticking over the mantel disturbed the quiet.

"Look, it's obvious that someone got to you and used Nicholas's safety as part of a threat. I just want a name, Neva."

"I don't know . . ."

Trask's fist coiled over her fingers. "Just one name!"

"Oh, Trask," she whispered, closing her eyes and slumping in the chair. "There is no name. . . ." Her voice was shaking and she let her head drop into her hands. "Oh, God, Trask, I'm so scared," she whispered. He placed his arms around her and she tried in vain to stem the flow of her tears. Instead she began to sob against his shoulder. "I've been getting these calls—horrible calls—"

"From whom?"

"I don't know. Some man. He threatened me. Told me that if I didn't convince you to forget about the horse swapping swindle that . . . that . . . he'd take Nicholas from me . . . hurt him." She was shaking violently. "I was afraid to tell anyone."

White-hot rage raced through Trask's blood and all of his muscles tensed. "You should have told me," he ground out, pushing away from the chair.

"Probably," she admitted. "For the first time in my life I didn't know what to do. And the man insisted that I wasn't to tell you anything, or—" her anguished eyes searched Trask's bruised face "—or one of us would be hurt. And now look at you . . . look what he did . . ."

"Nothing's going to happen to Nicholas," Trask swore.

"How can you be sure—look what happened to you!"

Trask's eyes sparked blue fire. "I'll see to it that

you're safe. Not only are we going to call Paul Barnett and tell him what's going on, I've got a friend, a private investigator, who'll put a twenty-four-hour watch on you and Nicholas." He checked his watch. "Paul's probably already on his way to the Lazy W." Quickly he punched out the number of the sheriff's department and got hold of Deputy Woodward, who promised to come directly to Neva's house.

"I don't need to be watched," Neva stated, gathering her courage as Trask hung up and immediately redialed the phone.

"Don't argue with me, Neva," Trask nearly shouted just as the groggy voice of John Davis answered the phone. Again, Trask told his story and John promised to send a detective to Neva's home as well as have someone survey the comings and goings at the Lazy W.

"What are you planning?" Neva asked, once Trask had hung up the phone and was slipping his arms through his shirt.

"A deputy from the sheriff's department, a man by the name of Greg Woodward is coming over here tonight."

"No."

"Just listen to me, damn it. Woodward is going to take your statement and wait until one of John Davis's men arrives. Then he's going to meet me and Sheriff Barnett at the Lazy W."

"You're going back to see Tory?"

Trask's face hardened and his eyes darkened murderously. "If someone is dead set on discouraging me, I'd be willing to bet that the next person they'll approach is Tory."

Neva's mouth went dry. "What do you mean?"

"I mean simply that I'm worried about her. While we were at Devil's Ridge, someone took a shot at us."

"No!" Neva looked half-crazed with fear. Her face went deathly white and she glanced from Trask to the loft where Nicholas was sleeping so peacefully and back again. "I can't believe this is happening. All because of some damned note!"

"Believe it."

"Oh, dear Lord," she whispered.

There was a sharp knock at the door and Trask opened it to find Deputy Woodward on the doorstep. After assuring himself that Woodward had contacted the sheriff and was following Barnett's orders, Trask half ran to the Blazer, shoved the truck into gear and drove toward the Lazy W.

A THUNDEROUS NOISE awakened Tory. She sat bolt upright in bed until her groggy thoughts began to make sense and she realized that someone was pounding urgently at the front door. Probably Keith. He had a habit of losing his key . . . .

She tossed on a robe and hurried down the stairs. "I'm coming, I'm coming," she called. "Hold your horses."

"Thank God," she heard a male voice say and grinned when she realized it belonged to Trask.

Jerking the door open, she felt her smile widen for the man she loved. "Well, Senator McFadden, what brings you back to the Lazy W at this hour?"

As she stepped onto the front porch, she was swept into Trask's arms as he crushed her desperately to him. "Thank God, you're all right," he whispered against her wet hair. "If I ever lost you again . . ." His voice caught and the arms around her held on as if he expected her to disappear. "Where were you?" he demanded.

"When?"

"About twenty minutes ago." Still he held her tightly, almost deliberately.

"I was here."

"But I called. No one answered."

"I was here," she repeated. "Maybe you caught me when I was in the shower. I thought I heard the phone ring, but by the time I got to it, no one was there."

"Lord, Tory," he whispered, closing his eyes. "You had me half out of my mind with fear." He slowly pulled his head back and stared into her eyes. "Where's Paul Barnett?"

"The sheriff?" she asked incredulously. "Trask, what's going on? Do you have any idea what time it is? Why would Paul Barnett be here?"

"Because I asked him to come. He's supposed to be here, damn it!"

"Slow down, will you? You're talking like a lunatic!"

The light from the hallway spilled onto the front porch and for the first time she noticed that his clothes were ripped and dirty and there were cuts below his right eye and on his chin. "Wait a minute," she said, drawing away and gently touching his beard-darkened jaw. "What in God's name happened to you?"

Trask's eyes fell on her face and then looked past her to the interior of the house. It was then she noticed his haggard expression and the fact that he walked with a slight limp. Worry crept into her voice. "Trask? What's going on?"

"Are you okay?"

"Looks like I should be asking you that one," she

observed, concern making her voice rough. "Trask, what happened?"

"Our friend from the ridge caught up with me."

"What?"

Trask walked into the entry hall and began snapping on lights before he started looking into the corners of the rooms on the ground floor. Once a quick, but complete search of the lower level was accomplished, he started up the stairs and Tory followed him. "I was worried about you," he finally explained, once all the rooms and closets were searched. "Are you alone?"

"Yes. You could have asked me, y'know, instead of walking in here and tearing the place apart like some kind of madman."

He ignored her sarcasm. "Where's Keith?"

"I don't know," she admitted. "Sometimes he stays out late—"

"Son-of-a-bitch!" Trask stalked into the den. All of his muscles became instantly tense.

"Oh, no, Trask," Tory whispered, following him into the study and understanding his anger. She tried to ignore the tiny finger of dread slowly creeping up her spine. "You're not seriously trying to blame Keith for this—" she pointed at the disheveled state of his appearance "—are you?"

"I was hoping that he had an alibi."

Tory's eyes widened in horror. "You think Keith did this to you?"

"Maybe."

"Oh, Trask, no! You can't be serious!" she said, her voice shaking as she clamped a hand over her mouth and tried to pull herself together. Reading the anger in his eyes she slowly let her hands fall to her side. "But you're just guessing aren't you? I take it you didn't see who attacked you?"

"Didn't have time. It was dark."

Tory felt a little sense of relief. This was all a big mistake. Keith wouldn't rough somebody up, not even Trask Mcfadden. "Have you seen a doctor?"

"Neva examined me."

"Neva! Good Lord, have you been there, too?" Tory pushed her damp hair out of her eyes.

"That's where it happened."

Tory's eyes turned cold. Too much was happening and she couldn't think straight. "Wait a minute, slow down. Come into the kitchen and tell me exactly what happened and when and where and why." She started down the hallway, Trask right behind her.

"Why? That's the kicker, isn't it?"

Tory frowned as she took down two cups and made a pot of tea. Forcing her hands to remain steady, she poured the tea into the cups. "So tell me, what did Neva say?"

"Other than that I should be more careful?" Tory didn't crack a smile. "She thinks I'll live."

"Some consolation." She handed him a cup of tea and tried to force a grin as her eyes slid down his slightly bruised chin to the torn shirt that displayed all too vividly his muscled chest and discolored abdomen. "You look awful."

"That's a cut above the way I feel."

"I really think you should go to the emergency room, and get some X-rays."

"Later." He set down his cup and his eyes took her in; the tousled damp hair that hung in springy curls around a fresh face devoid of makeup, the gorgeous green eyes now dark with concern, and the soft heather-colored robe clinched loosely over her small waist. "God, I was worried about you," he admitted, rubbing his hand over his unshaven jaw.

"It looks like I should have been the one worrying."

He took the cup from her hands and pulled her toward him. Lowering his head, he caught her lips with his and let the fresh feminine scent of her fill his nostrils and flood his senses. "From now on, I'm not letting you out of my sight," he vowed against her ear before reluctantly releasing her.

"Is that a promise or a threat?"

His uneven, incredibly charming grin flashed white against his dark skin. "However you want to take it."

"I'll think about it and let you know what I decide."

Trask's face sobered and his fingers toyed with the lapel of her plush robe. "As much as I find the thought distasteful," he said with a frown as he kissed her forehead, "I think you should get dressed. I asked Sheriff Barnett to meet us here."

"Tonight?"

"Yeah." He stepped away from her and patted her firmly on the behind. "Look, I'll explain everything when Paul gets here, just go put on something—" he lifted his palms upward as he looked at her soft terry robe and the white silk gown that was visible when she walked "—something less erotic."

"I've never heard of a terry-cloth bathrobe being called erotic."

"Only because I've never seen you in one before."

Tory laughed and shook her head. Against her better judgment she walked upstairs and changed into a pair of cords and a sweater. She was braiding her hair into a single plait as she stood on the landing when she heard the knock at the front door.

"I'll get it," Trask said. He'd positioned himself at the bottom of the stairs and was watching with interest as Tory wrapped the rubber band around the tip of her braid.

"Suit yourself."

His teasing expression turned grim. "And I think you'd better try and track down your brother. There are a few questions he'll have to answer." With one last glance upward in her direction Trask opened the door.

Paul Barnett and Detective Woodward were standing on the front porch. Tory's fingers curled around the banister as she walked slowly down the stairs and faced all three men.

"Come in, sheriff . . . Deputy Woodward." She inclined her head toward each man and wondered if it was obvious to them how nervous she felt. Not since the trial had she been uncomfortable with the police, but this night, with Trask beaten and Keith missing, she felt a nervous sweat break out between her shoulder blades. "I was going to make a pot of coffee. I'll bring it into the den."

Barnett pursed his lips and nodded his agreement. He was a slightly paunchy man with wire-rimmed glasses, cold eyes and a hard cynical smile. "Anyone else here?"

"No."

"No hands on the ranch?"

"Not tonight."

"What about that kid brother of yours?" the sheriff pressed, his graying bushy eyebrows lifting with each of her negative responses.

Tory felt herself stiffen. "Keith isn't home. He's in town, I think."

"But you don't know?"

"No. Not for sure."

Barnett pressed his thin lips tightly together but didn't comment. When the three men went into the den, Tory escaped to the kitchen and put on a pot of coffee. She tried to ignore the fact that her hands as well as her entire body were trembling.

Where was Keith? Everyone wanted to talk to her brother and she had no idea where he was. It was late, damned late and unlike her brother to be out on a weeknight.

The grandfather clock in the entry hall chimed one o'clock. The hollow notes added to Tory's growing paranoia.

Drumming her fingers on the counter as the coffee perked, she considered using the phone and trying to track down her brother, but discarded the idea. He was twenty-one and able to make his own decisions. Or so she silently prayed.

The murmur of voices from the den caught her attention and her heart began to pound with dread. Quickly grabbing the glass carafe, four mugs, the sugar bowl and creamer, she set everything onto a woven straw tray and carried it into the den. Trask looked up from his position in her father's leather recliner and smiled reassuringly.

"Okay, now let me get this straight," Barnett was saying, his graying mustache working as he spoke. "You two went up on Devil's Ridge looking for some sort of clue that might lead you to the fourth man who was supposedly involved in the Quarter Horse swindle. Right?"

"Right," Trask replied.

Tory caught Barnett's inquisitive stare and nodded curtly to his unspoken question. "However, it could be a three-man conspiracy," she said. "I still don't believe that my father was involved."

"Be that as it may, Ms. Wilson, your father was tried and convicted, so we'll have to assume that he was in on the swindle," Barnett said slowly before turning to Trask. "So, you believe the fourth man theory because of this piece of paper." He held up the anonymous letter, without waiting for a response. "And you think that because you've been poking around looking for some proof to support the fourth man theory, one of the calves from the Lazy W was shot, and someone tried to shoot you as well, this afternoon—"

"I'm not sure they were shooting at us, maybe just trying to scare us," Trask interjected.

"Nevertheless, a shot was fired in your general direction."

"Yes."

"And when that didn't work, whoever it was that fired the rifle followed you to Neva McFadden's place and beat the tar out of you."

Trask frowned, nodded his head and rubbed his jaw pensively. "That's why I think it was a warning. If they had wanted me dead, I would have been. I had to have been an easy target coming out of Neva's house."

"So that's all of your story?"

"Except that someone's been calling Neva and harassing her, making threats against her son," Deputy Woodward added.

"What!" Tory's face drained of color and she almost dropped her coffee. She turned her wide eyes on Trask. "No—"

Trask's jaw hardened and his eyes turned as cold as blue ice. "That's why Neva tried to talk both me and you out of the investigation. She was afraid for Nicholas's life."

"This has gotten completely out of hand," Tory whispered, leaning against the pine-paneled wall.

"You should have called me," Barnett said, leveling his gaze at Trask, "instead of trying to investigate something like this on your own. Could have saved yourself a lot of grief as well as a beating."

"I was just trying to keep it quiet."

Barnett frowned. “We could have done a better job. In case you’ve forgotten, that’s what my department gets paid to do. As it is, you’ve made one helluva mess of it.”

Trask’s lips twisted wryly. “Thanks.”

After asking Tory questions that confirmed Trask’s story about what happened on the ridge, the sheriff and his deputy finished their coffee, grabbed their notes and left.

“It gets worse by the minute,” Tory confided, once she was alone with Trask.

“Barnett’s right. I should have gone to the police in the beginning.”

“And then the police would have flocked back here, the press would have found out about it and the scandal would have been plastered on the front pages of the local papers all over again.”

“Looks like it’s going to end up that way regardless.”

“Nothing we can do about it now,” she said with a sigh. Walking toward the recliner Tory searched Trask’s face. His jaw was still strong, jutted in determination, but pain shadowed his blue eyes. The cuts on his face, though shallow, were slightly swollen and raw. “Are you okay? I could take you into Bend to the hospital.”

“Not now.”

“But your head—”

“It’s fine. It’ll wait until morning.”

“Oh, senator,” she said with a sad smile. “What am I going to do with you?”

His eyes slid seductively up her body to rest on the worried pout of her lips. “I can think of a dozen things . . .”

“Be serious.”

“I am.”

"Well, I'm not about to have you risk further injury." She glanced out the window and back at the clock. *Two fifteen, and still no sign of Keith.* "Besides, it's late."

"Are you trying to give me a less than subtle hint?"

"I'm tired." She touched his head fondly. "You should be, too."

"I'm okay. Go to bed."

"And what about you?"

"I'm staying here."

"You can't—"

"Watch." He settled into the recliner and folded his hands over his chest.

"Trask. Think about it. You can't stay here. Keith will be home soon."

"That's who I'm waiting for."

"Oh, Trask." The rest of her response was cut off by the sound of an engine roaring up the driveway and the spray of gravel hitting the sides of the barn as the pickup ground to an abrupt halt.

"About time," Trask said, pushing himself upward.

Tory's heart was beating double time by the time that Keith opened the front door and strode into the den. His young face was set with fierce determination and he scowled at the sight of Trask.

"What's he doin' here?" Keith demanded of Tory, as he cocked an insolent thumb in Trask's direction.

"Why don't you ask me?" Trask cut in.

Turning, Keith faced Trask for the first time. It was then that he noticed the bruise on Trask's chin and his rumpled dirty clothing. "What the hell happened to you?"

"Why don't you tell me?" Trask hooked his thumbs in the belt loops of his jeans and leaned his shoulders against the fireplace. His intense gaze bored into Keith's worried face.

Keith immediately sobered. "What're you talking about?"

Trask's eyes narrowed. "Someone followed Tory and me up to Devil's Ridge this afternoon. Not only did this guy have a rifle, but he decided to use it by taking a shot at us."

"What?" Keith spun and faced his sister. "What's he talking about? Why would you go up to the ridge with him after what he did to you?" Keith became frantic and began pacing from the den to the hallway and back again. "I knew that McFadden couldn't wait to bring up all the dirt again!" He glanced over his shoulder at Trask. "What's he talking about—someone shooting at you? He's not serious—"

"Dead serious," Trask said tonelessly. "Then later, at Neva's place, someone decided to use the back of my head for batting practice."

Keith's face lost all of its color and his cocky attitude faded with his tan. "You're not kiddin' are ya?"

"Hardly," Trask said dryly, approaching the younger man in long sure strides. "And that same person has been calling my sister-in-law, threatening her to get me to stop this investigation." Keith looked as if he wanted to drop through the floor. "I don't suppose you know anything about that, do you?"

"I . . . I don't know anything."

"So where were you tonight?" Trask ground out.

"Tonight? You think I did it?" Keith seemed genuinely astounded. He looked pleadingly at Tory before stiffening at the sound of Trask's voice.

"Where were you?"

"I've been in town."

"Until two in the morning?"

"Yeah. Rex and I went into town, looking for a part for the combine. When we couldn't get it, I stayed at the Branding Iron for dinner and a few beers. Later I went over to Rex's place. He and several of the hands had a poker game going."

"And someone was with you all night?"

"For most of it." Keith's indignation flashed in his eyes. "Look, McFadden, I've done a lot of things in my life that I'm not particularly proud of, but what happened to you and Tory today has nothing to do with me."

"Why do I have difficulty believing you?"

"Because I've made no bones about the fact that I hate your guts." He pointed a condemning finger at Trask. "You nearly single-handedly destroyed everything my dad worked all of his life to achieve; you not only sent him to prison, but you took away all of his respectability by using his daughter and publicly humiliating her."

Trask's face hardened. A muscle worked in the corner of his jaw and his eyes narrowed fractionally. "I've made my share of mistakes," he admitted.

"Too many, McFadden. Too damned many! And tonight is just one more in the string. I didn't have anything to do with what happened to you tonight." He was shaking with rage. "Now I think it's about time you left."

Trask's eyes glittered with determination. "I'm not going anywhere, Wilson." He sat down in one of the chairs and propped the heels of his boots on the corner of the coffee table. "As a matter of fact, I intend to spend the rest of the night right here."

"Get out!"

"Not on your life."

Keith glared at his sister. "He's your problem," he spat out before stomping out of the den and treading heavily up the stairs to his room.

Tory took a seat on the arm of Trask's chair. "You

were too hard on him, y'know," she reprimanded, her brow knotted in concern. "He's not involved in this."

"So he claims."

"You don't believe him," she said with a sigh.

"I don't believe anyone—" he looked into her worried eyes and smiled slightly "—except for you."

"Not too long ago you didn't trust me."

"Not you, lady; just your motives."

"Same thing."

Trask took her hand and pressed her fingers to his lips. "Not at all. But sometimes I think you'd lie to protect those closest to you."

She shook her head and smiled sadly. "Wrong, senator. Maybe I should have five years ago. Since Dad wouldn't say what happened, maybe I should have covered for him." She picked up a crystal paperweight from the desk and ran her fingers over the cut glass. "Maybe then he'd still be alive."

"And you'd be the criminal for perjuring yourself."

She frowned at her distorted reflection in the glass. "I guess there are no easy answers," she said, as she placed the paperweight on the corner of the desk. "You really don't have to stay, you know."

"Wouldn't have it any other way."

"It's ridiculous. Keith's here."

"Precisely my point." He looked up at her and wrapped his hand around her neck, drawing her lips to his. "I'm not taking any chances with your life."

"What about Neva and Nicholas?"

"A private investigator is with them."

"And you've assigned yourself to me as my personal bodyguard, is that it?"

"Um-hm." He rubbed his lips gently against hers, then murmured, "I'm going to stick to you like glue."

"I just can't believe that anyone would want to hurt Nicholas or you."

He smiled wryly. "Believe it."

He pulled on her hand and she tumbled into the chair with him. Though he let out a sharp breath as her weight fell against his ribs, he grinned wickedly. "Maybe it would be best if I came to bed with you," he suggested, his breath touching her hair.

"I don't think so."

"Are you worried about what Keith and the rest of the hands will think?"

She shrugged. "A little, I guess."

"Hypocrite." He nuzzled her neck and she felt her blood begin to warm.

"There's nothing hypocritical about it, I'm just trying to use my head. We both need sleep. You can stay in the guest room. It's only a couple of doors down the hall from mine."

"I remember," he said softly, his voice intimate.

Tory had to look away from him to ignore the obvious desire smoldering in his eyes. *Who was she kidding? How many times had he stolen into her room in the past? He knew the ranch house like the back of his hand.*

"Where does Keith sleep?"

"He, uh, moved into Dad's room when Dad passed away."

"And the rest of the hands?"

"Usually go home. Once in a while someone will stay in the bunkhouse, but that's pretty rare these days."

"What about tonight or, say, the past week?"

"No one is staying on the ranch except Keith and myself."

"And Rex?"

"He has his own place, just north of Len Ross's

spread. He and Belinda have lived there for over five years." *Five years!* Once again, Tory was reminded of the time when she was free to love Trask with all her heart. But that was before her world was destroyed by the horse swapping scam, Jason's murder and the trial.

She stood up and tugged on Trask's arm, hoping to break the intimacy that memories of the past had inspired. "Come on, mister, let me help you up the stairs." As he stood, she eyed him speculatively. "If you give me your clothes, I'll throw them in the wash so that you have something clean in the morning."

"Gladly," he agreed as they mounted the stairs.

"Just leave them in the hall outside your door."

"Whatever you say," he whispered seductively and a shiver of desire raced down her spine.

"What I say is that we both need some time to think about what happened today. Maybe then we can make some sense of it."

Trask's smile slid off his face. "None of this makes any sense," he admitted, grimacing against a sudden stab of pain.

A few minutes later Trask was in the guest room, his clothes were in the washer and Tory was lying on her bed wondering if she would ever get to sleep, knowing that Trask was only two doors down the hall.

Chapter Nine

PALE LIGHT HAD just begun to stream into the bedroom when Tory heard the door whisper open. She rolled over to face the sound and focused her eyes on Trask as he approached the bed. He was wearing only a towel draped over his hips. A dark bruise discolored the otherwise hard muscles of his chest and the cut on his chin was partially hidden by his dark growth of beard. As he walked the towel gaped to display the firm muscles of his thighs moving fluidly with his silent strides.

"What're you doing?" she whispered, lifting her head off the pillow and rubbing her eyes.

"Guess."

The sight of him in the predawn light, a mischievous twinkle dancing in his blue eyes, his brown hair disheveled from recent slumber, made Tory's blood begin to race with anticipation.

But the purple bruise on his abdomen put everything into stark perspective. Someone didn't want Trask digging into the past and that person was willing to resort to brutal violence to stop Trask's investigation.

"What time is it?" she asked, pushing the disturbing thought aside.

"Five." He stopped near the bed and looked down at her, his gaze caressing the flush in her cheeks then meeting her questioning eyes. "I couldn't sleep very well," he admitted, his fingers working the knot on his towel. "Knowing you were in the same house with me has been driving me crazy."

"You're absolutely indefatigable . . . or is it insufferable? It's too early to decide which," she murmured, gazing up at him affectionately. "Last night someone tried to beat the living daylights out of you. There's a good chance you could have been killed and here you are—"

"Intent on seducing the woman I'm supposed to protect." He let the towel slide to the floor and sat on the edge of the bed. Bending slightly, he pushed the tousled auburn hair from her eyes and gently kissed her forehead. "Any complaints?"

"None, senator," she replied as he threw back the covers and settled into the bed, his naked body pressing urgently against the softer contours of hers.

"I could get used to a job like this," he said as he held her face in his hands and gazed into her slumberous eyes.

Happiness wrapped around Tory's heart. A cool morning breeze carrying the faint scent of new-mown hay ruffled the curtains as it passed through the open window. Morning birds had begun to chirp and from far in the distance came the familiar sound of lowing cattle. Lying with Trask in her bed as the first silvery rays of dawn seeped into the room seemed the most natural thing in the world. There was a peaceful solitude about dawn and Tory loved sharing that feeling with the only man she had ever loved.

His arms wrapped around her, pulling her close to him. The warmth and strength of his body was welcome protection. It felt good to lean on him again, she thought. Maybe there was a chance they could forget the pain of the past and live for the future. Looking into his eyes,

Tory felt that there was nothing in the world that could possibly go wrong as long as he was beside her.

"God, I love you," he whispered as he lowered his head and kissed her almost brutally.

Through the sheer nylon nightgown, she felt his hands caress her skin. Deft fingers outlined each rib as they moved upward to mold around her breasts and Tory gasped at the raw desire laboring within her.

Her breast ached with the want of him, straining to be caressed by his gentle fingers. As he found one nipple and teased it to ripe anticipation, Tory moaned. The exquisite torment deep within her became white hot as he lifted the nightgown over her head and slowly lowered himself alongside of her. His hands pressed against the small of her back as he took first one hard nipple into his mouth and after suckling hungrily for a time, he turned his attention to the other ripe bud and feasted again.

Tory's blood was pulsing through her veins, throbbing at her temples in an erratic cadence. Sweat moistened her body where Trask's flesh molded to hers. She could feel the muscles of Trask's solid thighs straining against hers and the soft hair on his legs rubbed her calves erotically, promising more of the impassioned bittersweet torment.

"I love you," she cried, all of her doubts erased by the pleasure of his body straining against hers. Painful emotions were easily forgotten with the want of him. Her fist clenched with forced restraint and her throat ached to shout his name as he slid lower and kissed the soft flesh of her abdomen, leaving a dewy trail from her breasts to her navel.

"I'm never going to let you go again," Trask vowed, his breath fanning her abdomen, his hands kneading the soft muscles of her back and buttocks as she lifted upward, offering herself to him. "Don't ever leave me, Tory."

"Never," she cried, the fires within her all-consuming in the need to be fulfilled, to become one, to surrender to her rampant desire for this one, proud man.

Slowly he drew himself upward and his hands twined in the wanton curls framing her face. His moist skin slid seductively over hers. "I'll keep you to that promise," he said, his voice rough and his blue eyes dark with passion. "Make love to me."

As she stared into his eyes, she reached forward, her arms tightening around his muscular torso. The warm mat of hair on his chest crushed her breasts as he rolled over her and his knees gently prodded her legs apart. "I want every morning to be like this one," he said as he lowered himself over her. His lips once again touched hers and she felt the warm invasion of his tongue just as he pushed against her and began the slow rhythmic dance of love.

Closing her eyes, Tory held him tightly, her fingers digging into the hard muscles of his back and shoulders as he moved over her in ever more rapid strokes. Her heart was thudding wildly in her rib cage. The warmth within her expanded around him and her breathing came in short gasps as Trask pushed her to the brink of ecstasy time and time again before the rippling tide of sweet fulfillment rushed over her and she felt his answering surrender.

Sweat dampened her curls as the warmth of afterglow caressed her. With Trask's strong arms wrapped around her, Tory felt there was nothing that they couldn't do, as long as they did it together.

She snuggled closer to him and Trask kissed her hair. "I meant it, you know," he insisted, his voice low. "About never letting you go."

"Good, because I'm going to hold you to it."

Silently they watched as the pale gray light of dawn faded with the rising sun. Clear blue sky replaced the early-morning haze.

Tory looked at the clock and groaned. "I've got to get up, senator. Rex usually gets here between six thirty and seven."

"Why don't you call him and tell him to take the day off?"

Laughing at the absurdity of his request, she wiggled out of his arms. "It's easier to get a straight answer out of a politician than it is to get Rex to take a day off," she said teasingly.

"You're feeling particularly wicked this morning aren't you?" But he was forced to chuckle.

"And what about you? Are you going to take the day off and forget about going to visit Linn Benton and George Henderson in the pen?"

His voice became stern. "Not on your life."

"That's what I was afraid of." Concern clouded her eyes as she rolled off the bed and reached for the robe draped over a bedpost at the foot of the bed. "It wouldn't surprise me if they were behind what happened to you last night."

Tenderly rubbing his jaw, Trask shook his head. "They're in prison, remember?"

"Yeah, but Linn Benton's got more than his share of friends." She shivered involuntarily and cinched the belt of her robe more tightly around her waist.

"So do I."

"I don't think friends in Washington count. They can't help you here," she thought aloud. Mentally shaking herself, she then tried to rise above the worries that had been with her ever since Trask had forced himself back in her life with his damned anonymous letter.

As she stared at the man she loved, she had to smile. His brown hair was tousled, his naked body was only partially hidden by the navy-blue sheet and patchwork quilt and his seductive blue eyes were still filled with passion. "I'll go throw your clothes in the dryer."

"Don't bother. I already did. They're probably dry by now."

"You mean that you went creeping around this house this morning with only a towel around you?"

"I wasn't creeping. And the only people here are you and Keith." His grin widened and amusement sparked in his eyes. "Besides I know where the utility room is. Believe it or not, I have done my own laundry on occasion."

"Hmph. I suppose you have." With a shake of her head, Tory went downstairs and into the kitchen. After starting the coffee, she walked into the adjoining utility room and removed Trask's clothes from the dryer. As he had predicted, the jeans and shirt were warm and dry. She draped them over her arm, climbed the stairs and returned to her room.

Trask was still lying on the four-poster, his head propped up with both pillows, a bemused grin making his bold features appear boyishly captivating. Tory's heart beat more quickly just at the sight of him.

"There you go, senator," she said, tossing the clothes to him.

"Can't I persuade you to come back to bed?"

"Not this morning. I'm a working woman, remember?"

"Excuses, excuses," he mumbled, but reached for his clothes. She sat on the edge of the bed while he pulled on his jeans and slipped his arms through the sleeves of his shirt.

"So tell me," she suggested, eyeing his bruised ribs

and the cut on his chin. "Have you got any theories about who decided to use you as a punching bag?"

He looked up from buttoning his shirt. "A few."

"Care to share them?"

"Not just yet."

"Why not?"

"No proof."

"So what else is new?" she asked, leaning back against the headboard of the bed and frowning. Here, lying with Trask in the small room decorated in cream-colored lace, patchwork and maple, she had felt warm and secure. The worries of the night had faded but were now thrown back in her face, quietly looming more deadly than ever.

Trask stood and tucked in the tails of his shirt. "What's new?" he repeated. "Maybe a lot."

"This is no time to be mysterious."

"Maybe not," he agreed while cocking his wrist and looking at his watch. "But I've got to get out of here. I want to check on Neva and Nicholas, change clothes at the cabin and be in Salem by ten."

The thought of Trask leaving the ranch was difficult for Tory to accept. In a few short days, she had gotten used to his presence and looked forward to the hours she spent with him. The fact that he was leaving to face two of the men responsible for his brother's death made Tory uneasy. Though she knew that her father had been innocent, the ex-judge Linn Benton and his accomplice, George Henderson, had been and, in her opinion, still were ruthless men more than capable of murder.

"Look," he was saying as he walked to the door. "I want you to be careful, okay? I'll check with John Davis and make sure he has a man assigned to the Lazy W."

"I don't think that's necessary."

Trask's eyes glittered dangerously. "I hope not, but I'm a firm believer in the better-safe-than-sorry theory."

"Oh, yeah?" She stared pointedly at the cut on his chin and the bruise peeking out of his shirt. "Look where it's gotten you. And now you're going to talk to your brother's murderers!"

He frowned and crossed the room to hold her in his arms. Placing a soft kiss on the crown of her head he let out a long weary sigh. "Believe me, lady, someday this will all be behind us."

"You hope."

"I promise."

"Just don't tell me that in twenty years I'll look back at what we're going through now and laugh, 'cause I won't!"

He chuckled and hugged her fiercely. "Okay, I won't lie to you, but I will promise you that we'll have plenty of stories that will entertain our grandchildren."

"That's a promise?" *Grandchildren and children. Trask's children.* At this point the possibility of marrying Trask and having his children seemed only a distant dream; a fantasy that she couldn't dare believe would come true.

"One I won't let you get out of." He lowered his head and captured her lips with his. "The sooner we get all of this mess behind us, the better. Then we can concentrate on getting married and filling the house with kids."

"Slow down, senator," she said, her love shining in her eyes. "First things first, don't you think? Oh, and if you want a cup of coffee, I'm sure it's perked."

He shook his head. "Haven't got time. I'll be back this afternoon."

"I'm counting on it."

"Maybe then I'll get a chance to talk to your foreman, Rex Engels."

Tory stiffened slightly. “Are you going to put him through the third degree, too?”

“Nothing so drastic,” Trask promised. “I just want to ask him a few questions.”

“About last night?”

“Among other things.”

“You don’t trust anyone, do you?”

“Just you,” he said.

“Hmph,” she muttered ungraciously and crossed her arms over her chest. “I’ll tell Rex that you want to talk to him.”

“Thanks.” With a broad wink, he opened the door of her room and disappeared. She watched from the window as he walked out of the house, got into his Blazer and drove down the lane. A plume of gray dust followed in his wake and disturbed the tranquility of the morning. As the Blazer roared by the pasture, curious foals lifted their heads, pricking their ears forward at the noise while the mares continued to graze.

“When will it ever end?” Tory wondered aloud, taking one final look at the dew-covered grass and the rolling green pastures and dusty paddocks. With a thoughtful frown she turned away from the window and headed for the shower.

TORY WAS IN the den balancing the checkbook when she heard Keith come down the stairs. He walked by the study without looking inside and continued down the hall to the kitchen.

“I’m in here,” Tory called. When she didn’t get a response, she shrugged and continued sorting through the previous month’s checks. A few minutes later, Keith strode into the room, sipping from a cup of coffee.

He frowned as if remembering an unpleasant thought. "So where's our guest?"

"Trask already left for Salem."

Keith tensed. "Salem? Why?" His eyes narrowed and he lifted a hand. "Don't tell me: he plans on visiting Linn Benton and George Henderson in prison."

"That's the idea."

"He just won't let up on this, will he?"

"I doubt it. And now that the sheriff's department is involved, I would expect that Paul Barnett or one of his deputies will be out later to ask you questions."

"Just what I need," Keith said grimly and then changed the subject. "So how're you this morning?" He threw a leg over one of the arms of the recliner, leaned back and studied his sister.

"As well as can be expected after last night."

Keith scowled into his cup. The lines of worry deepened around his eyes. "What McFadden said, about you being shot at, was it true?"

Tory let out a long breath. "Unfortunately, yes."

Keith's eyes clouded as he looked away from his sister. "And you think it has something to do with this anonymous note business, right?"

"I don't know," she admitted, taking off her reading glasses and setting them on the corner of the desk as she stared at her brother. "But it seems to me that it's more than a coincidence that the minute Trask comes into town, all the trouble begins."

"Has it ever occurred to you that Trask may have initiated all this hoopla just to get his name in the papers? You know, remind the voters that he's a hero."

"I don't think he hired someone to beat him up, if that's what you mean. And I don't think that he would let someone terrorize Neva or Nicholas—do you?"

Keith squirmed uncomfortably. "Maybe not."

"So how do you explain it?"

He looked straight into her eyes. "I can't, Sis. I don't have any clue as to why someone would take a shot at you or want to hurt Neva. And it scares me, it scares the hell out of me!"

"But maybe someone was just interested in hurting Trask?" she said. "The rest of us might just have gotten in the way. After all, he was the one that took the punches last night."

Keith's head snapped upward and his jaw tightened. "I hate the bastard. It's no secret. You know it and so does he." Keith's voice faded slightly and he hesitated before adding, "And I hate the fact that he's back here, getting you all messed up again, but I wouldn't beat him up or shoot at him, for crying out loud."

Tory tapped her pencil nervously on the desk. What she was about to say was difficult. "I'm sorry, Keith. But I can't seem to forget that the first day Trask came into town you were in a panic. You came out to the paddock to tell me about it, remember?" Tory's heart was hammering in her chest. She didn't like the role of inquisitor, especially not with Keith.

"I remember."

"And later you said something about pointing a gun at him if Trask tried to trespass."

Keith squeezed his eyes shut and rubbed the stiffness out of his neck. "That was all talk, Tory." He leaned back in the chair. "I just wish he'd leave us alone." After finishing his coffee, Keith stood. "I don't want to see you get hurt again. Everything that's happening scares me."

"I'm a big girl, Keith. I can take care of myself."

Keith offered his most disarming smile. "Then I'll try not to worry about you too much."

"Good." She let out a sigh of relief and felt the tension in her tight muscles ease. She believed everything Keith had told her and wondered why she had ever doubted him. "Oh, by the way, how did you do in the poker game last night?"

Keith's grin widened and he pulled out his wallet. When he opened it, he exposed a thick roll of bills tucked neatly in the side pocket. "I cleaned everyone's clock."

"That's a switch."

"Thanks for the vote of confidence."

"So how'd you get so lucky?"

Keith took his hat off a peg near the entry hall and jammed it onto his head. "Haven't you ever heard that poker is a game of skill, not luck?"

"Only from the winners."

Keith laughed as he walked out the front door. "I'll be on the west end of the ranch helping Rex clear out some brush."

"Will you be back for lunch?"

"Naw, I'll grab something later."

Keith left and Tory began drumming her fingers on the desk. Her brother had never won at poker in his life. Just when she was beginning to trust him, something he did seemed out of character. It worried her. It worried her a lot.

"Cut it out," she told herself, pushing her glasses onto her nose and studying the bank statement. "Trask's got you jumping at shadows." But she couldn't shake the unease that had settled in her mind.

IT WAS NEARLY one thirty when Tory heard the sound of a vehicle coming down the drive. She had been leaning over the fence and watching the foals and mares as they grazed in the pasture. Shading her eyes against the glare of the afternoon sun, she smiled when she recognized Anna Hutton's white van.

Dusting her hands on her jeans, Tory met the van just as Anna parked it near the stables.

"How's our boy doing?" Anna asked as she hopped out of the van and grabbed her veterinary bag.

"Better than I'd expected. I took your advice about the cold poultices and he's even putting a little weight on the leg this morning."

"Good." Anna grinned broadly. "See, I told you. Sometimes we don't have to resort to drugs."

"He's in the paddock around back," Tory said, leading Anna past the stables to the small enclosure where Governor was being walked by Eldon.

The stallion snorted his disapproval when he saw the two women and his black ears flattened to his head.

"So walking him hasn't proven too painful for him?" Anna asked, carefully studying the nervous horse.

"I don't think so," Tory replied. "Eldon?"

The ranch hand shook his head and his weathered face knotted in concentration. "He's been doin' fine. If I thought walkin' him was causing him too much pain, I wouldn't have done it, no matter what you said."

"It's great to have employees who trust your judgment." Tory commented when she read the amusement in Eldon's eyes.

Anna seemed satisfied. "Let's take a look at you," she said to the horse as she slid through the gate, patted Governor's dark shoulders and gently prodded his hoof from the ground. "Come on, boy," she coaxed. "You should be used to all of this attention by now."

After carefully examining Governor's hoof Anna released the horse's leg. "He looks good," she said to

Tory. "Just keep doing what you have with the poultices. Keep walking him and consider that special shoe. I'll look in on him in another week."

"That's the best news I've had in two days," Tory admitted as Anna slipped through the gate and they began walking toward the house.

"I heard about what happened yesterday on Devil's Ridge," Anna commented.

Tory stopped dead in her tracks. "What? But how?"

With an encouraging smile, Anna met her friend's questioning stare. "You'd better be sure that your backbone is strong, Tory. All sorts of rumors are flying around Sinclair."

"Already? I don't see how—"

Anna placed her hand over Tory's arm. "Trask McFadden, excuse me, *Senator* McFadden is a famous man around these parts. What he does is news—big news. When someone attacks a man of his stature, it isn't long before the gossip mill gets wind of it and starts grinding out the information, indiscriminately mixing fact with fiction to distort the truth."

"But it only happened last night," Tory argued.

"And how many people knew about it?"

Tory smiled wryly and continued walking across the parking lot. "Too many," she admitted, thinking about Trask, Neva, Keith, the private investigator . . . The list seemed nearly endless.

"Then brace yourself; no doubt the press will be more than anxious to report what happened and how it relates to the horse swindle of five years ago as well as Jason McFadden's murder." Anna's voice was soft and consoling. "Your father's name, and his involvement in the scam, whether true or not, is bound to come up."

Tory let out a long breath of air. "That's just what I

was trying to avoid." The afternoon sun felt hot on the back of her neck and the reddish dust beneath the gravel was stirred up by the easterly breeze.

"Too late. The handwriting's on the wall."

Tory lifted her chin and her eyes hardened. Involuntarily her slim shoulders squared. "Well, what's done is done, I suppose. At least you've given me fair warning. Now, how about staying for a late lunch?"

"It sounds heavenly," Anna admitted, pleased that Tory had seemed to buck up a little and was ready to face the challenge of the future. "I thought you'd never ask!"

Tory laughed and found that she looked forward to Anna's company and sarcastic wit. She needed to think about something other than the mysterious happenings on the ranch and it had been a long time since she and Anna had really had a chance to talk.

"THAT WAS DELICIOUS," Anna stated, rolling her eyes as she finished her strawberry pie. "Denver omelet, spinach salad and pie to boot. Whenever you give up ranching, you could become a chef. It's a good thing I don't eat here more often or I'd gain twenty pounds."

"I doubt that," Tory said, pleased with the compliment nonetheless. "You'll never gain weight, not with the work schedule you demand of yourself."

"That's my secret," Anna said. "I never have time to eat."

Chuckling softly the two women cleared the dishes from the table and set them in the sink. "So we've talked about what happened here yesterday, and about my plans for the ranch, and about Governor's condition. Now, tell me about you. How're you doin'?"

Anna's dark eyes clouded. "Things have been different since Jim moved out." She held up a strong finger, as if to remind herself. "However, despite it all, I've survived."

"If you don't want to talk about it . . ."

Anna forced a sad smile. "There's nothing much to talk about. I was involved with starting my own veterinary practice. I worked long hours and was exhausted when I got home. I resented the fact that he expected me to be the perfect wife, housekeeper, you-name-it, and he got bored with listening to my dreams, I guess. I kind of ignored him and I guess he needed a woman. So I really can't blame him for taking up with someone else, can I?"

"I would," Tory said firmly. "It seems to me that if two people love each other, they can work things out."

"It's not always that easy."

Tory thought of her own situation with Trask. The love they shared had always been shrouded in deceit. "Maybe you're right," she finally admitted. "But I don't see why you should have to go around carrying all this guilt with you."

Frowning thoughtfully, Anna rubbed her thumb over her index finger. "Maybe I carry it because I was brought up to believe that a woman's place is in the home, having babies, washing dishes, enjoying being her husband's best friend." She leaned against the counter and stared out the window. "But I got greedy. I wanted it all: husband, home, children and a fascinating career. I didn't mean to, but somehow I lost Jim in the shuffle."

"Easy to do—"

"Too easy. But I've learned from my mistakes, thank you, and you should, too."

"What's that supposed to mean?"

Anna laughed grimly. "That I'm about to poke my nose in where it doesn't belong."

"Oh?"

"Look, Tory. I know you never got over Trask." Anna saw the protest forming on Tory's lips and she warded it off with a flip of her wrist. "There's no use denying it; you love him and you always have, regardless of all that mess with your dad. It's written all over your face.

"And, despite what happened in the past, I think Trask's basically a decent man who loves you very much. What happened with your dad was unfortunate and I was as sad as anyone when Trask took the stand against Calvin. But that was five years ago and it's over." She took a deep breath. "So, if Trask is the man you love, then you'd better do your damnedest to let him know it."

Tory couldn't hide the stunned expression on her face. "That's the last piece of advice I would have expected from you," she replied.

"I had a chance to think about it last night. Let me tell you, if fate dealt me another chance with Jim, I'd make sure that I held on to him."

"How? By giving up your practice and independence?"

Anna shook her head. "Of course not. By just being a little less stubborn and self-righteous. I still believe that you can have everything, if you work at it. But you have to give a little instead of taking all the time."

"But that works two ways," Tory thought aloud.

"Of course. But if you're both willing, it should be possible." Anna looked up at the clock on the wall and nearly jumped out of her skin. "Geez, is it really three? Look, Tory, I've got to cut this session short, if you don't mind. I'm supposed to be in Bend at four."

"I'm just glad you stopped by."

"Anytime you're willing to cook, I'm ready to eat. Thanks for lunch!" Anna was out the back door in a flash and nearly bumped into Keith as he was walking through the door to the back porch.

"Excuse me," Anna called over her shoulder, while running down the two wooden steps to the path that led to the front of the house.

Keith, his eyes still fastened on Anna's retreating back came into the kitchen and threw the mail down on the table. Dust covered him from head to foot and sweat darkened the strands of his hair. Only the creases near his eyes escaped the reddish-brown dust. He placed his hat on the peg near the back door and wiped the back of his hand over his face, streaking the brown film. "I suppose I missed lunch," he said, eyeing the dishes in the sink.

"I suppose you did," Tory replied. "Anna and I just finished."

"I saw her take off." He stretched the knots out of his back. "I have to go into town and pick up the part for the combine. Then I'll go talk to Paul Barnett—you did say that he wanted to see me?"

Tory nodded.

"After that I'll probably stay in town for a couple of hours and have a few beers at the Branding Iron. Do you think I could con you into making me a sandwich or something while I get cleaned up?"

"Do I look like a short order cook?" she asked testily. "Didn't I ask you if you'd be back for lunch this morning before you left?"

"Please?"

Keith could be so damned charming when he chose to be, Tory thought defensively. She managed a stiff smile. "Okay, brother dear, I'll see what I can scrape together, but I'm not promising gourmet."

"At this point I'd be thrilled with peanut butter and jelly," Keith admitted as he sauntered out of the kitchen and up the steps. In a few minutes, Tory could hear the sounds of running water in the shower upstairs.

By the time that Keith returned to the kitchen, some twenty minutes later, he'd showered, shaved and changed into clean clothes.

"I hardly recognized you," Tory said teasingly. She placed a platter of ham sandwiches next to a glass of milk on the table. It was then she saw the mail. Quickly pushing aside the magazines and catalog offers, she picked up the stack of envelopes and began to thumb through them.

"Bills, bills and more . . . what's this?" Tory stopped at the fifth envelope. The small white packet was addressed to her in handwriting she didn't recognize. There was no return address on the envelope but the letter was postmarked in Sinclair. Without much thought, she tore open the envelope. A single piece of paper was enclosed. On it, in the same unfamiliar handwriting that graced the envelope was a simple message:

STAY AWAY FROM MCFADDEN

"Oh, dear God!" Tory whispered, letting the thin white paper fall from her hands onto the table.

"What?" Keith set down his sandwich and grabbed the letter before staring at the threat in disbelief. As the message began to sink in, his anger ignited and his face became flushed. He tossed the letter onto the table. "That does it, Tory, I'm not going to listen to any more of your excuses. When McFadden gets back here you tell him that you're out of this investigation of his!"

"I think it's too late for that." She was shaken but some of her color had returned.

"The hell it is! Damn it, Tory. He was beaten. Neva's been getting threatening phone calls. You were shot at, for crying out loud! Shot at with a rifle! What does it take to get it through your thick head that whoever is behind this—" he pointed emphatically at the letter "—is playing for keeps!"

"We can't back out, the police are involved and the whole town knows what's happening."

"Who gives a rip? We're talking about our lives, for God's sake!" His fist curled angrily and the muscles of his forearms flexed with rage. "All of this has got to stop!" Pounding the table and making the dishes rattle, Keith pushed his chair backward and stood beside the door. Leaning heavily against the frame he turned pleading gray eyes on his sister. "You can make him stop, y'know. You're the only one he'll listen to."

"Not when he's set his mind to something."

"Then unset it, Tory!" He turned his palms upward and shook his hands. "What does it take to get through to you?"

Tory looked down at the note lying face up on the table and she trembled. For a moment she considered Keith's suggestion, but slowly her fear gave way to anger. "I won't be threatened," she said, "or compromised. Whoever sent this must have a lot to lose. I wonder what it is?"

"Well, I don't!" Keith nervously pushed his hair away from his face. "I wish this whole nightmare would just end."

"But it won't. Not unless we find the truth," she said.

"Oh, God, Tory, you're such a dreamer. You always have been. That's how McFadden tricked you the first time and now you've let him do it to you again. You're so caught up in your romantic fantasies about him that you don't see the truth when it hits you in the face!"

Tory leaned against the refrigerator. “Then maybe you’ll be so kind as to spell it out for me.”

“He’s using you, Tory. All over again. I just never thought you’d be dumb enough to fall for it!”

With his final angry words tossed over his shoulder, Keith stalked out of the room leaving Tory feeling numb. Within a few moments, she heard the sound of the pickup as it roared down the lane before squealing around the corner to the open highway.

For the rest of the afternoon, Tory waited for Trask to return as he had promised. She tried to make herself busy around the house, her anxiety increasing with each hour that passed without word from him. As the day darkened with the coming of night, Tory began to worry. What, if anything, had he found out from Linn Benton and George Henderson?

Both men had to hate him. Trask’s testimony had sealed their fate and sent them both to prison. What if they were somehow involved in his beating and the threatening calls to Neva?

When the phone rang at ten o’clock Tory felt relief wash over her. It had to be Trask.

She answered the telephone breathlessly. “Hello?”

“Tory? It’s Neva.” Tory’s heart fell through the floor. “I was wondering—actually hoping—that you’d heard from Trask.” All of Tory’s fears began to crystallize.

“I haven’t seen him since this morning,” she admitted.

“I see.” There was a stilted silence. “Do you know if he went to Salem?”

“That’s where he was headed when he left here.”

“Damn.” Neva waited a second before continuing.

“Maybe he went to the cabin,” Tory suggested hopefully, though she already guessed the answer.

“I was already there, about an hour ago. His Blazer’s gone and no one answered the door. I have a key and let myself in. I'm sure he hasn't been there since early this morning."

Tory's heart began to pound with worry. "And I assume that he hasn't called you?"

"No."

"Have you called the sheriff?"

"Not yet."

"What about the investigator, John what's-his-name?"

"Davis," Neva supplied. "He knows I'm worried. He's already contacted a couple of his men."

Tory slid into a nearby chair and felt the deadweight of fear slumping her shoulders. "So what do we do now?"

"Nothing to do but wait," Neva replied. "You'll call if you hear from him?"

"Of course." Tory hung up the phone and a dark feeling of dread seemed to seep in through the windows and settle in her heart. Where was Trask? The question began to haunt her.

Dear God, please let him be all right!

Chapter Ten

THE ROAD FROM the Willamette Valley was narrow. It twisted upward through the Cascades like some great writhing serpent intent on following the natural chasm made by the Santiam River. With sheer rock on one side of the road and the deep ravine ending with rushing white water on the other, the two-lane highway cut across the mountains from the Willamette Valley to central Oregon.

At two in the morning, with only the beams from the headlights of the jeep to guide him, Trask was at the wheel of his Blazer heading east. And he was dead tired. He had spent all of the morning and most of the afternoon at the penitentiary asking questions and getting only vague answers from the low-lifes Henderson and Benton.

Trask's hands tightened over the steering wheel as he thought about the ex-judge's fleshy round face. Even stripped of his judicial robes and garbed in state-issued prison clothes, Linn Benton exuded a smug untouchable air that got under Trask's skin.

Linn Benton had been openly sarcastic and when Trask had asked him about another person being involved in the horse swindle, the judge-turned-inmate had actually had the audacity to laugh outright. Trask's slightly battered condition and obvious concern about what had happened five years past seemed to be a source of amusement to the ex-judge. Trask had gotten nowhere with the man, but was more convinced than ever that somehow Linn Benton was pulling the strings from inside the thick penitentiary walls. But who was the puppet on the outside?

George Henderson had been easier to question. The ex-vet had been shaking in his boots at the thought of being questioned by a man whose brother he had helped kill. But whether Henderson's obvious anxiety had been because of Trask's stature as a senator, or because of previous threats he may have received from his prison mate, Linn Benton, Trask couldn't determine.

With an oath, Trask downshifted and the Blazer climbed upward toward Santiam Pass.

All in all, the trip hadn't been a complete waste of time, Trask attempted to console himself. For the first time he was certain that Linn Benton was still hiding something. And it had to be something that he didn't expect Trask to uncover, or the rotund prisoner wouldn't have smirked so openly at his adversary. It was as if Benton were privy to some private irony; an irony Trask couldn't begin to fathom.

"But I will." Trask squinted into the darkness and made a silent vow to get even with the men who had killed his brother. If another person was involved in Jason's death, Trask was determined to find out about it and see to it that the person responsible would pay.

For over six hours, Trask had been in the Multnomah County Library in Portland. He had searched out and microfilmed copies of all of the newspaper clippings about the horse swindle and Jason's murder, hoping to find something, anything that would give him a hint of what was happening and who was behind the series of events starting with the anonymous letter. If only the person who had written the letter would show his face . . . tell his side of the story . . . let the truth be known once and for all . . . then justice could be served and Trask could put the past behind and concentrate on a future with Tory.

THE NIGHT SEEMED to have no end. Tory heard Keith come in sometime after midnight. She tossed and turned restlessly on the bed, alternately looking at the clock and staring out the window into the dark night sky. *What could have happened to Trask?* she wondered for what had to be the thousandth time. *Where was he? Why hadn't he called?*

She finally slept although fitfully and when the first streaks of dawn began to lighten the room, Tory was relieved to have an excuse to get out of bed and start the morning chores. If she had had to spend another hour in bed staring at the clock, she would have gone out of her mind with worry about Trask.

She had changed, showered and started breakfast before she heard Keith moving around in his room upstairs.

Coffee was perking and the apple muffins were already out of the oven when Keith sauntered into the kitchen. She turned to face her brother and he lifted his bands into the air as if to ward off a blow. "Truce, Sis?" he asked, grinning somewhat sheepishly.

The corners of Tory's lips curved upward and her round eyes sparkled with affection for her brother. "You know I don't hold a grudge. Well, at least not against you."

"Or Trask McFadden," he pointed out, walking to the stove and pouring them each a cup of coffee.

"I think five years was enough," Tory said.

"For sending Dad to prison where he died? Give me

a break!" He offered her a mug of steaming coffee, which she accepted, but she felt her smile disintegrate.

Tory set the basket of muffins on the table and tried to ignore Keith's open hostility toward Trask. "Did you say something about a truce?"

"A truce between you and me. Not with McFadden!" Keith frowned, sat down in his regular chair and reached for a muffin. "By the way, where is he this morning?"

"I don't know," she admitted, biting nervously at her lower lip and trying to hide the fact that she was worried sick about him. She glanced nervously at the clock. It was nearly seven.

"Did he visit Benton and Henderson yesterday?" Keith had his knife poised over the butter, but his eyes never left his sister's anxious face. It was evident from the circles under her eyes and the lines near the corners of her mouth that she hadn't been able to sleep.

"I don't know that either. No one's seen or heard from him since he left here yesterday morning."

Keith set the knife aside. "So you're worried about him, right?"

"A little."

"He can handle himself."

"I wish I could believe that," Tory said.

"But you can't? Why not?"

"Think about it," Tory said with a sigh. "His brother was murdered for what he knew, Trask was beaten up the night before last and someone shot at him on Devil's Ridge." Her voice trembled slightly and she took a long swallow of coffee. "I think I have a reason to be worried." She glanced nervously out the window before taking a seat at the table. "If I don't hear from him this morning, I'm calling Paul Barnett."

"Maybe Trask's with Neva," Keith said as gently as he could.

Tory felt the sting of Keith's remark and she paled slightly. "He wasn't with Neva," she whispered. "Neva called here last night. She's worried, too."

"Look, Tory," Keith cajoled. "A United States senator doesn t just vanish off the face of the earth. He'll be back flashing that politician's smile of his. The man's a survivor, for crying out loud."

Tory didn't answer. She swirled the coffee in her mug and silently prayed that this time Keith was right.

The sound of Rex's pickup caught her attention. Still wrapped in her own worried thoughts, Tory poured the foreman a cup of coffee without really thinking about it. By the time that Rex came in through the back door, she had already added a teaspoon of sugar to the cup.

"'Mornin'," Rex greeted, noting the lines of worry disturbing the smooth skin of Tory's brow.

"How about some breakfast?" Tory asked.

Rex eyed the muffins and the sliced fruit on the table. "Looks good, but no thanks." He patted his flat abdomen. "Already ate with Belinda." He paused for a moment and shook his head. "I just wanted to let you know that I fixed the combine late yesterday afternoon and that I'm planning to cut the yearling calves from the herd today. There's a rancher who lives in Sisters and he's interested in about thirty head. He'll be here around eleven." Rex pushed the brim of his hat farther up on his forehead as he accepted the cup of coffee Tory offered. He warmed his gnarled fingers around the ceramic mug. "He might want to look at the horses, too."

Tory managed a smile. "Good. You can show him the mares and the foals as well as the yearlings."

Keith didn't bother to hide his surprise. He frowned, causing a deep groove in his forehead between his eyebrows. "You plan on selling some of the mares?"

"Maybe. If the price is right."

Her brother leaned back in his chair and his eyes narrowed thoughtfully. "Because you know that once this scandal hits the papers no one, even if his life depends on it, will buy a Quarter Horse from the Lazy W."

"That's exaggerating a little, I think. But the note from the bank is due soon and we'll need all the cash we can get."

"Don't remind me."

"I'll try not."

"Okay," Rex said, noticing the simmering hostility between brother and sister. "I'll show the man from Sisters around, see if I can get him interested in any of the horses."

"I thought you wanted to keep the mares another year at least and wait until the foals were born," Keith persisted.

Tory pursed her lips and shook her head. "I think we'd better go with the bird in the hand theory." She leveled her concerned eyes at Rex. "If the buyer wants any of the mares, they're for sale."

"What about stallions?" Rex asked.

Tory clenched her teeth. "They're for sale, too. For the right price."

"Even Governor?" Rex asked.

"All of them," Tory whispered.

"Tory, I can't let you do this—" Keith began to interrupt and looked as if he wanted to say more, but Tory cut him off.

"I don't think we've got a choice. I have a meeting with the bank scheduled for the end of next week, and for once I'd like to show that the Lazy W has a positive cash flow. You were right when you first told me we'd have to sell—it just took a while for it to sink in. Selling some of the cattle and a few horses might get us out of the red for the month of June. Even if it's only one month, it would say a lot and help me convince the loan officer to lend us more operating capital."

"Hmph! How was I to know you'd listen to me for once?" Keith replied. Then, not having an argument against her logic, but worried just the same, Keith set down his empty coffee cup, got up from the table and explained that he would be working with some of the men who were cutting hay.

Rex and Keith walked out of the house together. Tory was left alone with the dirty dishes as well as her worries about what may have happened to Trask.

TWO HOURS LATER, as she was finishing feeding the horses and wondering which, if any of the stock, would sell to the buyer from Sisters, she heard the sound of Trask's Blazer rumbling down the drive. Her heart seemed to leap inside her. She looked out the dusty window of the stables to confirm what her ears had told her and a smile grew from one side of her face to the other as she watched Trask's vehicle stop near the house. He got out of the Blazer and stretched, lifting his hands over his head, and making his flat abdomen appear almost concave with the unconscious, but erotic movement. He was dressed in worn cords and a shirt with the sleeves pushed up to his elbows. The sight of him brought tears of relief to Tory's eyes.

He started for the house, but she pounded on the window of the stables. Trask turned, squinted against the sun and his wonderful slightly crooked smile stole over his jaw when he noticed her. That was all the encouragement she needed. Without caring that they might be seen, Tory ran out of the stables and straight into his arms. He held her so tightly that her feet were pulled from the ground as he spun her around.

Bending his head, Trask kissed her passionately, sending warm bursts to every point in her body.

"What happened to you?" she asked breathlessly, once the lingering kiss was over. His arms were still around her, locking her body next to his, pressing her curves against the hard muscles of his thighs and torso. "I was worried to death!"

"I should have called," he admitted, kissing her forehead and letting the faint scent of lilacs from her hair fill his nostrils. All of the frustrations that had knotted the muscles in the back of his neck since visiting the penitentiary seemed to melt away just at the sight of Tory's enigmatic smile and the feel of her warm body pressed eagerly to his.

"At the very least you should have called! You had Neva and me out of our minds with worry."

"Neva, too, huh?" he asked with a frown.

"What did you expect would happen when you disappeared?"

"I had no idea I was so popular," he said with a smile and she laughed, her hands still clutching his shoulders. Through the light cotton fabric of his shirt, she could feel the corded strength of his muscles tightening around her as he kissed her once again before lifting his head. His blue eyes smoldered with aroused passion.

"Why didn't you come back last night?" she managed to ask, though her thoughts were centered on the feel of his body pressed tightly against her.

"It didn't cross my mind that it would take all day and half the night to finish what I'd set out to do. I didn't get back to the cabin until two thirty and even if I had a phone there, I wouldn't have called. I thought you'd already be in bed." That thought brought a seductive curve to his lips.

"I was!" she retorted, trying to sound angry and

failing. She lovingly traced the rugged set of his jaw with a finger. "I was in bed tossing and turning and wondering what horrible fate had come to you." Unconsciously she touched the cut on his chin. "You don't have a great track record for keeping yourself safe, you know. I stared at the ceiling and the clock all night long."

"I'm sorry," he said, refusing to release her and grinning broadly. His blue eyes twinkled with the morning light and he kissed her finger when it strayed near his mouth. Her breath caught in her throat at the feel of his tongue on her fingertip. "You paint a very suggestive picture, y'know," he whispered hoarsely. "I would have done just about anything to be with you last night." Familiarly his hands slid up her back, drawing her still closer to him, letting her feel the need rising within him. Instantly her body began to react and as his head dipped again, she parted her lips, anxious for the taste of him. How right it felt to be held in his arms with the warmth of the morning sun at her back.

"Maybe we should make up for lost time," he suggested against her ear.

She had to clear her throat and force herself to think rationally. The feel of Trask's body pressed urgently against hers made it difficult to think logically. "Later, senator," she said, trying to ignore the sweet rush of desire flooding her veins. "I've got work to do and I want to hear everything you found out yesterday."

"Can't it wait?" His breath fanned her ear.

She swallowed with difficulty and the feel of his palms pressed against the small of her back made refusing him incredibly difficult. Tory was tempted to say "yes" but she couldn't forget the threatening letter she had received just the day before. "I don't think so," she replied, reluctantly slipping out of his embrace and taking his hand to lead him toward the house. "You're not the only one who has something to say."

For the first time he noticed the trace of worry in her gray-green eyes. "Something happened last night?"

They were approaching the path leading to the back of the house. Alex, who had been lying under his favorite juniper bush, tagged along behind them and slid through the screen door when Tory opened it.

"Yesterday," Tory clarified. She poured them both a cup of coffee, placed a plate of leftovers on the floor for Alex's breakfast and retrieved the note from a drawer in her father's desk in the den.

Trask's eyes narrowed and glittered dangerously as she studied the single sheet of paper. "This has gone too far," he muttered. His fists clenched in frustrated rage and the muscles of his forearms flexed. "First Neva was threatened, and now you."

"Apparently someone has something to hide."

"And he'll go to just about any lengths to keep his secret hidden." Trask let out a long sigh and leaned against the counter. "Have you talked to the sheriff?"

"Not yet."

"What about any of John Davis's men?"

Tory shook her head. "The one man assigned to the ranch keeps a pretty low profile. He's only been inside the house a couple of times, but several of the hands have commented about his presence."

Trask's head snapped upward. "And what have you told them?"

"That I'm trying to prevent another one of the calves from being shot, you know, protecting the livestock."

"And they bought that story?" His dark brows raised suspiciously.

Tory shrugged. "I doubt it. The hands are too smart to be conned. They know when someone is trying to pull the wool over their eyes and can see through lies, just about any lie. Though they don't go poking around in my business, it's hard to ignore the fact that a United States senator showed up here, sporting a rather ugly cut on his chin. Especially since there was a scandal he was involved in a few years ago." She looked pointedly at Trask. "It hasn't helped that the rumors and gossip are already flying around Sinclair like vultures over a dying animal. So you see, it's really too much to expect the hands to think that the only reason a detective is on the ranch is to protect the cattle."

"I suppose so." He looked down at the letter again. "I don't like this, Tory."

She shuddered and took a sip of her coffee. "Neither do I."

Trask wearily pushed the hair from his face and began to pace across the kitchen floor.

"Cut that out," Tory admonished softly and then explained. "Pacing drives me nuts."

"You really are on edge aren't you?"

"I think we both are. Why don't you call Neva and let her know that you're all right? Then you can sit down and tell me everything that happened yesterday with the judge and his accomplice."

Trask reluctantly agreed and while he was on the phone to Neva and Paul Barnett, Tory fixed him a breakfast of muffins, fresh fruit and scrambled eggs. She was just placing the eggs on a platter when Trask walked back into the kitchen.

"You're spoiling me," he accused with a devilish twinkle in his eyes.

"And you love it." She looked up and pointed at a chair near the table. "Now, sit, senator, and tell me everything there is to know about Linn Benton."

Trask slid into his chair and began eating. "Benton

seemed to think it was a joke that I was there, but Henderson was scared spitless. I think Henderson would have talked, but he was afraid that Linn Benton would find out."

"So you didn't learn anything you didn't already know?"

"Nothing specific," Trask admitted. "But I've got a gut feeling that somehow Linn Benton is involved in what's happening here. He was so amused by the whole thing, especially the fact that someone had beat the hell out of me." Puzzled lines etched across Trask's forehead.

"But you can't figure out exactly what he's doing or with whom, right?"

He looked away from her and his blue eyes grew as cold as the morning sky in winter. "I'm working on it. John Davis is checking out Benton's friends and the people that still work for him on his ranch near Bend, and after I was through at the penitentiary, I drove to Portland and did some research."

"What kind of research?"

"I made copies of all the newspaper accounts of what happened five years ago. Everything I could find on Jason's murder as well as the Quarter Horses and the swindle."

Tory felt her back stiffen. "But you were at the trial, heard and gave testimony. You already knew what happened; at least you thought you did."

"But I wanted to get a new perspective on the scam. I thought I could find it in the press accounts of the investigation and the trial."

"You must have read all those articles a hundred times," she whispered.

"I did five years ago under . . . a lot of stress and conflicting emotions," he said quietly. He finished his breakfast and again noticed the threatening letter. "So who do you think sent you this?" He pointed to the single white sheet of paper.

"I don't know."

"But surely you could hazard a guess," he coaxed.

"The only people I can think of are Linn Benton and George Henderson because we already know that they were involved. Benton has powerful allies outside of the penitentiary, people who are still on his payroll or owe him favors—"

The front door opened with a bang. "Tory?" Keith's anxious voice echoed through the house.

"In the kitchen," she called out to him.

"Thank God you're here," he said, striding to the back of the house and stopping short when he met Trask's cool stare. "I've got a bone to pick with you, McFadden."

Trask smiled wryly. "Another one?"

"Rex found another calf—shot just like the last one," Keith said, his face twisted with worry. He jerked his hat off his head, tossed it carelessly onto the counter and slid into the chair facing Trask.

Tory's slim shoulders slumped. Yesterday the note, today another calf . . . when would it end. "Where is it?" she asked.

"Rex found it on the south side of the pasture, near the lake. He's already taken care of the carcass."

"What was he doing in that pasture?" Trask asked.

"He works here, damn it!" Keith replied, his fist coiling angrily. "He was laying irrigation pipe—why the hell am I explaining all this to you?"

Tory held up her hands, forestalling the fight before it got started. "The calf was shot just like the other one?"

"Right. Near as we can tell, someone jumped the fence, picked out a victim and blasted it."

Tory felt her blood run cold. She looked at Trask and noticed that every muscle in his face had hardened.

"This all happened because of you," Keith pointed out as he leaned against his elbows on the table and rubbed a dirty hand over his brow, leaving streaks of dust on his face. "Everything was going along okay until you started poking around here."

A muscle in the corner of Trask's jaw began to work convulsively and he set his coffee cup on the table. When he stood, he towered over Keith and felt older than his thirty-six years. "I know that because I returned to Sinclair, I've put the ranch in danger. Believe me, it wasn't intentional."

"Hmph." Keith stared insolently up at the man who was responsible for all of the pain in his life. Tory's brother had to close his eyes and shake the feeling of dread that had overtaken him in the last few days.

"You don't have to worry about what's happening—"

"Like hell!" Keith's head snapped upward. "Another calf's been killed and we got this . . . this threat, for crying out loud!"

"I'll take care of it."

"Like the way you took care of Dad?" Keith demanded.

Tory's stomach was in knots. "I don't think bringing up the past will help—"

"Hell, Tory, that's what this is all about—the past—or have you forgotten?"

"Of course not!"

"Maybe we should all just cool off," Trask suggested, staring pointedly at Keith.

The silence in the kitchen was so thick Tory could feel the weight of it upon her shoulders. When Rex came through the back door, she was glad for the excuse of pouring the foreman a cup of coffee.

"We lost another one," Rex stated, frowning slightly

at the sight of Trask in the house. He took off his Stetson and ran his hand over his forehead.

"Keith told us about it," Tory said.

"What are your theories about how it was killed?" Trask asked, leaning his elbows against the counter, stretching his legs in front of him before crossing his ankles and folding his arms over his chest. Though he tried to appear casual, Tory noticed the grim set of his jaw and the determination in his eyes.

Rex shrugged and accepted the cup of coffee Tory offered. "Don't really know."

"Surely you must have some thoughts about what happened?"

Rex stared at Trask over the rim of his cup. "All I know is that the trouble started when you arrived."

Trask's eyebrows cocked. "So you think it was more than a coincidence?"

"I'd stake my life on it."

"Tell me, Rex," Trask cajoled and Tory was reminded of the one time she had seen him working as a lawyer in the courtroom. Her blood chilled at the memory. It had been two or three months before the scandal involving her father had been discovered. Trask's country-boy charm and affable smile had won him the confidence of everyone in the courtroom, including a few of the prosecution's witnesses. He coaxed one woman, a witness for the prosecution, into saying something the D.A. would rather have remained secret. Dread began to knot in Tory's stomach as Trask began to question Rex in his soft drawl. "Tell me how long you've been with the Lazy W."

"More years than I'd want to count," Rex replied, returning Trask's stare without flinching. "What're you getting at, McFadden?"

Trask overlooked the question. "And why did Calvin hire you?"

Tory felt the air in the room become thick with suspicion. "Trask—"

"What's this got to do with anything?" Keith demanded.

The foreman disregarded Keith's interruption and drained his cup, never once taking his eyes off Trask. "Calvin needed help with the Lazy W, I guess. And I needed a job."

"And you've stayed all these years."

"Yep."

"Even after Calvin died." Trask made it sound as if Rex's loyalty were some sort of crime.

"I'm too old to jump from spread to spread."

"Trask," Tory interjected, her voice wavering slightly. "There's no need for this. Rex doesn't have to explain himself."

"Just a few friendly questions," Trask replied coldly.

Tory wondered what had happened to the warm caring man he had been only moments before.

"Well, let me ask you a few," Keith cut in. "You seem to be pointing fingers at nearly everyone you meet, McFadden. But what about you? How do we know that the letter you brought here isn't a phony? How do we know that you haven't been the one calling Neva, sending threatening letters to Tory or shooting the calves?"

If Trask was outraged, he managed to hide it. His lips twisted into a grim smile but his eyes became as cold as the deepest well at midnight.

"And you think I took a shot at myself, too?" Trask returned.

"You could have hired someone to fire a shot when you were up on Devil's Ridge. After all, you were the only one who knew you'd be up there. As for what happened to you—" Keith's palm flipped upward as he pointed to the discoloration under Trask's eye "—you could have hired that done as well, for authenticity's sake!"

"You know, Wilson, you have one hell of an imagination," Trask said with genuine amusement. "Why would I bother?"

"I think your motives are pretty obvious. Sure it looks like you're on the up and up; that way you could worm your way back into Tory's heart, not to mention the fact that you'd look good to the press. All the rumors and publicity that are bound to spring from your investigation aren't going to hurt your career, are they? And they'll serve to remind the voting public of the reason you were elected in the first place, proving beyond a shadow of a doubt that you're still the hard-nosed, filled-with-integrity candidate you were four years ago!"

"I just want to find out if another man was involved in Jason's death."

"You've got your vengeance and more," Keith said. "Because my father wasn't involved with Linn Benton or George Henderson."

"Then why didn't he say so, declare his innocence? He had his chance."

"I . . . I don't know," Keith said, his cocky attitude slipping a little.

"So we're back to square one, aren't we?" Trask thought aloud. "Well, not for long. I intend to figure out what happened back then." Trask's eyes glittered so fiercely that Tory felt a needle of fear pierce her heart.

"And what if your anonymous letter is a phony? How about that?" Keith persisted. "Then you've brought us all this trouble for no reason."

"I don't think so."

"Neither do I," Tory said with conviction as she looked at the cut on Trask's face.

"Oh, God, Tory, you can't believe him, not again!"

"It sure takes a helluva lot to convince you, Wilson," Trask said tiredly before returning his gaze to Tory. The warmth returned to his eyes. "Look, I'm going to be gone for a few days, do some checking around. But I'll be back. And, while I'm gone, one of John Davis's men will be here." He looked pointedly at Rex and Keith before letting his gaze fall back on Tory. "I think you should call Paul Barnett and report what happened to the calf."

"I will," she promised.

"Here we go again," Keith muttered as he grabbed his hat and walked out the door.

Rex shifted uncomfortably before wiping his hand nervously over his brow. "I just want to clear the air," he said.

"About what?"

"The reasons I came to the Lazy W."

"Rex, you don't have to—"

"I've got nothing to hide, Tory. I couldn't get work anywhere because of my first wife. She claimed that I . . . that I'd get angry with her, drink too much and . . . rough her up." Rex closed his eyes and sadly shook his head. "Marianne swore that on several occasions I'd beat her; but it just wasn't so. The only time I slapped her was after a particularly bad fight and, well, she had a butcher knife, said she was going to use it on me if I came near her. I took the knife away from her and slapped her. She filed charges against me."

"Which were later dropped," Trask added.

"You knew all about it?" Rex asked with a grimace.

Trask nodded and Tory felt sick inside that Rex had been forced to bare his soul.

"Even though I was acquitted, no one would give me work."

"Except for Calvin Wilson."

Rex's chin jutted outward. "I've been here ever since." He set down his cup and started toward the door. "I'll be in the stables if you want me," he said to Tory. "The buyer from Sisters still wants thirty head of cattle."

Still slightly numb from the scene she had just witnessed, Tory found it difficult to concentrate on the work at hand. Her eyes offered Rex a silent apology. "What about horses?"

Rex frowned and shook his head. "He said he'll wait to decide about the horses, though he looked at a couple of yearlings that he liked." Forcing his hat onto his head, Rex walked out the back door. Tory didn't have to question him any further. She knew that the sale of the horses wasn't completed because of the Quarter Horse swindle her father was supposedly involved in five years ago. Even though it had happened long ago and her father was dead, people remembered, especially now that Trask was back. So the paranoia of the past had already started interfering with the future.

When she heard Trask move toward the door, she impaled him with her eyes. "That was uncalled for, senator," she rebuked.

"What?"

"You didn't have to humiliate Rex. Especially since you knew all the answers anyway. That's called baiting, senator, and I don't like it. It might work in Washington, D.C., but I won't have it here, on the Lazy W, used against my employees."

"I just wanted to see if he would tell the truth."

Hot injustice colored Tory's cheeks. "And did he pass the test?" she demanded.

"With flying colors."

"Good. Then maybe you'll quit harassing everyone who works on this ranch and concentrate on Linn

Benton or whoever else might have a grudge against your brother."

"I didn't mean to upset you," he said softly.

"You don't mean to do a lot of things, but you do them anyway, despite anyone else's feelings."

"Not true, Victoria," he countered, coming up to her and placing his hands over her shoulders, his blue eyes searching hers. His fingers gently massaged the tense muscles near the base of her neck, warming her skin. "I'm always concerned about you and what you feel."

"You weren't five years ago."

A shadow of pain crossed his eyes. "I only told what I thought was the truth and you still can't forgive me, can you?"

She closed her eyes against a sudden unwanted feeling that she would break down and cry. "It . . . it was very hard to sit by and know that Dad was dying . . . alone in some god-awful jail cell all because of what I told you."

"It's not your fault that you overheard Linn Benton discussing plans with your father."

"But it's my fault that you found out about it," she whispered.

Trask frowned and took her into his arms, but the response he got was cold and distant. "You can't keep blaming yourself."

She let out a tired sigh. "I try not to."

He hesitated a minute. "Are you okay?" She nodded mutely and took hold of her emotions to force the tears backward.

"Good." He kissed her softly on the forehead. "I've got to go. I'll be back in a couple of days."

"Where are you going?"

"I wish I knew," he admitted. "I'll start by visiting John Davis in Bend and showing him all these clippings.

Maybe he can come up with something; a new angle. I'll be back . . . soon."

"I'm counting on it, senator," she whispered before he gathered her into his arms and kissed her with all of the passion that had fired his blood since the first time he had seen her. His tongue caressed and mated with hers and she leaned against him, her knees becoming soft. Once again she was caught up in the storm of emotions that raged within her each time she was near him, and when he finally released her, she felt empty inside.

Tory stood on the back porch and watched him leave. When his Blazer was out of sight, she tried to think of anything but Trask and his reasons for returning to the Lazy W.

Pouring hot coffee into her cup, she walked into the den and sat at the desk, intending to concentrate on preparing a financial statement to take to the bank later in the week.

But the numbers were meaningless and her mind wandered. She found her thoughts returning to the conversation she had overheard between her father and Linn Benton five years ago . . . in this very study.

THE SUMMER NIGHT had been breathlessly hot and humid. Tory had come downstairs for a glass of lemonade when she heard the muted whispers behind the closed doors to the study. Her father's den had never been off limits, but that night, the night that Linn Benton had stormed into the house, everything changed and the pieces of the argument that drifted to her ears caught her attention and made her hesitate on the lowest step.

"Don't be so goddamned sanctimonious," the judge had said in his high-pitched wheezing tone. "You're in this up to your neck, Wilson."

Tory slipped down the final step and stood frozen in the entry hall, eavesdropping on a conversation she wished later that she had never overheard.

"I should never have gotten involved with you," her father replied brusquely.

"Too late for second thoughts now."

"If it weren't for the kids . . ." Her father's voice had drifted off and her heart grew cold. Calvin was entangled with Linn Benton because of her brother and her. Her father was doing something he didn't believe in just to support his children! She reached for the door, but the self-satisfied laughter of Linn Benton made her withdraw her hand. Tory realized that it would be better if she waited until she could speak to her father alone before confronting him.

The rest of the angry conversation was muted and she only heard parts of it, just enough to know that whatever the two men were arguing about wasn't aboveboard. She silently worried in the outer hall before going upstairs and pacing the floorboards of her room.

When she heard the judge's car roar down the drive, she raced down the stairs, intent on confronting her father and begging him to abandon whatever it was that involved Linn Benton.

But Calvin was no longer in the study. The door to the den was open, and thick cigar smoke still lingered in the air. Two half-empty glasses of whiskey sat neglected on the desk.

"Dad?" she called, starting for the kitchen and glancing out the window just in time to see her father reining his favorite gelding out of the stables and kicking the horse into a full gallop in the moonlight. Head bent against a mounting summer wind, Calvin Wilson raced through the pastures toward the mountains and Devil's Ridge.

Tory ran to the front door, jerked it open and let the hot dusty wind inside. *"Dad!"* she called again, this time screaming at the top of her lungs from the front porch. Either Calvin didn't hear her voice over the sound of his horse's racing hoofbeats and the whistling wind, or he chose to ignore her.

Tory was just about to follow him when Trask arrived. She was already leading a mare from the stables as his truck approached. Tory's nerves shattered with fear for her father's life and she quickly explained about the strange conversation she had overheard to the man she loved and trusted with all of her heart. Trask muttered an angry oath and his eyes blazed with angry lightning.

His jaw set with furious resolve and with only a few abrupt commands telling her to stay on the ranch and wait for his call, Trask wheeled his jeep around and followed Calvin through the open fields. Like a fool she had trusted him and obeyed, keeping her lonely vigil through the night, pacing in the den, praying that the phone would ring and end her fears.

Early the next morning, when Trask finally returned, she learned the horrible truth: Jason McFadden had been found dead—the result of a monstrous plot conceived by Linn Benton, George Henderson, and, according to Trask, her own father. Tory was numb with disbelief when she learned that Calvin Wilson had been charged with murder.

Chapter Eleven

NEARLY TWO QUIET weeks had passed when Trask found himself staring into the self-satisfied smile of the private investigator. Trask was sitting in one of the soft leather chairs near the desk, but his body had gone rigid.

"You found out *what*?" Trask demanded, staring at the private investigator in disbelief.

"Just what I told you," John Davis replied, settling back in his chair and casually lighting a cigarette. Behind him, through the second-story window of his office, was a bird's-eye view of the bustling downtown area of the city of Bend.

"Damn!" Trask's fist coiled and he slapped it into his other palm. His dark brows drew together.

"I thought you wanted the truth."

"I did. I did." Trask sounded as if he were trying to convince himself. "It's just that . . . Hell, I don't know." His thoughts were jumbled and confused. The past couple of weeks had eased by in a regular routine. Fortunately there had been no more threatening letters, dead calves or violence. He had spent most of his time with Tory on the Lazy W. The days had been pleasant; the nights filled with passionate exhilaration. And now this unexpected news from John Davis was about to change all that. The damned thing was that it was exactly what he had been asking for.

"You're sure about this," Trask said, already knowing the answer as he stared at the damning report in John's hands.

The private investigator stubbed out his cigarette and studied his client through thick lenses. "Positive, and even if you're entertaining thoughts about keeping it quiet, I can't. I've got some responsibility to the law, y'know." He tossed the neatly typed report across the desk.

"As well as your clients."

"Doesn't matter. If you want to keep something the size of this quiet, Trask, you'll have to use every bit of senatorial pull you have in this state. Even that might not be enough."

"I didn't say I wanted to keep it quiet."

"Good. Now, if you're worried about your career once the truth is known . . ." The young man shrugged and smiled.

"I don't give a damn about my career!"

"Still the rogue senator, right?"

Trask's face tensed and his eyes dropped to the damning document lying on the polished mahogany of the desk. He picked it up and folded it neatly into the manila envelope John offered. "This is going to be one hell of a mess," he thought aloud.

"But it will be over," John replied. The investigator's voice sounded like a trumpet of doom.

"Yes, I suppose it will," Trask replied. "I guess I should thank you." He placed the thick envelope in his jacket pocket and tossed the coat over his arm.

"I guess maybe you should," John replied with a smile, though his eyes remained sober.

Trask strode out of the office feeling as if the weight of the world had been placed upon his shoulders. *So Tory had been right all along: Calvin Wilson had been innocent! But not so her younger brother, Keith.* And that news would destroy her. No doubt she would blame Trask.

Trask's blood began to boil with anger when he thought about how many times Keith had lied through his teeth, not only to Trask, but to Tory as well. Letting out a descriptive curse, Trask walked down the short flight of stairs to the ground floor. According to John Davis's report, which the investigator had double-checked, Keith Wilson and not Calvin Wilson had been involved in the Quarter Horse swindle five years past. All Trask's testimony at the original trial had been in error. Calvin Wilson had only been trying to protect his teenaged son from prosecution.

"Crazy old fool," Trask muttered as he walked out of the building and climbed into his Blazer. He threw the truck into gear and let out a stream of oaths against himself and the whole vile mess that Linn Benton had conceived. The aftermath of the ex-judge's illegal scam was ruining the lives of the only people he really cared about. Tory, Neva and Nicholas had all been innocent victims of a plot so malicious it had included the murder of his brother.

Trask's mouth twisted downward and he could feel his jaw clench at the stupidity of Keith Wilson. All of Tory's precious trust would be shattered when she found out the truth about her brother and that Trask had helped send her father, an innocent man, to prison. "Damn it, Wilson," he swore, as if Calvin were in the Blazer with him. "Why couldn't you have said something before being so goddamned noble!"

TORY WALKED OUT of the bank and into the blazing heat of midafternoon. Her head throbbed and the muscles in the back of her neck ached. For the past two hours she had explained the profit and loss statements, as well as going over the assets and liabilities of the Lazy W to a disinterested young loan officer.

"I'll let you know," the bored young man had said. "But I can't make any promises right now. Your loan application, along with the financial statements and a status report of your current note with the bank will have to be reviewed by the loan committee as well as by the president of the bank."

"I see," Tory had replied, forcing a discouraged smile. She knew, whether the young man admitted it or not, that he was peddling her nothing more than financial double-talk. The Lazy W didn't have a snowball's chance in hell of receiving more funds from this particular bank. "And how long will it take before I can expect an answer?" Tory had asked.

"The loan committee meets next Thursday."

"Fine." She had stood, shook the banker's soft hand and walked out of the building, certain that the Lazy W would have to secure operating capital from another source.

After stopping by Rasmussen Feed for several sacks of oats and bran for the horses, Tory made her weekly visit to the grocery store and bought a local newspaper along with her week's supply of groceries. Once the sacks were loaded in the pickup, she glanced at the headlines on the front page of the paper.

The article was small, but located on page one. In five neatly typed paragraphs it reported that Senator Trask McFadden was back in Sinclair looking into the possibility that there may have been a fourth conspirator in his brother's death as well as the Quarter Horse swindle of five years past. The *Sinclair Weekly* promised a follow-up story the next week.

"Wonderful," Tory muttered with a groan, tossing the newspaper aside and heading back to the Lazy W.

The past two weeks had been quiet and Tory had ignored her earlier doubts about the past to the point that she had let herself fall completely and recklessly in love with Trask all over again. There had been no threats or violence and oftentimes Tory would allow herself to forget the reason that Trask had come back to Sinclair. She had even managed not to dwell on the fact that he would be leaving for Washington, D.C., very shortly.

Though she was still worried about the threats of violence that seemed to have accompanied him back to the Lazy W, Tory had thought less and less about them as Trask's wounds had healed and there hadn't been any further incidents. Unfortunately, the *Sinclair Weekly* decided to stir things up.

Just let me love him without the rest of the world intruding, she silently prayed.

Of course her hopes were in vain. With the article in the newspaper, everything came crashing back to reality. No longer could she ignore the real reason Trask had returned to Sinclair. Nor could she forget that he would leave as soon as he had finished his investigation.

And then what? she asked herself. *What about all his words of love, promises of marriage? Is that what you want? To be married to a United States senator who lives in Washington, D.C.? And what if he isn't sincere? What if this has all been an adventure for him—nothing more. He left you once before. Nothing says he can't do it again.*

"But he won't," she said as she parked the pickup near the back door. "He won't leave me and he'll never betray me again!" Hearing her own voice argue against the doubts in her mind, she experienced a sudden premonition of dread.

Tory unpacked the groceries and after changing from the linen business suit she had worn to meet with the bank's loan officer, she drove the pickup to the stables, unloaded the heavy sacks of grain and stacked them in the feed bins against the wall.

Her eyes wandered lovingly over the clean wooden stalls, and she noted the shining buckets that were hung near the mangers. The smell of horses, leather and saddle soap combined with the sweet scent of oats and freshly cut hay. Tory gazed through the window. Against the backdrop of long-needled pines, Governor was grazing contentedly, his laminitis nearly cured. A distant sound caught his attention. He lifted his graceful dark head and pricked his ears forward before pawing the ground impatiently and tossing his head to the sky. Tory's heart swelled with pride as she watched the magnificent stallion, a horse she had cared for since he was a fiery young colt.

She walked outside and closed the door of the stables behind her. Her eyes scanned the horizon and the rolling fields leading toward the craggy snowcapped mountains. What would she do if she lost the Lazy W? Leaning against the fence she could feel her brows draw together. The thought of losing the ranch was sobering and her small chin lifted in defiance against the fates that sought to steal her home and livelihood from her.

I can't, she thought to herself, slowly clenching her fists. *No matter what else happens, I can't lose this ranch.* Tory had always believed that where there was a will, there was a way. So it was with the Lazy W. She would find a way to keep the ranch, no matter what. Livestock could be sold, as well as pieces of machinery, if need be. And there were several parts of the ranch that could be parceled off without really affecting the day-to-day operations. The fields used for growing hay could be sold and she could buy the hay she needed from other ranchers. And there was always Devil's Ridge. Though Keith now owned that parcel, it could be sold or mortgaged.

She leaned on the fence and sighed. If things had gone differently, Devil's Ridge would now be where her father and mother would have retired and Keith would be running the ranch. Tory could have married Trask, and had several precious children to love . . .

"Stop it," she muttered to herself, slapping the fence post and dismissing her daydreams. "If wishes were horses, then beggars would ride."

Trying to shake the mood of desperation that had been with her since leaving the bank, Tory saddled her favorite palomino mare and mounted the spirited horse. After walking through the series of paddocks surrounding the stables, she urged the small horse into a gallop through the fields surrounding the main buildings of the ranch. Tory really didn't know where she was going, but she felt compelled to get away from the problems at the Lazy W.

The mare was eager to stretch her legs and Tory leaned forward in the saddle, encouraging the little horse. The only sounds she could hear were the thudding of the mare's hooves against the summer-hard ground and the pounding of her own heart. As the palomino raced toward the lake in the largest pasture, Tory felt the sting of the wind tangle her hair and force tears to her eyes. As if stolen by the wind, the pressures of running the ranch ebbed from Tory's mind and she gave herself up to the breathless exhilaration of the horse's sprint.

"You're just what I needed," she confided to the mare as she slowly reined the horse to a stop. Tory slid out of the saddle and let the horse drink from the clear lake. The late-afternoon sky reflected on the spring-fed pond and the scent of newly mown hay drifted over the land. *Her land.* The land both she and her father had worked to keep in the family.

While the mare grazed nearby, Tory propped her back against a solitary pine tree and stared at the horizon to the west. Misty white clouds clung to the uppermost peaks of the craggy snow-covered mountains in the distance. Closer, in the forested foothills, the distinct rocky spine of Devil's Ridge was visible.

Despite her earlier vows to herself, Tory's thoughts centered on the ridge and the afternoon she had spent with Trask just a few short weeks before.

Trask. His image flitted seductively through her mind.

He was the one man she should hate but couldn't. Despite the deceit of the past, and the uncertainty of the future, Tory loved him with all of her heart. The past few weeks even Keith seemed to have thawed and for the first time Tory thought there was actually a chance of a future with the man she loved. She tossed a pebble into the lake and watched the ever-widening circles spread over the calm water.

So what about the anonymous note, the dead calves, the rifle shot on Devil's Ridge, the threats? her persistent mind nagged.

With lines of concern creasing her brow, Tory plucked a piece of grass from the ground and twirled it in her fingers. *When all of this is behind us,* she thought, envisioning Trask's face, *then there will be time for you and me. Alone. Without the doubts. Without the lies . . .*

The sound of an approaching horse caught Tory's

attention. The mare lifted her head and nickered softly to the approaching horse and rider before grazing again.

Tory shielded her eyes from the sun with her hand and recognized a large buckskin gelding and the man astride the horse. A smile eased over her features at the sight of Trask riding the gelding. Dressed in jeans and a cotton shirt, bareheaded to the sun, he looked as comfortable in the saddle as he did in a Senate subcommittee.

Tory forced herself to her feet and dusted her hands together as Trask dismounted and tethered the gelding near Tory's mare. "I was just thinking about you," she admitted, her lips lifting into a welcoming smile. "How did you know where to find me?"

"One of the hands, Eldon—at least I think that's his name—" Tory nodded. "He saw you leave and told me which direction to take after saddling the buckskin for me."

"So much for privacy," she murmured.

"I didn't think you'd mind." He walked over to her and gently pulled her against him. Immediately she felt her body respond and the dormant stirrings of desire begin to waken deep in her soul.

"I don't, senator. Not much, anyway," she said teasingly, cocking her head upward to gaze at him. The late-afternoon sun caught in her hair, streaking the tangled auburn strands with fiery highlights of gold.

When she looked deep into his eyes she noticed the worry lingering in his gaze. The tautness of his skin as it stretched over his cheekbones and the furrow of his brow made her sense trouble. "Something's wrong," she said, feeling her throat constrict with dread.

He tried to pass off her fears with a patient smile, but his blue eyes remained intense, dark with a secret. "I was just thinking that it's about time we got married."

"What!" Though what he was saying was exactly what she wanted to hear, she couldn't hide the astonishment in her eyes.

"Don't look so shocked," he said coaxingly, kissing her tenderly on the forehead and squeezing his eyes shut against the possibility that he might never hold her again. "You know that it's something I've been talking about for the past three weeks."

"Wait a minute. What's going on? I thought we had an understanding that we had to get things settled between us. What about the note and the dead calves and your theory about another person being involved in the Quarter Horse swindle—"

"None of that will change." His voice was calm, his jaw hard with determination.

It was then that real fear gripped her throat. "You know something, don't you?" she asked, with the blinding realization that he was hiding something from her. She pulled away from his embrace and felt her heart thud with dread.

The pain in his eyes was nearly tangible and the lines near his mouth were grim with foreboding. "I want you to marry me, as soon as possible."

"But there has to be a reason."

"How about the fact that I can't live without you."

"Level with me, Trask."

"I am. I want to spend the rest of my life with you and I thought you wanted the same."

"I do . . . but something isn't right. I can see it in your eyes. What happened?" she demanded.

Trask pushed his hands through his hair and his broad shoulders slumped. "I just came from John Davis's office," he admitted.

John Davis. The private investigator. Tory's voice trembled slightly. "And?"

"And he came up with some answers for me."

"Answers that I'm not going to like," she surmised, taking in a deep breath.

"Yes."

"About Dad?"

"No."

Trask turned and met her confused gaze. "John Davis did some digging, thorough digging. He even went back to the penitentiary to double-check with George Henderson about what he'd discovered. George decided to come clean."

"About what?"

"Your father was innocent, Tory. Just as you believed."

So that was it! Trask's guilt for condemning an innocent man to prison was what was bothering him. Relief washed over her in a tidal wave and tears of happiness welled in her eyes. If only her father were still alive he could be a free man. "But that's wonderful news," she said, stepping closer to him.

The look he sent her could have cut through steel. "There's more. Your father wasn't involved with Linn Benton and George Henderson but someone else was." She froze and the first inkling of what he was suggesting penetrated her mind. "Who?"

"Your brother, Tory. Keith was an integral part of the horse swindle."

Tory didn't move. She let the words sink in and felt as if her safe world was spinning crazily away from her. Cold desperation cloaked her heart. "But that's impossible. Keith was only sixteen. He didn't even know Judge Benton or . . . George . . ."

"He knew George Henderson, Tory. George was the local vet. He'd been out to the ranch more times than you can remember. He liked your brother. Keith had even gone hunting with him on occasion."

"But he was just a boy," she said, feeling numb inside. "It just doesn't make any sense, none of it."

"Why do you think Keith reacted so violently to my return to Sinclair?"

"He has reason to hate you."

"And fear me."

Tory's mind was clouded with worried thoughts, pieces of the puzzle that weren't fitting together. She walked away from Trask, pushed her hands into the back pockets of her jeans and stared into the lake, not noticing the vibrant hue of the water. The gentle afternoon breeze lifted her hair from her face. "I don't believe you," she whispered. "If Keith had been involved with Linn Benton and George Henderson, it all would have come out at the trial."

"Unless your father paid for your brother's crime."

"No!" She whirled to face him. Her eyes were wide with new understanding and fear.

"Why else wouldn't Calvin defend himself?" He reached forward and grabbed her upper arms, his fingers digging into the soft flesh. She was forced to stare past the anger of his eyes to the agony in his soul. "Your father sacrificed himself, Tory. So that your brother wouldn't have to go to some correctional institution or prison."

"No! I won't believe it!" A thousand emotions raged within her: love, hate, anger, fear and above all disbelief. "You're grasping at straws because that investigator found out that Dad was innocent."

"God, woman, do you think I made this up?" he asked, his voice cracking with emotion. "Do you think I enjoy watching you fall apart? Do you think I wanted to come out here and tell you that I was wrong, that I'd made some horrible mistake about your father and that your only living relative was the real criminal?"

She placed her head in her hands and closed her eyes. "I don't know, Trask."

"Marry me," he said, desperately trying to hold on to the love they had shared. "Don't think about anything else, just marry me."

"Oh, God, are you crazy?" she threw back at him, her chest so tight she could barely breathe. "After what you just told me, you want to marry me." Her eyes became incredibly cold.

"I don't want to lose you again," he said, his fingers clutching her upper arms in a death grip.

Again she buried her face in her hands trying hopelessly to make some sense of what he was telling her, trying not to let her feelings of love for this man color her judgment. She swallowed with difficulty before lifting her eyes and meeting his stormy gaze. "I . . . I just can't believe any of this."

"Can't or won't?"

"Same thing," she pointed out, feeling suddenly alone in an alien world of lies and deception. "I won't believe it and I can't. Keith was with me at the trial, helped me here at the ranch. He's grown into a good man and now you're trying to make me believe that he was capable of swindling the public, being a part of a gruesome murder and letting my father go to prison in place of him? How would you feel if I'd just said the same thing to you?" Tory was shaking, visibly fighting to keep from breaking down.

"I don't know," he admitted, his voice harsh, "because I've lived the past five years without my brother."

"It's all happening again," Tory whispered, swallowing back the lump forming in her throat. "Just like before." She felt as if her heart was slowly being shredded by a destiny that allowed her to love a man who only wanted to hurt her. "And you're the one to blame." She shook her head and let the tears run freely. "I suppose you think that Keith beat you up, shot the calves and wrote threatening notes to both me and Neva?"

"I don't know," Trask said. "But I wouldn't rule it out."

"And what does your crackerjack ace detective think?" she asked, her voice filled with sarcasm.

"He knows he's found out the truth. He knows that some of the testimony of the original trial was faulty at best and maybe downright lies at the worst."

"Including yours?" she asked. Trask's jaw hardened and his eyes glittered dangerously, but Tory couldn't help the outrage overtaking her. *Keith. A criminal!* It couldn't be. She wouldn't sit still and let her only brother be given the same sentence as her innocent father. She had to fight back against the fates that were continually at odds with her happiness. "And I suppose Mr. Davis feels obligated to set the record straight."

"It's his job."

She smiled bitterly through her tears. "And what about you, senator? Is it your duty as well?"

"I've only wanted two things in my life: the truth and one other thing."

"I don't want to hear it," she whispered.

"You can't hide from it, Tory. I want you. All of you. No matter what else happens, I want you to be with me for the rest of my life." He lifted his head proudly and she realized just how difficult confronting her had been for him.

Her heart felt as if it were breaking into a thousand pieces. "Then why do you continue to try and ruin me?" she choked out, her eyes softening as she looked past the pain in his. "Must we always be so close and yet so distant?"

He reached for her, but she drew away. Her eyes were filled with tears and she didn't care that they ran down her cheeks and fell to her chest. "Please, just trust me," he asked so softly that she barely heard the words.

"I don't know if that's possible," she replied. She straightened her spine and attempted to tell herself that she could live without him. She had before. She would again, despite the gripping pain in her chest. "I . . . I think we should go back to the house." She turned toward the mare but the sound of his voice stopped her dead in her tracks.

"Victoria?" he said, and she pivoted to face him. "I'll always love you."

She squeezed her eyes tightly shut, as if in so doing she could deny the painful words. *How desperately she had loved Trask and now she wished with all of her heart that she could hate him.*

They rode back to the house in silence, each wrapped in private and painful thoughts. Though dusk was gathering over the meadows, painting the countryside in vibrant lavender hues and promising a night filled with winking stars and pale light from a quarter moon, Tory didn't notice.

Keith's pickup was parked near the barn. Tory's heart began to race at the thought of the confrontation that was about to take place. She silently prayed that just this once Trask was dead wrong.

After Eldon offered to unsaddle and cool the horses, Tory walked with Trask back to the house. They didn't touch or speak and the tight feeling in Tory's chest refused to lessen.

"About time you showed up," Keith shouted down the stairs when he heard Tory walk into the house. "I'm starved." The knot in the bottom of her stomach tightened at the sight of her brother as he came down the stairs. His shirt was still gaping open and he was towel drying his hair. "What say we go into Bend and catch a movie and then we'll go to dinner—my treat . . ." His voice faded when he saw Trask. He lowered the towel and smiled grimly. "I guess you probably have other plans." He stopped at the bottom step and noticed her pale face. "Hey, what's wrong?"

"There's something Trask wants to ask you about," Tory said, her voice quavering slightly.

"So what else is new?" Keith cast an unfriendly glance at Trask before striding into the kitchen.

"It's a little different this time," Trask remarked, following the younger man down the short hallway.

"Oh yeah? Good." Keith chuckled mirthlessly to himself. "I'm tired of the same old questions." He seemed totally disinterested in Trask's presence and he rummaged in the refrigerator for the jug of milk.

Alex was whining at the back door and Keith let the old collie into the house. "What's the matter, boy?" he asked, scratching the dog behind the ears. "Hungry?" The sight of her brother so innocently petting the dog's head tore at Tory's heart. "Keith—" Tory's words froze when she noticed Rex's pickup coming down the drive.

"What?"

"Maybe we should talk about this later," she said.

"Talk about what?" Keith poured a large glass of milk, then drank most of it in one swallow.

"About what happened five years ago," Trask stated.

"I thought you said you had come up with some new questions."

"I have." The edge to Trask's voice made Keith start.

"Not now—" Tory pleaded, desperation taking a firm

hold of her. She had already lost her father and the thought of losing Keith the same way was unbearable.

Though he felt his stomach tighten in concern as he studied the pale lines of Tory's face, Trask ignored her obvious dread, deciding that the truth had to be brought into the open. "No time like the present, I always say." He watched with narrowed eyes as the foreman climbed out of his pickup and started walking toward the house. "Besides, Rex should be part of this."

"Part of what?" For the first time Keith noticed the worry in his sister's eyes. "What's going on?" he insisted. "Don't tell me we got another one of those damned notes!"

"Not quite."

"Oh, Keith," Tory whispered, her voice cracking.

Rex rapped on the back door and entered the kitchen. His eyes shifted from Tory to her brother before settling on Trask and he felt the electric tension charging the air. "Maybe I should come back later—" he said, moving toward the door.

"No." Trask swung a chair around and straddled the back. "I think that you can help shed a little light on something I've discovered."

"You're still going at it, aren't you?" the foreman accused. He lifted his felt hat from his head and worked the wide brim between his gnarled fingers. "You're worse than a bull terrier once you get your teeth into something."

"Trask's private investigator has come up with another theory about what happened five years ago," Tory explained, her worried eyes moving to her brother.

Keith bristled. "What do you mean 'another theory'?"

"John Davis seems to think that your father was innocent," Trask said, silently gauging Keith's reaction.

"Big deal. We've been telling you that for years."

"But you wouldn't tell me who Calvin was protecting."

"What!" Keith's face slackened and lost all of its color.

Tory felt as if her heart had just stopped beating.

"John Davis seems to think that your father was covering for you; that you were the man called 'Wilson' that was involved with Linn Benton and George Henderson."

"Wait a minute—" Rex cut in.

Tory's eyes locked with the foreman's anxious gaze. *Oh, my God, he knows what happened,* she realized with a sickening premonition of dread. Her chest felt tight and she had to grip the counter for support.

"What do you know about this?" Trask turned furious eyes on the foreman.

"Keith wasn't involved with the likes of Henderson and Benton," the foreman said, his face flushed, his grizzled chin working with emotion.

"Davis can prove it," Trask said flatly.

Dead silence.

"How?" Tory asked.

Trask took the envelope from his jacket and tossed it onto the table. "Someone, a man who worked for Linn Benton when he was judge, saw Keith. George Henderson verified the other guy's story."

"No!" Tory screamed, her voice catching on a sob. *Not Keith, too. She wouldn't, couldn't lose him.*

"Back off, McFadden," Rex threatened, his eyes darting to the rifle mounted over the door before returning to Trask.

Keith's shoulders slumped and he looked up at the ceiling. "No, Rex, don't. It's over—"

"Shut up!" the foreman snapped, his cold eyes drilling

into Trask and his gnarled hands balling into threatening fists. "You just couldn't leave it alone, could you?"

"Why are you standing up for him? Were you involved, too?" Trask suggested.

"Save it, Rex," Keith said, his eyes locking with those of his sister. "He obviously knows everything." Keith's hands shook as he opened the envelope and skimmed through the contents of John Davis's report. "Not everything. Maybe you can fill in a few of the missing blanks."

"Oh, God, Keith," Tory said, shaking her head, her voice strangling in her throat. "You don't have to say anything."

"It's time, Sis. I knew it the minute McFadden showed up here. I let Dad cover for me because I was young and scared. I don't have those excuses to hide behind any more."

"Please," she whispered.

"You promised your father," Rex reminded Keith.

"And it was a mistake. A mistake that you and I have had to live with for five years," Keith said. "I know what it's done to me and I can see what's happening to you."

"You were in on it, too?" Trask said, his voice stone-cold.

"No, he wasn't involved," Keith said.

"Wait a minute," Tory said, realizing that Keith was about to confess to a man who would ultimately want to see him sent to prison. "You don't have to say anything that might incriminate you—you should talk to a lawyer. . . ."

"Forget it, Tory. It's time I said what's on my mind. Even if McFadden hadn't come back, I would have told the truth sooner or later. It wasn't fair for Dad to take the rap for me, or for Dad to expect Rex to protect me."

A deathly black void had invaded her heart and she felt as if her world was crumbling apart, brick by solid brick. *All because of Trask.*

"What happened?" Trask asked persistently. Every muscle in his body was tight from the strain of witnessing what this confrontation was doing to Tory. Maybe he'd been wrong all along, he thought, maybe, as Keith and Neva had so often suggested, he should have forgotten it all and just fallen in love with Tory again. As it was, she was bound to hate him. He could read it in her cold gray-green eyes.

"George Henderson approached me," Keith was saying. "He asked me if I would help him with some horses he wanted hidden up on Devil's Ridge. All I had to do was keep quiet about it and make sure that no one went up to the ridge. I was stupid enough to agree. When I found out what was going on, how he and Linn Benton were switching expensive Quarter Horses for cheaper ones, I told George I wanted out. George might have gone for it, but the judge, he wouldn't let me out of the deal . . . told me I was an accomplice, even if an unwitting one. And he was right. No doubt about it, the judge knew the law from both sides. And I did know that something shady was going on. I just didn't realize how bad it was . . . or . . . or that it could mean a stiff jail sentence."

"So you were in over your head," Trask said without emotion.

Keith nodded and Tory's eyes locked with her brother's dull gaze before he looked ashamedly away from her.

"But you could have come to me or to Dad," Tory said, feeling dead inside. *First her father and now Keith!*

Her chest felt so tight she had to fight to stand on her feet. Closing her eyes, she leaned against the wall for support.

"No way could I have come to Dad or you. How could I let you know how bad I got suckered, or that I had let someone use our property to conduct illegal business? I was already a failure as far as Dad was concerned; you were the responsible one, Sis."

"We were a family, Keith," she moaned. "We could have helped you—"

"What about the horses? The ones from the Lazy W?" Trask cut in, knowing that he had to get this inquisition over fast before Keith could think twice about it. And Tory. God, he wished there was a way to protect and comfort her.

"I switched the horses," Keith admitted. "I figured that I was in too far to back out. If I didn't agree, Benton promised to tell Dad."

Trask's fingers rubbed together and a muscle in the back of his jaw clenched and unclenched in his barely concealed rage. "So what about my brother?" he asked, his voice low and cold.

"I had no idea that Jason was onto us," Keith said, his gray eyes filled with honesty. "I knew that Benton and Henderson were worried about being discovered but I didn't know anything about the insurance company investigation or your brother's role as an investigator."

"He's telling the truth," Rex admitted, wearily sliding into a chair and running his hands through his thinning hair.

"But what about the conversation that Tory overheard?"

Tory's disbelieving eyes focused on Rex.

"It was part of the ruse. Staged for your benefit," Rex

said, returning Tory's discouraged stare. "Once Linn Benton approached your father and told him about Keith, Calvin was determined as hell to sacrifice himself instead of his boy. He had to make everyone, including you, Tory, believe that he had been a part of the swindle. He didn't know anything about the plot to kill Jason McFadden. That was Linn Benton's idea."

Tears had begun to stream down Tory's face. She swiped at them with the back of her hand, but couldn't stem the uneven flow from her eyes. She shuddered from an inner cold. "So Dad wouldn't testify on the stand because he wanted to protect Keith?"

"That's right," Keith said, tears clouding his vision. Angrily he sniffed them back.

"Your dad knew he was dying of cancer; it was an easy decision to sacrifice himself in order that his son go free," Rex explained.

"And you went along with it," Tory accused, feeling betrayed by every person she had ever loved.

"I owed your dad a favor—a big one."

Tory took in a shuddering breath. "I don't want to hear any more of this," she said with finality. "And I don't want to believe a word of it."

"We can't hide behind lies any longer," Keith said, squaring his shoulders. "I'll call Sheriff Barnett tonight."

"Wait!" Tory held up her hand. "Think about what you're doing, Keith. At least consider calling a lawyer before you do anything else!"

Keith came over to her and touched her shoulders. "I've thought about this too long as it is. It's time to do something—"

"Please . . ." she begged, clinging to her brother as if by holding on to him she could convince him of the folly of his actions.

Keith smiled sadly and patted her back. "If it makes

you feel any better I'll call a lawyer, just as soon as I talk Barnett into coming out here and taking my statement."

"I wish you wouldn't—" Rex said.

"You're off the hook," Keith said, releasing his sister and walking from the kitchen and into the den. Tory sat in a chair near the doorway and refused to meet Trask's concerned gaze.

"So you were the one who shot the calves, right?" Trask asked the foreman once Keith had left the room.

Rex frowned and lifted his shoulders. He couldn't meet Tory's incredulous gaze. "I thought you would stop the damned investigation if you discovered any threats to Tory."

"So you sent the note?" Tory asked.

"I'm not proud of it," Rex admitted, "but it was all I could think of doing." His chin quivered before he raised his eyes to meet Tory's wretched stare. "I promised your old man, Tory. You have to believe I never meant to hurt you or the ranch . . . I . . . I just wanted to do right by your dad." His voice cracked and he had to clear his throat. "Your father hired me when no one else in this town would talk to me." He turned back to Trask. "I just wish it would've worked and you would've gone back to Washington where you belong instead of stirring up the lives of good decent people and making trouble."

Tory's head was swimming in confusion. So Keith had been involved in the Quarter Horse swindle and her father had only tried to protect his young son. And Rex, feeling some misguided loyalty to a dying man, had kept the secret of Keith's involvement. Even the foreman's fumbling attempts to deter Trask were in response to a debt that had been paid long ago.

"I reckon I'd better talk to the sheriff as well," Rex

said, forcing his hat back on his head and walking down the hall to the den where the soft sound of Keith's voice could be heard.

Trask got out of the chair and walked over to Tory. He reached for her but she recoiled from him. Not only had Trask put her father in jail five years earlier, but now he was about to do the same to her brother.

"Tory—"

"Don't!" She squared her shoulders, stood, shook her head and looked away from him while her stomach twisted into painful knots. *How could this be happening?* "I don't want to hear reasons or excuses or anything!" Cringing away from him she backed into the kitchen counter.

"This had to come out, y'know."

"But you didn't have to do it, did you? You didn't have to drag it all out into the open and destroy everything that's mattered to me. First my father and now my brother. God, Trask, when you get your pound of flesh, you just don't stop, do you? You want blood and tears and more blood." Tears ran freely down her cheeks. "I hope to God you're satisfied!"

Trask flinched and the rugged lines of his face seemed more pronounced. He ran his fingers raggedly through his windblown hair and released a tired sigh. "I wish you'd believe that I only wanted to love you," he whispered.

"And I wish you'd go to hell," she replied. "I'd ask you if you intend to testify against my brother, but I already know the answer to that one, don't I?"

His lips tightened and the pain in his eyes was overcome by anger. "I had a brother once, too. Remember? And he was more than a brother. He was a husband and a father. And he was murdered. *Murdered,* Tory. Keith knew all about it. He just didn't have the guts to come clean."

"That's all changed now, hasn't it? Thanks to you."

"I didn't want it to end this way," he said, stepping closer to her, but she threw up her hands as if to protect herself. He stopped short.

"Then you should never have started it again. Face it, senator, if there was ever anything between us, you've destroyed it. Forever!"

"There are still a lot of unanswered questions," he reminded her.

"Well, just don't come around here asking for my help in answering them," she retorted. "I'm not a glutton for punishment. I've had enough to last me a lifetime, thanks to you."

Trask stood and stared at her. His blue eyes delved into her soul. "I won't come back, Tory," he warned. "The next move is yours."

"Just don't hold your breath, senator," she whispered through clenched teeth before turning away from him. For a moment there was silence and Tory could feel that he wanted to say something more to her. Then she heard the sound of his retreating footsteps. They echoed hollowly down the hallway. In a few moments she heard the front door slam shut and then the sound of Trask's Blazer roaring down the lane.

"Oh, God," she cried, before clamping a trembling hand over her mouth. Tears began streaming down her face. "I love you, Trask. Damn it all to hell, but I still love you." The sobs broke free of her body and she braced herself with the counter.

"Get hold of yourself," she said, but the tears continued to flow and her shoulders racked with the sobs she tried to still. "I never want to see him again," she whispered, thinking of Trask and knowing that despite her brave words she would always love him. "You're a fool," she chastised herself, lowering her head to the sink and splashing water over her face, "a blind lovesick fool!"

Knowing that she had another investigation to face this night, for surely Sheriff Barnett and his deputy would arrive shortly, she tried to pull herself together and failed miserably. She leaned heavily against the counter and stared into the dark night. Far in the distance she saw the flashing lights of an approaching police car.

"This is it," she said softly to herself. "The beginning of the end . . ."

Chapter Twelve

THE COURTROOM WAS small and packed to capacity. An overworked air-conditioning system did little to stir the warm air within the room.

Tory sat behind Keith. She tried to console herself with the fact that Keith was doing what he wanted, but her heart went out to her brother. He hadn't been interested in hiring an attorney; in fact, he had petitioned the court to allow him to represent himself. Even the district attorney was unhappy with the situation, but Keith had been adamant.

He looks so young, Tory thought as she studied the square set of her slim brother's shoulders and the proud lift of his jaw. *Just the way Dad had faced his trial.* Tory had to look away from Keith and swallow against the thick lump that had formed in the back of her throat.

The district attorney had already called several witnesses to the stand, the most prominent being George Henderson, who had been accompanied by a guard, when he testified. Not only did George tell the court that Keith, not his father, Calvin, had been in on the Quarter Horse swindle, but he also explained that Linn Benton had blackmailed Calvin into admitting to be a part of the scam.

According to Henderson, Linn Benton had been interested in recruiting Keith as a naive partner in order to have some leverage over Calvin Wilson and the Lazy W. Linn Benton knew that Calvin would never let his son go to prison and a deal was made. Calvin would accept most of the guilt in order to keep Keith's name out of the scam.

"Then what you're suggesting, Mr. Henderson," the soft-spoken D.A. deduced, "is that Calvin Wilson's only crime was that of protecting his son."

"Yes, sir," an aged Henderson replied from the stand. He had thinned considerably in prison and looked haggard. While he continuously rubbed his hands together, a nervous twitch near his eyes worked noticeably.

"And that Linn Benton was blackmailing Calvin Wilson with his son's life."

"That's about the size of it."

"Then Keith Wilson knew about the horse swindle."

"Yes."

Tory cringed, but Keith didn't flinch. A murmur of disapproving whispers filtered through the hot room.

"And he was aware of the deal struck between his father and Judge Linn Benton?"

Henderson nodded.

"You'll have to speak up, Mr. Henderson. The court reporter must be able to hear you. She can't record head movements," the elderly judge announced.

Henderson cleared his throat. "Yes, Keith Wilson knew about the blackmail and the deal," he rasped.

The district attorney paused and the courtroom became silent. "And did he know about the plan to kill Jason McFadden?"

George Henderson's wrinkled brow pulled into a scowl. "No."

"You're sure?"

"Yes," George answered firmly. He met Keith's stony gaze before looking away from him. "Benton did it all on his own. He only told me a few minutes before Jason McFadden's car exploded. By then it was too late to do anything about it." The old vet's shoulders slumped from the weight of five years of deceit.

"And why didn't you go to the police?"

"Because I was afraid," George admitted.

"Of being apprehended?"

"No." George shook his head and the twitch near his left eye became more pronounced. "I was afraid of crossing Linn Benton."

"I see," the district attorney said, sending a meaningful look to the jury. "No further questions."

Keith refused to cross-examine Henderson, as he had with all of the prosecution's witnesses. Tory felt sick inside. It was as if Keith had given up and was willing to accept his fate. For the past week, she had tried to get him to change his mind, hire an attorney and fight for his freedom, but her brother had been adamant, insisting that he was finally doing the "right" thing by his father.

"Don't worry about me," he had said just before the trial. "I'll be fine."

"I can't help but worry. You're acting like some sacrificial lamb—"

"That was Dad," Keith answered severely. "I'm just paying for what I did. It's my time."

"But I need you—"

"What you need is to run the ranch yourself, or better yet, make up with McFadden. Marry the guy."

"Are you out of your mind?" she had asked. "After everything he's done? I can't believe you, of all people, are suggesting this."

Keith just shook his head. "I did hate him, Tory, but that was because of fear and guilt. I knew, despite what I said, that Trask wasn't responsible for Dad being sent to prison and dying. It was my fault. All McFadden ever wanted was the truth about his brother and you can't really blame him for that."

"How can you feel this way?" she asked incredulously.

"It's easy. I've seen how you are when you're around him. Tory, face it, you were happier than you'd been in years when he came back to Sinclair." His gray eyes held those of his sister. "You deserve that happiness."

Tears had formed in her eyes. "What about you?"

"Me, are you kiddin'?" he had joked, then his voice cracked. "I'll be having the time of my life."

"Seriously—"

"Tory, this is something I've got to do and you won't change my mind. So take my advice and be happy . . . with McFadden."

"He's responsible—"

Keith lifted a finger to her lips. "*I'm* responsible and it's time to pay up. Believe me, it's a relief that it's all nearly over."

Several other witnesses came to the stand, all painting the same picture that Keith was an ingrate of a son who had used his martyred father to protect himself.

When Trask was called to the stand, Tory felt her hands begin to shake. Until this point he had sat in the back of the courtroom and though Tory could feel his eyes upon her, she had never looked in his direction, preferring to stare straight ahead and watch the proceedings without having to face him or her conflicting emotions.

Trask seemed to have aged, Tory thought, her heart twisting painfully at the sight of him. He looked uncomfortable in his suit and tie. His rugged features seemed more pronounced, his cheeks slightly hollow, but the intensity of his vibrant blue eyes was still as bright as ever. When he sat behind the varnished rail of the witness stand, he looked past the district attorney and his eyes

she, too, leave no stone unturned in the apprehension of the guilty parties?

She twisted her handkerchief in her lap and avoided Trask's stare.

"So tell me, senator, how you found out that the defendant was part of the horse swindle."

"I had a private investigator, a man by the name of John Davis, look into it."

"And what did Mr. Davis find out?"

"That Keith Wilson, and not his father Calvin, was a partner to Linn Benton and George Henderson."

Tory felt sick inside as the questioning continued. The D.A. opened his jacket and rocked back on his heels. "Did Mr. Davis find out who sent you the first anonymous letter to Washington?"

"Yes."

Tory's eyes snapped up and she felt her breath constrict in her throat. *Who was responsible for bringing Trask back to Oregon? Who knew about Keith's involvement and wanted to see him go to prison?*

"The letter came from Belinda Engels," Trask stated. Tory took in a sharp breath. "Belinda is the wife of Rex Engels, the foreman of the Lazy W."

"The same man who was sworn to secrecy by Calvin Wilson before he died?"

"Yes."

"Thank you, Senator McFadden. No more questions."

When Keith declined to cross-examine Trask, the senator was asked to step down. With his eyes fixed on Tory, Trask walked back to his seat, and Tory felt her heart start to pound wildly. Even now she couldn't look at him without realizing how desperately she loved him.

The district attorney called Belinda Engels to the stand and Tory watched in amazement as the young woman with the clear complexion and warm brown eyes explained that she had spent five years watching her husband's guilt eat at him until he became a shell of the man she had married.

"Then you knew about Keith Wilson's involvement in the horse swindle?"

"No," she said, looking pointedly at Keith. "I only knew that Rex was sure another man was involved. One night, not long after it happened, Rex woke from a horrible nightmare. Against his better judgment, he told me that he was covering for someone and that Calvin Wilson wasn't involved in the murder. I just assumed that the other man was someone connected to Linn Benton. I . . . I had no idea that he was Keith Wilson."

"And even though you knew that an innocent man was on trial five years ago, you didn't come forward with the information."

Belinda swallowed. "I . . . I thought that Rex might be charged with some sort of crime and I didn't think he'd be given a fair trial because of his past . . . with his ex-wife." Tory sitting silently, watched as the red-haired young woman struggled against tears.

"But you and your husband both knew that Calvin Wilson was innocent."

Belinda leveled her gaze at the district attorney. "My husband's a good honest man. He promised to keep Calvin's secret. I did the same."

Tory closed her eyes as she pictured her father and all of the suffering he had accepted for Keith's involvement with Linn Benton. Tears burned at the back of her eyes but she bravely pushed them aside.

The rest of the trial was a blur for Tory. She only remembered that Keith spoke in his own defense, explaining exactly what happened in thc past and why. Since he had pleaded guilty to the charges, the only question was how stiff a sentence the judge would impose.

When Tory left the courtroom, her knees felt weak. She held her head high, but couldn't hide the slight droop of her shoulders or the shadows under her eyes. The past few weeks had been a strain. Not only had the trial loomed over her head, but she had been forced to deal with nosy reporters, concerned friends, and worst of all the absence of Trask in her life. She hadn't realized how difficult life would be without him. She had grown comfortable with him again in those first warm weeks of summer. Since he had discovered Keith's secret, there was a great emptiness within her heart, and life at the Lazy W alone was more than Tory could face at times.

Lifting her head over the whispers she heard in the outer hallway of the courthouse, she walked down the shiny linoleum-floored corridor, through the front doors and down the few concrete steps into the radiant heat of late July in central Oregon.

She stepped briskly, avoiding at all costs another confrontation with the press. At the parking lot, she stopped short. Trask was leaning against her pickup watching her with his harsh blue eyes.

After catching the breath that seemed to have been stolen from her lungs at the sight of him, Tory lifted her chin and advanced toward Trask. Her heart was pounding a staccato beat in her chest and her pulse jumped to the erratic rhythm, but she forced her face to remain emotionless.

Trask pushed his hands deep into his pockets, stretching his legs in front of him as he surveyed her. Dressed in a cool ivory linen suit, with her hair swept away from her face, Tory looked more like royalty or a sophisticated New York model than an Oregon rancher. He grimaced slightly when he noticed the coldness of her gaze as she approached. She stopped in front of him, her head slightly tilted to meet his gaze.

"Are you happy?" she asked, inwardly wincing at the cynicism in her words. She noticed him flinch.

His teeth clenched and a muscle worked in the corner of his jaw. The hot summer wind pushed his hair from his face, exposing the small lines etching his forehead. The sadness in his eyes touched a very small, but vital part of Tory's heart.

"No."

"At least satisfied, I hope."

He frowned and let out a long sigh of frustration. "Tory, look. I just wanted to say goodbye."

She felt a sudden pain in her heart. "You're . . . you're leaving for Washington," she guessed, surprised at how hard it was to accept that he would be on the other side of the continent. *If only she could forget him, find another man to love, someone who wouldn't destroy all she had known in her life.*

"The day after tomorrow."

She stiffened. "I see. You wanted to stick around for the sentencing, is that it?"

His face hardened, but the agony in his blue eyes didn't diminish and her feelings of love for him continued to do battle in her heart. Rex and Keith had been right all along. Trask had used her to promote himself and his damned political career. Already the papers were doing feature articles about him; painting him as some sort of martyred hero who had come back home to capture his brother's killers. *Only Keith hadn't killed anyone!*

"I just hoped that we could . . ." He looked skyward as if seeking divine guidance.

"I hope that you're not going to suggest that we be friends, senator. That's a little too much to ask," she said, but the trembling of her chin gave away her real feelings.

"I wish that there was some way to prove to you that

I only did what I had to do, and that I didn't intend to hurt you." He lifted a hand toward her and she instinctively stepped backward.

"Don't worry about it. It won't happen again. All my family is gone, Trask. There isn't anyone else you can send to prison." She walked around to the driver's side of the truck and reached for the door handle, but Trask was there before her. His hand took hold of hers and for a breathless instant, when their fingers entwined, Tory thought there was a chance that she could trust him again. God, how she still loved him. Her eyes searched his face before she had the strength to pull away. "I have to go."

"I just want you to be careful, some things still aren't clear yet."

She shook her head at her own folly of loving him. "Some things will never be clear. At least not to me."

"Listen . . . I thought you'd want to know that I've instructed John Davis to keep watching the ranch."

"What!"

"I think there still may be trouble."

"That's impossible. It's all over, Trask."

"I don't think so."

"Call him off."

"What?"

"You heard me!" She pointed an angry finger at Trask's chest. "Tell Davis that I don't need anyone patrolling the ranch. Furthermore, I don't want him there. I just want to forget about this whole damned nightmare!" Her final words were choked out and she felt the tears she had managed to dam all day begin to flow.

"Tory . . ." His voice was soft, soothing. His fingers wrapped possessively over her arm.

"Leave me alone," she whispered, unable to jerk away. "And tell that private investigator of yours to back off. Otherwise I'll have the sheriff arrest him for trespassing."

"I just want you to be safe."

"And I want you out of my life," she lied, finally pulling away and jerking open the door of the pickup. With tears blurring her vision, she started the truck and drove out of the parking lot, glancing in the rearview mirror only once to notice the defeat in Trask's shoulders.

TORY HADN'T BEEN back at the Lazy W very long before the telephone rang. She had just stepped out of the shower and considered not answering the phone, but decided she couldn't. The call could possibly be from Keith.

Gritting her teeth against the very distinct possibility that the call was from another reporter, she answered the phone sharply.

"Hello?"

"Ms. Wilson?" the caller inquired.

Tory grimaced at the unfamiliar voice. "This is Victoria Wilson."

"Good. Don Morris with Central Bank."

The young loan officer! Tory braced herself for more bad news. "Yes?"

"I just wanted to let you know that the loan committee has seen fit to grant you the funds you requested." Tory felt as if she could fall through the floor. The last thing she expected from the bank was good news. Nervously she ran her fingers through her hair. "Thank you," she whispered.

"No problem at all," the loan officer said with a smile in his voice. "You can pick up the check the day after tomorrow."

"Can you tell me something, Mr. Morris?" Tory asked

cautiously. She didn't want to press her luck, but the bank's agreement to her loan didn't seem quite right. She felt as if she were missing something.

"Certainly."

"The last time I came to see you, you insisted that I didn't have enough collateral for another loan with the bank. What happened to change your mind?"

"Pardon me?" She could almost hear the banker's surprise.

"You haven't had a change of policy, have you?"

"No."

"Well?"

The young banker sighed. "Senator McFadden agreed to cosign on your note."

Tory's eyes widened in surprise. "What does Senator McFadden have to do with this?"

"He talked with the president of the bank and insisted that we lend you the money. The senator owns quite a chunk of stock in the bank, you know. And the president is a personal friend of his. Anyway, he insisted that he cosign your note."

Blood money! "And you agreed to it?"

"You did want the loan, didn't you? Ms. Wilson?"

"Yes . . . yes. I'll clear things up with the senator," she replied, her blood rising in her anger as she slammed down the phone. "Bastard," she whispered between clenched teeth.

It occurred to her as she towel-dried her hair and pulled on her jeans that Trask might have cosigned on the note to the bank as a final way of saying goodbye to her. After all, he did appear sincere when he said he hadn't wanted to hurt her.

"Oh, God, Trask, why can't we just let it die?" she wondered aloud as she took a moment to look out the window and see the beauty of the spreading acres of the ranch. As August approached the countryside had turned golden-brown with only the dark pines to add color and contrast to the gold earth and the blue sky. And Trask had given her the chance to keep it. It wasn't something he had to do. It was a gift.

"And a way of easing his conscience," she said bitterly, trying desperately to hate him.

Without really considering her actions, she ran outside and hopped into the pickup with the intention of confronting Trask one last time.

DUSK HAD SETTLED by the time that Tory reached Trask's cabin on the Metolius River. Even as she approached the single story cedar and rock building, she knew that Trask wasn't there. His Blazer was nowhere in sight and all of the windows and doors were boarded shut.

He'd already gone, Tory thought miserably, her heart seeming to tear into tiny ribbons. As she ran her fingers over the smooth wooden railing of the back porch, she couldn't help but remember the feel and texture of Trask's smooth muscles and she wondered if she would ever truly be free of him, or if she wanted that freedom.

With one last look at the small cabin nestled between the pines on the banks of the swift Metolius, Tory climbed back into her pickup and headed into Sinclair. On the outskirts of the small town, she turned down the road where Neva McFadden lived.

Trask's Blazer was parked in the driveway.

Maybe he had turned to Neva. Keith had said that Neva was in love with him. A dull ache spread through her at the thought of Trask with another woman, any other woman.

With her heart thudding painfully, Tory walked up the sidewalk and pounded on the front door. Almost immediately, Neva answered her knock.

"Trask!" she shouted before seeing Tory. The color drained from Neva's face. "Tory?" she whispered, shaking her head. "I thought that you might be Trask . . ." The blond woman's voice cracked and she had to place a hand over her mouth.

Tory felt her blood turn to ice water. "What happened? Isn't he here?" She lifted her hand and pointed in the direction of the Blazer but Neva only shook her head.

"I guess you'd better come in."

Neva led Tory into the house. "Where's Trask?" Tory asked, her dread giving way to genuine fear.

"I don't know. He . . . he and John Davis and Sheriff Barnett are looking for Nicholas."

Tory stood stock-still. When Neva lifted her eyes, they were filled with tears. "Where is Nicholas?" Tory asked.

"I . . . I don't know. Trask and I assume that he's been kidnapped."

"Kidnapped?" Tory repeated, as she leaned against the wall. "Why?"

"Because of the trial. Trask thinks Linn Benton is behind it."

"But how—?"

"I don't know. George Henderson told everything he knew about the swindle and that included some pretty incriminating things against Linn Benton. The blackmailing alone will keep him in the pen several more years," Neva said.

"Wait a minute, slow down. What about your son?"

"I came back from the trial and he was gone. There

was just a note saying that I hadn't kept Trask from digging up the past and I'd have to pay."

"And you're sure that Nicholas didn't go to a friend's house?"

"Yes." Neva could stand the suspense no longer. Her tears fell freely down her face and her small body was racked with the sobs.

Tory wrapped her arms around the woman and whispered words she didn't believe herself. "It's going to be all right, Neva," she said. "Trask will find your son."

"Oh, God, I hope so! He's all I have left."

Gently Tory led Neva to the couch. "I think you should lie down."

"I can't sleep."

"Shh. I know, but you're a nurse; you've got to realize that the best thing to do is lie still. I'll . . . I'll make you some tea."

Neva reluctantly agreed. She sat on the edge of the couch, staring at the clock and wringing her hands with worry.

Tory scrounged around in Neva's kitchen and found the tea bags. Within a few minutes, she brought two steaming cups back to the living room.

"Thank you," Neva whispered when Tory offered her the cup. She took a sip of the tea and set it on the arm of the couch, letting the warm brew get cold.

"They're going to kill Nicholas," she said firmly, and tears ran in earnest down her cheeks.

"Don't talk that way—"

"I should never have told Trask. Oh, God—" Neva buried her face in her hands. "I'll never forgive myself if they hurt my baby—"

The knock on the door made Neva leap from the couch. "Oh, God, it's got to be Nicholas," she whispered, racing to the door to discover Deputy Woodward on the front steps.

"What happened?" she cried.

The grim deputy looked from one woman to the next. "We've found your boy, Mrs. McFadden."

Neva looked as if she would faint in relief. "Thank God. Is he all right?"

"I think so. He's in the hospital in Bend, just for observation. He appears unharmed. I'd be happy to drive you there myself."

"Yes, please," Neva said, reaching for her purse.

"Where's Trask?" Tory asked.

"Senator McFadden is in the hospital, too."

Tory felt sick inside and she paled. *What if something had happened to Trask? What if she could never see him again? What if he were dead?* Tory couldn't live without him.

Neva turned and faced the young deputy. "What happened?"

"The senator got into a fistfight with the man who kidnapped your son. It looks as if this guy might be the one that knocked Senator McFadden out and beat him up a few weeks ago—the guy who was shooting at you on Devil's Ridge."

"Who is he?" Tory demanded, fear and anger mingling in her heart.

"A man by the name of Aaron Hughs. He's the foreman of Linn Benton's spread, just north of Bend."

"And Hughs still works for him?"

"Appears that way." The deputy turned his attention to Neva. "Anyway, if it hadn't been for the senator, your boy would probably be across the state line by now. According to the sheriff, McFadden should be awarded some sort of medal."

"Then he's all right?" Tory asked.

"I think so."

"Thank God."

"How did you know where to find Nicholas?" Tory asked.

"Senator McFadden, he thought your son had to be somewhere on Linn Benton's ranch. As it turns out, he was right. The kid was tied to a chair in the kitchen."

A small cry escaped from Neva's lips. "Come on, let's go."

The trip to the hospital seemed to take forever. Tory closed her eyes and imagined Trask lying in a stark, white-sheeted hospital bed, beaten beyond recognition. *Oh, God, I've been such a fool,* she thought, knowing for the first time since Keith had been arrested that she would always love Trask McFadden. The few fleeting minutes that she had thought he might be dead had been the worst of her life.

Deputy Woodward took them into the hospital and straight into the emergency ward. Nicholas was sitting up on a stretcher looking white, but otherwise none the worse for wear. At the sight of his mother, he smiled and let out a happy cry.

Neva raced into his small arms and lifted him off the portable bed. "Oh, Nicholas," she cried, her tears streaming down her face. "My baby. Are you all right?"

"I'm not a baby," the boy insisted.

Neva laughed at Nicholas's pout. "You'll always be my baby, whether you like it or not."

It was then that Tory noticed Trask. He was seated on a gurney, his legs dangling over the side. His hair was messed and there was a slight bruise on his chin, but other than that he appeared healthy.

Tory's heart leaped at the sight of him and tears of relief pooled in her eyes. Without hesitation, Tory walked up to him and stared into the intense blue of his eyes.

She placed a hand lovingly against his face. "Thank God you're alive," she whispered, her voice husky with emotion.

"You thought my constituents might miss me?" he asked, trying to sound self-assured. The sight of her in the noisy emergency room had made his stomach knot with the need of her.

"It wasn't your constituents I was concerned about, senator. It was me. I'd miss you . . . more than you could ever imagine," she admitted.

He cracked a small smile. "How did you know I was here?"

"I came looking for you." She wrapped both of her arms around his neck.

His eyebrows shot up, encouraging her to continue. "Because you were going to beg me to marry you?"

"Not quite. I was going to give you hell about cosigning on my loan."

"Oh." He let out a long groan. "I thought maybe you'd finally come to your senses and realized what a catch I am."

Her smile broadened and the love she had tried to deny for many weeks lighted her eyes. "Now that you mention it, senator," she said, pressing her nose to his and gently touching the bruise on his jaw, "I think you're right. You need me around—just to make sure that you stay in one piece. Consider this a proposal of marriage."

"You're not serious?"

"Dead serious," she conceded. "I love you, Trask, and though I hate to admit it, I suppose I always have. If you can see your way clear to forgive me for being bullheaded, I'd like to start over."

His arms wrapped around her slender waist and he

held her as if he was afraid she would leave him again. "What about Keith?" he asked softly.

"That's difficult," she admitted. "But he made his own mistakes and he's willing to pay for them. I only hope that he doesn't get a long sentence. I can't say that I feel the same about Linn Benton."

"I've already taken care of that. There are enough charges filed against him including blackmail and kidnapping to keep him in the penitentiary for the rest of his life.

"As for Keith, I talked to the judge. He's a fair man and I think he realizes that Keith was manipulated. After all, he was only sixteen when the Quarter Horse swindle was in full swing. That he finally turned himself in and confessed speaks well for him and he was absolved in the murder. My guess is that he'll get an extremely light sentence, or, if he's lucky, probation."

"That would be wonderful," Tory said with a sigh.

Trask slid off the bed and looked longingly into her eyes.

"Are you supposed to do that? Don't you have to be examined or something?"

"Already done. Now, what do you say if I find a way to get released from the hospital and you and I drive to Reno tonight and get married?"

"Tonight?" She eyed him teasingly. "Are you sure you're up to it?"

"A few cracked ribs won't slow me down." He nuzzled her neck. "Besides I'm not taking a chance that you might change your mind."

"Never," she vowed, placing her lips on his. "You're stuck with me for the rest of your life, senator."

"What about the Lazy W?"

"I guess I can bear to be away from it for a little

while," she said. "Just as long as I know that we'll come back home after you've finished terrorizing Capitol Hill."

"That might be sooner than you know. I'm up for reelection pretty soon."

"And if I get lucky, you'll lose, right?"

Trask laughed and held her close. "If you get lucky, we'll be in Reno by morning," he whispered against her ear.

"Trask!" Neva, holding a tired Nicholas in her arms, ran up to her brother-in-law. "Thank you," she said, her joy and thanks in her eyes. Her smile trembled slightly. "Thank you for finding Nicholas."

Trask grinned at Nicholas and rumpled his hair. "Anytime," he said. "We good guys have to stick together, don't we?"

"Right, Uncle Trask. Come on, Mom, you promised me an ice-cream cone."

"That I did," Neva said, shaking her head. "Now all I have to do is find an all-night drive-in. Want to come along?"

"Please, Uncle Trask?" Nicholas's eyes were bright with anticipation.

Trask shook his head. "Another time, Nick." Trask looked meaningfully at Tory. "Tonight I've got other plans. Something that can't be put off any longer."

Neva's smile widened and she winked at Tory. "I'll see you later," she said. "Good luck." With her final remark, she packed her son out of the hospital.

"So now it's just you and me," Trask said. "The way it should have been five years ago."

"Senator McFadden?" A nurse called to him. "If you just sign here, you're free to go."

Trask signed the necessary forms with a flourish. "Let's get out of here," he whispered to Tory, gently pulling on her hand and leading her out of the building.

"You're sure about this, aren't you?" he asked, once they had crossed the parking lot and were seated in his Blazer.

"I've never been more sure of anything in my life," she vowed. "I've had a lot of time alone to think. And even though I tried to tell myself otherwise, even as late as this afternoon, I discovered that I loved you. There was a minute when I thought you were dead . . . and . . . I can't tell you how devastated I was. Thank God you're alive and we can be together."

He lifted his hands and held her face in both palms. "This is for life, you know. I won't ever let you go."

"And I won't be running, senator."

When his lips closed over hers. Tory gave herself up to the warmth of his caress, secure in the knowledge that she would never again be without the one man she loved with all her heart.

Zachary's Law

Chapter One

THE REALIZATION THAT Zachary Winters was Lauren's last hope, perhaps her only chance of ever seeing her children again, was a grim but undeniable conclusion. And Lauren was stuck with it.

Swallowing hard, she withdrew her keys from the ignition of the car and closed her eyes, fighting a growing sense of desperation. The tears threatening her green eyes were as hot and fresh as they'd been for nearly a year, but she refused to give in to the overwhelming desire to cry.

How many tears had she already wasted? How many times had her hopes of finding her children soared only to be dashed against the cold, cruel stones of reality?

This time, she silently vowed to herself, she wouldn't fail. And if Zachary Winters was her only hope of finding Alicia and Ryan, then Lauren would have to plead her case to him and ignore the rumors and mystery surrounding the roguish lawyer.

As she stepped out of the car, Lauren realized just how little she knew about the man who held her destiny in his hands. What she had pieced together in the last two weeks was sketchy. Rumor had it that at one time, long before she had moved back to Portland, Seattle-born Zachary Winters had been one of the finest attorneys in the Pacific Northwest. However, because of some scandal revolving around his dead wife, Winters's practice, as well as his name, had suffered.

The tarnish on Zachary Winters's reputation didn't deter Lauren, however. Her only concern was for the welfare of her children. Nothing else mattered. If there was a way to reach Winters and interest him in her case, she would find it. She had no choice; her options had run out.

Lauren walked the short distance from her car to the Elliott Building, where the offices of Winters and Tate were housed. It began to rain, and though it was only mid-October, the chilling promise of winter lingered in the wind blowing across the murky Willamette River. Gray clouds shrouded the city of Portland, and water collected in clear pools on the uneven concrete sidewalk.

Lauren didn't notice. She gathered her raincoat more closely around her and took in a long breath as she approached the brick building located in the heart of Old Town on the western shores of the river.

Old Town was slowly being renovated and older, once decrepit buildings were being revamped into their original grandeur. The clean lines of contemporary concrete and steel skyscrapers towered over their older, Victorian counterparts and gave the city an eclectic blend of modern sophistication and turn-of-the-century charm.

The oak and glass doors of the once elegant Elliott Building groaned as Lauren shouldered her way into the office building. Without glancing around the interior of the lobby, she strode into a waiting elevator car and pushed the button for the eighth floor. As the elevator ascended, she leaned against the paneled walls and steeled herself against the possibility of rejection by the one man who could help her. What if Winters refused the case? Despite her determination, there was a chance that the unpredictable attorney would close the door in her face . . . and destroy the little remaining hope she had of seeing Alicia and Ryan again. New fear, ice cold and desperate, clutched at her heart. She closed her eyes for a second and tried to pick up the shattered pieces of her life.

It had been a little over a year and the pain was as fresh as if it had been only yesterday when she had opened the door of the house and found that everything was gone . . . including her beloved children.

The elevator stopped with a jolt and Lauren was forced back to reality. The soft line of her jaw hardened, and her fingers whitened as she clutched her purse. Resolutely, she walked down a short hallway before hesitating slightly at the glass door. *Please be here, Zachary Winters. I need you,* she thought before leaning heavily on the door and pushing her way inside the sparse suite of offices.

A red-haired woman whose unlined face indicated that she was no older than twenty-five looked up from the scattered paperwork on her desk and smiled pleasantly. "May I help you?"

Lauren returned the smile uneasily. "I'd like an appointment with Mr. Winters. My name is Lauren Regis."

Recognition flashed in the secretary's gray eyes at the mention of Lauren's name. Her brows pulled into an anxious frown. "Ms. Regis. You've called the office, haven't you?"

"Several times," Lauren replied. "Is Mr. Winters in?"

The redhead, whose brass name plate indicated that she was Amanda Nelson, shook her head, and her smile faded slightly. "I'm sorry, but I don't expect Mr. Winters this morning."

Lauren's piercing green eyes never wavered from the

woman's concerned face. Amanda Nelson seemed more than slightly perturbed.

"And he wasn't in yesterday or the day before or the day before that. Is he out of town?" Lauren asked.

There was a hint of defiance in Ms. Nelson's even features. "No. What Mr. Winters is—is busy."

Lauren's dark eyebrows arched at the pointed remark. "I don't mean to be pushy, Ms. Nelson, but it's very important that I speak with Mr. Winters," she explained, glancing at the empty reception area before returning to the secretary's face. "Is it possible to make an appointment with him?"

Amanda tapped her pencil on the desk. "As I said, he's very busy. Let me give Mr. Winters your number, and he'll arrange an appointment with you at a time convenient for you both."

"Can't *you* do that?" Lauren asked, wondering at the odd procedure. Her voice was tiredly impatient. She was weary of playing cat-and-mouse games with the man.

Amanda Nelson managed a stiff smile, and her composure slipped a bit. "Usually I can. But right now Mr. Winters is unavailable. Let me take your card and number."

"No."

"Pardon me?" The secretary's eyes hardened.

"I phoned last week and left my number; Mr. Winters didn't bother to call. I phoned again two days ago . . ."

The secretary didn't seem surprised. "And Mr. Winters didn't bother to contact you?" she asked, already surmising the answer.

"No."

Amanda's lips pursed in frustration, and Lauren had a premonition that there was something intangibly but undeniably wrong in the law offices of Winters and Tate.

"I suppose you hear this all the time," Lauren said,

her voice and eyes softening a little, "but I really do have to see Mr. Winters as soon as possible. He's been referred to me by my attorney, Patrick Evans."

At the mention of the prestigious lawyer's name, the corners of Amanda's mouth tightened.

"Do you mind if I wait?" Lauren asked.

Amanda eyed Lauren skeptically and then lifted her shoulders in a dismissive gesture. "I don't think he plans to come into the office," she replied.

"I've got a little time," Lauren responded firmly. "I may as well spend it here." Thank God for Bob Harding—the rotund co-worker had agreed to see all of her clients this morning.

Lauren dropped into a side chair and picked up a glossy-covered business magazine, casually tossing her thick auburn curls over her shoulder. Her nerves were stretched to the breaking point, but she carefully hid that fact behind a facade of poise. Her gaze swept over the top of the magazine, and she noted that there were no other clients in the reception area. The plush gray carpet was slightly worn near Amanda's desk, and the modern tweed chairs and couch looked as if they had seen better days. Spiky-leaved plants seemed lifeless and out of place on the eighth floor of the elegant old building.

The once revered firm of Winters and Tate looked as if it were slowly dying from neglect. Again Lauren experienced the uneasy feeling that something wasn't right in the hushed law offices.

If Lauren hadn't been so desperate, and if two other lawyers in town hadn't failed her, she would never have crossed the threshold of Winters and Tate. As it was, she had no other choice.

Bob Harding, the man now holding down the fort at the bank, had been the first to mention Winters's name.

Bob had insisted that Zachary Winters was the one man in Portland who could help her.

"I don't care what other people seem to think," Bob had stated emphatically, frowning and shaking his balding head. "If anyone can find those kids, Winters can. His methods might not be . . ."

"Ethical?" Lauren had asked, eyeing her friend as he tugged at the knot of his tie and adjusted his glasses.

Bob had pursed his thin lips and scowled at the ledgers on the desk. "I was going to say 'conventional.' In my experience with Zachary Winters, everything he did was aboveboard." Bob had looked through thick lenses, and his myopic eyes had pierced the doubt in Lauren's gaze. "And even if his methods were 'unethical,' as you suggested, would it make any difference to you?"

"No," Lauren had replied in a rough whisper. She'd been through a lot in her twenty-nine years. Even if Winters turned out to be slightly unscrupulous, she was sure she could handle him. Past experience had taught her well. Her first attorney, Tyrone Robbins, had proved to be nothing more than a self-serving, second-rate lawyer whose interest in her case was limited to his fascination with her as a woman. As bad as the experience had been, Lauren had learned a lesson and was still undaunted in her quest for locating her children. She'd been able to handle Tyrone—Zachary Winters could certainly be no worse.

"Then take my advice—talk to the man," Bob had insisted.

Perhaps she should have asked Bob Harding about the scandal that had nearly ruined Zachary Winters. But she hadn't inquired, because she hadn't cared. Her only thought was of finding her children.

Lauren had already decided to follow Bob's well-intentioned advice when the second attorney she had employed, Patrick Evans, had haltingly mentioned Winters's name less than a week later.

"Five years ago, I would have recommended Zachary Winters for the job," the sharp-minded lawyer had thought aloud, pensively rubbing his chin while studying his client.

"And now?" Lauren had asked.

Patrick Evans had wavered only slightly. "It depends on how serious you are about this, Lauren."

"Dead serious," she had returned, green eyes glinting with righteous indignation and defiance. "We're talking about my children, for God's sake."

Patrick had shrugged defeatedly, settling into his comfortable desk chair in his well-appointed office. "Then you might look him up."

Patrick had withdrawn a yellowed business card from his wallet and handed it to Lauren. "Just remember—things have changed for Zack. He might not accept the case," Evans had cautioned.

Lauren had left the opulent offices of Evans, Peters, Willis and Kennedy, Zachary Winters's card clutched tightly in her fist, with renewed determination. . . .

From somewhere down the hall a clock softly chimed, bringing Lauren back to the present. She checked her watch and realized that she had waited forty minutes already for the elusive attorney. As she shifted uncomfortably in the chair, Lauren straightened the hem of her skirt. The door from the outer hall swung forcefully inward, and the man she had been trying to track down for the better part of two weeks entered the reception area.

Zachary Winters's windblown sable-brown hair looked nearly black from the mixture of rain and sweat clinging to the dark strands. It had begun to curl slightly at the nape of his neck and near his ears. Moisture was trickling down his ruggedly handsome face and neck to collect in a dark triangle on his worn gray sweatshirt. He was breathing heavily from the exertion of his run along the waterfront. With only a fleeting glance and polite smile in Lauren's direction, he wiped the sweat from his forehead with his hand and approached the secretary's desk.

Amanda Nelson, who had seemed to lose more than a little of her composure at the sight of her employer, quickly managed a patient smile for him, while her worried eyes darted to Lauren and then returned to Winters.

She covers for him, Lauren thought in angry amazement. *Amanda Nelson is trying to hold this office together, and one of the partners in the firm doesn't give a damn.*

"Mr. Winters," Amanda was saying, loud enough so that Lauren could overhear the conversation. "I didn't expect you in today."

"I'm not." The tall attorney with the piercing dark eyes and rough-hewn features reached into a nearby closet, withdrew a towel, looped it behind his neck and wiped his face with the edge of the terry fabric. "I just thought I'd pick up the McClosky deposition—is it ready?"

"On your desk."

"Good."

Without further comment, Zachary Winters started down the corridor behind Amanda's desk. Lauren, whom the lawyer had barely noticed, realized that the man she had been waiting for was about to make a quick exit. As his long strides took him around a corner, Lauren grabbed her purse and stood.

"Is it possible to see him now?" she asked the nervous Amanda, who was staring after her boss and chewing on her lower lip in frustration.

"Oh . . . no, he's just in to pick up something."

"He's been avoiding me."

"I don't think so. . . ." But the expression on the young woman's face belied her words.

"It's important," Lauren stated, her nerves beginning to fray. She couldn't let him slip out a back stairway. Too much was at stake.

"Let me talk to him—"

"I think it would be best if I handled it myself," Lauren decided, and without waiting for the secretary's approval, she strode down the short hall in the direction of the retreating attorney.

"Wait a minute—"

Lauren ignored Amanda's command and rounded the corner, only to stop abruptly. Zachary Winters filled the hallway. He was leaning against the windowsill, stretching tired leg muscles. His hands were braced against the painted sill, and his head was lowered between broad, muscular shoulders.

His faded navy-blue running shorts were wet and clung to his buttocks. Lean, well-muscled thighs strained as the cramps from the long run slowly eased out of his calves.

Lauren's eyes fastened on the straining features of his face. "Mr. Winters?"

He lifted his head, turned his near black eyes on her and managed a slightly embarrassed smile as he straightened. Though he was more interested in relieving the tension from the back of his neck with his fingers, he cocked a dark, inquisitive brow in her direction. "Yes?" he replied in a clipped voice.

It was apparent she was disturbing him, but Lauren extended her hand and met his slightly inquisitive stare. "I'm Lauren Regis." Winters's rugged features didn't indicate that he had ever heard of her before—or that he cared. "I've been trying to reach you for over two weeks."

His dark, knowing eyes were rimmed with ebony-colored lashes and guarded by thick, slightly arched brows. They glimmered with respect when he took her small palm in his strong fingers and gave it a cursory shake.

The man staring at her was a far cry from what she had expected. He smelled faintly of fresh rain mingled with the earthy scent of musk, and he wore an inquisitive, slightly cynical smile on his handsome face.

In Lauren's mind Zachary Winters had worn an expensively tailored three-piece suit and polished leather shoes; he'd radiated a formidable self-assurance, wielded a deadly charm . . . Or so she'd hoped.

"I told her you were busy," the secretary explained nervously as she approached, obviously trying to protect her boss and provide him with an easy excuse to avoid Lauren if he wanted to. Amanda's lips were compressed in a thin, worried line.

Winters's interested grin widened to a dazzling smile, and he held up a silencing palm in the redhead's direction. "It's all right, Mandy," he said, his quiet brown eyes never leaving the elegant contours of Lauren's face. "I've got a few minutes—I can talk to Ms. Regis. We'll be in my office."

Amanda started to protest but thought better of it when she caught her employer's warning glance.

Zachary's gaze returned to Lauren. "Right down the hall, first door on the left. . . ." He nodded in the direction of his office and smiled at Lauren. "We can talk now, if it's convenient."

Relief swept over Lauren. Maybe now, after a long, agonizing year of running in circles, she would, with the help of this man, find the path leading to Alicia and Ryan.

ZACHARY WINTERS FELT an uneasy stirring at the sight of the proud woman standing before him. There was an intriguing sadness in her soft green eyes that suggested she'd been through more than her share of pain. The defiant tilt of her finely sculpted chin and the cautious arch of her dark brows lent a quiet vulnerability to her air of sophistication.

Though he knew instinctively that he should dismiss Lauren Regis and whatever business she'd her mind set on, Zachary found it difficult. Her eyes were the most intriguing shade of green he had ever seen. Round and softened by the gentle sweep of dark lashes, they were darkened by an intelligence and pride that he didn't often find in the opposite sex. It was a rare quality in a woman, and it touched a very dark and primitive part of him. A seductive mystique was evidenced by the pout on her lips, and her auburn hair fell around her face in somewhat tousled, layered curls that added the right amount of sophistication to the soft allure of her eyes.

You're a fool, he thought inwardly, *a damned fool who's intrigued by a beautiful face. Didn't you learn your lesson five years ago—with Rosemary?*

ZACHARY LED HER to an inauspicious office near the back of the building. Though it had a window view of the Broadway Bridge spanning the dark Willamette River, the office itself was a small, confining room littered with documents and worn law books.

Despite the austere suite of offices and Winters's attempts to brush her off, Lauren began to feel hopeful.

Maybe, at last, she'd found someone who could help her. She tried to temper that hope with reality. *Don't expect miracles,* she silently cautioned herself. *You've been this far before, and where did it lead? Only to a dead end.* She couldn't begin to count the times in the last year that all her hopes had been scattered like dry leaves in the wind. Each time she'd had to start the agonizing search for her children all over again.

"Have a seat," the lawyer suggested as he scooped up a stack of law journals haphazardly occupying one of the leather side chairs near his desk. He opened the window a crack, letting the brisk autumn breeze filter into the airless room, then placed the journals on the floor near a crowded bookcase. When he settled into the desk chair, it groaned as if unaccustomed to his weight. Zachary rotated his head to wipe a fresh accumulation of sweat from his brow with the towel still draped around his neck, then once again faced Lauren.

She looked at the disorganization in the office and felt an uncomfortable knot forming in her stomach. It was becoming clear that Zachary Winters practiced very little law these days. All the mysterious rumors surrounding the man came hauntingly to mind, and she frowned at the papers strewn on his desk. The untidiness of the office and the studious gaze of the attorney made her uncomfortable.

The lawyer must have read her thoughts. "Maid's day off," he explained with a charming, slightly rueful smile. After straightening a few papers on the desk, he looked around his office as if noticing the clutter for the first time.

Lauren sat on the edge of her chair and dropped her hands into her lap. She wondered if she had made a mistake in forcing herself upon the lawyer . . . jogger . . . whatever he was.

"What can I do for you?" Winters asked as he pushed up the sleeves of his sweatshirt to expose tanned, rock-hard forearms. He leaned back in the desk chair.

Lauren drew a long breath. "Mr. Winters—"

"Zachary." When she didn't immediately respond, he grinned. It was a killer grin—slightly off-center but devastating nevertheless—and it did strange things to her insides. When he used it in court, it probably coaxed witnesses into divulging secrets better left unsaid. "It just makes things simpler."

She nodded, slightly taken aback by his lack of formality. She needed a lawyer—a strong, decisive attorney who would be ruthless in his quest for the truth and single-minded in his search for her children. The man sitting before her, wearing jogging shorts and a sweatshirt, didn't fit the image she had in mind.

"So—you need an attorney. Right?" His interest appeared genuine as his brown eyes met hers.

"Yes. Patrick Evans recommended you." At the mention of the other attorney's name, Zachary flinched. "He gave me your card." She handed the yellowed business card to Zachary, who extracted a pair of glasses from his top desk drawer, studied the embossed card and set it aside.

"You're a client of Pat's?"

"I was."

Zachary's fingers drummed nervously on the arm of his chair, but his eyes never left Lauren's face. "And he couldn't help you?"

"No," she whispered, avoiding his probing stare. The lump in her throat made speech difficult. "And . . . your name came up in another conversation."

"Go on."

"I work with Bob Harding. He told me that you were the one man in Portland who might be able to help me."

Zachary nodded curtly, removed his reading glasses and set them on a stack of legal documents on the corner of his desk. "That was several years ago!"

"He insists you're the best in Portland."

A humbling grin spread across the attorney's bold features. "Like I said, a lot of time has passed since I worked on Bob's case—water under the bridge."

"I need help," Lauren stated, suddenly fearing that he was about to turn down her request. Her heart thudded painfully in her chest at the thought of another dead end. This man was about to close the door again on her chances of finding the children, unless she could convince him of the desperation of her plight.

Zachary inclined his head, encouraging her to continue.

"You see . . . my husband . . . my ex-husband, kidnapped my children." She tried in vain to keep her voice from shaking, and her hands trembled in her lap.

Her green eyes turned cold as the bitterness she felt at the injustice of her situation deepened. It was still difficult to talk about the circumstances that had left her feeling bereft and empty.

Zachary's eyes glittered with concern, and his square jaw tightened a fraction. "How long ago was this?"

"A little over a year—about thirteen months," she whispered, tears gathering in the corners of her eyes.

He expelled a long whistle. "And so why did you wait this long to start looking for them?"

"I didn't! I've spent every waking moment of the last year searching for them. I hired a private investigator and two other attorneys." *All who failed miserably,* she added silently.

"One being Pat Evans."

"Yes."

"And the other?"

Lauren swallowed the sickening feeling rising in her throat at the thought of the first man she had enlisted to help her. "Tyrone Robbins," she replied.

Zachary's lips twisted downward at the familiar name. "Robbins? How did you end up with him?"

"I didn't. I started with him . . . It . . . our professional relationship, that is, didn't work out." *Not by a long shot.*

"I'll bet," Zachary mumbled as if to himself, and his dark eyes flashed with scorn.

He waited for a further explanation, but Lauren didn't elaborate. She wasn't about to let what had transpired between herself and Tyrone Robbins cloud the current issue—the *only* issue that mattered. She wanted Zachary Winters to help her find Alicia and Ryan, nothing more. The problem with Tyrone Robbins she could handle herself.

A muscle worked convulsively in the corner of Zachary's jaw as he tried to push aside his personal feelings for Tyrone Robbins. "I assume, because you're here, that both your previous attorneys came up empty-handed," Zachary surmised. He swiveled in the desk chair and stared out the window as he pondered the problem at hand. Lauren's case wasn't the first of this type to cross his desk. But they never got any easier. And they only served to remind him of his own tragic past.

"Doug didn't leave any clues."

"Doug is—was your husband?"

"Yes."

Zachary turned to face her again. "Do you keep in contact with any of your husband's family—his parents . . . a brother, sister, cousin, anyone?"

Lauren shook her head and her auburn curls fell forward. The feeling of utter hopelessness she had learned to live with overtook her. "Doug had no brothers or sisters, and his parents were killed when he was young. The only family he has is the children."

Zachary tapped his fingers thoughtfully over his lips. "What about close friends?"

Again Lauren shook her head. "We hadn't lived in Portland long enough to make any really close friends. I called all the people we knew, everyone I could think of—even people I hadn't met, people who had sent Christmas cards to Doug—but no one knew where he was, or at least they wouldn't tell me."

"How long had you been divorced?" Zachary asked, his eyes glinting fiercely.

"About six months . . . but we had been separated for nearly a year." She didn't understand his sudden wariness but was thankful that he was interested. If only he would help her find Alicia and Ryan.

"And you had custody of the kids—right?"

"Yes. He came and took them, supposedly for a weekend at the coast and . . . and . . . he never came back."

"What about a forwarding address?"

"General delivery, here in Portland." She stood and looked out the window. Her shoulders sagged with the weight of the memory. "A private investigator, a man hired by Patrick Evans, tried to track him down, and couldn't."

Zachary frowned and rubbed his chin. "But school records—"

"Alicia was just about to enter kindergarten and Ryan was just two." Lauren's lips quivered slightly, and tears welled in the corners of her eyes. "He took my babies," she whispered, swallowing hard. Her fingers curled into fists of frustration and helplessness. "He took them, and he has no intention of ever bringing them back!"

Zachary rubbed his chin, and a muscle began to work

in the corner of his jaw. "What about work records? Your husband's employer must have had to send him withholding statements, in order that he prepare his taxes."

"He worked for Evergreen Industries. They haven't heard from him. And I didn't get any further with the IRS or the Social Security Administration." She shrugged her shoulders. "Either he hasn't yet filed a tax return . . . or the IRS hasn't processed it . . . or they're not telling me where he is." Her lips trembled slightly, and she ran her fingers through her hair. "For all I know, he could have changed his name, used an alias or left the country . . ."

Zachary took a long, steadying breath. His dark gaze held hers, and the look on his face was serious but filled with compassion. He phrased the next question carefully. "Lauren," he said softly, aware that she was near tears and damning himself for feeling compelled to explore every angle to her story, "have you considered the possibility that your children might not be alive?"

"No!" She let out a shuddering sigh and lowered her eyes. "Oh, dear God," she murmured. "I . . . I just can't believe that." She shook her head in physical denial of her blackest fears. For a moment she thought she might break down completely.

Zachary cursed himself silently and felt an overwhelming urge to comfort her. When she lifted her flushed face, he saw that she was fighting a losing battle with tears.

"I have to find them, Mr. Winters," she said hoarsely, determination burning in her sea-green eyes. "Will you help me?"

Rubbing the tension from the back of his neck, he wondered why he couldn't just say no to this woman. His narrowed gaze held hers. "I don't know if I can," he admitted with obvious reluctance. "It sounds as if you've exhausted all your resources."

"Bob Harding swears by you," she whispered, desperation creeping into her voice.

"Harding's case was a simple matter of locating a lost relative, one that *wanted* to be found."

"Don't you think my children want me to find them?"

Zachary studied the anguished lines of her face and noticed the trembling of her lower lip. How easy it would be to lie to her, to accept her case, make a good fee, and then come up dry . . . just as the others had done. But he couldn't. Basically, despite public sentiment and a few skeletons in his closet, he was an honest man. And the thought that she'd sought help from scum like Tyrone Robbins stuck in his craw. To top it off, Pat Evans had had the nerve to recommend him; the wily s.o.b. had thrown a challenge in his face, daring him to accept the case. The entire situation didn't sit well with Zachary, not at all. "I don't know, Lauren. Your children were very young when they were taken away from you, and it's been—"

"A year. A little more. It happened in early September."

"So now your daughter is . . . what? Seven?"

"Six."

"And your son is three?"

"Yes," she whispered while remembering Ryan's cherubic face. How he must have grown in the past year. . . .

"They might not even remember you," Zachary said gently.

Lauren forced a sound of protest past the constriction in her throat. "They have to, Mr. Winters. I'm . . . I'm their mother, for God's sake." Her fist opened and closed as she tried to control the indignation and rage enveloping her. How could he sit there, across the desk, and slowly destroy all her hopes of finding her children?

Zachary felt as if a knife were being slowly twisted in his stomach. Old wounds were reopening. His eyes were soft but direct. "Look, I'm not trying to be cruel, but you have to understand what you're up against. For all we know your husband could have remarried and another woman is raising your kids."

Lauren's face drained of all color. Everything this man was saying brought out her worst fears. She wrapped her arms over her waist. "I can handle that," she said breathlessly.

"Can you? Can you come face-to-face with the fact that they might not want to return? That they might call another woman 'Mommy' and cling to her when you show up on their doorstep?"

Lauren was trembling. Fear, rage, hatred and jealousy roiled within her. Two large tears slid down her face. "I can handle just about anything, Mr. Winters, except not knowing what is happening to them." She brushed the tears away with the back of her hand. "Do you have children, Mr. Winters?"

He hesitated slightly, and his broad shoulders tightened beneath his sweatshirt. "No."

"Then you can't possibly understand the torture I've been living with." She raised her chin defiantly. "Usually I'm a proud woman, a woman who wouldn't beg a man for anything, but these aren't usual circumstances. I'm at the end of my rope, and I *need* your help."

He understood more than he wanted to admit. Zachary Winters had experienced more than one personal tragedy in his thirty-five years. He'd suffered the anguish of losing a loved one, had known the emptiness of living alone. But that had no bearing on this case. This time he wouldn't allow what had happened to him personally to affect his business.

His hands formed a tent shape under his chin. "I'd like to help you," he admitted with a hint of reluctance.

Lauren braced herself for the rejection she heard in his voice.

"But I seriously doubt that I can do what others haven't. I wouldn't want to mislead you, or incur expenses that may all be for the sake of a dead end. . . ." *Or be the one who has to tell you that your children are dead,* he silently added.

"I don't care," she insisted, placing her palms on the desk and holding his intense stare.

"I understand what—"

"No, you don't," Lauren cut in, her voice shaking as her palm slapped the corner of the desk. "No one can. No one who hasn't been a parent can possibly understand the loss—the pain—the agony of this nightmare I'm living.

"I was told by people I trust that you might be able to help me, and that's why I'm here, asking, *begging* you to help me. I love my children, Mr. Winters, more than I love anything in this life, and I'll do anything, *anything* to get them back!"

Chapter Two

ZACHARY WATCHED THE agitated woman in amazement. She rose from her chair and stood proudly before him. "I came here thinking that you were my last hope," she told him, her green eyes darkening with anger. "But maybe I was wrong. Because if you don't help me, I'll find someone who will. My children are alive, and they need me . . . and . . . and I need them. I'd go through hell and back to find them," she proclaimed, visibly trembling. "And I'll do it with or without you."

"I didn't say I wouldn't help you," Zachary said, his voice softened, calming. "I just wanted to point out the pitfalls we may encounter."

Lauren's heart was pounding so loudly it seemed to echo in the small room. "Does that mean you'll accept the case?"

"Let's just say I'll do some preliminary checking. If I think we have a chance of locating your children, I'll give it my best shot. If there's nothing to go on, I won't flog a dead horse." His dark eyes were sincere and honest, and they were sharply penetrating. "That is, I want you to know from the start that I'm not a magician. I can't make people appear out of thin air."

"Is that a kind way to tell me not to get my hopes up?"

"I just want you to be realistic."

"I am, Mr. Winters."

"A year is a long time," he pointed out. "And just for the record, the name's Zachary. Remember?"

"Zachary," she repeated. "Well, *just for the record,* I've lived that year, and it's been the longest of my life." Her voice had grown husky, but she firmly extended her hand toward the roguish lawyer with the windblown hair and worn gray sweatshirt.

He took her palm in his fingers as he stood, and the warmth of his hand filled her with renewed hope.

"I'm not making any promises, you understand."

"Of course." *How quickly he had interjected a legal disclaimer,* Lauren thought. Probably a habit of his profession. She withdrew her hand from his and rummaged in her purse. When she found the manila envelope, she handed it to him. In the slim packet were her only clues to the whereabouts of her children. "The reports from the private investigator and the lawyers," she explained, realizing how wretchedly thin the packet of information was.

Without examining its contents, Zachary placed the envelope on the desk. It blended with the rest of the clutter as if it were no more important than the legal documents littering his seldom-used desk. "I'll look over the reports, make a few calls and get back to you in a couple of days—or however long it takes. I'll need your phone number and address, and probably some more personal information from you, *if* I come to the conclusion that I can be able to help you."

Some of Lauren's fear and anger slowly dissipated. She managed a feeble smile. "My phone number and address, along with my business number, are in the envelope."

"Good."

He seemed satisfied, and Lauren realized that the impromptu meeting was over. "Mr. Wint—Zachary?"

His bold eyes darkened in response, and he arched a brow inquiringly. In an unconventional way, he really was incredibly handsome. And though she hated to admit it, Lauren decided that the ragged sweatshirt, windblown hair and lines of cynicism bracketing his mouth only added to his rugged masculinity.

"Thank you." Quickly clutching her purse to her chest, she walked out of the law office with the feeling that, if nothing else, she had one reluctant ally in the bitter struggle to find her children. Once outside the building, she felt as if she could breathe again.

Zachary watched her leave and again wondered what had possessed him to agree with her request. He generally made it a practice to avoid sticky family disputes. At least he had since Rosemary's betrayal.

"You've gotten yourself into a helluva mess this time," he told himself before getting up from the desk, stretching bone-weary muscles and walking over to the lower cupboard of his bookcase, which a few years ago had served as a private bar. The bottles within the cabinet were dusty. He extracted a half-full fifth, studied the label and frowned.

Swearing under his breath, he grabbed an empty water glass from the shelf over the dusty bottles and splashed a stiff shot of Scotch into the glass. Taking an experimental sip of the warm liquor, he returned to the desk and only then noticed that it wasn't yet noon.

"Bad way to start the day," he warned as he cleared a spot on the desk and set the drink on the worn wooden surface. He reached for the manila envelope, opened it and began looking through the sketchy reports from the private investigator. He frowned darkly when he came across a letter from Pat Evans. There was nothing from Tyrone Robbins.

"Great," he mumbled to himself when he found nothing substantial in the first few pages.

But when his eyes encountered the last page, he felt an unwelcome emotion sear through his body. His lips thinned to a hard line and he reached for the Scotch.

Attached to a plain piece of typing paper was a photograph of four people—the Douglas Regis family.

Zachary's gaze narrowed as he studied the photograph. He recognized Lauren. Though she seemed somewhat pale, her green eyes were filled with happiness. She was dressed in a loose-fitting sweater and comfortable jeans, and her auburn hair was pulled into a casual ponytail. Seated on her lap was a chubby, curly-headed baby of about six months. With rosy cheeks and two tiny teeth, the baby was laughing merrily at the camera. A little girl, the one he supposed was Alicia, stood near her mother and baby brother. Alicia had Lauren's fair skin, somber blue eyes and a shy smile.

Standing behind the small family, his hand poised possessively on Lauren's shoulder, was the man whom Zachary assumed to be Doug Regis. Of medium height, with curly brown hair, a tight smile and impeccable clothes, he seemed out of place in the photograph—a stiff interloper rather than an integral member of the family.

"You miserable son of a bitch," Zachary muttered before tossing the offensive photograph onto the desk and taking a long swallow of warm liquor. Every one of his razor-sharp instincts told Zachary that he was about to make a monumental mistake—one he might regret for the rest of his life.

The hell of it was that it wouldn't be the first time—and probably not the last.

With a sound of disgust, aimed primarily at himself,

Zachary finished his drink in one swallow. It burned the back of his throat and did nothing to quiet the demons shrieking inside him.

LAUREN FELT DRAINED by the time she made it back to the quiet, well-appointed trust department of Northwestern Bank. Located in the bank tower at Fifth and Taylor, the trust offices had been decorated in understated elegance. The furnishings hinted at a conservative opulence, from the brass lamps perched on the corners of the desks to the thick emerald-green carpet running throughout the sixth floor of the building.

Lauren paused by the receptionist's desk to pick up her telephone messages, then walked into her office. After hanging her raincoat on one of the curved spokes of the brass tree adorning her private office, she settled into the chair behind her desk.

She was just sorting through the phone messages when Bob Harding walked into her office and closed the door behind him.

"How'd it go?" he asked as he settled into one of the winged chairs near her desk and stuck two fingers behind his tight collar.

"All right, I guess," she replied with an uncertain smile. "What about here? Were you able to help Mrs. Denver?"

"No problem. She was just worried about the terms of her father's trust and the allocations to her children. One of the boys will be turning of age in February, and she doesn't want to see him get a lump sum of nearly two hundred thousand dollars."

Lauren nodded, understanding Stephanie Denver's concern. "Not much she can do about it, I'm afraid.

When the kid turns twenty-one, he gets his share of his grandfather's trust. That's the way Mrs. Denver's father wanted it." Lauren settled back in her chair and arched a dark brow. "Anything else?"

Bob shook his head. "Nope. It's been pretty quiet around here."

"Good. Thanks for bailing me out."

"No sweat." Bob's eyes narrowed behind his thick glasses. "So what happened with Winters?"

"He agreed to take the case," Lauren replied.

Bob's round face sparked with enthusiasm, and he slapped his knee emphatically. "I knew he would."

"He wasn't all that anxious. And there's a catch."

"Oh?"

"If he doesn't think he can locate the children after he's done a little nosing around, he won't continue." Lauren couldn't hide the note of concern in her voice or the worry in her large green eyes.

Bob let out a long sigh. "Same old thing." He nervously ran his fingers over his mouth, then noticed the defeated slump of Lauren's slim shoulders. "Hey, look, what are you worried about? Zachary Winters said he'll take the case. You're on your way." He winked encouragingly. "He'll leave no stone unturned, let me tell you."

"God, I hope not," she said fervently, pushing her hair away from her face with her fingers. "I should have listened to you when you first brought up his name."

Bob shrugged. "Maybe. But you thought Pat Evans would find them."

"I hoped." Bob made a move to get out of his chair, but Lauren lifted her hand in a gesture to make him stay. "You said that Winters helped you find your aunt, right?"

Bob nodded.

"How long ago was that?"

After hesitating for a moment, Bob replied, "'Bout eight years, I think."

"And how long did it take?"

"Six weeks—no, more like two months, I'd guess. We hired him in February, and Aunt Myrna was home by Easter."

Pensively, Lauren tapped her fingers on the edge of her desk. "Pat Evans also referred me to Zachary Winters," she mused aloud.

Bob nodded at the mention of the prestigious Portland attorney. The firm of Evans, Peters, Willis and Kennedy had referred many clients to the trust department of Northwestern Bank, and Evans sat on the board. Patrick Evans was one of the sharpest lawyers in the city.

"And?" Bob prodded.

"Patrick seemed to think that Zachary Winters wasn't quite as . . . dependable as he used to be. He said that he would have recommended Winters five years ago, but that things had changed for him." Lauren watched as Bob shifted uncomfortably in the winged chair near her desk. "And you said something about rumors surrounding the man and his wife—something about his being unethical."

"Unconventional is the word I used . . ." Bob corrected with a frown. "You were the one discussing ethics. And I thought it didn't matter."

Lauren studied her friend and tapped her pencil on her lips. "It really doesn't. I'd just like to know what I'm dealing with," she explained with a smile. "So what are we talking about here? Idle gossip? Or fact? What happened to Zachary Winters?"

Bob hoisted himself out of the chair and paced between the window and the door. He was obviously uncomfortable with the conversation. "No one knows for certain. . . ."

"But it had something to do with his wife."

"Right." Bob sighed, and his round shoulders tensed beneath his suit jacket. "Look, I don't really put much stock in rumors, and I don't know what happened . . . not for sure. I just know that Zachary Winters helped me when I needed him. As to all that business about his wife . . . it's just idle speculation in my book."

"But *something* happened to him. I was there, Bob. His office looked as if he hadn't been in it in days—maybe weeks. And his receptionist . . . Lauren shook her head. "That poor girl didn't know whether she was coming or going. She was as surprised as I was when Winters literally jogged into the office."

"I told you—he's unconventional."

"That you did." Lauren looked up at him. "Now, are you going to tell me anything else about him?"

Bob shrugged. "I don't know much more: When I dealt with him eight years ago, he had moved here from Seattle. He'd been in Portland about two years, I think. He was married, had been for a while, seemed to adore his wife—" Bob walked over to the window and stared at the gray clouds surrounding the west hills of Portland. Rain was slanting from the dark sky, and tiny droplets ran down the glass.

"The trouble started several years later, I guess. No one really knows what happened because Winters has been pretty closemouthed about it, but his wife died unexpectedly in a single car accident at three in the morning . . . somewhere on the coast."

"That must've been hard for him," Lauren whispered, feeling a sudden chill. At least she understood a little of the pain she had seen in Zachary's eyes.

"It gets worse."

"What?"

"Turns out his wife was pregnant."

"Oh, no." Lauren remembered the stiffening of Zachary's shoulders when she'd self-righteously asked him if he had any children. She closed her eyes again at the image.

Bob turned back to Lauren. "It wasn't more than three weeks later that Zachary Winters's partner, Wendell Tate, was found dead in his home. Overdose of some prescribed medication, I think. No note, but the police thought it was probably suicide."

"Oh God," Lauren murmured, wishing she'd never pressed Bob for the truth. Zachary Winters had suffered his own private hell.

"You may as well know the rest of it," Bob continued. "Seems that somehow Zachary blamed himself for both deaths. Who knows why? Anyway, he took it upon himself to see that Tate's kid, Joshua, finished law school and became a full partner of the firm within three years of passing the bar exam."

Lauren let out a weary sigh and stared blankly at the neatly stacked account folders on the desk.

"You asked," Bob reminded her.

"And I'm sorry I did."

"Like I said, no one really knows how much truth there is to all the rumors surrounding the man. For reasons known only to himself, Zachary prefers to remain silent about the whole thing."

"And in the meantime, he's let his practice slide," Lauren said.

"I don't know. The only thing I'm certain of is that if I ever need any legal or investigative work again, I'll contact Zachary Winters."

Lauren smiled at the portly trust officer. Bob Harding was certainly loyal. And that meant a lot. Without Bob's friendship, Lauren wondered how she would have made it through the past thirteen months.

The telephone rang and Bob moved toward the door. "I'll talk to you later," he said as he left the room. Lauren paused before picking up the receiver. Slowly, she took a deep breath and forced all thought of Zachary Winters and her children aside . . . for now.

THE CLOCK ON THE bookcase indicated it was nearly seven when Lauren walked into her small house in Westmoreland. It was the same house she had shared with Doug and the children. From the living room and front porch she could watch the ducks gather on the man-made lake, witness a softball game in progress or see children playing under the fir trees that shaded the small creek running the length of the park.

Things had changed in the course of a year; the picket-fenced backyard still had a swing set, which had become rusty from the rain, and the boards in the sandbox were beginning to rot. Still, Lauren couldn't bear the thought of removing her children's playthings.

The day had been long and tiring. Because she'd been gone from the office for nearly two hours in the morning, she had decided to make up for if by staying late.

She didn't mind. The nights alone in the house were the worst. It had been over a year and she still found herself listening for the sound of Alicia's ever-racing footsteps or the soft gurgle of Ryan's laughter.

Lauren couldn't move out of the house. There was always the possibility that Doug might return with the children or that Alicia would remember her home.

After taking off her coat, she walked over to the fireplace and studied the portrait of her children that sat on the mantel. Looking at the portrait was a ritual she observed every evening, and though it brought tears to her eyes, she couldn't take the picture down. It would have been like giving up. And that, she vowed, she would never do.

How was Alicia doing in school? By now she would be starting first grade, learning how to read, would know how to ride the bus, maybe be able to comb her beautiful dark hair by herself. And Ryan. He would be walking and talking like a little boy, no longer a pudgy toddler. A painful lump rose in her throat, and she closed her eyes and sagged against the wall.

"Oh, dear God," Lauren murmured, "let them be alive and safe and . . . and please let me find them . . . please. . . ." Her voice caught, and she thought of Zachary Winters. "He's got to help me," she whispered fiercely. "He's got to!"

Why had Doug taken them? she wondered for the thousandth time. The divorce was supposed to have been amicable, a friendly parting that wouldn't pit one parent against the other. Best for the children. *And a lie! Doug's lie.*

When she thought back to her marriage, Lauren shook her head in wonder. She'd been so young, and naive enough to believe in a romantic fantasy. It had all come crashing around her feet.

Lauren walked into the kitchen and put on a pot of tea. Her movements were automatic as she considered the unfortunate set of circumstances that had led her into marriage with Douglas Regis.

Lauren's parents had been happily married but poor. Her father was a vagabond who moved from city to city, always believing the grass would be greener somewhere else. Both her mother and father had adored their only child. Lauren never felt unhappy or unloved . . . until both Andrea and Martin Scott had died unexpectedly in a boating accident on the Willamette River.

Lauren, who was staying with a friend, had been told the news by the welfare authorities, since she was still a juvenile. Then she'd been unceremoniously delivered by a kind but busy social worker to her only living relative, a maiden aunt approximately forty years old.

Aunt Lucy hadn't been pleased to have a sixteen-year-old pauper dumped on her, and she'd made no bones about the fact. "It's just like your father to do this to me," the woman had complained, shaking her curly blond hair. Then, adding a heartfelt sigh, she'd said, "Martin never did have a lick of sense. Well, there's nothing I can do about it now, I suppose. Family's family."

Begrudgingly, Aunt Lucy had converted her small attic into a sleeping loft for her only niece, and Lauren moved in. Absorbed in her grief, Lauren didn't question what had happened to the few personal possessions left her. Much later she realized that Aunt Lucy must have sold everything and kept the money, which probably wasn't enough to cover the cost of raising a teenager for two years.

Lucille Scott was a flamboyant woman who despised responsibility and avidly pursued the good life, which was provided by several older gentlemen who were introduced to Lauren only by their first names. They provided Lucy with some relief from the boredom of a spinster's life and a low-paying government job.

It was obvious that Aunt Lucy didn't want or need an orphaned niece. Lauren promised herself that she would find a way to leave "home" as quickly as possible. She spent as many hours as she could at school, in the library or in her room with the books that were her escape. She applied herself to her studies with fervor, taking college courses offered by the high school while earning her diploma.

The scholarship she was awarded provided the funds for tuition and books, and with a part-time job, Lauren was able to move out of Aunt Lucy's house and into a small apartment near campus.

At the end of four years in college, Lauren not only had a B.A. but also was working on her master's. That's when she'd met Doug, an assistant professor of economics. And she'd fallen in love with his boyish smile and flashing gray eyes—at least she thought she had. During high school and college, she'd rarely had time to date. Doug Regis was the first person since her parents had died who had told her she was loved.

When she and Doug were married, she felt as if the world were at her feet. She worked until Alicia came along and then felt the supreme joy of motherhood.

The marriage had started to deteriorate after the birth of Alicia. Without Lauren's income finances were tight, and to make matters worse, Doug lost his job at the university because of budget cuts. Two years and several jobs later, Doug had decided to move north.

With each employment failure, Doug had grown more bitter. The pattern was always the same—no matter where he worked, he was convinced someone in the firm was out to get him fired. No job lasted more than a year.

Then he began to drink.

The small family moved to Portland just after Lauren gave birth to Ryan. Lauren was incredibly happy with her two children. Though a little worried about Doug, she was certain that here, in a new city, they could begin again and find the happiness that had begun to elude them.

She'd been concerned about her husband's erratic

behavior, of course, but was convinced that if given the right breaks, Doug would once again become the charming, self-confident man she had married.

When Doug found employment with an investment firm in downtown Portland, he and Lauren celebrated by uncorking a bottle of champagne, most of which Doug consumed himself. That night, while making love to Lauren, he unwittingly called her by another woman's name. The effect was chilling. For the first time, Lauren began to see Doug for the man he really was and not as the prince in a fairy-tale fantasy. He fell asleep, but she was haunted by the thought that once again she was unloved.

Doug's job with Dickinson Investments lasted less than six months.

When Doug came home with the news that he had been let go, he was already drunk. His tie was undone and banging loosely around his neck; his jacket was slung carelessly over his arm.

Alicia was playing in the backyard, Ryan was napping and Lauren was preparing dinner.

She looked up from the stove when Doug noisily entered the room and slammed his briefcase on the small kitchen table.

"It happened again," he said flatly. "Goddamn it, I knew that Dickinson was out to get me from day one!"

Although Lauren no longer believed that it was everyone else's fault when Doug was fired, she tried to be understanding.

"You'll find something else," she said with a reassuring smile. "You always do."

"Well, maybe I'm tired of working my ass off!"

Surprised by his vulgarity, Lauren leaned against the

kitchen counter and dried her hands. “I could get a job,” she suggested.

“No!”

“I’ve got a degree—”

“And two kids!”

“It would only be temporary.”

“I said forget it!” Doug raged. “It’s bad enough that I got canned, but then you come up with some goddamned idea about going back to work.”

“Just to help out—”

“My ass!” he exploded. “You’ve always expected so much from me. More money, bigger houses, more clothes—”

“That’s not true, Doug. All I’ve ever wanted was for us to be happy . . . like we used to be.”

His gray eyes narrowed. “Like hell!”

“I don’t understand what’s going on here,” she replied to his sudden outburst. His face was flushed with anger, and he was nearly shaking.

“Oh, no? Then let me tell you. You’re trying to emasculate me, that’s what’s going on.”

“Oh, Doug, no!” she cried, hurt that he would think she could be so cruel. Despite the unhappiness, he was her husband, the father of her children. “Getting a job . . . it was only a suggestion . . . to make things easier.”

“Sure.”

“What do you want me to do?” she asked, refusing to release the tears of frustration stinging her eyes.

“Lay off, Lauren. Just lay the hell off.”

He strode to the refrigerator and took out a can of beer. Pulling the tab and letting the foam spill onto the floor, he threw back his head and guzzled the cold liquid.

Lauren had never seen him so angry. It was as if he

felt it was *her* fault that he'd gotten fired. Holding her temper in check, she grabbed a sponge and knelt to start wiping the floor where he'd spilled the beer.

She felt a numbing pain in her hand when Doug kicked the sponge away from her.

"Stop it," she hissed, holding her hand and looking up angrily at him. "Get a hold of yourself."

"Ha!" He laughed unevenly, and when she started to rise, he pressed a booted foot menacingly against her abdomen. She stared at him, aghast at the threatening glitter in his eyes. For the first time she was afraid—for her children as well as herself. Never before had Doug threatened her physically.

"Let me up," she demanded, "and don't you ever, *ever* do anything like this again."

The heel of his boot ground into her stomach. "You're no better than your Aunt Lucy," he spat out, crinkling the aluminum can in his fist and tossing it toward the garbage can. He missed, and the can rolled noisily on the linoleum floor to rest near the sponge. "You're a whore just like she was."

Lauren's temper flared and she tried to rise, but his foot dug deeper into her abdomen. Doug seemed to take immeasurable pleasure in watching her futile efforts. "She was always looking for an easy ticket, too," Doug continued. "Some old John to keep her in negligees—"

"Move your foot," Lauren said, her voice filled with anger and disgust.

Doug smiled and ground his boot heel into her ribs. "I don't think so."

Knowing that it might infuriate him further, Lauren took both her arms and swung at his leg. At the same time she tried to slither backward. Doug's drunken state was his undoing, and he lost his balance. His boot gouged her stomach, but Lauren was able to rise as he came crashing down on the linoleum.

"Mommy. . . ." Alicia's worried voice and racing footsteps announced her entry, even before the screen door banged behind her. The little girl's eyes widened in fear as she noticed her father writhing on the floor, clutching his leg, his face white. When Alicia turned to Lauren, her lower lip trembled at the disheveled appearance of her mother.

"It's all right, honey," Lauren whispered, trying to sound calm as she reached for her daughter, and held her tightly to her chest.

"I'm hurt, goddamn it!" Doug screamed.

With an effort, still carrying a sobbing Alicia, Lauren went to the phone and called for an ambulance while smoothing Alicia's hair and kissing the top of her daughter's head. Once she was assured that the ambulance was on its way, she offered Doug an ice pack for his rapidly swelling ankle. Not once did she let go of her trembling child.

"It's broken, you know," Doug accused, wincing against a sudden stab of pain. "All because of you. . . ." He meant to say more, but the furious, indignant glint in Lauren's eyes stopped him. "I've lost you, too, haven't I?" he asked softly, and Lauren didn't have the heart to answer.

When the ambulance came, she clutched Alicia and Ryan to her as if fearful of losing them, whispering words of comfort that were meant for herself as well as her children. She waited nearly two hours before summoning up the courage to go to the hospital, where Doug was suffering from an acute ankle sprain.

It had been the first and last time Doug had threatened her physically. He had managed to get a job at Evergreen Industries a few weeks later, and Lauren sensed her marriage was slowly disintegrating. The new job wouldn't last; they never did. All the hope she had once harbored for herself and Doug was gone.

She had suggested that he get professional counseling, and he had scoffed at her and called her every kind of fool.

She had discovered that he was having an affair, and it didn't surprise her when he asked for a divorce. She didn't fight him. The marriage had been over for months. And despite all the pain, she had her children.

While the courts had allowed him some rights as a father, Lauren wouldn't permit him to be alone with Ryan or Alicia until he'd sought the services of a psychiatrist and apparently turned over a new leaf. She didn't doubt that he loved the children, and she knew that he would never hurt them. As he himself had said, they were all he had left in the world.

When he had come to take the children to the coast, supposedly for the weekend, Lauren had had no idea that he'd been fired from his job at Evergreen Industries.

She'd spent most of that Sunday working at the office, and when she'd returned home late that afternoon expecting Doug and the kids to be waiting for her, the house had been stripped of everything belonging to Alicia and Ryan—except for the one precious picture above the mantel on the fireplace.

That had been thirteen months ago. . . .

"Damn you, Doug Regis, damn your miserable hide!" Lauren muttered to the empty house as the teapot began to whistle and bring her out of her unhappy memories. She brushed the tears away from her eyes. *I'll get them back,* she promised herself. *As long as there's a breath of life in my body, I'll keep looking until I find my children, and I'll bring them home!*

Chapter Three

ON THURSDAY MORNING Lauren walked into her office and found a note on her desk stating that Zachary Winters had called. Her heart stopped for a moment as she stared at the slip of pink paper. Had he found something about the children, or was he merely calling to say that he'd had second thoughts and was dropping the case?

The phone number on the note wasn't the one she had called when trying to reach him at the office.

With trembling fingers Lauren dialed the number on the message and waited, eyes closed, silently counting the rings, until he answered.

"Zachary Winters." His voice was curt, authoritative and somehow comforting.

"Hi. This is Lauren Regis."

"Lauren." Did she imagine it, or did his voice soften a little? "I know this is short notice," he was saying, "but I thought it would be a good idea if we met soon. If possible, today. Maybe over lunch?"

Lauren's eyes slid to the calendar on her desk. She was scheduled for a trust board meeting at nine, and the remainder of the morning was filled with appointments. "Of course," she replied, mentally juggling the various meetings. "But I'm a little swamped. What time?"

"Whenever you suggest."

"I don't think I'll be able to get out of here until one or one thirty," she admitted reluctantly. Her heart was thudding erratically with the hope that he had found something, *anything* that might lead to the children.

"How about one hirty at O'Donnelly's?" he suggested. "Can I pick you up?"

Lauren hesitated. Zachary Winters's arrival at the office might cause undue speculation. After all, he *had* been one of the most sought-after lawyers in town a few years back. Lauren didn't like the thought of any idle gossip about her personal life by her co-workers. Bob Harding was the only employee of Northwestern Bank who knew everything about her past, and she preferred to keep it that way—at least until Alicia and Ryan were safely back with her. "I'll walk," she replied after an uncomfortable pause. "It's only a couple of blocks from here."

"See you then."

"Wait!" she pleaded, unable to contain her agitation. "Please, tell me. Have you found anything?"

"Nothing to pin your hopes on," he admitted, reluctance evident in his voice. "There's one more lead I want to check out before I see you. Maybe then I'll be better able to evaluate the situation."

A feeling of desperation seized her. "All right," she said. "I'll meet you at O'Donnelly's. . . . Right. Bye." Softly she hung up the phone. Zachary Winters was going to drop the case; she was sure of it.

The door to her office burst open and Bob Harding walked in, making a great show of looking at his watch. "You'd better get a move on, girl," he suggested. "Zero hour is less than ten minutes away." If Bob noticed that she was preoccupied, he had the decency not to mention it.

Lauren managed a thin smile and tried to hide her

depression. "You make it sound as if I'm walking into a lion's den."

"Near enough. It's D-day."

"Why so?"

"The Mason trust—remember? The heirs are suing the bank for the tune of two million dollars."

"Oh, of course. How could I forget?" she replied, shaking her head. Her telephone conversation with Zachary Winters had driven everything else from her mind.

"Anyway, rumor has it that the president of the bank is on the rampage and ready to fire anyone connected with the account."

Lauren eyed her friend suspiciously. "What are you trying to do? Scare me?"

"No." Bob shook his head. "I just want you to be ready for the grilling of your life."

"The investment mistakes in the Mason trust occurred because the heirs chose a disreputable investment firm. They wouldn't listen to the bank's advice," Lauren stated. "You know that as well as I do."

"You have the correspondence to back you up?"

Lauren picked up the Mason file, patted the cardboard exterior and tucked it securely under her arm. "Right here."

"Good. At least we have some ammunition. Let's just hope that you can convince our illustrious leader that we were in the right," Bob said as he opened the door with one hand. He made a sweeping, chivalrous gesture with his arm. "After you."

"Coward." Lauren laughed and walked out of her office toward the boardroom at the other end of the plushly carpeted corridor.

* * *

THE BOARD MEETING went better than Lauren had hoped. As Bob had surmised, the small, wiry president of Northwestern Bank, George West, had been tight-lipped throughout the discussion of the Mason trust lawsuit. However, Lauren was able to placate him a little by giving him, as well as the other members of the trust board, copies of the correspondence that clearly proved the bank had not been negligent in handling the funds of the Mason trust.

Bob Harding had sat through the meeting alternately tugging at his tie and adjusting his glasses. He'd backed up Lauren's assessment of the situation, which had occurred three years ago, before Lauren was administrator of the account. To Bob's immense relief, Pat Evans, legal counsel for the bank, concurred with Lauren. George West relaxed as well when Pat convinced him that the plaintiffs didn't have a legal leg to stand on.

By the time the lengthy meeting had ended and Lauren had finished with two other short appointments, it was after one o'clock; Zachary was probably waiting for her. Quickly she forced her arms through the sleeves of her raincoat, grabbed her umbrella and raced out of the building into the Portland rain.

Lauren hurried along the redbrick-and-concrete sidewalk, unconsciously trying to sidestep puddles and slower pedestrians on her way to O'Donnelly's. She paused only to shake the rain from her umbrella before closing it at the door of the authentic Irish establishment.

Her cheeks were reddened from the brisk walk, and wisps of coppery hair had blown free of the sleek chignon coiled loosely at the nape of her neck. Disregarding her disheveled appearance and summoning her courage, she shoved open the cut-glass-and-oak door of the restaurant. The interior was dim and Lauren hesitated while her eyes adjusted to the light.

O'Donnelly's was a popular restaurant and bar in the heart of the city. Known for its spectacular clam chowder and imported Irish beer, the restaurant did a brisk business at all hours of the day. Today was no exception. Patrons crowded around the bar, and conversation hummed throughout the smoky interior.

Zachary must have noticed Lauren's arrival. Before she could explain to the inquiring hostess that she was looking for him, he strode up to the front desk, took her arm and propelled her toward a private table near the windows.

Lauren couldn't help but smile as she sat down. Unconventional was the word Bob Harding had used to describe Zachary Winters, and it fit him to a tee. Lauren found it difficult to imagine this rugged man doing anything as confining as studying law journals, pacing in front of the jury or straightening an imported silk tie.

Once again Zachary was dressed down, wearing soft brown cords and what appeared to be a blue oxford shirt peeking up from the crew neck of a cream-colored sweater. His jacket, which was tossed over one of the unused chairs, was a soft brown tweed.

"What would you like?" he asked, motioning to the menu as a slim waitress came to take their orders.

"Just a bowl of chowder," she replied softly. Her stomach was in knots, and she didn't think she could swallow anything. Nervously Lauren twisted her linen napkin in her lap.

Zachary frowned at her response and looked back at the waitress. "Two bowls of chowder, two salads from the salad bar, whole wheat rolls and two beers—"

"No beer for me," Lauren broke in, turning to smile briefly at the waitress. "Water will be fine." At Zachary's questioning look, she replied, "I have to go back to work. Besides which, I want to keep a clear head while I listen to what you have to tell me."

Zachary shook his head, but he didn't argue, and the waitress disappeared after pointing in the general direction of the salad bar. Zachary forced a smile, stood and helped Lauren out of the chair.

"I really don't think I can eat all this," Lauren murmured as she placed various greens and vegetables onto her chilled plate and walked slowly around the spectacular array of condiments and specially prepared salads in the long, ice-covered carousel that served as "the bar."

"Sure you can," Zachary assured her matter-of-factly. He flashed her a rakish smile that nearly took her breath away. For the first time, Lauren realized that she was responding to Zachary as a woman to a man. *I can't let this happen,* she thought to herself as she walked back to the table, incredibly aware of his presence at her side. *This is the man who might help me find Alicia and Ryan—purely professional, strictly business. No other relationship can cloud the issue. No other emotions can be involved!*

Back at the table, she met his dark gaze steadily and tried to conceal the fact that he was having such an effect on her. "Tell me what you found out," she requested.

The corners of his mouth tightened as he took a swallow of beer. "Not much," he admitted. "I sorted through all the reports you gave me."

"And?"

"And they're fairly complete. I looked for loopholes, anything that Pat Evans or his investigator might have missed. But—" he shrugged his broad shoulders "—as usual, Pat was pretty thorough. I can't say the same for Tyrone Robbins."

The bite of bread she'd just taken seemed to stick in her throat. "Mr. Robbins was my attorney for just a few months," she murmured unsteadily.

"Why?" It seemed an innocent enough question; Zachary displayed only mild interest.

"It didn't work out. I didn't think he was putting all of his efforts into locating my children." She kept her eyes lowered, staring at her neglected salad.

"He probably spent more time trying to convince you that it would help your professional relationship if you got to know him better personally—dated socially, that sort of thing." There was an underlying edge to his words.

More than that, she thought, but resolutely pushed the disturbing thoughts aside. "Something like that," she said. "Sounds as if you know Mr. Robbins fairly well."

Zachary smiled grimly. "I've had the pleasure of dealing with him in court a couple of times."

Swallowing hard, Lauren stared directly into Zachary's eyes. "So what does all this have to do with my case?"

His dark eyes hardened with self-reproach. "Not much."

"Meaning?"

"That I came up dry."

"Nothing new?" she whispered.

"Nothing." Zachary felt an overwhelming need to apologize and explain himself. A muscle flexed in the corner of his jaw.

"That just can't be. . . ."

"Look, I'm sorry." He noticed the skepticism in her gaze. *"Really."* He tossed his napkin onto the polished wood of the table and took a long swallow from his glass mug before setting the beer back on the table. "I rechecked everything—even pursued a few new leads. I talked to the people who had worked where your husband worked, called the list of friends, visited the IRS. And—" he shook his dark head disgustedly "—nothing."

Lauren had trouble keeping her voice from shaking. "What about the new lead you were talking about this morning on the phone? What happened?"

"Nothing's come of it." He folded his hands in his lap and studied her. "Why do you think your husband took the children from you?" he asked suddenly, his eyes returning to the elegant features of her face. God, she was beautiful. Escaping tendrils of red-brown hair framed her gently sculpted face, color highlighted the elegant curve of her cheeks, and her eyes. . . . God, those intelligent green eyes seemed to reach into his mind and read his darkest thoughts.

"I wish I knew. I've asked myself the same question a thousand times. . . ."

"Do you think he wanted them because he needed to be a part of their lives . . . or because he wanted to hurt you?"

"I don't know," she admitted, her voice rough.

Zachary's dark eyes held hers. "Do you still love him, Lauren?" he demanded softly. Though it had little bearing on the matter at hand, it was a question that had interrupted his sleep for the past three nights. He had to know what he was dealing with—what kind of emotions were involved.

Despite the urge to cry, Lauren managed a cynical smile. The question was so absurd! She shook her head, and the recessed lights of the restaurant reflected in fiery highlights throughout her hair. "No," she said quietly. "I wonder now if I ever did."

"But he hurt you?"

"Yes," she admitted, swallowing against the dryness in her throat. She lowered her eyes and pretended interest in her water glass. "There were other women."

Zachary stiffened. "Do you know their names?"

Lauren shook her head. "I didn't want to—tried to pretend that they didn't exist." She shrugged slightly and met his concerned gaze. "It was stupid of me, I know . . . but at the time, with the kids, I preferred to bury my head in the sand." She reached for her water glass and found that her fingers were shaking. "My idea of fidelity in marriage and Doug's were worlds apart." She lowered her gaze and stared briefly at the linen tablecloth to compose herself. Then, managing a frail smile, she took a sip of water.

"I want to help you," he insisted quietly.

"But you can't," she finished for him, her voice toneless. The fire in her eyes had suddenly died, and she was left with a cold feeling of emptiness.

"I don't think it would do any good."

"A waste of your time?"

"And yours. Lauren, look at me." Slowly, her green, lifeless eyes lifted. One of his hands reached across the table and took hers. "You're a young, beautiful woman. Your whole life is ahead of you." The conviction in his voice pierced her heart. "You can't live in the past."

"I don't," she replied, her throat uncomfortably tight. She fought the tears stinging her eyes.

"Then accept the fact that your children are gone."

"No!" Her hand crashed into the table, rattling the silverware and plates. Eyes, sparked with fury, burned into his. "I'll *never* accept that." Her back was rigid, her head held high as she stood. "Obviously you don't understand that I'd be willing to pay any price to find Alicia and Ryan."

Zachary stared up at her and watched in silence as two tears trickled from her brimming eyes. Suddenly four years seemed to slip away, and he was transported back in time to a place where another woman had once stood, head held high, her eyes condemning and filled with hatred.

"I just don't think that I can find them for you," he said as the image of Rosemary faded. "I wish that I could tell you differently, but I won't lie to you or protect you."

"Protect me?"

"From the truth."

"Which is?" she asked.

Zachary rose slowly from his chair and placed a comforting hand on her shoulder. His eyes were kind, as if he understood her agony. "That I don't think you'll ever see those children again, unless your husband wants you to. And that, after a year, seems very unlikely. Whether he enjoys hurting you or is afraid to come back, I don't know. But it's obvious that he doesn't want to be found, and while your kids are minors there's not much they can do about it."

She suppressed a sob of anguish and turned to leave the cozy restaurant, but the fingers gripping her shoulder restrained her. "I can't believe that," she whispered, still trying to walk out with as much dignity as possible.

Zachary was at her side, still holding her arm, unable to break the fragile contact. "Or won't?"

"Doesn't matter. I intend to find them."

"And when you do? What will you do? Steal them away from your husband?"

She whirled to face him, determination flashing in her eyes. "If I have to."

"You think he'd allow that to happen after he's been so careful to cover his tracks? He's cut himself off from all of his family and friends, just to insure his secrecy. You don't have a chance."

"The courts are on my side. They gave me custody."

"*In Oregon.* Unless I miss my guess, he's taken them out of state—maybe out of the country."

She'd heard it all before. Within the restaurant she could hear the sound of muted laughter, merry conversation and glasses clinking familiarly together. The sounds were distorted and vague, in direct contradiction to her feelings of despair. Shaking her head, she turned to face him, her green eyes filled with pride and determination. "Whatever it takes, I'll find them, and when I do, I won't rest until I bring them home . . . for good."

"Lauren," he said sharply, "think about what you'll be doing to those kids if you uproot them."

She withdrew as if she'd been struck. "I think about my children every day. I *know* they belong with me. *Not just for my well-being, but for theirs as well.* No one can love them the way I love them. No one." She was shaking with the intensity of her conviction. "The courts will agree. My only mistake was thinking that you would help me." With that, she turned on her heel and strode out of the restaurant and into the slanting rain.

The pain of his rejection overwhelmed her. She thought she had prepared herself for the possibility that he might not help her, but his withdrawal from the case seemed to bleed her soul of all hope. She threw her coat over her shoulders, clutched the lapels together and opened her umbrella against the rain.

When she returned to the office, she repaired her makeup and tucked the untidy wisps of hair back into the neat coil at the base of her neck. It took all her concentration to return to the problems in the office. The

Mason trust lawsuit paled in comparison to the problem for which she was steadily running out of solutions—that of finding her children.

It was nearly five o'clock when Lauren finally decided on a new, more visible way of locating her children. After looking up the telephone listing for KPSC television, Lauren punched out the number and prayed that someone in the news department would be able to help her.

What she was planning was a long shot, and if it blew up in her face, she would lose all chance of finding Alicia and Ryan again.

But without Zachary Winters's help, she had no other choice.

Chapter Four

ZACHARY HAD JUST stepped out of the shower when he heard someone knocking on his door. Swearing softly, he rubbed his hair with a towel, quickly smoothed the wet strands with the flat of his hand and stepped into his favorite pair of worn jeans. "Hold on a minute . . . I'm coming," he called in the direction of the front door as the loud pounding continued.

Who the hell would be stopping by his home? He could count on one hand the number of visitors he'd had since building the cabin four years ago . . . shortly after Rosemary's death. With the help of an able contractor he'd constructed a house better suited for the pine-covered slopes and sweeping farmland of Pete's Mountain, the edge of the grassland two short miles from the freeway leading to Portland.

He walked down the hall from the master bedroom toward the front door in his bare feet. The glossy hardwood floors felt cool and solid against his skin. Muttering ungraciously, he opened the door to find his partner on the doorstep. Joshua Tate, dressed as always in a crisp business suit and starched white shirt, was leaning on a roughly hewn post supporting the roof of the porch. His tawny eyes took in the state of Zachary's undress.

"Am I interrupting something?" he asked hopefully, a knowing smile curving his lips.

"Only a shower."

"Alone?"

Zachary laughed mirthlessly. "Yeah. Alone." He stepped out of the doorway to let the younger man inside.

"Aren't you supposed to be working?" Zachary inquired as he followed Joshua down the half flight of stairs into the living room.

"I am." Joshua took a seat on the leather couch and placed his briefcase on the coffee table. Snapping it open, he withdrew a sheaf of papers.

"What's that?"

"The McClosky deposition. The one you wanted so badly and then left on your desk last week."

Frowning at himself, Zachary shook his head. He hadn't been thinking straight for the past ten days. Lauren Regis had not only stolen his sleep but had somehow managed to muddle his usually clear thinking. He took the papers from Joshua's outstretched hand. "Thanks."

"No problem. I thought maybe it was time we touched base anyway." He tugged at his tie, tossed his suit jacket over the arm of the couch and loosened his cuffs.

Zachary shrugged. "I suppose so." Joshua Tate had learned his lessons from Zachary well, and despite everything that had happened between them, the kid seemed to like him. Zachary never really understood why. By all rights, Joshua should hate him, regardless of the kindness he'd shown him after Josh's father's death.

"Have you eaten?" Zachary asked, watching as Joshua casually turned on the TV and began shucking peanuts, just as if he owned the place. Like a kid coming home. That's how Joshua acted whenever he dropped by.

"No. How about you? Want to grab a pizza?"

Zachary shook his head and smiled. Along with his jacket, Joshua had cast aside any pretense of sophistication. "I've got some leftover ham sandwiches. . . ."

"Sounds great." Joshua was focusing his attention on the TV, catching up on the latest football scores.

McClosky deposition my eye, Zachary thought. The kid's lonely. And he'd probably hate being called "the kid." After all, Joshua had to be nearly twenty-seven. He'd passed boyhood years ago. And Zachary Winters was the only family he had left.

"Hey, Zack," Joshua called from the living room. "Ya got a beer?"

Zachary smiled to himself. Josh was so predictable. But smart. The kid had finished both high school and college early and breezed through law school—once Zachary had straightened him out. Joshua Tate wasn't much like his father.

At the thought of his ex-partner, Zachary's mood shifted. Scowling, he grabbed two beers and the sandwiches from the sparsely stocked refrigerator. He slapped the sandwiches onto a paper plate, tore off some paper towels from the roll and balanced the hasty meal in his hands as he returned to the living room.

"Take a look at this, will ya?" Joshua requested in mild admiration, eyes trained on the television set. "Isn't that the woman that Amanda was talking about—the one that wants to find her kids—what's her name? Regal, or . . . no, Regis—Lauren Regis."

Already Zachary's eyes were riveted to the television. He set the food on the coffee table without breaking his stare. "What the devil is she doing?" he demanded as he straightened again.

The television show was a half-hour program that usually dealt with some of the more pressing social issues of the day. At the end of the program, for one five-minute segment each week, the news team would explore a personal problem of a citizen who had not been able to receive help through the usual channels. With the power of the press behind it, KPSC news was sometimes able to get results for the victim. The problems televised had included discrimination, consumer fraud, grievances against government agencies and the like. Never before had Zachary seen a segment dedicated to finding a child abducted by a parent.

A muscle worked tensely in his jaw as he watched the raven-haired anchorwoman interview Lauren.

"So what you're saying, Mrs. Regis, is that your ex-husband, under the guise of taking the children for the weekend, took them away from you."

"That's right." Lauren's hair fell to her shoulders in soft auburn layers, and her cheeks were highlighted by a rosy shade of pink. Her emerald-green eyes, partially hidden by the sweep of dark lashes, shifted uncomfortably from the reporter to the camera and back again. She was, without a doubt, the most beautiful woman Zachary had met in a long, long while.

"That was over a year ago and you still don't know where he is?" the dark-haired reporter persevered.

"I have no idea." Lauren spoke softly, but Zachary recognized the underlying thread of steel in her voice.

"And no one has been able to help you find them?"

"Several have tried."

"Without any luck, I take it."

"None," Lauren replied softly. Zachary's shoulders stiffened.

"And you feel like you have nowhere to turn."

Lauren hesitated, and her neck muscles tightened a

bit, barely discernible on screen. But Zachary noticed, and his teeth ground together in frustration.

"Essentially, yes. I've tried the police, private investigators and lawyers. They've all attempted to help me, but so far . . . no one has been able to find even a trace of my children."

Her voice quavered, but she was able to hang on to her composure. When Lauren looked into the camera, Zachary felt as if her incredible green eyes were reaching into his soul. "Damn," he muttered under his breath, his eyes fastened on the screen.

"What about the juvenile services?" asked the reporter, continuing the emotional interview.

Lauren smiled sadly and shook her head. The anchorwoman stared into the camera. "Mrs. Regis would like your help." The image changed and a picture of Lauren's children flashed onto the screen as the reporter spoke to the viewing audience. "Remember, this portrait is over eighteen months old. It's the last picture Lauren Regis has of her children. If you have seen either of these children, or have some information as to their whereabouts, please get in touch with your local police or call station KPSC at this number. . . ."

"Son of a bitch!" Zachary cried as a telephone number for the television station flashed onto the screen.

"Is that the same woman?" Joshua asked, reaching for his beer and unscrewing the cap. "The one that got past Amanda—"

"Yes."

"And you turned her *down*?" Joshua didn't bother to hide his amazement. "Bad move, Zack." He lifted the bottle to his lips and took a long swallow, his tawny eyes never leaving the harsh features of his visibly irritated partner.

"There was nothing to go on."

"But a case like this—it could bring us a lot of recognition . . . publicity. Which, I might add, we could use. Find those kids and you'd be a hero. Maybe even get some national attention." Joshua Tate stared at Zachary over the top of the beer bottle.

"You're beginning to sound like a politician."

"Not yet, but just give me a couple of years." The cocky young attorney laughed, picked up his sandwich, then paused before taking a bite. His bright eyes narrowed pensively. "Seriously, Zack, I think you should call her and tell her you'll help her."

"Even if I can't?"

"Why the hell not? She's already been on television, for crying out loud. The media will jump on this faster than a flea on a dog. It could be worth a lot—and I'm not just talking about legal fees. . . ."

"I know what you're talking about and I'm not interested."

Joshua frowned in frustration. "She's a good-looking lady, and the publicity surrounding her case could really give us some media attention. It'll be Christmas in a few months, and you know how the press loves a tear-jerker type story at that time of the year. We could get a little recognition. . . ."

"Which we don't need."

"That's the problem, isn't it?" Joshua decided after taking a bite of his sandwich and washing it down with a long swallow of beer. "You really don't give a damn about the business. Or anything else, for that matter."

"I managed to save your scruffy neck, didn't I?" Zachary dropped wearily onto the couch and ran a hand over his suddenly tense shoulder muscles.

"You felt obligated."

Inclining his head in mute agreement, Zachary

reached for his bottle of beer, discarded the cap and took a long swallow. It helped . . . a little. "Maybe so. Doesn't matter. If I hadn't bailed you out, you would have been working on the other side of the law by now. You were already on your way."

"Yeah, well, if I forgot it then, 'thanks.'"

Zachary grinned wickedly. "You're a mean bastard, aren't you?"

"Guess I've had a good teacher."

The two men laughed together and finished the haphazard meal in silence.

Hours later, once twilight had settled and Joshua had returned to the city, Zachary threw away his well-intentioned restraint and decided to visit Lauren Regis.

THE TELEVISION INTERVIEW had been more difficult than she had imagined. By the time she got home that evening, Lauren was dead tired. After placing the portrait of the children back on the mantel, she took off her coat and sagged against the fireplace. "I hope I did the right thing," she whispered.

Then, trying to shake off the depression that had been with her ever since the interview at the television studio, she changed into her favorite pair of jeans and a soft lavender sweater before lighting a fire and preparing dinner.

By the time she had finished eating, the flames were beginning to crackle against the pitchy fir and the living room was scented with the odor of burning wood. She kicked off her boots and curled her feet beneath her in her favorite overstuffed chair. Tucking a faded patchwork quilt over her lap, she picked up the suspense novel she had just started reading and tried to concentrate on the book's reluctant hero.

Involuntarily, her thoughts wandered to Zachary Winters. What would he say if he had seen her plead her case on the news program? How would he react? Would he even care?

Probably not. He'd made it perfectly clear that he wasn't interested in helping her. He was probably glad to be rid of such a problem case.

But no matter how hard she tried, she could never convince herself that Zachary Winters was an arrogant, self-serving bastard so caught up in his own problems that he couldn't see his way clear to help someone else. She'd seen the regret in his dark brown eyes, the lines of pain bracketing his mouth when he'd told her that he'd found no new clues in the search for her children. He cared. Whether he admitted it or not, Zachary Winters cared!

With a start, she realized that she could fall for the handsome man with the roguish grin and the dark, knowing eyes. She'd been hurt and in despair when he'd dashed her hopes of ever finding Alicia and Ryan. But a part of her had been disappointed simply because his rejection meant she'd no longer be seeing him.

"Don't be an idiot," she admonished with a sigh. The feelings she had for Zachary were tied to the emotional situation regarding her children. She was confusing her hope that he would help her with something else. Because she needed his help so desperately, she had managed to convince herself that she was attracted to him. "You're a fool," she chastised aloud. "And you should know better—especially after Doug and Tyrone Robbins." At the thought of her ex-husband and the smooth-talking attorney who had turned out to be so much like Doug, she shuddered. It was ironic that she was attracted to Zachary Winters after her disgusting experience with Tyrone Robbins. "Damn it, Lauren, you're *not* attracted to Zachary Winters. You need him, yes, but *only* to find the kids!" *And he isn't going to help you, no matter how much you want him to.*

"No," she said aloud at the coldly betraying thought, as if by physically rejecting her feelings for him, she could expunge the frightening emotions from her heart. But even as she did so, she thought how easy it would be to fall in love with Zachary Winters. *You picked the wrong man once before. Whatever you do, don't make the same mistake again. It will only cause you more pain and won't help you find the kids. Besides which, he's out of your life. He made that choice, and he doesn't want to deal with you or your problems.*

A loud knock on the door caught Lauren off guard. She glanced at the grandfather clock mounted near the door just as it chimed half-past eight. She wasn't expecting anyone—who would be calling? And then she knew. It had to be someone with news of the children, someone who had seen her on television. Her heart began to pound in anticipation.

Tossing aside the quilt and suspense novel, she scrambled up from her favorite chair and forced herself to walk slowly to the door. Though she told herself to remain calm, she half expected a reporter from KPSC to be standing on her porch, ready to share the good news that the children had been located. Nervously she leaned on one of the long, narrow windows beside the door, flipped on the porch light and stared out.

Her heart nearly missed a beat as she recognized Zachary Winters. When he saw her anxious face pressed against the window, he smiled the same dazzling smile that had touched her heart before. Lauren returned his grin hesitantly.

Either he had seen the television program, or he had new information on the whereabouts of Alicia and

Ryan. Lauren's pulse raced at the thought. Her fingers fumbled as she unbolted the door and opened it.

"Hello, Lauren," he said, his eyes resting on the elegant contours of her face.

His effect on her was immediate—and this time, undeniable. "Come in," she murmured, and stepped away from the door, leaving enough room for him to enter.

His friendly smile faded somewhat as he walked into the living room and scanned the modest interior. The small, one-story, 1920s vintage house was decorated with a blend of antique tables, overstuffed chairs and baskets filled with leafy green plants. A small, navy-blue velour couch rested before the glowing coals in the brick fireplace, and a brass kettle on the hearth was filled with pieces of oak and fir. A slightly faded, cranberry-colored chair sat near a window, and a worn patchwork quilt was tossed haphazardly over one of the overstuffed arms. Small calfskin boots were placed near a matching footstool.

It was a warm room, quietly intimate. Gleaming hardwood floors were visible around the edges of a well-worn Oriental carpet in soft hues of blue and dusty rose.

Zachary's eyes shifted from the floor to the mantel, and he noticed the portrait of the children. He walked over to the fireplace and studied the picture.

"I saw you on TV," he said, getting straight to the point.

"And—what did you think?" Lauren returned to her position in the chair, watching his reaction as she folded the quilt.

Turning slowly to face her, he leaned against the red bricks of the fireplace and felt the warmth of the flames heat his calves. "I think it was the most foolish thing you could have done."

Lauren's heart lurched. "Why?" Slowly, she placed the folded quilt in a wicker basket.

"Because you just gave your husband a warning. If he lives anywhere around here—or somehow saw you on television—he knows that you're still looking for him." Zachary rammed his hands into his pockets in frustration. "And even if he didn't see the program, you can bet that someone he knows did. He'll be warned."

"It was a chance I had to take," Lauren replied stubbornly. "I'm running out of options."

Zachary's shoulders sagged, and he closed his eyes as he leaned the back of his neck against the mantel. "Oh, Lauren," he whispered in a caressing tone. "I wish I had all the answers and that I could find those kids for you."

When she didn't immediately respond, he looked at her once again and she saw the agony in his eyes.

"I can't give up," she said, her throat tightening with emotion. She swallowed hard and crossed her arms under her breasts.

Impatiently he raked his fingers through his rich, sable-brown hair. "I don't expect you to."

"And what, exactly, is it that you do expect of me?"

"I wish I knew."

"That, counselor, is called hedging."

He shook his head and smiled sadly. "Wrong. It's called the truth."

"So why did you come here tonight?"

"To apologize."

She raised her eyebrows inquisitively and with a hand gesture encouraged him to continue. Having him here, in her home, was doing strange things to her. She had to force her eyes away from the strong, sensual line of his mouth.

"I didn't give you enough credit."

"I don't understand—"

"What I'm trying to say, Ms. Regis, is that I want another crack at finding your children." He turned his head to study the photograph again, then returned his eyes to her face. "Maybe I *can* help you."

"Didn't you insinuate that it would be a waste of time?" she asked, barely believing her ears. Not only was he here, but he was prepared to help her.

"It still might."

"Then forget it. I want someone who's dedicated, who'll leave no stone unturned, follow any lead . . . I've wasted too much time as it is on attorneys and private investigators who squeezed me into their already full case loads."

"And I want a client who will put all her trust in me and not go spouting off to some two-bit reporter anytime the going gets rough. It's got to be my way or no way."

Lauren was held captive by the intensity of his gaze, mesmerized by the deadly gleam in his eyes. Someone had once said that he could be ruthless in pursuit of the truth. She hoped to God that it was true.

"All right," she agreed suddenly. Instinctively she knew that he was the one man who could help her.

"You'll call the shots and I won't do anything to sabotage you, even unintentionally."

Slowly he relaxed. "I'd appreciate that." Then, cocking his head in her direction, he asked, "Are you ready to get to work?"

"Now?"

"As soon as I get my briefcase out of the truck. Soon enough for you?"

She smiled in amusement. "You know how I feel about this. But before we get started, I want to know one more thing—what made you change your mind?"

He tensed slightly, and when his eyes searched hers, she felt as if he were reaching into her soul. "You did, lady," he said simply. His sensual gaze stripped her bare, and she caught her breath at the smoldering passion lurking within the depths of his eyes. "I want to help you. I fought the attraction I've felt for you and I lost the battle."

"Then . . ." she began, her voice a hoarse whisper. "It wasn't because of the television interview."

"That was the catalyst, but I would have been back, anyway." He thought fleetingly of Joshua's remarks about the publicity surrounding Lauren's case, but kept silent. In all truth, that had nothing to do with his reasons for driving to Westmoreland this evening.

"What made you think I'd agree?"

"Because you need me."

She couldn't deny what was so patently obvious. "All right, counselor," Lauren said with a smile intended to break the tension in the room. "How do we start?"

"It's simple. You make the coffee, and I'll get my notes and tape recorder."

"Tape recorder—why?"

"We're going to start at the beginning," he declared, his jaw tightening in resolve.

"But I've gone through this all before. You have the reports from Pat Evans and—"

"And I prefer to do things my own way. Now, do you want to find your children or not?" Without waiting for her response, he walked across the small room and went outside to his truck.

When Lauren returned to the living room with the coffee, Zachary was waiting for her. What was it about him that made her little house seem like home? Was it his dazzling smile, the bold thrust of his chin or his eyes, first compassionate and kind, then sensual and intimately dangerous?

He was kneeling on the hearth and placing fresh logs on the fire. The light, worn denim stretched across his buttocks, and his shirt tightened over his shoulders as he adjusted the logs with a poker. His masculine presence seemed to fill the room. When the flames began to crackle, he dusted his hands and positioned himself on the floor, his back braced against the bricks. "Not bad for a guy who never made it to an Eagle Scout," he said with a smile.

She laughed. "Not bad at all."

"Sit down, sit down, let's get on with this." He patted one of the cushions of the couch and accepted the mug of steaming coffee she offered.

"Cream? Sugar?"

He smiled. "Black."

Lauren sat on the couch facing him. She tucked her feet under her and watched as he took an experimental sip.

"Okay," Zachary said, crossing his legs. "Let's get started." He flashed her a disarming smile before assuming an expression of intense interest. "Why don't you start by telling me a little of your background and then explain how you met your husband, where he was from. I want to know where you met, who your friends were, who *his* friends were, where he comes from . . . everything."

She hesitated slightly as she realized how difficult it would be to talk about her personal life. With the other attorneys, telling her story had been strictly a matter of business, but she sensed that with Zachary Winters it would be different. With all of her efforts to convince him to take her case, she had begun to know him—more than she wanted to. Perhaps more than she should.

She held on to her cup and stared into it as she began to talk. She told Zachary about her parents' death, living with Aunt Lucy, going to college in Medford, and meeting Doug when he was an assistant professor of economics and she a graduate student. Tears filled her eyes when she told Zachary about the birth of her first child, and the happiness she experienced at becoming a mother. Then she explained about Doug's inability to hold down a job. She mentioned his feelings of inadequacy. The beginning of his drinking problem. The fact that he blamed her for his failures. Finally, she explained about Ryan's birth and the move back to Portland.

She tried not to leave anything out. Though her eyes burned when she explained about the frequent arguments, it wasn't until she repeated the story of the terrifying day Doug had lost his job at Dickinson Investments, when he had pressed his boot into her abdomen, that tears began to slide down her cheeks. And when she spoke haltingly of the day she'd come home to find that he had stolen the children, her shoulders began to shake and she could fight the stream of tears no longer.

Zachary had been quiet throughout most of her story, only interjecting questions to clarify something he didn't understand. He'd watched her fight a losing battle with the emotions ripping her apart, but he'd pressed her further, hoping to find anything that might lead him to her children.

She wiped her eyes and took a deep breath. "That was the last time I saw them—or heard from them," she said.

Zachary set his pad on a table nearby and crossed to her, placing his hands on her shoulders. "It'll be all right," he promised, tilting her trembling chin with one strong finger and forcing her to look into his eyes. "We'll find them."

"How . . . how can you be sure?"

He hesitated only slightly. Then his rugged features hardened with emotion and his eyes glittered. Lauren could feel the tension in his touch. "We'll find them," he repeated, his voice steely with resolve, "because I won't rest until I do."

A small, thankful cry broke from her lips as his strong arms gathered her close.

Chapter Five

AT LAST, LAUREN thought, *at last I've convinced him to help me.* Tears of gratitude welled in her eyes. For the first time in weeks, she was filled with hope.

Zachary held her gently, pressing his comforting lips to her forehead and gathering her close. She felt his strong arms around her and the seductive tease of his breath on her hair. She didn't withdraw from the embrace but accepted the strength he offered. It had been years since she had leaned on a man. Usually, she hated the thought of it, but with this enigmatic lawyer, her feelings had changed. Intuitively, she knew that accepting his strength wasn't a sign of weakness. For over a year she had depended only upon herself, and now, at last, she had a friend . . . an ally in the struggle for her children. Tears of relief slipped from the corners of her eyes.

Zachary's arms tightened around her slim shoulders. It was as if he were suddenly aware of the intimacy of the embrace and was struggling within himself to let her go. . . . Lauren recognized the signs of his conflicting emotions; they mirrored her own inner turmoil.

Zachary tried to restrain himself, but the feel of Lauren's body pressed against his chest brought back sensations he had thought long dead. *What the hell are you doing?* he asked himself. He wasn't usually a stupid man—he'd earned a reputation as an intelligent, sharp-witted lawyer by proving himself to be shrewd, intuitive and incisive. He recognized that holding Lauren was nothing short of lunacy; yet he couldn't release her. As crazy as it was, he wanted her, more desperately than he had ever wanted a woman before.

The salt taste of Lauren's tears lingered on Zachary's lips; the fragrance of her hair drifted into his nostrils; her soft breasts pressed intimately against his chest, forcing sensually erotic images to his mind—dangerous images that burned in his brain and would not be ignored.

The sobs that had been racking her body eased a bit as he held her, but still he found it impossible to let her go. His fingers slid up from her neck and wound in her thick auburn hair. God, he couldn't let himself get involved with her. . . .

Lauren must have felt the tension in his muscles, because she began to draw slowly away from him. What was it about her that made him react so irrationally? True, Lauren was a beautiful woman, but he couldn't afford to get involved with any woman, especially a client. In all his years of practicing law, he'd never succumbed to even the most tempting of advances from women who had employed him. Usually the ones who threw themselves at him were suffering emotional crises of their own, and in any event Zachary considered himself smart enough to avoid emotional entanglements with his clients.

Until now. But then, Lauren wasn't throwing herself at him. If anything, she seemed to be experiencing the same conflict that was slowly ripping him apart.

Lauren took a shuddering breath. "I'm . . . I'm sorry," she apologized, wiping the tears from her eyes with her fingers. "I didn't mean to get so upset."

"It's okay."

"You've had your share of emotional clients?" she asked, attempting to lighten the mood and dissipate the tension clouding the air.

The corners of his lips twitched. "A few. Comes with the territory."

Lauren nodded, once again experiencing the urge to weep. Her voice broke as she explained, "It's just that usually I'm a fairly rational person—"

"Except where the kids are concerned."

"Yes," she whispered. "Except where the kids are concerned."

Zachary cleared his throat. Thinking it would be best to put some distance between her body and his, he walked across the room to lean against the warm bricks of the fireplace. "Look, maybe we should call it a night," he said as he reached for his tape recorder and placed it, along with his legal pad, into his briefcase.

Anxiously, she searched his face for a clue of what he thought of her story, but his expression was unreadable. Now that she had explained everything, perhaps he could find the children. . . . She forced herself to ask the question. "Do you have enough information to go on?"

"No." He rubbed the tension from the back of his neck, and his thick brows knotted together in concentration. "But it's late."

Then he couldn't leave. Not yet. "I can make some more coffee. Please stay until you find something, *anything* that might help."

A look of tenderness crept into his eyes, and Lauren suddenly realized how desperate she must sound . . . how desperate she had become.

Zachary walked back toward her, reached forward as if to touch her shoulder, then let his hand drop before shoving it into the pocket of his jeans in frustration. "I'll come back," he said, fighting the urge to stay with her, "after I've gone over my notes and double-checked some of the places that Evans and his private investigator looked into."

"Will that do any good?"

His lips compressed angrily. "Probably not."

"Then why waste your time?"

"Because we don't have a lot to go on, Lauren," Zachary replied honestly. "I want to make sure that no one, including Evans, made any mistakes—overlooked anything."

"Surely Patrick Evans can be trusted."

Zachary glanced skeptically in her direction. "Can he?"

Suddenly Lauren felt uneasy. Zachary didn't seem to trust anyone. . . . But maybe that was good. "He's on the board at the bank. He recommended you," she pointed out. *For God's sake, Patrick Evans is a respected member of the Northwestern Bank Board of Directors as well as legal counsel for the bank. His reputation as a lawyer is beyond reproach!* "His reputation is—"

"A lot better than mine," Zachary finished for her. He scowled and his eyes locked with hers. "What about Tyrone Robbins?"

Lauren drew in a quick breath. "That was a mistake," she admitted, hoping to close the subject. "*My* mistake."

Zachary muttered something unintelligible that Lauren deduced to be profane. "And I'm just trying to be careful, so that we don't make any more mistakes. Doing things my way might take a little more time, but it'll be worth it."

"You're sure?"

"No, but I'll do my damnedest to get those kids back

to you," he promised with a slow, genuine smile that concealed all his reservations. "Trust me."

"I do," she replied, adding silently to herself, *whether I want to or not. You're my last hope. I hope to God that you're as good as Bob Harding and Pat Evans think you are.*

"Good. Then I'll call you in a couple of days." He strode to the door, and she followed him, placing a hand on his arm.

"Zachary?"

"Yes."

Lauren smiled, though her green eyes still glistened with tears. "Thank you."

His shoulders tensed slightly. He looked as if he were about to say something, and for a moment his eyes embraced hers. Then he opened the door, stepped into the night and was gone.

Lauren waited until the sound of his truck faded into the darkness. Then she locked the door and sagged against the smooth wood. Between working most of the day, being interviewed by the news reporter at KPSC and recounting her life to Zachary Winters, Lauren was exhausted. Ignoring the stack of dishes in the kitchen sink, she headed for the bathroom, pulling her sweater over her head as she went. Once there, she knelt by the tub and turned on the water, testing the temperature now and then by running her fingers through the clear liquid, as she had done hundreds of times while preparing a bath for her small children.

She could almost see Ryan's cherubic face as he splashed in the water, his blond curls becoming dark ringlets as he played. He kicked his legs, thinking proudly that he was swimming as he crawled along the bottom of the white enamel tub.

"He's not swimming," Alicia had said as she looked

disdainfully down at her younger brother splashing happily in the water. The little girl had sat on the linoleum floor surrounded by a mound of dirty clothes. As Alicia tugged on her dusty socks, she'd frowned disapprovingly at Ryan.

"He thinks he is," Lauren had replied. Ryan squealed happily, put his face in the water and then lifted it up again, his blue eyes shining.

"Good boy."

The pudgy baby grinned, showing off his two teeth.

"But his hands are touching the bottom of the tub," Alicia pointed out with all the wisdom of a four-year-old.

"That's the way you used to swim, too." Lauren pulled the hooded pink sweatshirt over her daughter's head and dropped it into the growing pile of dirty clothes.

"When I was a baby?" Alicia's round, earnest eyes delved into her mother's, and Lauren laughed at her daughter's serious expression.

"Yes, honey. When you were a baby."

The memory was so vivid that Lauren smiled to herself. Suddenly she noticed that the tub was nearly overflowing; she turned off the water and took a long, steadying breath. "I'll find you," she whispered fiercely. "I promise. This time, I'll find you, both of you, and I'll bring you home! This time I've found someone who will help me."

ZACHARY'S FINGERS TIGHTENED over the steering wheel and he cursed himself for being the worst kind of fool. For the first time in four years he had let his emotions get in his way and cloud his judgment.

"Son of a bitch," he muttered angrily. How could he have been such an idiot as to promise that he would find those kids? Hell, it was probably impossible. Doug Regis probably had them stashed away in the wilds of British Columbia or maybe even in the desert in Mexico. Or, worse yet . . . for all Zachary knew, the lot of them could be dead. And he'd been foolish enough to promise Lauren that he'd locate them!

His fist slammed into the steering wheel in frustration, and his eyes narrowed against the darkness. He had turned off the freeway and was winding his way up the familiar, unlit country road that curved up the gradual slope of Pete's Mountain toward his secluded cabin.

Why had he been such a damned fool? Maybe it was seeing Lauren on television, or maybe it was because Josh was right—Lauren Regis's case could be news. Big news. Or perhaps it was a chance to get back at Tyrone Robbins one more time. Whatever the reason, Zachary had made promises that would probably prove impossible to keep. Unless he got lucky.

"Boy, you've got it bad," he muttered to himself, diagnosing his problem as an unwanted attraction for Lauren. "Why should you think you can succeed when Patrick Evans gave up?" *And why did Evans recommend you in the first place?*

He turned on the radio, hoping that the throbbing beat of a sixties rock classic would drown out the unanswered questions spinning crazily around in his mind. It didn't. Zachary's thoughts flitted uncomfortably to Lauren Regis, her husband and her first attorney, Tyrone Robbins. How the hell had Lauren gotten involved with the likes of Robbins? he wondered, frowning. He told himself it didn't matter, but he could still recall Tyrone's smug face and the satisfied gleam in the younger man's eyes when Tyrone had served Zachary with the divorce papers four years ago. Robbins had had the audacity to come with the court-appointed messenger, just to witness the shock in Zachary's expression as he was handed the documents that had shattered his life.

"Happy anniversary, Zack," Tyrone had taunted, knowing that he had timed it so that Zachary was served the papers on the fifth anniversary of his stormy marriage to Rosemary. Tyrone had sauntered back to his car, smiling to himself as Zachary had stared numbly down at the documents in his hands, unable to believe that Rosemary actually planned to go through with the divorce. Less than a month later she was dead. Zachary wondered if Tyrone had taken the news any better than he had.

That's what you get for defeating the poor bastard so many times in the courtroom, Zachary thought. *And now it's your chance to get even—to get back at Robbins by succeeding where he's failed.*

So where was the sense of satisfaction, the lust for revenge that should be coursing through his veins?

He downshifted and turned into the lane that led to his house. His headlights caught the interlaced branches of the fir, maple and oak trees that grew naturally along the gravel drive. Finally he pulled the truck up near the garage and hopped out, angrily striding up the two steps to the front door.

Just what the hell am I doing?

He had no more chance of finding Lauren's children than the proverbial needle in the haystack. The odds were stacked against Ms. Regis, and in all honesty, Zachary seriously doubted that he could help her.

Then why all the promises?

Because I'm a fool; a goddamned hypocritical fool who's attracted to a beautiful, intelligent woman. Just like before. With Rosemary!

He walked inside the house, kicked the door shut behind him and headed straight for the liquor cabinet.

THE NEXT MORNING, as she walked into the suite of offices of the trust department, Lauren saw several of her co-workers staring curiously at her. Obviously, more than one of the employees of Northwestern Bank had seen the television program. She was reminded of Zachary's warning that Doug may also have seen the show. Going public with her personal problems may have been a horrible mistake. Lauren braced herself for what promised to be a long, uncomfortable day.

Don't second-guess yourself, she thought as she picked up her messages from the receptionist and smiled at the petite blonde, who quickly returned the smile and then avoided any further eye contact.

So it's already started. Lauren groaned inwardly and turned toward her office. *If you hadn't done the television show, Zachary wouldn't have accepted the case. And then where would you be? Back to square one.*

As she was about to enter her office, Lauren was confronted by Della McKeen, the securities cashier for the trust department. Della was a quick-witted, petite woman in her late fifties who'd worked at several brokerage houses before coming to work for the bank. She smiled sincerely and ran nervous fingers through her curly gray hair as Lauren approached.

"Good morning," Lauren said.

"Same to you." Della looked a little self-conscious. "I . . . I, uh, well, I saw you on the news last night."

"You and half the staff. I suppose I'm the main topic of conversation in the lunchroom," Lauren replied with a good-natured grin. This was going to be harder than she had imagined, but she tried to look unruffled.

"I—" Della shrugged "—I don't really know what to say. I had never guessed that your husband took the kids from you." She shook her head. "It's just awful. That's what it is. Gawd-awful. I've got two kids of my own. They're grown now, but I can't imagine what it would have been like to lose them. . . ." Realizing that she'd blundered and inadvertently voiced Lauren's feelings, Della quickly added, "But don't give up, mind you. If I were you, I'd hire the best attorney in town and chase that husband of yours down!" Della's small brown eyes blazed furiously from behind her silver-rimmed glasses.

"That's exactly what I'm trying to do."

"Good!" Della replied emphatically. "I hope it all works out for you. If there's anything I can do—"

"I'll let you know. But I doubt that anyone can help now." *Except Zachary.*

"But maybe someone who saw the program?"

"Maybe," she murmured. But she didn't have much hope of that.

"Well, honey, if it's any consolation, I think that husband of yours should be strung up by his . . . hamstrings." The cashier patted Lauren affectionately on the arm and continued talking under her breath as she stalked down the long corridor.

"Yep. It's going to be a long day," Lauren muttered, glancing at her watch and noting that it was barely eight thirty. She walked into her office, hung her coat and umbrella over the brass hall tree and sat down at her desk. She had just begun to check her appointment book when Bob Harding strolled leisurely into the room. He closed the door behind him, placed a cup of steaming coffee on the corner of the desk and then did a quick double take as he looked at Lauren.

"I didn't expect to find you here."

"What?" Good Lord, what was Bob talking about? Lauren put down her pen and focused her attention on her friend. He was still gazing at her with overly dramatized awe and a twinkle in his myopic eyes.

He shrugged. "I thought someone else must be occupying this office."

"Someone else?" she repeated. "Why?"

"I have it on good authority that some infamous Hollywood star is supposed to be here."

"Don't I wish!" She shook her head and rested her chin in her palm as she eyed her friend. "Are you going to tell me what this is all about?"

"You first. I caught your act on television last night, and from the sound of all the gossip ripping through the lunchroom, a few others saw you, too."

Lauren groaned as she imagined the excited knots of bank employees sitting around the Formica-topped tables and whispering about her. "Is it that bad?"

"Not really." He settled into one of the chairs near the desk and dropped his teasing facade, to Lauren's immense relief. "Actually, from what I understand, everybody feels sorry for you. You know, they're all wondering what they can do to help. That sort of thing."

Lauren was touched, but she was also realistic. "I don't need sympathy, Bob, just answers."

"I hear that the operations staff is taking up a collection—"

"What!" Her bright eyes impaled her co-worker. "Tell me you're kidding."

"Okay. I'm kidding." He shrugged his round shoulders and sipped his coffee.

"Not funny, Bob," she told him, chuckling. She reached for her cup and cradled it in her hands. "Thanks," she said, indicating the coffee.

Bob rested his elbows on the arms of the chair and placed his hands over his belly. "I just thought you could use a laugh or two."

She smiled. "You thought right."

"Don't I always?"

"Most of the time. Say about seventy percent."

"At least you think so," he replied. "The powers that be might disagree." He frowned into his cup, and Lauren had a sudden, chilling premonition. All of Bob's teasing was to get her to relax because the ax was about to fall. She could sense it.

"Meaning?"

He waved away her obvious concern, but the lines of worry creasing his forehead didn't disappear. "I'll get to it in a minute. Tell me, what's really going on with you? Why did you agree to be on that program yesterday?"

Lauren set her cup on the desk and rotated her pen between her fingers. "To find my kids."

"Because Zachary Winters wouldn't take your case," her friend deduced. He studied her closely, and Lauren suddenly felt he was keeping something from her, to protect her.

"Right," she agreed somewhat hesitantly. "But it seems that he's changed his mind."

Bob took a deep breath. "I don't know if that's so good," he said.

"What're you talking about?" Lauren stared at Bob incredulously. "You're the one who recommended the man to me. You've been insisting for the past six or seven months that I should switch attorneys and try to get Winters interested in my case."

"That was before."

"Before what?" Her voice had risen and she had to force herself to remain calm. "If this is another joke—"

"No joke, Lauren." The eyes behind the thick lenses saddened slightly. "I still think that Zachary Winters is the best attorney in Portland . . . maybe even the entire West Coast."

"But?"

He cleared his throat. "We've had some bad news," he said with a grimace. "The date of the Mason trust lawsuit is on the docket."

"What does that have to do with retaining Winters as my attorney?"

"I'm getting to that. The heirs of the Mason trust are out for blood."

Lauren was having trouble switching gears. What did the Mason trust have to do with Zachary Winters finding her children? Trying to keep her patience, she began tapping the tip of her pen on the polished surface of the desk. "So they're really going to take this to the limit?"

"The bank won't settle, and the heirs have hired another lawyer on a contingency. He's pushing it through, hoping that all the bad press will force the bank into settling out of court." Bob slid photocopies of the documents across her desk. "We're in court on December fifth, unless the bank decides to settle, which we won't. George West has decided to fight the suit with all we've got. He figures that if we lose this, it will open doors for lawsuits of a similar nature. And that could be bad."

"You're telling me." Lauren could envision the result. Anyone who'd ever lost a dime on an investment—even one initiated by an adviser the account holder himself had hired—ould try to sue the bank. Even if Northwestern Bank won the case, the legal fees would be enormous.

"So who's the brilliant attorney who decided to put the bank through the wringer?" she asked.

"You're not going to like the answer to this one."

Lauren's heart skipped a beat. "Who is it, Bob?"

"Joshua Tate. Zachary Winters's partner."

Lauren felt as if she were suffocating; she couldn't seem to breathe properly. "When . . . when did he take the case?"

"Just last week."

"After I'd met with Winters?"

Bob rubbed the top of his bald head. "Looks that way."

"So Zachary may have accepted my case just to get close to me and find out what the bank was planning," she said slowly, numb at the insinuations in her mind. After all, she was the administrator of the Mason trust. Why else had he decided to help her after telling her that locating the kids was next to impossible? Lauren stared at the desk and felt all her hopes slowly die.

Bob was shaking his head. "I don't think so. The man is basically honest."

"With more than a little dirt on his reputation," Lauren murmured. How could she have been so foolish as to believe that he cared about her or the children?

"Gossip."

Lauren sighed and placed her head in her hands. The morning had barely started and already she had a blinding headache. "No one knows for sure."

"Except Winters."

Lauren closed her eyes and thought about the enigmatic man with the dark brown eyes and cynical smile. She knew he was the only person who could help her, and that thought rekindled her determination. "I won't let him go," she said, half to herself.

"Pardon me?" Bob shifted in his chair and tugged at his collar uneasily.

Lauren lifted her head, her green eyes glittering with resolve. "He said he'd take my case, and he meant it. I'm not taking him off it."

"I agree with you. You know that."

"But?"

"If George West finds out about it, he might go through the roof."

Lauren's jaw tightened. "What I do with my life outside the office is my business. It has nothing to do with George West or Northwestern Bank."

"Except that now you've made a public issue of your life by going on that television show last night. And to top things off, you've hired Zachary Winters as your lawyer."

"Just following your advice," she reminded him.

"I know. I know." Bob got up and paced restlessly to the window to stare at the overcast sky. "But now his partner has taken on a case against the trust department of the bank you work for. More than that, the Mason account is under your administration. Whether you were handling the account when the alleged investment errors were made is irrelevant. The important thing is that there seems to be a conflict of interest. The law firm attacking the bank is the one you've hired for your own personal use."

"And I'm the administrator for the Mason trust . . . she said softly, her heart thudding irregularly.

"Yes." Bob frowned as he noticed how pale she had become.

"I can't . . . won't believe it's all that cut and dried."

"God, I hope not," Bob said worriedly as he wiped his sweating brow. "Because, despite everything, I still think Winters is the right man to locate those kids."

"So do I."

"Let's just hope George West agrees."

"It's none of his business," Lauren said firmly.

"Yet."

Bob checked his watch, then straightened his jacket

and walked to the door. “If it’s any consolation, I’m on your side.”

“I know.”

“Well . . . good luck.”

“Let’s just hope I don’t have to rely on luck.” She took a sip of her cold coffee as she watched Bob disappear from her office. *Yes,* she thought again, *it’s going to be a long day, and it’s probably going to get a lot worse.*

Chapter Six

"YOU DID *WHAT*!" Zachary demanded incredulously. He was seated in his desk chair, glaring at his partner past the various law books, journals and documents that littered the scarred oak desk. Joshua Tate, his crisp three-piece suit, gold cuff links and satisfied smile smugly in place, returned the older man's stare as he dropped into the leather chair nearest the window and watched the first drops of rain drizzle down the glass.

"I agreed to represent the Mason trust beneficiaries in their lawsuit against Northwestern Bank," Joshua replied. Gold eyes filled with challenge, he rotated to face Zachary and braced himself for a dressing-down.

Zachary leaned back in his chair, took off his reading glasses and rubbed his temples, as if to ease a suddenly throbbing headache. Sweat trickled down his temple and stained the front of his sweatshirt in a dark V, evidence of the exertion of his recent run along the waterfront. He'd only stopped by the office to make a few calls. Just for fifteen minutes! Then Joshua had calmly sauntered in and dropped this—this *bomb.*

"You can't represent Hammond Mason or the trust," Zachary declared wearily. He was familiar with the Mason trustees. The most vocal of the angry heirs, Hammond Mason, was the kind of man who would never be satisfied, no matter what. If Hammond had been left two million dollars from a relative he'd never known existed, it wouldn't be enough.

"Of course I can."

"It's a no-win situation," Zachary cut in impatiently.

"Maybe. . . ." Joshua let his voice trail off suggestively.

"Just what the hell are you trying to prove?" Zachary asked tiredly as he pushed aside a stack of mail and leaned his bare forearms on the desk.

Josh's eyes darkened. "I'm trying to prove that Winters and Tate is still a firm to be reckoned with. Look around you. Haven't you noticed what's been happening here? We're dying on the vine! We're supposed to be in the business of practicing law, Zack—something you've been avoiding for some time."

Zachary couldn't argue with that one—the kid was right. "Go on," he said quietly.

"And I thought—no, make that you told me, very emphatically, I believe—that you weren't interested in taking on Lauren Regis's case or looking for her kids."

"I wasn't."

"But you've changed your mind?"

"Yeah." Zachary got out of the chair and stretched. He thought about pouring himself a drink, then decided against it. Alcohol wouldn't help. Not much would. The whole set of circumstances—Lauren, her children and her position at the bank as administrator of the Mason trust—was a mess, a damned bloody mess.

"And now you expect me to drop *my* case because of a *possible* and highly unlikely charge of conflict of interest." Joshua crossed his arms over his chest, awaiting further battle.

Zachary realized that arguing with Josh would get him nowhere. Josh was a master at verbal attack and defense. So he decided to change tactics. "Why didn't you bother to tell me about your discussion with Hammond Mason?"

"I meant to."

"When?"

Joshua shrugged and looked away. "Oh, hell, Zack. I don't know. Like I say, I intended to—"

"Yeah, well. it's a little late."

"It's not like you hang around here much, y'know," Josh pointed out, knowing he was hitting a sensitive nerve. He cleared his throat and the angle of his jaw hardened determinedly. "I'm not letting go of the Mason case."

"Why?"

Josh rolled his eyes heavenward. "You haven't been listening to a word I've said, have you? We need a case, Zack, a strong case that will get us a little publicity."

"Even if we lose?" Zachary rubbed his hands together and guiltily eyed a stack of unanswered correspondence on the corner of his desk. Maybe the kid was right. Maybe he didn't spend enough time in the office and therefore had no right to exercise his prerogative as senior partner of the firm. In all honesty, Zachary had to admit that Josh had been all but running the firm for the past couple of years.

"We won't."

Josh was sure of himself; Zachary had to give him that. "You don't have a prayer."

"Old man West will settle."

"I doubt it." Zachary folded his hands behind his back and stretched, attempting to relieve the tension in his shoulders. As he shook his head, he leaned one hip on the window ledge. "He's out to beat you, Josh, and he's got Patrick Evans on his side."

"Evans is over the hill."

Zachary's eyes narrowed. "No way." He frowned

slightly. "I thought the first lesson I taught you was never to underestimate the opposition. As for Evans, he's the best Portland has to offer."

"Since you gave up."

Zachary tensed, and the muscles between his shoulder blades knotted uncomfortably. "Evans has always been good."

"Then it's time he came down a peg."

Zachary sighed and studied the angry planes of Joshua's even-featured face. "When are you gonna get rid of that chip on your shoulder?" he asked. "It's not doing either one of us a damned bit of good."

"As if you care." Joshua pushed himself out of the chair. "You haven't given a damn about anything for four years." He made a sweeping gesture with his arm that encompassed everything in Zachary's office—the seldom-used law journals, the stack of mail, unanswered letters and dust-covered volumes on the shelves. "Look at this mess! You call this an office?" Sarcasm edged his words. "I remember the way it used to be, Zack. Y'know, when Dad was alive and Winters and Tate was the most sought-after law firm in the Pacific Northwest."

Zachary's eyes glinted at the mention of Wendell Tate. "That was a long time ago."

"Not so long."

"But I let it slide." Zachary's dark brows lifted challengingly.

Joshua backed off a little. "Lots of things happened. Rosemary and Dad dying . . . well, no one blamed you for packing it in, but now—Christ, Zack, it's been six years! With the right case we could have it all again." He held out his hand and curled his long fingers into a fist, as if he were reaching for something tangible.

"And what would it be worth?"

Josh's gold eyes glittered. "It's what it's all about, old man, money and prestige."

"Whatever happened to justice?" Zachary asked cynically.

"If we're good enough, justice will come along for the ride."

Zachary smiled sadly and shook his head. "Just like that?"

Josh grinned—a flash of white teeth and good humor. "I didn't say we didn't have to work at it."

"And in the case of the Mason trust?"

"I plan to wait and see, but I'm willing to bet that justice will prevail."

"In the form of a huge out-of-court settlement."

Joshua's grin broadened.

"You could lose big," Zachary warned.

"And you think you've got a better chance with Lauren Regis and her kids?" Joshua folded his arms over his chest and eyed his partner skeptically.

"It won't be easy," Zachary admitted, raking his fingers through his damp hair and staring out the window at the drizzly autumn day.

"So why'd you agree to do it?"

Zachary raised an eyebrow. A sticky question. He considered lying to Josh, but he'd never yet had to resort to dishonesty with his younger partner, and he didn't want to start now: "The lady needs help," Zachary finally responded. That much wasn't a lie.

"And she was on television the other day," Josh thought aloud, grinning as he looked at his partner. "We're already talking about major publicity, aren't we?"

"Nothing to do with it."

"It could be big, Zack." Joshua pursed his lips and his eyes narrowed into speculative slits.

"And it could blow up in my face."

"Maybe. But life's a gamble," Josh pointed out. "At least that's what you've always told me."

"And you insist on throwing it back in my face every chance you get, don't you?"

"Only when you need a kick in the ass."

"Like now?"

Josh glanced at Zachary, and a slow-spreading smile inched across his face. "Yeah," he replied with a quick nod of his head. "Like now." He started to leave the room, but Zachary's voice stopped him.

"Drop the Mason case, Josh. It won't work."

Zachary very rarely issued orders, at least not since making Joshua a full partner, and the ultimatum rankled. "Can't do it, Zack. The challenge of it all, y'know." He turned and faced the man he'd come to think of as a second father. "I'll never know that it won't work until I've tried," Josh stated evenly. "After all, I've got nothing to lose but a little time."

"And Northwestern Bank?"

"Can afford it."

"Even if they're in the right?"

"Then George West will have the chance to prove it, won't he?" He reached for the doorknob.

"What about Lauren Regis?"

Josh turned and again surveyed Zack calmly, shrewdly. Suddenly a glimmer of understanding flickered in his eyes. "That's what this is all about, isn't it? The woman herself, not her case. Lauren Regis. She's gotten under your skin. That's why you took her case."

"One reason," Zachary drawled.

"And the others?"

Zachary's mocking grin slowly widened. "Maybe I think that you're right—it's time I took a little interest in the office."

Joshua snorted in disbelief and opened the door.

"Maybe," he said, shaking his head as he gazed at the clutter in Zachary's office. "But then again . . . maybe not."

LAUREN WAS SNAPPING her briefcase closed when the intercom buzzed. She glanced swiftly at the clock. Six thirty. Most of the employees had already left the bank, and Lauren was about to join them. It had been an exhausting, disappointing day. She was anxious to get home to see if she'd received any calls on the answering machine concerning Ryan's or Alicia's whereabouts. After that, a long, leisurely bath and a glass of wine, not necessarily in that order.

When the intercom buzzed again, Lauren frowned but pressed the button on the receiver and answered, "Yes?"

"Ms. Regis? Mr. West would like to see you," the receptionist said.

Lauren's throat tightened with dread. "When?"

"In about ten minutes, if you're not too busy."

Lauren smiled despite her unease. George West was nothing if not a gentleman, but whenever he issued a polite request, he expected it to be followed through as if it were an imperial command.

"I'll be there," Lauren said as she clicked off. Great. So even the president of the bank had seen or heard of her television appearance. He probably knew that she'd hired as her personal attorney the senior partner in the firm that was attempting to sue Northwestern Bank to the tune of two million dollars on behalf of the Mason trust beneficiaries.

Her heart was pounding irregularly by the time she had slipped on the jacket of her wine-colored business suit and was heading for the elevator. Once inside the confining car, she punched the button for the eleventh floor, where the bank's corporate headquarters were located.

George West's secretary, a competent, unsmiling woman in her mid-forties, escorted Lauren into the large corner office which faced both south and west. A bank of ceiling-high windows on the outside walls of the office offered a panoramic view of the west hills of Portland. Modern skyscrapers, Gothic church spires and elegant old hotels rose in the foreground. In the distance were the lush, forestlike grounds of the gently sloping west hills. Some of the most expensive homes in the city were hidden behind a private curtain of regal Douglas fir and autumn-burnished maple and oaks. Tudor and Victorian mansions peeked through the colorful trees from their lofty vantage points.

George West was sitting at his desk, which was angled by the corner of the room, with the commanding view of the city at his back. Thick imported carpet in a subtle shade of ivory silenced Lauren's footsteps. Spiky-leaved green plants sprouted from porcelain vases, and gold plaques awarding honors of city consciousness adorned the two mahogany-paneled walls.

"Lauren," George West said familiarly, rising from his padded leather chair as Lauren approached. "Please . . . take a seat." He motioned toward one of the winged chairs near his desk and dropped back into his own chair to survey her shrewdly with eyes that for sixty-two years had seen life solely from the viewpoint of the very rich. George West had been born with the proverbial silver spoon in his mouth, and had managed first to double, then triple his family's fortune by investing wisely in real estate.

As Lauren lowered herself into the oxblood leather

chair, the president of the bank checked his watch and then got straight to the point. "I heard that you were on the KPSC news program last night . . . what's it called? *Eye Contact*?"

"Yes."

"Didn't see it myself, but Ned Browning did."

Ned Browning was vice-president in charge of personnel. Lauren's heart sank as she realized she'd already been the subject of at least one closed-door upper echelon meeting. She managed a stiff smile but didn't comment on George's observation, preferring to wait until he asked her a question.

"I didn't realize what had happened between you and your husband," George explained with a thoughtful frown. "Of course, I knew that the kids weren't with you, but I just assumed that your husband had custody." His frown deepened. George West prided himself on knowing his officers fairly well, but this was becoming increasingly difficult as Northwestern continued to grow. "This is a nasty business," he stated.

"Yes," Lauren agreed, wishing that the uncomfortable interview were over. She shifted uneasily in her chair but held her head high, waiting for a direct question—or command—from her boss.

"Brownings said you'd hired several attorneys and a private investigator."

"That's right. I worked with Tyrone Robbins and then Patrick Evans."

"And?"

She shook her head. "Nothing. At least not so far."

"Pat Evans couldn't help you?" George asked, clearly skeptical.

"No," she responded, waiting for the ax to fall.

"And now you've hired Zachary Winters."

Lauren nodded.

George thoughtfully drummed his fingers on the mahogany desk. "Did he suggest you go on television?"

The question surprised her, especially considering Zachary's reaction to the program. Still, she was careful. Something in the set of George's jaw discouraged confidence. "No, actually, he hadn't accepted my case at that point."

"He accepted *after* you were on last evening's show."

Lauren folded her hands carefully in her lap. "Yes."

George thought for a minute, scratching his temple pensively. Then he said, "You know, of course, that Winters and Tate are attorneys for the Mason beneficiaries."

"I found out about it this morning. Bob Harding brought me all of the documents from Winters and Tate. I looked them over carefully and found no evidence that Zachary Winters is involved in any way. Joshua Tate is the attorney of record. I'm working solely with Mr. Winters."

George shook his head and discounted her excuse with a wave of his hand. "All the same outfit," he muttered, as if to himself. "You can see what we're up against, can't you? Whether Winters intended it or not, it *appears* that he took your case knowing that his firm was representing the Mason trust. Sticky business, if you know what I mean."

Lauren saw no reason to hedge. "You think there may be a conflict of interest?"

"Appears so." He patted his hands together, pleased that she had caught on so quickly. Lauren Regis was as smart as she was attractive, he decided. "Winters knew you were an employee of Northwestern Bank?"

"Yes."

"In the trust department?"

She nodded, her face losing some of its color.

"Did he have any idea that you were the administrator of the Mason trust?"

Lauren had anticipated the question; she had been thinking it of herself for most of the afternoon. "I don't think so. No, he couldn't have. At least not from me."

"But the beneficiaries of the trust—who's the guy that's spearheading this suit—Hammond Mason? Yes, that's the name. He could have talked with Winters before he did business with Tate. Or, for that matter, Winters could have talked to Joshua Tate himself or even seen some of the documents. No doubt your name appears on various correspondence from the bank."

Lauren placed her hands on the arms of the chair and curled her fingers around the padded arms. "Yes."

George took off his glasses and tiredly rubbed a hand over his face. "You see what we're up against here, don't you? The bank's position is clear—we have to go to court and prove that we weren't the least bit negligent, in order to discourage these ridiculous lawsuits."

"And you're afraid that if it ever leaked out that I was using Zachary Winters as my counsel, the members of the board and the stockholders of the bank would be upset."

"To put it mildly." He straightened his tie. "They'd be out for blood." He didn't have to say whose blood. "If we lost, which I admit is highly unlikely, but still a possibility, the bank would lose two million dollars plus the cost of the trial. There might be an investigation."

"All because I hired Winters," she finished for him.

"Precisely." George seemed pleased that she understood the bank's position so well.

"You want me to find another lawyer."

George smiled a little. "It would make things much easier."

Lauren could feel herself breaking out into a cold sweat. She couldn't fire Zachary as her attorney. *Wouldn't.* He was reputed to be the best, and she couldn't believe that he would use her: He wasn't like Doug or Tyrone Robbins. He couldn't be!

"Legally, you can't ask me to fire Winters," she managed to say calmly.

"I realize that."

"Are you saying that my job is on the line?"

He shook his head slowly, as if he were extremely tired: "I just want you to think, Lauren. You've made an excellent career for yourself here at Northwestern Bank. You have a brilliant future as well. I wouldn't want you to make any rash decisions that might jeopardize it. You're up for a promotion within the next few months, and I see nothing that should affect it . . . so far."

Lauren began to tremble in frustrated rage. Sometimes it seemed as if the entire world were against her, all because she wanted to be with Alicia and Ryan. "We're talking about my children," she said. "You have to understand, Mr. West, that I'll do anything to get them back. They're the most important part of my life."

"And your job with the bank?"

"Is secondary," she admitted without hesitation.

George sighed and looked at the framed photograph of his granddaughter on the corner of his desk. "That's how it should be," he agreed. "I understand your feelings . . . and I admire them, but I can't run this bank on emotion. I have stockholders who expect me to protect the bank's reputation and get the best performance I can from each of its employees."

Lauren stared at the small man seated at the big

desk, her heart pounding with dread. "So you are suggesting. . . ."

"That you find yourself another attorney."

Even though she'd been expecting the president of the bank to say just that, she felt betrayed; trapped. "Patrick Evans referred me to Winters."

George's eyes rounded and he rubbed a hand over his chin. "I see," he said, frowning. "Then I imagine that you know all about Winters and you're not worried about the scandal that surrounded him a few years back."

"No." Her green eyes blazed defiantly. "I don't know all about it, but I don't really care what happened. His personal life doesn't concern me. All I want from Zachary Winters is for him to locate my children and bring them back to me."

"Whatever the cost?"

"Whatever the cost!" she repeated, her voice shaking with emotion. "You know that I would never do anything to jeopardize Northwestern's reputation or undermine the bank's defense, but I have to do everything in my power to find Alicia and Ryan."

"Yes. Well, I suppose you do." He pressed his hands flat on the desk and smiled slightly as he stood, indicating that the interview was over. "Thank you for talking with me."

"You're welcome," Lauren replied dully as she straightened from her chair, smoothed the hem of her skirt and headed toward the double doors of the opulent office. Anger seethed through her at the unfairness of it all, and she had to force herself to walk proudly, to keep the slump of defeat from her shoulders.

"I hope you find your children, Lauren," George said as she reached the doors.

She turned back to face him and noted that he was still standing in front of the large plate-glass windows.

Threatening storm clouds, dark with the promise of rain, had begun to gather over the west hills. "Thank you. So do I." With that she slipped through the heavy doors and hurried away.

In the elevator, she thought back on the interview. If nothing else, she'd been honest with the president; now it was up to him to decide how to deal with the problem. Sighing, she stepped out of the car, returned to her office to pick up her things and hurried out of the building.

Thank God it's Friday. She had two free days before she had to return to the bank. Maybe by then the gossip about her appearance on television would settle down. Maybe she would know something more about Alicia and Ryan. And maybe she would be out of a job.

The downpour had just begun as she walked out of the building. A heavy breeze caught in her umbrella, and the rain began in earnest, chilling her face and hands as it slanted down from leaden skies.

"Damn it!" Lauren muttered as she dashed across the wet pavement of the parking lot and unlocked the car door. She slid her hands over the wheel and fought to quiet the rage storming in her heart.

All she wanted was her children. Was that so much to ask? Tears gathered in her eyes, and her small hands, curled into impotent fists, pounded mercilessly on the steering wheel.

She'd fight them. She'd fight them all! Douglas Regis, George West, Joshua Tate, even Zachary Winters if he tried to thwart her. She was the woman who had given birth to Alicia and Ryan, and if she accomplished nothing else in her life, she would find her children, no matter who stood in her way.

Chapter Seven

ZACHARY'S PICKUP WAS parked on the street in front of her house. Lauren's fingers tightened on the steering wheel in tense anticipation. Maybe he'd already found out something, anything, about her children!

Or maybe he'd come to report that he had to drop the case because Joshua Tate had already agreed to represent Hammond Mason. Fleetingly, she wondered if he had come to extract information from her, then discarded the idea. If gaining some sort of advantage in the Mason trust trial had been his objective, he would have tried to pump her for information already, before the bank caught on to his scheme.

As she turned into the driveway and parked, she realized her feelings for Zachary ran deeper than anxiety over the children or worry about the Mason trust lawsuit. Yes, she desperately wanted to know about the kids, and the bank's attitude about her attorney concerned her. But she was also glad that Zachary had come to the house searching for her. Somehow it eased her earlier doubts about his integrity.

Silently chastising herself for her foolish thoughts, Lauren climbed out of the car, dashed to the mailbox and hurried up the wooden steps to the front door, sifting through the bills and various pieces of junk mail as she ran. Wet leaves in hues of orange and brown littered the steps and caught on the heels of her boots.

Zachary watched Lauren approach as he stood lazily on the small veranda that ran the width of the cream-colored house. Wide pillars supported the roof, and a half wall constructed of the siding that covered the house afforded the roomy porch some privacy. Cobalt-blue shutters and trim provided a striking contrast to the ivory exterior. All in all, the small house seemed cozy, well-kept and inviting, to Zachary's way of thinking. But maybe that was because of the intriguing woman who lived there.

Lauren forced a wary smile as she approached the enigmatic man she had hired as her attorney. His legs were stretched out in front of him, his ankles crossed, and he was supporting his weight with his hands on the half wall. He wore a bulky-knit camel-colored sweater, tan cords and soft leather loafers. A slight breeze caught his dark hair, mussing it and softening the harsh angles of his face. He was still dressed down, but his casual attire and unconventionality only added to his sensuality. She felt comfortable with Zachary, relaxed. Maybe even the clothing was part of an act to gain her confidence. He'd acquired a reputation as a roguish lawyer, she reminded herself, and wondered just how unconventional, even dishonest, he might be if pushed.

At the sight of Lauren, a grin spread slowly across Zachary's face to display straight white teeth and the traces of what had once been a dimple in his cheek.

Despite the scandal of Zachary's past, and George West's doubts about his integrity, Lauren found that there was something reassuring about coming home to him. It seemed so natural and comfortable; she felt he was a man she could live with and enjoy. The mystery surrounding him and the seldom-seen twinkle in his eyes intrigued her. If it hadn't been for the fact that he was her attorney, hired for the specific purpose of finding her children, she could imagine herself falling for him. *Crazy,* she chided herself. *You're thinking like a crazy woman.*

Before she could say anything, he pushed away from the short wall and reached for the briefcase she had been juggling between her umbrella, her purse and the mail. "I thought I'd better come over and explain a few things," he began.

"A few things?" she echoed, attempting to keep the indignation out of her voice as she recalled her uncomfortable meeting with George West. "Like Joshua Tate and the Mason trust?" she asked, fumbling in her purse for her keys and finally unlocking the door.

Zachary averted his gaze. "For starters."

"Good." Her emerald eyes darkened with reawakened anger. "Because I've been hearing about it all day, and I hope to God that you've got some answers for me. Everyone at the bank thinks I'm out of my mind for hiring you!" She opened the door and tried to remind herself that this man was only her attorney, nothing more. If he was really interested only in using her, she'd have to get rid of him. *And then where will you be?* Her heart filled with desperation at the thought, and unconsciously her eyes moved to the portrait of Alicia and Ryan on the mantel.

"And do you think you're . . . uh, 'out of your mind'?" he asked.

"I don't know what to think. The way I've been treated the last few hours, you'd think I'd changed my ame to Benedict Arnold!" She saw the unconscious tightening of his jaw and immediately felt remorseful. Unsteadily, she pushed aside the windblown wisps of hair that had pulled free of her chignon. "Oh, God,

Zachary, I'm sorry," she said, her chin trembling slightly. "I didn't mean to take it out on you. It's just that today has been a total disaster. If people weren't smothering me with sympathy, they were treating me as if I were some kind of traitor." She shook her head and closed her eyes wearily. "Dear Lord, I've made such a mess of this. I guess I shouldn't have gone on the air last night. . . ."

"You did what you had to," he replied as he touched her shoulder reassuringly. "Now, what about you? Are you all right?"

The concern in his brown eyes touched her, and she nodded mutely, struggling to maintain her poise. "Yes . . . or I will be, once I calm down."

After she had tossed her coat over the back of the couch and set her briefcase on the rolltop desk, she quickly rewound the tape on the recording machine and listened for her messages. There was only one—it was from Zachary, explaining that he wanted to see her and felt it would be better if he came to her home rather than meet with her at the bank.

"I didn't think George West would appreciate my visit," Zachary said when Lauren turned off the machine.

"You thought right," she agreed with a mirthless laugh.

"I was surprised that you weren't here when I drove in, but I waited, figuring you'd show up."

"I had an unscheduled meeting with the president of the bank."

"Let me guess—the Mason trust."

"And the attorney representing it," she replied distractedly. Her thoughts weren't on George West or the Mason trust as she rewound the tape and turned off the recording machine. There was no call about Alicia or Ryan. No one who'd seen the program had contacted her. For a few seconds she couldn't turn around and face Zachary. She was bitterly disappointed—and angry at herself for putting too much confidence in the broadcasting of *Eye Contact*. Airing her problem had been a long shot, but Lauren had prayed that someone who had seen the show would be able to help her.

"It's only been one day since the program was aired," Zachary said quietly, as if reading her troubled thoughts.

"I know, but I thought—well, I hoped—that I'd hear something by now, while the program was still fresh in the audience's mind. I expected a quick response. The more time that goes by, the sooner the public will forget and the less likely I'll hear anything." She raised her hands, then let them fall limply to her side in a gesture of frustration.

"You don t know that," he said softly.

"It's been a long day, Zachary," she replied, shaking her head. "I just hoped—"

"That someone would call with information about your kids," he concluded, touching her gently on the shoulder.

"Yes." Tears threatened, but she refused to release them. She would not break down in front of him again. "I don't suppose you've come up with anything?" she asked.

"Other than a pain in the neck from my partner, no." He noticed that beneath the rich weave of her burgundy jacket, her shoulders sagged a little. Her fingers played distractedly with the silky tie of her pale pink blouse.

Zachary reached forward and tilted her chin up with one finger, forcing her to stare into his eyes. "It's only been one day for me, too," he told her, determination flashing in his eyes. "Give it a little time."

"Oh, Zachary, I have—it's been over a year!"

"Come on, let me buy you dinner."

Her frail smile faltered. She didn't want his sympathy or his kindness. Her feelings about him were confused enough as it was. Slowly, she shook her head. "I don't think so."

"You're beat."

"I know, but I think we have things to discuss."

"And we could just as well talk over dinner. I don't know about you, but I'm starved."

She hesitated. "What about the phone? Someone may call about the kids." Even as she said it, she realized that pinning her hopes on *Eye Contact* was probably foolish.

"Put on your answering machine again."

"Yes, I suppose you're right. There's no sense in waiting around for someone to call," she replied, and turned on the recorder. Zachary grabbed her raincoat from the back of the couch and slipped it over her shoulders as he led her back out the door.

The restaurant, which proudly boasted an authentic German cuisine, was a small, turn-of-the-century home that had been converted into an eating establishment. Large apple trees still stood in what had once been a front yard. A redbrick path led to the open porch of the gray house, where an elegant hand-painted sign displayed the hours of operation in black letters. The entrance was softly illuminated by sconces mounted on either side of the narrow windows surrounding the carved oak door.

Zachary and Lauren were seated at a private table near the fireplace in what appeared to have been the living room of the cozy home. Glossy wooden tables were covered with ivory-colored linen cloths. The elegant wallpaper, frilly Austrian shades covering paned windows and hand-painted ceramic tiles over the fireplace were all a beautiful moss green. Fresh-cut flowers and brightly polished oak floors gave the restaurant a certain old-world charm that was enhanced by the softly glowing fire.

A waiter with a trim, waxed mustache, laughing blue eyes and a thick Bavarian accent brought the food and wine to the table. Lauren began to relax over the meal of thick brown bread, lentil soup and fresh trout. The conversation remained light and companionable, as if both she and Zachary were deliberately avoiding anything serious.

The tension Lauren had experienced all day seemed to drain from her as she sat with Zachary in the intimate surroundings of the restaurant. After a dessert of cinnamon-flavored apple strudel, Zachary ordered brandied coffee for them both.

"So," Zachary began as he settled back, cradling his warm drink and studying Lauren intently, "you already knew that Joshua had agreed to represent the Mason trust."

Lauren shook her head. "Not before I walked into the bank this morning. Apparently, George West received notice of the change in attorneys just yesterday."

Zachary observed Lauren over the rim of his cup as he drank. "And George guessed that I was your attorney?"

"Yes."

"How did he know?"

Lauren shrugged, and her finely arched brows drew together pensively. "Probably from Patrick Evans or Ned Browning in personnel. I suppose it really doesn't matter, though. When he asked about you, I told him that you had agreed to represent me . . . as of yesterday evening."

"*After* he'd learned that Joshua had taken on the Mason trust," Zachary muttered. "Great! He probably thinks I planned it that way. I don't suppose that West wants you to find another attorney?" he asked sarcastically.

"As soon as possible."

The muscles around Zachary's mouth tightened. "And?"

"I told him I wouldn't," Lauren replied softly, holding his gaze with her own.

Zachary smiled. "I doubt if he liked that."

"Not much he could do about it."

"He could fire you," Zachary said carefully, watching her reaction.

Lauren winced a little at the thought. She couldn't afford to be out of a job. "Not legally."

Zachary shook his head, and firelight reflected off the sable-brown strands of his hair. "He could find a reason, have your supervisor make the appropriate notes in your file, make it look as if you were doing unsatisfactory work."

"Sounds as if you've had some experience yourself in this type of deception, counselor," she observed uneasily. *Just how ruthless was he?*

"I've practiced law a long time. It wouldn't be the first case of fraudulent employee records I've come across."

Lauren held on to her cup with both hands and watched as the fragrance steam rose from the dark liquid. "I don't think George West would resort to those kinds of backstabbing tactics. Too obvious," she mused. "I've had good employment reviews so far. Besides, it's not his style," she reasoned, trying to convince herself as well as Zachary. "He's not the sneaky type, and I think he genuinely likes me. It would be my guess that if he felt he was being backed into a corner, he would transfer me to another department rather than do a hatchet job on my employment records. He would have it seem as if the transfer were a promotion and then make damned sure I had absolutely no access to any records surrounding the Mason trust."

"Except that you already have had access," Zachary reminded her. "If you wanted to give me any information on the Mason trust, you could have done it already."

Something in Zachary's tone struck a nerve. Lauren forced herself to look directly into Zachary's dark, probing eyes and ask, "Is that what you expected of me when you took my case?"

A muscle throbbed in the corner of his jaw. "Of course not. Last night I told you why I took your case."

"And I believed you," she replied, her face taut. "But you have to admit, it looks bad . . . very bad . . . for everyone involved."

"I know."

"And now that I've made the search for the kids a public issue, the press is involved," she continued, lowering her voice slightly.

"So what do you want to do?" Zachary asked.

"What I've wanted for more than a year," she replied softly. "I want to find my kids. And I want you to help me."

"What about the Mason trust?"

She glanced at the ceiling and shook her head. One hand lifted in a gesture of bewilderment. "I don't know," she answered honestly. "I guess I'll have to cross that bridge when I come to it."

Zachary was silent for a long, tense moment, and Lauren wondered what was going through his mind. Finally, he sighed. "I don't want you to risk your career, Lauren," he said, his voice grave with concern.

"There are other banks in Portland."

"But you're happy with Northwestern."

How well he could read her. Already. After knowing her only a few short weeks. Zachary Winters was more than shrewd—he was insightful, and this worried her a little. "Yes, I'm happy at the bank. At least I was."

"If it's any consolation, I tried to talk Joshua out of handling the Mason trust."

"And?"

"He flat-out refused, accused me of pulling rank on him."

Lauren set down her cup and smiled cynically as she remembered the first time she had set foot in Zachary's seldom-used office. Zachary's neglect and disinterest had been obvious. Joshua Tate had probably decided to take the bull by the horns. "Do you blame him?"

Zachary shook his head. "No. He's been waiting a long time for a big case—a chance to prove himself—and he sees the Mason trust as just that opportunity."

"He'll lose," Lauren predicted.

"Maybe so, but he's willing to gamble." Zachary's brown eyes burned into hers. "Just like you."

"Maybe he feels like me. That he's really got nothing to lose and everything to gain from the lawsuit."

"Maybe."

"Then I guess there's nothing either of us can do," she said. "I want you to find my children. And I trust you not to weasel information out of me about the Mason trust." Her green eyes suddenly turned cold. "It certainly wouldn't do any good to try."

She was about to get up from the table when Zachary's hand reached out and caught her wrist. His dark gaze burned with honesty, and in a low, intense voice he said, "I want you to know Lauren, that whatever else happens, I would never . . . *never* use you."

Her gaze moved from his face to her wrist and back again to the conviction in his dark eyes. Her heart began to pound.

"If you don't believe anything else," he continued,

"know that you can trust me. Otherwise we have no reason to continue the search for your children. If I'm going to work with you, I'll have to know that you're with me—not against me."

She slipped her hand away from his. "All right, Zachary," she agreed, wondering how many words of his impassioned speech were sincere and how many were the well-rehearsed legal theatrics of a convincing trial lawyer.

In the end it didn't matter, she supposed, as long as Zachary continued to help her find Alicia and Ryan.

The short drive from the German restaurant in Sellwood was undertaken in a strained silence that made it impossible for Lauren to relax. Night had descended upon the city and the interior of the pickup was dark, illuminated only by the flash of oncoming headlights, or by the ethereal streetlights, which gave the city and the cab of the truck a bluish tinge. Rain poured from the heavens, spattering against the windshield before being pushed aside by the rhythmic wipers.

The subject of Joshua Tate and the Mason trust lawsuit had been left at the restaurant, and Lauren was too tired now to think about how the situation might affect her or her job. There was no point in spending her weekend second-guessing George West. Monday would come soon enough, whether she worried about her job or not.

Zachary braked slowly and parked the pickup by the curb in front of her house. He let the engine idle for a minute, his hand cocked over the ignition before he turned the key and allowed the rumbling motor to die.

In the silence that followed, rain began to collect on the windshield. "Would you like to come in?" Lauren offered, knowing that her business with him wasn't concluded and unable to face the cold, dark house alone. Once she had loved the little cottage across from Westmoreland Park, but now, without the sounds of the children's laughter and their high-pitched arguments, she could barely stand the place. The nights were the worst. She turned to face Zachary, the invitation still in her eyes.

God, if she only knew what she did to him, Zachary thought. "I do have a few more things to discuss," he admitted, avoiding her eyes and rubbing his hand around the back of his neck as he watched the headlights of an oncoming car. It roared past and sprayed the truck with water from the street. "But the questions won't be too pleasant."

"Will they help me find the kids?" she asked.

"I hope so."

Lauren supposed that was all she could expect. She didn't hesitate, despite the uneasiness she saw in the tense lines of his face. "Then, of course I'll answer them. Come on, counselor," she said, trying to dispel the growing tension between them, "just give me a few minutes to change and I'll make you a cup of coffee."

He smiled tentatively. "I can't turn down an offer like that," he said with a trace of reluctance as he grabbed his briefcase and helped her out of the pickup.

Once inside the house, Lauren quickly put on the coffee, then stepped into the bedroom. She took off her wool suit and donned a blue sweater and a pair of soft gray corduroy slacks. By the time she had changed, the water had run through the coffeemaker and the kitchen was filled with the enticing aroma of freshly ground coffee. Zachary had taken it upon himself to start a fire in the living room, and as she poured the coffee into ceramic mugs, she could hear the pleasant sound of crackling flames igniting against mossy wood.

Zachary was on his haunches, leaning into the fireplace, when Lauren entered the living room. His sweater had pulled away from the waistband of his low-slung cords, and she stood there for a few moments, fascinated by the play of muscles in his back and thighs as he placed a chunk of oak onto the fire.

Suddenly he straightened, and the intensity of his stare told her that he knew she had been watching him. He dusted his hands together but didn't comment as she blushed and handed him a steaming mug. Sitting cross-legged on the floor near the warmth of the fire, she peered at his handiwork. "You sure you weren't an Eagle Scout?" she teased, trying to disperse the tension in the intimate room.

"Not on your life. My folks had a wood stove to heat their cabin in the Cascades. It was my job to start the fire every morning, and I learned quickly. It's pretty cold in the mountains at five in the morning. Even in June."

She laughed a little, enjoying the easy feeling of companionship. Then, deciding that she couldn't put off the inevitable any longer, she looked up at him through the sweep of long, black lashes and said, "Okay, counselor, what's up? You said you had questions."

"I need some more information," he replied, staring at her steadily as he sipped his coffee. He was leaning against the fireplace, one shoulder propped on the mantel.

As long as the questions don't have anything to do with the Mason trust. "Shoot." She took a long sip of her coffee and waited.

"I've started checking over everything I got from Patrick Evans and his investigator. So far I haven't found anything that will do us much good, I'm afraid. Evans is still the best in town, and his investigation was thorough."

"Oh." She couldn't hide her disappointment. "Nothing?"

"Not so far."

"Then what about the information from Tyrone Robbins?" she asked reluctantly, the name of the arrogant attorney nearly sticking in her throat. It was a long shot, but she had to make sure that Zachary had looked over every piece of evidence she'd given him.

Zachary snorted disgustedly. "What Tyrone Robbins came up with isn't worth the price of a snowball in Alaska."

Lauren felt her tired muscles stiffen. "I guess I already knew that much," she admitted.

"So why did you hire him?"

"A friend of mine gave me his name."

"Some friend," Zachary replied sardonically.

"You have to understand that I had never dealt with any lawyers, aside from those I knew from the bank, and I didn't think it would be wise to deal with someone in my capacity as a trust administrator as well as on a personal basis."

"As you're doing with me, because of the Mason trust."

"Exactly." She looked up at him apprehensively. "You have to admit, everything's become more complicated now that Tate's representing Hammond Mason and the rest of the beneficiaries."

His dark eyes glittered. "Go on. How did this 'friend' of yours come up with Robbins?"

"Sally, a girl I used to go to school with, gave me his name. He'd helped her with her divorce, and she claimed that he was . . . 'terrific,' I think was the term she used."

Lauren shuddered a little as she thought about Sally's earnest face. "Tyrone Robbins is the best in Portland," Sally had promised. "And his fees are . . . negotiable." The brunette had smiled knowingly, but Lauren hadn't questioned her words. At the time, Lauren had been frantic; Doug had just taken off with the kids. She'd needed a good attorney quickly and had latched on to Tyrone Robbins like a drowning woman to a life raft.

"Terrific?" Zachary shook his head. "You don't strike me as the naive type, Lauren. You work with lawyers every day."

"That was the problem."

"What about the guy who handled your divorce?"

"He moved out of the state," she answered, frowning. "Look, you have to understand that I was desperate and . . . well, I went to see Robbins. As far as I knew, he didn't represent any of the trust accounts I was overseeing, and he didn't have any ties with Northwestern Bank."

"And?"

She looked away from Zachary and stared into the fire. The flames crackled and hissed, and the scent of burning wood mingled with the aroma of the coffee. "Robbins seemed interested in helping me and . . . and . . ." Lauren's voice caught at the vivid memory of Tyrone attempting to unbutton her blouse after their second meeting, which had turned out to be an intimate dinner instead of the business meeting that had been planned. The turquoise silk had ripped as she'd pulled away from him, but neither that nor her violent protests had deterred him. If anything, her rejection had seemed to backfire, making him more bold. She still shivered as she thought about his soft hands clutching her bare shoulders. "It . . . didn't work out."

From the ashen color of Lauren's face, Zachary could well imagine what had happened. He knew from his own experience that Tyrone Robbins was a snake of an attorney who didn't deserve his license to practice law. Tyrone had twice been before the bar on charges that hadn't stuck. Somehow the slimy lawyer had always managed to avoid disbarment. Zachary felt the muscles at the base of his neck tightening in sudden rage at the thought of Tyrone's slippery hands on Lauren. He had to force himself to appear calm. "Do you want to talk about it?" he asked.

"Not particularly," she admitted, composing herself. "Let's just say that Tyrone Robbins seemed to think that he could help me find my children, or at least relieve some of my tension and lower his attorney's fees by seducing me. I didn't see it that way. When I finally convinced him he was wrong about me, he nearly tripped over himself with apologies, but I'd already decided to find another attorney."

"You could have sued him for malpractice," Zachary suggested darkly, imagining his fingers around Tyrone's throat.

"But that wouldn't have helped me find Alicia and Ryan." Lauren's color returned. "What happened with Tyrone was . . . an unpleasant situation that I decided to chalk up to experience."

"So that's when you hired Evans."

"Right. At that point I didn't care that Patrick worked with the bank. At least he was someone I could trust. I . . . well, I practically begged him to take my case." She set her cup on the hearth and leaned back against the couch. "That's why it took me over a year to end up with you; when Patrick couldn't find the kids, he recommended you."

"With some reservations, I'll wager."

"A few," she conceded. "So now, counselor, you know all of my darkest secrets, right?"

"Not quite."

"Pardon?" She heard the hesitation in his voice. "What're you talking about?"

"Your secrets. I need to know more about them."

"I don't understand."

"Specifically about the other people in your life—that is, the friends you had when you were married to Doug. It doesn't seem likely that he would disappear without a trace and not contact one single person in the last year. There must be someone he befriended, cared about enough that he would keep in touch."

"I already explained about our friends. . . ."

"What about *his* friends? The ones you didn't meet."

Her blood turned cold as she realized what he meant.

"The other women, Lauren," he said, kneeling next to her. "Can you tell me the names of any of the women your husband was involved with during your marriage—or better yet, after the separation?

"I don't know them," she replied, burying her gaze in the bright, hungry flames of the fire. "I told you that much last night. It was just easier if they remained nameless and faceless."

"But you're sure he was unfaithful?"

"Yes." Dear God, she was certain. Even when she'd tried to believe that Doug was not involved with other women, she'd known her hopes of his fidelity were futile and naive.

"How?"

Lauren shifted her eyes to his. "A woman knows," she said. "I . . . Look, I don't see what this is going to accomplish."

"Lauren, think! One of those women might know where Doug and the children are." Zachary's face was grim, as if he knew the pain he was putting her through. "Think back. Certainly you had your suspicions."

"Nothing I can prove."

Now he was getting somewhere. "Did you mention them to either Tyrone or Pat?"

"No . . . well, yes, but nothing came of it. . . ."

"And you're sure you can't remember any names?"

Lauren looked away. "This—this isn't my favorite subject," she faltered, avoiding his gaze.

He reached out and grasped her shoulders, forcing her to face him. "Dammit, look at me," he ordered, his fingers tightening over her sweater. "I'm trying to help you. But I can't, not unless you tell me *everything*."

"I have."

His fingers continued to grip her upper arms, and his dark eyes pierced hers. "Then give me a name. You said yourself that a woman knows when her husband is having an affair. Surely there was one who you think may have been involved with Doug." He pressed his hand against her cheek. "I know this is painful, but I don't have anyone else I can ask, Lauren. I have to trust your intuition."

As all the old memories, filled with torment and fear, resurfaced, Lauren found she was having trouble breathing. "Doug was very discreet," she said, her hands curling into fists of frustration as she forced herself to recall what she'd sought to blot out for so long—the grim, deceitful side of her marriage. "I never caught him . . . not on the phone, not going out." She paused for a moment: "Once, a woman called when he wasn't home, and I wondered . . . Well, nothing came of it."

"Did she leave a message or her name?" Zachary persisted, hoping for any shred of evidence, just one tiny lead.

Lauren shook her head. "No . . . she wouldn't say who she was. That's why I became suspicious."

"Damn." His hands fell to his sides. "I know this is hard for you," he murmured, pinching the bridge of his nose thoughtfully. "I wouldn't ask if I didn't think it would help, but it might be our only chance of finding your children."

Lauren stared into the fire, trying to reconstruct the painful nights when she'd been alone in the double bed, waiting for Doug, knowing he was with another woman. In the beginning, she hadn't been sure he was lying to her. She'd forced herself to believe his excuses of working late, but eventually she'd been faced with the simple truth that he was having an affair, one of many.

Her hands twisted uncomfortably in her lap, and she had to clear her throat as she began to speak. "There was one time," she whispered.

Zachary's eyes narrowed. "What happened?"

Lauren fought to control the tears that were forming behind her eyes. She'd sworn that night nearly two years ago that she would never cry another tear for Doug Regis. It had been a promise to herself that she'd broken time and time again.

"Lauren?" Zachary prodded, his voice filled with kindness.

"Doug had just gotten the job with Dickinson Investments," she began. "He was ecstatic and came home with a bottle of champagne to celebrate the occasion. I thought . . . anyway, I *hoped* that this job would be a new beginning for us." She closed her eyes and forced her voice to remain steady. "We drank the champagne and went to bed . . . and while we were making love . . . he called me by another woman's name." A solitary tear slid down her cheek, and she hurriedly brushed it aside. *No more tears, not for Doug.*

Zachary gritted his teeth as he saw the anguish in her glistening green eyes. All because of a bastard by the name of Douglas Regis. "What was her name?" he asked, tenderly touching her chin with the tip of his finger.

"I can't remember," she replied, pursing her lips. "Maybe I never wanted to know."

"Lauren, please. *Try.*"

She sighed. "I don't know." Closing her eyes, she could almost see Doug's face, flushed from the alcohol in his bloodstream, as he bent over her and placed a sloppy kiss on her neck. "Oh, baby," he'd whispered thickly, stretching anxious hands over her abdomen and breasts. "Please . . ." And then, as painful as if he'd slapped her face, he'd called her by another woman's name.

Lauren's stomach knotted as she tried to concentrate. "I can't remember, but I think it was something common like Susan or Sandra or Sharon." None of the names sounded quite right. But then it had been several years ago, and she tried hard to forget that night.

"When you heard the name, you didn't connect it with any of the women you knew or that Doug may have worked with?"

"No." Every muscle in her body was taut with the memory.

Zachary rubbed his thumb tenderly along her jaw. "I'm sorry," he murmured, watching her reaction. Her cheeks were flushed, and the dark twist of her hair had begun to fall free, framing her face in tangled burnished curls that reflected the firelight. Her green eyes were filled with pain. It occurred to Zachary that Lauren might still be in love with her ex-husband, and that thought only served to harden the set of his jaw.

"It's okay," she said, sniffing a little and trying to regain her composure.

"Lauren, are you sure you want to continue looking for your children?"

"What?" Her head snapped up, and she saw that he was serious. "Of course I do."

"How will you feel when you see your ex-husband again?" he asked, damning himself for needing to know.

"Angry," she replied without hesitation.

"You're sure?"

"He's put me through hell. Every day I wake up wondering where Alicia and Ryan are, if they're all right, if they'll remember me, if I'll ever find them . . . if they're alive."

Zachary's eyes narrowed as he studied her. "I just want you to be certain that you're not in love with Doug, or out for revenge; that you're only thinking of the children."

"Of course I am," she snapped. "But if I weren't, would it matter?"

"It would to Alicia and Ryan."

She pointed a condemning finger directly into his face. "*What kind of a mother do you think I am?* All I want is to get my children back. What happens to Doug I don't care, except for how it will affect Alicia and Ryan."

"You're certain of that?" He leaned against the couch and searched the soft contours of her angry face.

"Yes."

"And the love you once felt for your husband?"

"Is dead. He killed it." Lauren took a deep breath, then returned her gaze to Zachary. It was imperative that he understand her. "I know that probably sounds callous, Zachary, but I loved Doug once, trusted him, dreamed with him, planned my life with him, and he didn't want me or the kids. That's what came as such a shock, I suppose, that he would take them away from me. I *never* thought he would do anything so horrible. I didn't even think he wanted the kids, but I guess I was wrong. It was just me he didn't want."

Zachary felt the need to comfort her, but she faced

him dry-eyed. "Don't get me wrong, I'm not feeling sorry for myself because I lost Doug; he and I were never right for each other, and I should have been smart enough to realize it before I married him. But I wasn't, and in one respect I'm glad I married Doug—because of the kids." She leaned back on the couch and ran her fingers through her hair. "If only I could find them."

She felt the hot tears begin to slide down her cheeks. How could she hope for Zachary to understand? "Maybe you should go," she whispered. But when his strong arms encircled her waist, she didn't resist. She swallowed hard and tried to stop the tears. "Look, Zachary, I can't wind up crying on your shoulder every night."

"Sure you can," he said fervently, the passion in his voice startling her. "Every night if you want." He kissed the top of her head tenderly, and she felt the warmth of his lips against her hair. She clung to him, glad of his strength and warmth. Her body was touching his, her hips and thighs fitting snugly against his muscular legs. "You don't have to worry, lady," he said. "I'll be with you . . . help you. . . ."

The doubts that had lingered with her for the better part of a day faded away silently. "I trust you," she whispered, touching his rough cheek.

"That's how it's supposed to work between client and attorney." His lips brushed hers tentatively, and the tenderness of the gesture brought fresh tears to her eyes.

"You're almost too good to be true," she murmured.

"I bet you weren't thinking that this afternoon."

"No . . . my thoughts about you were rather unkind."

"I'll bet." His fingers reached up and slowly removed the pins from her hair. The auburn twist gently unwound to fall in a thick braid at her shoulders. Zachary's fingers twined in the red-brown silk and brushed against the curve of her neck. When his lips touched the hollow of her throat, she shivered with pleasure.

This can't be happening, she thought, but she couldn't find the words to halt what her body longed to feel. The pliant pressure of his tongue as it lazily rimmed her collarbone should have sobered her—should have reminded her of Doug, of Tyrone Robbins, of all the men who had used her—but it didn't. She was aware only of awakening feelings of desire, and she moaned Zachary's name in response.

His lips found hers and softly molded to her mouth. She reached forward and wound her arms around his neck, drawing him closer as the magic of his tongue gently urged her lips apart to taste the liquid warmth within. Gladly she opened to him, her blood beginning to race wildly through her veins, her heart pounding erratically.

You're a fool, she thought as the weight of his body pressed solidly against hers, forcing her to the floor in front of the fire. She felt his chest crushing her breasts and became vaguely aware that her sweater had slipped up as she felt the rough texture of the faded carpet rubbing against her skin.

Zachary saw the parted invitation of her mouth before he lowered his head and took her lips with his. Warmth invaded her body, filled her soul with yearning.

It had been so long since she had been with a man, years since she had wanted to be caressed. But now she ached for more, wanting to be fulfilled by this man who had such power over her—over her future, over her happiness. Perhaps that was it—the danger of it all, the intrigue of becoming involved with the one man she shouldn't. Every instinct screamed that she was making a monumental mistake, but when she looked up and stared into the mystery of Zachary's eyes, she knew that she was lost to him . . .

He groaned her name aloud, an ancient agony ringing in his voice. His hand brushed over her ribs to capture one straining breast, and the silky fabric of her bra rubbed urgently against the budding nipple.

Dear God, how desperately she wanted him. Her skin was flushed from the fire in her blood, her lips were swollen with the sweet torment of his kisses. When he lifted the sweater over her head, she didn't resist, anxious to touch him, to feel his body molding to hers.

He tossed her sweater onto the couch and quickly added his own. When he once again faced her, his torso was bare. Dark hair curled over rock-hard muscles and arrowed downward to his belt, emphasizing the flat, rippling muscles of his abdomen.

He looked down upon her, his eyes smoldering. "God, you're beautiful," he murmured. His gaze lingered at the gentle swell of her breasts, the creamy skin rounding over the edge of the sheer bra. Beneath the white lace, rose-colored nipples protruded deliciously, invitingly. With tentative fingers, Zachary outlined the beautiful buds, his eyes returning to Lauren's heavy-lidded gaze. Tangled red-brown hair framed her face, and desire darkened her intriguing green eyes. Zachary had to fight the urge to strip her of the rest of her clothes and take her at once.

"I don't want you to do anything you might regret," he said, his voice husky with desire.

"I won't."

"You're certain?"

She hesitated, then sighed and slowly shook her head. "Oh, Zachary, I'm not certain of anything right now," she admitted.

Gently he kissed her forehead and twined his fingers

in her long, shining mane. The flames from the fire reflected in his brown eyes, and Lauren wound her arms around his chest, holding him close, as if she were afraid he might vanish into the stormy night.

The feel of her pressed against his bare flesh made him groan in frustration. "If only you knew what you do to me."

When she tilted her face up to look at him, he brushed gentle lips across her cheeks and tasted the salt traces of her tears. She felt his muscles, taut with restraint, press against her thighs and hips.

He wants you, she thought, *with as much passion as you feel storming through your veins. He wants you. Tonight.*

"Lauren," he murmured against the fiery curtain of her hair, "I'm sorry."

She sensed his battle, knew that he was trying to strain himself, and her heart wrenched at the desperation in his apology. Still, he didn't let go but held her more closely, his arms tightening around her as he willed the tides of passion to subside. "I . . . I shouldn't have let things go so far," he said softly.

With more strength than she thought herself capable of, Lauren pushed him gently away, hoping she would find the courage to tell him that what had happened tonight would never be repeated. But she couldn't. It would have been a lie.

Chapter Eight

ZACHARY KISSED HER forehead softly, his lips lingering against her skin. "I'll wait for you, Lauren," he promised, "until you realize that what I feel for you won't interfere with locating Alicia and Ryan, and you can give me some sort of commitment. I think you know how I feel about you."

Dear God, what was he saying? "I really can't think about any commitments other than that of finding the children," she said softly, hoping that he would understand.

Involuntarily, her eyes lifted to the mantel, to the picture of the two smiling children. God, what she would do just to see them again, talk to Alicia, watch Ryan smile. "I just need time," she said, wondering if she were releasing the one man who might change her life. She knew that Zachary was asking for more than a simple night of passion; his feelings for her ran far deeper than a casual one-night stand. But Lauren wasn't ready for an affair—not when her life was so unbalanced. Loving Zachary and knowing that someday they would part was more than she could handle at the moment. Everyone she had ever loved in her life had abandoned her—first her parents, killed in the boating accident; then her husband, lost to fate and the wiles of other women; and now her children, taken from her so heedlessly by a man she had trusted. She couldn't bear the thought of learning to love Zachary only to have him leave her as had all the other people she'd loved.

That she was beginning to love him came as a surprise, and she told herself she was confusing love with dependence. She *needed* Zachary to help her find her children, not as a woman needs a man. She reached for her sweater, but Zachary's hand clamped firmly over her wrist.

"I want you, Lauren, but I won't push. I have to know that my feelings are returned."

"You know I care about you."

"Do you? Is it me or the fact that I might be able to find the children?"

"Both."

His thick brows drew together, and his eyes reached into hers, searching. "I won't push you, Lauren," he promised, relaxing the fingers on her wrist slightly, "but I'm not a patient man."

"And I'm not a patient woman."

His lips quirked in the hint of a warm smile. "Thank God for small favors."

She retrieved the sweater and pulled it hastily over her head, lifting the thick curtain of her hair through the neck and looking from Zachary to the picture on the mantel. Zachary saw her contemplative expression as she gazed at the portrait of the children. *First things first,* he reminded himself. Gently, he drew away from her and stretched his aching back and shoulder muscles. Then he stood and grabbed his sweater.

He hesitated a minute before dressing hastily. "I'd better go," he said when he saw the reluctance in her wide eyes, "while I still can."

She attempted a smile but failed. "I'm not trying to

drive you away, you know. It's just that . . ." She lifted her palms expressively.

"You're going through a difficult period in your life. And you don't want anything to interfere."

"Yes." She caught her lower lip between her teeth. "I didn't think that you'd really understand."

He made a deprecating sound. "Oh, I understand, lady, probably better than I should." He picked up his briefcase and notepads and stuffed them under his arm. "Good night, Lauren." He turned on his heel and walked to the door. By the time that Lauren had managed to stand, he was gone.

SATURDAY AND SUNDAY passed quickly but quietly. The phone didn't ring and Lauren didn't hear anything about the children. Nor did Zachary call or come over. The small house seemed strangely quiet and cold. When Zachary had finally left her on Friday night, Lauren had felt lonelier than she'd ever thought possible. Without the children the little house seemed gloomy, but without Zachary it suddenly felt like a cage without a key.

Lauren couldn't shake her dismal mood, and the weather didn't help. Throughout the starless night the rain had pelted the windows and gurgled through the overflowing gutters. Lauren had tossed and turned until early morning, caught up in restless, unresolved dreams of Alicia, Ryan and Zachary. In retrospect, the next morning, Lauren thought it odd that Doug hadn't been in the dream at all. Maybe subconsciously she'd decided that Douglas Regis no longer had rights as a husband or a father.

Trying to shake her moodiness, Lauren spent most of the rainy weekend inside the house, working on a project she'd been putting off for weeks—wallpapering the kitchen. Now that she'd been able to locate an attorney who had the expertise and desire to help her find the children, she could dedicate some time to the repairs and renovations the little house so desperately needed.

If the weather permitted, he also intended to stack the cord of wood lying haphazardly against the garage onto the back porch out of the rain.

"That's a tall order," Lauren told herself as she threw on a pair of her favorite faded jeans and a sweatshirt that still had splotches of house paint on it from the last project she'd completed. Eyeing the drizzly day outside, she started gluing wallpaper to the kitchen walls.

As she applied wet paste to the strips of wallpaper, Lauren considered the fact that she had been willing, even eager, to make love to Zachary the night before. Never had she wanted a man so desperately. Her feelings were completely irrational, she decided, and the sexual attraction she felt for him had to be ignored, at least until he'd located the children. She had to get Zachary Winters, the man, off her mind and concentrate on him only as the attorney she'd hired to find her children. The task proved impossible. She found that she was humming to herself and thinking of Zachary as she worked.

It took most of the weekend to finish the wallpapering, but by late Sunday afternoon it was done and most of the mess had been cleaned. Lauren looked at her handiwork with a practiced eye and smiled to herself. The new print, a muted gray with a striped basket weave design in cream, tan and blue, gave the kitchen a much-needed face-lift. She decided that next weekend she would tackle painting the scratched wooden cabinets in the kitchen. A solid ivory color would brighten the room . . . and complement the steel-blue counters.

Her conscience bothered her a little at the thought of the firewood still lying on the wet ground, a tarp thrown hastily over the top of the mound to protect it from the rain. *So much to do,* she thought while sipping the final dregs of her cold coffee and setting the cup aside, *and never enough time.* "Oh, well, Rome wasn't built in a day," she told herself philosophically as she headed for a hot shower to remove the dirt and relieve the aches in her tired muscles.

She'd showered, combed out her hair and was sipping a mug of steaming hot soup when the phone rang. The clock had just chimed five o'clock. Her first thought was that the caller had to be Zachary, and her pulse began to race as she answered the telephone.

"Hello?" she called into the receiver.

"Mrs. Regis?" asked an unfamiliar, weak female voice.

Someone who knows something about Alicia and Ryan. Her heart skipped a beat. "Yes?"

"My name is Minnie Johnson," the elderly voice said. "I saw you on that program, *Eye Contact*, the other night."

Lauren's palms began to sweat and her fingers curled around the phone until her knuckles whitened. "And you think you know where my children are?" she asked anxiously.

There was a pause. "Well, that's just it. I'm not sure, but there are a couple of kids in this neighborhood, living with their dad, about the right ages, y'know, and I thought that they might be yours. "I really didn't know how to call you or whether I should, but I called the television station, couldn't get an answer and found your number in the book."

Lauren's thoughts were spinning crazily. This was the first positive piece of information she'd received in over a year. Though she knew that it might turn out to be only a coincidence that didn't involve Alicia and Ryan, she couldn't help the anticipation she felt. "Where do you live, Mrs. Johnson?"

"Out here in Gresham. East County."

Oregon. Less than thirty miles away. Tears began to gather in Lauren's eyes, and she had trouble keeping her voice steady. "Do you know the family?"

"Not much. Keep to myself most of the time, don't y'know? I don't get out much. . . ." The old voice faded and then returned, with more conviction. "But I've seen the neighborhood kids."

"And they took like mine?"

"Yep. A girl 'bout seven or eight, I'd guess, and a boy a couple of years younger. The dad, he goes by the name of Dave Parker, but well, I figured that husband of yours could have changed his name easy enough."

Alicia will be seven in three weeks. Lauren's heart was thudding so wildly, she had trouble hearing the woman's soft responses. "And the children? Do you know their names?"

"No. I'm sorry. Like I said, I don't pay much attention, at least I didn't until I saw you on TV and put two and two together."

"I understand," Lauren replied, her hopes soaring. *Was it possible? Could Alicia and Ryan be barely a half hour away? All this time? Oh, God.* "But you think this boy and girl might be Alicia and Ryan?"

"That's why I called. Look," said the elderly woman, "here's the address." She repeated the street and cross street where the Parker family resided, and Lauren scribbled the information on the notepad near the phone.

"Thank you so much for calling," she said with heartfelt enthusiasm.

"You're welcome. I just hope those kids are yours, or if not, I sure hope you find yours soon. It's not right, a mother being away from her kids like that." There was a short pause in the conversation, as if the elderly lady wanted to say something more and then thought better of it. "Please let me know how it all turns out."

"Thank you, I will."

"I'm praying for you."

Tears of gratitude for the woman's kindness streamed from Lauren's eyes. "Thanks."

Lauren replaced the receiver and stared at the single piece of paper with the vital name and address. *Please,* she prayed, *let me find them.*

She dropped into the chair at the old desk and picked up the receiver again, anxiously punching out the number of Zachary's home. When he answered, she closed her eyes in relief.

"Hello?"

"Zachary, it's Lauren. I've got wonderful news! A woman just called and she thinks the kids might be in Gresham. She gave me the address. A man lives alone with two kids, about the ages of Alicia and Ryan. Can you believe it, right here in Oregon—"

"Hold on a minute," Zachary interrupted, then hesitated. He hated to burst her frail bubble of anticipation, but he had to be realistic. It was more than his job. He cared about Lauren and didn't want to see her hopes crushed again. "What makes the woman think they might be your kids?" he asked.

"She saw the picture of Alicia and Ryan on *Eye Contact.*"

Zachary hesitated, and Lauren could sense his reluctance to share her enthusiasm. "That picture was nearly two years old," he reminded her.

"Just the same, she thinks Alicia and Ryan are there."

"I think it's highly unlikely that Doug is in Gresham."

Lauren knew that Zachary was just trying to force

her to remain calm and prepare her for a possible—make that probable—disappointment. But this was her first real lead as to the whereabouts of her children! "We have to check it out," she said, her voice rising a little.

"Of course we do. In the morning—"

"Now!"

"Lauren, think about it. You can't go barging into a man's house at six o'clock at night, demanding to see his children. What if your information is wrong?"

"I have to know!"

"What you've got to do is keep things in perspective. Even if we go to Gresham and this guy, what's his name—"

"Dave Parker," she supplied impatiently.

"Even if Parker turns out to be Regis, which I doubt, what would you do?"

"Oh, God, Zachary, I'd hold my children," she said, her voice cracking. "I'd call the police, steal the kids, do *anything* I had to and then take them home with me."

"I don't think—"

"You don't *understand*!" she cried passionately. "It's been over a year since I've seen them, Zachary. *A year!* I'm going out to that address and I'm going to find out if my children are there. I'm going with you or without you. Your choice." She tapped her foot angrily on the carpet, waiting for his response.

He muttered something unintelligible, then let out a breath of air exasperatedly. "All right, wait for me. I'll be at your place in about . . . forty minutes."

"Good. I'll see you then." Lauren hung up and dashed into the bedroom, stripping off her robe and pulling on her favorite cream-colored slacks and a rose-hued sweater. After combing her hair until it shined, she repaired her makeup and then paced from the living room to the kitchen and back again, constantly checking the time while she waited impatiently for Zachary.

When she heard the familiar sound of his truck in the driveway, she grabbed her jacket and dashed out of the house clutching the precious piece of paper.

Zachary was halfway up the rain-slickened stairs and waited on the third step while Lauren locked the door. Her fingers were shaking and her cheeks were flushed. "Maybe you should stay here and wait," he suggested, seeing the hope shining in her beautiful green eyes. She was setting herself up for a monumental fall. He could feel it in his bones.

"Not on your life, counselor. I've waited over a year for this moment, and I'm not about to let you go alone." She was already down the short flight of stairs and striding toward his pickup with purposeful steps. He had to jog to catch her. When he was within arm's length, Zachary reached for her arm and twirled her around to face him, his fingers wrapping possessively over her coat sleeve. Zachary hated himself for what he had to do.

"I want you to be realistic, Lauren," he said as he felt the rain slip down his face. "This could be a disappointment, you know."

"I know that." She jerked her arm free. "But I can handle it," she assured him, turning back to the car. She was wasting precious time; time he could be spending with her children.

Lauren climbed into the pickup and slid to the passenger side of the cab. Zachary reluctantly followed her and shut the door. "You're sure . . . that you'll be okay—if this turns out to be a bad lead?"

Her green eyes burned into his. "I know the chances of this working out are slim, Zachary. But I can't help the fact that I'm as nervous as a cat about the possibility of facing Doug again and seeing Alicia and Ryan." In the fragile light of evening, her eyes narrowed into angry slits. "You can't possibly imagine the hell it's been for me this past year. Now, maybe—just maybe—I'll see Ryan, talk to Alicia, hold them both again . . . forever."

"If they're really in Gresham."

She smiled uncertainly, her incredible eyes darkening somewhat. "I can handle it if this all blows up in my face," she promised, her lower lip trembling.

Zachary sighed and settled behind the wheel. He could tell that there was no changing Lauren's mind. "Okay, I just have one condition."

She turned her head in his direction. "What's that?"

"That I go to the door, ask the questions." His dark eyes impaled hers. "Without you."

"Why?" she asked suspiciously.

"If Doug sees you, he may decide to bolt. And that's the last thing we'd want, considering what you've already been through."

"How could he?"

"The same way he did last time. He might get scared, pack the kids in the car tonight and run. Are you willing to take that gamble?"

"No," she whispered. She didn't think she could face losing the children a second time.

"Okay. So I'll go to the door. You stay in the truck and we'll see if the old lady knows what she's talking about."

"You're saying that even if my children are there, I won't be able to see them."

"I think it might be best," he agreed as he inserted the key into the ignition. "It's more important that we get them back to you for good rather than just for a quick look. Agreed?"

"Agreed," she said, wondering how she would be

able to restrain herself if, indeed, the children were her beloved Alicia and Ryan.

DAVE PARKER WAS not Douglas Regis. Not by a long shot. As Zachary stared into the inquisitive brown eyes of the short man, he knew without a doubt that Lauren's hopes would be cruelly dashed once more. Silently, he cursed himself for letting Lauren talk him into bringing her out to Gresham on this wild-goose chase.

"Yes, I'm Parker," the man had replied to Zachary's inquiry. Dave Parker's face was honest; he didn't seem to be hiding anything, and Zachary had seen enough bluffs on the witness stand to recognize honest curiosity. "And I've got an eight-year-old daughter and a four-year-old son." Parker frowned a little at the visitor's unlikely questions. "Why are you interested in Ellen and Butch? What's all this about?"

"A mistake, I'm afraid," Zachary admitted with a disarming grin. He caught a glimpse of a red-haired girl standing behind her father. The girl bore very little resemblance, if any, to Lauren's Alicia.

Zachary explained that he was a local attorney who was representing Lauren Regis, a woman who was desperately searching for her lost children.

"And you think I could help you?" Parker was clearly dubious.

Zachary shifted from one foot to the other. "We're checking out every possibility, no matter how remote."

"But I've never heard of this guy—Regis, or whatever his name is, and the kids don't have any classmates by the names of Alicia or Ryan. . . ." He lifted his shoulders. "Sorry. I'd like to help the lady, but I can't."

Parker followed Zachary back to the pickup, his

children following happily in his wake despite the rain and their lack of jackets.

"You kids go inside," he growled good-naturedly as he approached Lauren's side of the truck, "before you get soaked to the skin. Go on. Scat." The children ignored their father, and Parker turned to Lauren as she rolled down the window. She looked into the curious faces of the two small children and realized with a severe sense of disappointment that she was no closer to locating Alicia and Ryan than she had been a year ago.

"Hate to disappoint you," Parker said regretfully, "but I've never heard of your husband or your kids. Whoever told you that I might have some information about them gave you a bum steer."

"It's okay, Mr. Parker—"

"Dave."

"Dave," she repeated with a courageous smile. Her eyes returned to Parker's children. Though the girl held no resemblance to Alicia, the blond boy with the round blue eyes did have facial characteristics similar to Ryan's. Lauren's heart began to ache all over again.

The two kids scampered around the back end of the truck after Parker glared at them in mock anger.

"Sorry I can't be of more help," he concluded as Zachary opened the door of the truck. "I can't imagine why anyone would think that I would be able to help you."

"Just an anonymous tip," Zachary replied, handing the short man his business card. "If you do learn anything, please call me, either at the office or home."

"Will do." Dave smiled at Lauren and then turned his attention to his children. "Come on, you two, dinner's probably burned already. We'd better eat and then you've got some homework to attend to." He patted his daughter's head affectionately.

Lauren watched the retreating figures wearily. She leaned her head against the back of the seat and fought the urge to cry.

"I should have listened to you," she said, forcing her gaze out the window as Zachary started the truck and eased into the uneven flow of traffic. He shifted gears, and then his large hand covered hers.

"You couldn't. You were too excited."

"And foolish."

"It's not foolish to want to see your kids, Lauren," he said, his voice soothing, "but you've got to face the fact that this is just one of what might be a long string of false starts. Your ex-husband is clever, and he definitely doesn't want to be found. Unless I miss my guess, he's in another state . . . or country."

Lauren shook her head despondently. "We may never find them," she whispered as the black void of uncertainty loomed before her.

"Sure we will." He lifted his hand to the side of her face and gently brushed aside a tear with his thumb. "It's just going to take time, that's all."

THE NEXT TWO WEEKS were tedious. The tension in the bank was so thick that at times Lauren felt as if she would scream. On the first Monday back on the job, she'd been informed by George West that due to the circumstances involving her relationship with Zachary Winters, the Mason trust was no longer under her administration. From that day forward, Bob Harding would be in charge of the account.

Bob had regarded her with woeful eyes, knowing that she saw the transfer of authority as a slap in the face. Lauren tried to tell herself that it didn't matter, that the Mason trust was more trouble than it was worth, but she felt a little disappointed that the president of the bank had so little faith in her integrity.

"Be thankful you've still got a job," she told herself two weeks later as she reflected on the last several days.

After Minnie Johnson's call, what had started out as a trickle had quickly become a flood. Lauren was deluged with messages on her recording machine from people who were certain they had seen her children. Both she and Zachary sifted through the information, sorting fact from fiction, fantasy from truth, crank calls from sincere offers of help. Nothing had come of any of the leads, and with each passing day Lauren had grown more dejected. Sometimes the enormity of the task made finding her children seem impossible.

Working so closely with Zachary had been difficult. The attraction she felt for him continued to grow steadily, though, true to his word, he'd made no more advances upon her. She watched him while he sat at her kitchen table, and a warmth spread through her. His glasses were perched on the end of his nose as he meticulously went over each piece of information that came in. His legal pads were filled with notes to himself, clues to check, ideas beginning to hatch. *If nothing else,* she thought, *he's thorough.* And that's what she wanted. Lauren didn't doubt that, given enough time, Zachary would find the children. Her fears rested on the length of time involved. As each day slipped into the next, she felt the chasm between herself and the kids widening. Would they remember her? Would they run and hide when she opened her arms to them? When, oh, God, when would she see them again? Only time would tell.

Despite the worries clouding her mind, Lauren found that the conversations and quiet time she shared with Zachary had come to mean a lot to her. She welcomed the sound of his voice, smiled when she heard his truck in the driveway. And Mason trust or not, she was glad she'd hired him as her lawyer, for he was fast becoming her friend. Occasionally an unspoken invitation lingered in his dark eyes; she knew she had only to accept and they would become lovers.

The hours they spent together seemed to strengthen a bond between them; Lauren began to feel as if Zachary were as committed to finding the children as she was. She also knew that once the children were safely home, there would be no reason to see him, and his interest in her would certainly wane. Today she represented a challenge; once the children were found, he would go on to the next seemingly impossible task.

Though he was still kind to her, it seemed to Lauren that he'd purposely built a wall around himself . . . and under the circumstances, she thought it was a wise precaution. She reasoned that he'd finally realized an affair with her would be too sticky, what with the Mason case and all. Only once in a while, when he thought she wasn't looking, did she catch him staring at her with a flame of passion in his intense brown eyes.

FRIDAY DIDN'T COME soon enough to suit Lauren. The hours at the bank were torture. Though she still worked on the private trusts, the fact that she was excluded from all conversation regarding the Mason trust drove her to distraction. Bob Harding would still drop by her office to chat, but even he seemed distant, nervous whenever the conversation strayed to the forbidden territories of Hammond Mason, Zachary Winters or Joshua Tate.

For once Lauren was relieved to return to her lonely house in Westmoreland. She didn't mind that the weekend stretched before her. Anything was better than the tension at the bank. She kicked off her shoes, rewound the tape on the recording machine and was disappointed that no one had called with information about the children.

After changing into comfortable jeans, a thick plum-colored sweater and worn tennis shoes, she stood in her bedroom and began extracting the pins from her hair. She was just shaking it loose when she heard the far rumble of Zachary's truck. Glancing into the mirror, she noticed that she was smiling. Like it or not, she was falling in love with the man.

She was already at the front door when Zachary knocked.

"I didn't expect you tonight," she said, not bothering to hide her pleasure at seeing him.

"I thought it was time for a change," he replied cryptically, and for the first time in two weeks, he drew her into the possessive circle of his arms.

"A change, counselor? What kind of change?"

"Of scenery."

"Oh?"

"Pack your things. We're going to the coast," he said, kissing her lightly on the forehead.

"Tonight?"

"Right now."

"But I can't," she replied, trying to pull out of his persuasive embrace.

"Why not?" He nuzzled her neck and a tingling sensation whispered across her nape. "I've been as patient as I can, lady, and I won't take no for an answer."

A dozen excuses formed in her mind, all of them sounding incredibly frail. "I might get a call—"

"The machine will take care of it."

"Someone might come by—"

"They'll come back or leave a message."

"But Alicia and Ryan. Maybe someone is bringing them home to me right now."

Zachary tightened his arms around her and lifted his head to gaze into her eyes. "You and I both know that's not going to happen." One finger reached up and traced the worried arch of her brow. "What are you afraid of, Lauren? Is it me?"

"Of course not."

"Did Doug hurt you so badly that you're afraid to be with another man?"

"No."

"I promise that I won't ask you to do anything you don't want," he vowed, his dark eyes gazing intently into hers.

"I know that." For two weeks he'd kept to himself, treating her casually, remaining distant. She knew she could trust him with her life, but she wasn't so certain about her own feelings.

"We both need a break," he reasoned persuasively. "You more than I. The sea air will give us each a chance to think differently, more clearly, and when we get back, who knows? Maybe we'll just solve this riddle."

"You don't believe that any more than I do," she challenged.

"You won't know until you give it a try."

He was trying to buoy her spirits, and they both knew it, but Lauren couldn't fault his judgment. "All right, counselor," she said with a coy toss of her head, "you've got yourself a deal."

"Finally," he groaned, and released her. "So come on, get a move on. I'd like to get to the cabin before midnight."

Without further argument she went into the bedroom, threw a few things into her overnight bag and paused only for a moment to consider the fact that she was about to spend a weekend with a man for the first time since she'd been married. She should shrug it off, she thought, be a little more avant-garde, but she couldn't. She was falling in love with Zachary Winters, and the decision to spend a weekend alone with him couldn't be made lightly. Though it wasn't as if she were a seventeen-year-old virgin dashing off to a midnight rendezvous with her college boyfriend, Lauren wasn't the kind of woman who could sleep with a man and forget him overnight.

"Second thoughts?" he asked, suddenly standing in the doorway to the bedroom, leaning one shoulder against the jamb.

"A few."

His shoulder slumped a little, and he raked his fingers through his sable-dark hair. "You want to talk about them?" he asked, his eyes kind and understanding.

She gathered her courage and faced the obvious—she was falling in love with Zachary Winters. Avoiding him or denying her own physical urges wouldn't stop that. "Sure. But let's wait till we're at the beach," she replied, caressing him with her eyes. With renewed determination she snapped the overnight bag closed and lifted it from the bed. "After you, counselor."

Chapter Nine

THE SMALL CABIN was positioned on a cliff high above the ocean offering what Lauren supposed was a commanding view of the stormy Pacific Ocean. As Zachary drove down the short lane to park near a dilapidated garage, Lauren squinted through the windshield for her first peek at the rustic coastal retreat.

"Here it is," Zachary announced as he stared at the cabin in which he had last seen Rosemary alive. "Home away from home." He turned off the ignition and looked at Lauren. "I guess we'd better go inside."

Though she detected a note of reluctance in Zachary's voice, Lauren was anxious to see the cabin and get a glimpse of the personal side of Zachary's life. Although she had spent as much time with him as was possible in the past two weeks, she realized that she didn't know much more about him personally than she had on the first day she'd entered his office nearly a month before.

Grabbing her overnight bag, she dashed through the slanting rain and down a slightly overgrown path. Zachary was right behind her. He carried his canvas bag as well as the sack of groceries they'd purchased at the market in Cannon Beach. He also managed to train the beam of a flashlight onto the sandy path leading to the front door of the cabin.

The wind blowing off the ocean howled and threw

Lauren's hair into her face. Raindrops fell heavily from the black sky and splashed against her cheeks to chill her skin. The salty smell of the ocean permeated the air. Lauren paused for a moment to scan the dark, westerly sky and listen to the roar of the surf, but Zachary nudged her forward.

"I just want to see the ocean, she said over the sound of the ocean and rising wind.

"It's too dark. Wait till we're inside and I'll try to switch on the exterior lights."

With one last glance at the inky, raging ocean, Lauren followed Zachary to the door.

After several attempts, he was able to turn the key in the seldom-used lock and reach inside to snap on the lights. He propped the door open with his body and cocked his head toward the brightly lit interior. "Go on in. It's not much to look at, but at least we'll be alone." That thought was all the encouragement she needed to carry her over the threshold. Two solid days alone with Zachary. No phones, no Mason trust or Northwestern Bank, she thought gratefully. Then she realized that also there were still *no children*. Despondently, she walked through the doorway and into the tiny cabin overlooking the ocean.

The furniture was worn, but sturdy; a few mismatched pieces seemed to blend into a comfortable eclectic design. The walls were yellowed pine, the ceiling boasted exposed beams and the windows were composed of small panes, most of which faced west toward what she suspected was a panoramic view of the ocean. A corner fireplace of blue stone was blackened and empty, and the cabin felt cold, as if it hadn't been lived in for years.

Zachary tossed his overnight bag onto the couch and set the paper grocery sack on the counter separating kitchen from living area. "I haven't been here in a while," he admitted as he watched her look around.

"How long?"

He shrugged as if her question were insignificant, and his lower lip protruded thoughtfully. "I don't know—four, maybe five years."

"Why not?" She eyed the cabin discerningly. It could be a warm, comfortable home away from home, and she would have expected Zachary to spend quite a bit of time here.

"I don't know," he replied. "Too busy, I guess."

"With all the work at the office?" she quipped, not intending to sound sarcastic. He looked up sharply and impaled her with dark, knowing eyes. "I'm sorry," she said quickly. "I didn't mean it the way it sounded!" She tossed her jacket over the back of the couch.

"This place brings back a lot of unpleasant memories," he admitted, obviously uncomfortable with the subject. His gaze moved familiarly over the objects in the room; the slightly worn, wine-colored couch, an overstuffed tan chair, two scratched end tables.

For the first time Lauren realized that Zachary was referring to his dead wife. Hadn't Bob Harding told her that Rosemary, Zachary's wife, who had been pregnant at the time, had been killed in a single-car accident near the coast? It had probably happened while she and Zachary were spending a quiet weekend together. No wonder he hadn't returned to the little cabin overlooking the ocean. Rosemary, the beautiful wife he had adored, had died not far from here.

Lauren rubbed her hands over her forearms as if experiencing a sudden chill. "I didn't mean to pry."

"You didn't." He started toward the door. "Why don't

you try to find your way around the kitchen? I'll work on the fire, if I can find any dry wood."

"Just like home," she said, thinking about the comfortable routine they'd established together the past couple of weeks at her home in Westmoreland.

Zachary hesitated at the door, his gaze momentarily locked with hers, and he flashed her an endearing smile that warmed her heart. "Yeah, just like home."

She familiarized herself with the rustic kitchen as she reheated the Irish stew they'd purchased at a restaurant near the grocery store in Cannon Beach, warmed French bread and tossed a salad. Zachary worked at the fireplace, alternately cursing the poorly functioning damper and stoking the sodden logs that had to be coaxed to ignite.

An hour later they had consumed the hearty meal and were sitting together on the floor of the living room, boots discarded, bare feet warming on the stone hearth. Zachary's arm was around Lauren's shoulders, and her back was propped against the burgundy couch as she sipped clear wine from a cut-glass goblet.

When the conversation began to lag, Lauren listened to the storm and imagined she heard the powerful breakers pounding the rocky beach with thunderous intensity. The wind whipped noisily around the tall grass surrounding the cabin and through the contorted pines that clung to the rocky cliffs.

"So who keeps this place up for you?" Lauren asked as she sipped her wine.

"There is a maid service in Cannon Beach. Someone comes in once a month, more often if I request. I called them early in the week and asked that someone clean the place before we arrived. I didn't think you'd want to spend the weekend dusting furniture and mopping floors."

"Oh, I don't know. I'm pretty good at it. Lots of practice, you know," she said, smiling. "Besides, the company would have been great." She looked at him, her eyes twinkling. "And you would have gotten all of the hard work. I don't do windows."

"What you do, lady," Zachary said, his voice low, "is fascinate the hell out of me."

Caught off guard, she looked into his eyes and was lost in the depths of his dark, omniscient gaze. She twirled the wineglass nervously in her fingers. Reflections of the fire's shadows caught in the glass, seeming to turn her wine golden. "What would you have done if I'd had other plans this weekend?" she asked.

"I thought about that." He turned his gaze back to the quiet flames. "I decided to come back here anyway."

"Alone?"

He looked up sharply. "What kind of question is that?"

"I just wanted to make sure that I wasn't the third or fourth woman who was offered an invitation."

Zachary laughed hollowly and shook his head. A lock of sable-brown hair fell over his eyes, and he pushed it away. "You shouldn't have to ask."

"I don't know much about you," she said. "And you know everything about me. My life is a series of files, cross-files, notes on legal pads and tapes. You've examined my work record, my marriage, even my sex life."

"Does that make you uncomfortable?"

"A little."

Zachary studied her luminous green eyes and frowned. "I had to ask all those questions. I needed to know everything about you and your family life in order to start searching for your children."

"I know, but in the process you've managed to avoid any questions about *your* private life."

"I'm the attorney, remember?"

She set her empty glass on the raised hearth and turned to look at him. "But not tonight, right? Tonight has nothing to do with finding the kids, or the fact that I hired you. Tonight we're here as friends."

"At least," he replied, smiling.

"Then you understand."

"What? That I should tell you everything there is to know about me? I'm afraid I'd bore you to tears."

"Not a chance, counselor," she disagreed with a cautious grin. "And I don't want to know everything, I suppose," she pointed out, catching her lower lip between her teeth. "Though it would be nice. I guess what I really wanted to know was that you weren't seriously involved with another woman."

He laughed. "Keeping up that kind of relationship would be a little difficult, don't you think, considering the amount of time I've spent with you lately."

Lauren knew she was blushing and wished there was a way she could stop. "I just wanted to be sure."

"Oh, Lauren, if you had any idea what I've been going through the last couple of weeks . . . seeing you, talking with you, working with you and not being able to touch you." His dark eyes searched hers. "I thought I'd go out of my mind."

"That works two ways, counselor," she said, smiling uncertainly.

"You're a tease, you know," he remarked, setting down his empty glass.

"Hardly."

He brought his face close to hers and looked deeply into her eyes. "I should have ignored all your ridiculous reasons for keeping me at arm's length."

"I don't remember saying anything ridiculous." Lauren swallowed with difficulty. His warm breath caressed her face, and his eyes—God, his gentle brown eyes seemed to be looking into her soul. Her heart began to pound.

"I'm too old to play games," he said.

"I don't think you're exactly over the hill."

"But I'm tired of playing cat and mouse with you. It's child's play. Both of us have been married before. We know what it means to be intimately involved with someone who is important to us." He shifted a little and settled back, caressing the nape of her neck with his fingers.

She forced her eyes to meet his directly. "What are you asking, Zachary?"

"Only that you accept your feelings for what they are and that you don't hide behind any excuses—your marriage, your kids, the Mason trust lawsuit. All of that is back in Portland. This weekend, it's just you and me."

"Naked to the world?" she asked, trying to dispel the tension in the room.

"To each other." He brushed her lips softly with his, and Lauren closed her eyes. She felt him shift his weight and realized that she was slipping backward onto the heavy braided rug. She didn't care.

The pressure on her lips increased as Zachary's passion intensified. His kiss deepened, and willingly she parted her lips to the supple invasion of his tongue. The pounding of her heart echoed in her ears, and she felt the dormant fires of womanly need ignite deep within her.

His hands found the hem of her sweater and he slid it slowly up her back, warming her skin, fanning the restless flames of her desire. She felt his thumb outline the back of her ribs, tracing sensual circles against the muscles of her back.

"Let me love you," he whispered into her ear. He lifted the sweater over her head and stared down at the beauty of her breasts straining against the sheer lace of her bra. His head lowered, and he kissed the dusky hollow between the luscious mounds, letting his tongue slide up to press against the hollow of her throat. Her pulse quivered expectantly.

Deftly, he unbuttoned his shirt and tossed it aside. Lauren feasted her eyes on his rock-hard abdomen and chest, bronzed and glistening in the golden glow of the fire. Beads of sweat had collected on his forehead, and his corded shoulder muscles vividly displayed the restraint under which he held himself.

Lauren twined her fingers in the thick waves of his dark hair, and she moaned his name when his fingers found the catch of her bra and released it, allowing her breasts to fall free. The tip of his tongue touched one dark peak and then the other, the nipples hardening expectantly. Lauren had to fight the urge to plead for an end to the exquisite torture, to beg him to fill her aching body with his.

"I love you," he whispered, and Lauren found herself wanting desperately to believe his words. No one, except perhaps her two small children and her dead parents, had ever loved her. Certainly no man had ever really cared about her.

Gently, he rotated their bodies, positioning her above him. His hands gently massaged the muscles of her back as he stared into her flushed face. He pressed her forward with his palms, took one taut nipple between his lips and slowly suckled.

Lauren was supporting her weight with her hands placed on the carpet on either side of Zachary's face. As he filled his mouth with the ripeness of her breasts, she threw back her head and let the exquisite sensations overtake her. While he feasted from one creamy mound, his hands massaged the other ripe peak, preparing it for the plundering of his lips and tongue.

A sheen of sweat dampened his skin and reflected in the fire's glow; every muscle of his body was taut. Her fingers traced the outline of a male nipple, and Zachary sucked in his breath.

"Oh, God, Lauren," he murmured, his eyes closing with the feel of her fingers against his skin. "Let me love you and never stop."

He touched the waistband of her jeans, and his fingers pressed urgently against the velvet-soft skin of her midriff. She heard the zipper slide down, felt the gentle tug of her jeans as they slid over her hips and down her calves.

Her heart was throbbing by the time he'd removed her jeans and his own. Then his lips captured hers once again. His arms encircled her waist, pressing her against him, letting her feel the urgency of his need. Touching her intimately, he pushed her to the floor and covered her yielding body with his own.

His fingers caressed her thighs and kneaded her buttocks until she groaned in exquisite agony.

"Zachary, please," she pleaded. "Please, love me."

"I do, sweet lady," he replied, lowering himself upon her and gently urging her legs apart with his knees. "I'll love you forever, if you let me."

"Oh, God, yes," she cried, as she felt the warmth of his body gently pierce hers. She gasped as he settled upon her and began to fill her with swift, sure strokes of love that urged her higher, forced her soul to soar in physical and spiritual ecstasy.

Moist heat surged within her, urged forward with the possessive thrusts of Zachary's body. Her breath came in short, shallow gasps until she felt the splendor of his lovemaking explode in a series of earth-shattering waves that ripped through her body as well as her mind.

He fell against her, crushing her breasts with his weight, pressing her back into the soft coils of the rug. In the fire's glow, with the sound of the sea thudding tirelessly against the beach, they lay entwined in spirit and body, one man and one woman.

Lauren had never felt more secure with a man in her life.

"I do, you know," he said at length as he gazed down upon her and stared into her intense green eyes. Her hair fanned seductively over the tan carpet, framing her face in long, fire-gilded curls.

"Do what?"

With a reluctant shake of his head, he rolled to his side, one hand resting possessively at the bend in her waist. "I love you." He said the words sincerely, all the while staring into her eyes. Lauren didn't doubt that at this moment, while they were away from the strain of the city, locked in intimate embrace, Zachary meant what he said; he truly loved her.

"And I love you," she whispered. *Only it isn't just for this night, or for the weekend, or a year. I'll love you forever.*

He smiled softly. "Then I think we should do something."

"Do something?" she repeated. "What're you talking about, counselor?"

"I think we should consider the fact that you could get pregnant."

She nodded absently. "I'd thought of that."

"And?"

"And I'm not ready to raise a child alone . . . at least not until I can find my other children. It would be like giving up, almost . . . betraying them somehow."

"Shh." He took her hand in his and held it. "That's

not what I meant. I would never expect you to care for my child, our child, alone." He nodded slightly, as if emphasizing his words. "When the time comes, I want to be a part of his or her life; but right now . . ."

Obviously, Zachary was caught up in the moment, and Lauren couldn't find the strength to bring him back to reality. "I understand," she murmured.

"I don't think you do," he said, his eyes never leaving hers. His hand moved upward to stroke her cheek. "I love you, Lauren. And I want to marry you."

For a moment she was silent. He couldn't mean it! "Just because we made love, you don't have to propose," she said with a tremulous smile.

"Making love has nothing to do with it," he said. "Being in love does. I'd ask you to marry me tomorrow if it weren't for the fact that I want to find your kids, resolve the problems with the Mason trust lawsuit and put all the past behind us before we start a future together. I think we should start out on the right foot."

God, how desperately she wanted to believe him. "I . . . I don't think we should . . . spoil this weekend with what-ifs and maybes and whens," she said. "Let's just take one day at a time and forget about all the problems in Portland. That's what this weekend was all about, wasn't it, counselor? No heavy stuff?"

He smiled that special, rakish smile that touched her heart, glanced at the ceiling and back to her again. "Right, lady. No heavy stuff. At least not tonight."

He tugged gently on her arm, forcing them both to stand, and kissed her passionately. Then, lifting her off her feet, he headed for the small alcove that served as a bedroom—the bedroom he had shared with Rosemary.

Lauren tried to forget her jealousies of a wife long dead, but she couldn't quite shake the feeling that she was trespassing on private property.

"What's wrong?" Zachary asked as he gently lowered

her onto the bed. The ice-blue comforter was cold against her bare skin.

She looked at him with eyes filled with love. "Just hold me, darling," she murmured, clutching him to her and ignoring her doubts. Tonight she was with Zachary, and nothing else, save her concern for her children, would disrupt the bliss she felt in his arms.

"Willingly," he said as his lips claimed hers in a kiss that promised to last all night long.

Lauren awoke to the odors of perking coffee, sizzling bacon and burning wood. She was alone in the bed but could hear Zachary rustling around in the kitchen. She smiled to herself and stretched, looking around the bedroom for the first time. The gray light of morning filtered into the room through lacy curtains. Near the sturdy maple bed, there was an antique dresser with an oval mirror, and a small desk was pushed into a corner of the room. The walls were the same yellowed pine as the rest of the cabin, but the plank floor was bare and felt cold to her feet as she lowered herself from the bed.

Zachary had placed her overnight bag near the foot of the bed, and she zipped it open, threw on her robe and reached for her brush. After cinching the tie of the royal blue robe around her waist, she stood before the mirror and tried to brush the tangles free from her long auburn hair. She stared at her reflection and wondered just how many times Rosemary Winters had stood before this very mirror.

Tossing off her morbid thoughts, Lauren headed for the kitchen. Zachary was busy at the stove. A smile tugged at the corners of her mouth when she noticed that he was dressed in the same gray sweatshirt and navy running shorts he'd been wearing the first time she'd seen him. The sleeves of the sweatshirt were pushed up to expose his forearms as he poked the bacon. Sweat was running down his face and had collected in a dark

V on his chest as well as his back, discoloring his shirt. A fluffy orange towel was looped over his neck. It was obvious that he'd just returned from a long run along the beach. Realizing he was being watched, he looked up and offered Lauren a devastating smile. "About time you woke up," he said as he walked over to her and circled his arms around her small waist. "God, you look good."

"And you look like you're on the way to work," she joked, eyeing his lean frame.

"Not funny, lady," he replied with a wave of the spatula, his dark eyes sparkling. "Any more talk like that and I'll wreak my vengeance on you and have my way with you right here—on the kitchen floor."

"Promises, promises." She laughed, and Zachary thought it was the most precious sound he had ever heard.

"I'm warning you," he said as he dropped the spatula and gripped her shoulders, pulling her unresisting body against his. Lazily his lips claimed hers, and she parted her mouth, ignoring everything but the tides of desire beginning to flood her senses. His fingers undid the tie at her waist to explore the hidden valley between her breasts. "You make me crazy, y'know," he whispered against her hair, gently caressing a soft, rounded breast.

She laughed a little and slowly drew away. "If we don't stop this right now, your bacon will burn."

"Who cares?" he murmured, nuzzling her neck.

"I do. I'm always starved when I wake up."

"So am I." His hands slid under the lapels and lowered to the soft hill of her hips. She moaned and he knelt on the floor, working at the knot of the robe with his teeth, letting his lips brush lightly against her abdomen as he parted the soft barrier of cloth. Finally he pushed the robe down to the floor, letting his tongue and lips caress the soft skin of her abdomen. She quivered with longing.

"Zachary—" She gasped as he nipped her lightly, his hands dancing lightly across her buttocks. Then he stood, turned off the stove and pushed the bacon off the burner.

"No more excuses," he said, and reached beneath the bend of her knees to carry her back to the bed. Lowering her slowly onto the comforter, he shed his running clothes and placed his long, hard body next to hers.

Sweat glistened on his chest, abdomen and thighs, and she ran her fingers over his damp skin as he closed his eyes and moaned her name. She touched him boldly then, making him growl deep in his throat in anticipation.

"I love you, Lauren." He swallowed with difficulty as her fingers caressed his chest, traced the length of his lean torso, dug into his buttocks. "You're a fascinating, teasing witch," he muttered, "and I love you."

He pulled her on top of him and stared at her with smoldering brown eyes. "Make love to me," he ordered, lifting his hips off the bed and rubbing sensuously against her. "Make love to me all morning."

She felt the soft hair on his thighs brushing against her legs, watched as his abdomen rippled when he pushed up to her, saw the passion glazing his eyes. "Anything you want, counselor," she whispered, lowering her head and touching her lips to one dark male nipple.

He groaned and his fingers twined in the fiery curls of her hair, holding her head against him as he moved beneath her.

"Lauren, please," he begged, his voice raw with passion.

Slowly, she lowered her body, sliding over him until with one sharp thrust he entered her. Then his hands, pressing against her upper thighs and buttocks, started the sweet, gentle motion of love.

"I want—"

"Shh," she whispered, closing her eyes as the tension within her mounted. She rocked in rhythm to it, her mind soaring, her body propelled by the driving force of Zachary's love. "Oh, God," she moaned as the spasms of love burst within her. Her body bent over his, and she felt him stiffen, then explode in a series of shock waves of hot passion. "I love you, Zachary," she cried, wondering why the words sounded so tormented.

His hands reached forward and twined in the curling silk of her hair, forcing her to lift her head and stare into his eyes. "Then marry me, Lauren. When we find your children, please, marry me."

Tears gathered in her round green eyes as she witnessed the tenderness and sincerity in his gaze. She smiled. "Of course I'll marry you, Zachary." Bending forward, she placed a kiss on his forehead while her hands brushed a lock of hair away from his face. "And once I do, I'll never let you go."

He returned her smile. "You couldn't shake me if you tried, lady. When we get married, it's forever." He shifted his weight slightly. "Now, how about a shower?" he asked.

"With you?"

"Why not?" His dark eyes twinkled mischievously. "I don't know about you, but I certainly could use one."

"Lead on." She laughed, rolling off him and standing by the bed. His gaze slid sensuously up her body.

"This could be interesting," he announced devilishly. "Very interesting."

* * *

TWO HOURS LATER, the shower and breakfast were finished. Lauren felt more satisfied than she had in years. It was as if the woman she'd hidden away for so long had finally emerged.

After the dishes were done, Zachary suggested they go for a walk along the beach, and Lauren didn't disagree. He helped her down the slightly unsteady steps that led to the stretch of beach far below the face of the cliff.

The sand was moist and the fog that had settled after the storm was beginning to lift. The horizon wasn't yet visible, but dark, black rocks near the shoreline loomed in the gray tide pools. Foamy waves slipped onto the wet sand, trying to retrieve the lost treasures they had deposited the night before during the fury of the midnight storm.

Sea gulls dipped and arced over the water, their lonesome cries piercing the air above the soft roar of the now quiet surf. Broken shells, sodden driftwood, near-black seaweed and shiny pebbles littered the sand. The salty smell of the sea lingered in the air.

Lauren was walking with Zachary, her arms linked with his, the wind pushing her hair away from her face. The only other impressions in the sand were the footprints from Zachary's early-morning run. "It's beautiful here," Lauren observed with a sigh.

"I like it."

"But you don't come here often?"

"Not anymore." He stopped and stared out to sea. The happy light faded from his eyes and his jaw hardened as if he were experiencing some inner turmoil.

"Because of Rosemary?" she asked.

His dark eyes sharpened, as if focusing on some distant object on the horizon. "Yes."

"You don't have to talk about it."

"No, it's time." He looked back to her and smiled idly. "And it's not fair to you. It's not that I have any great secret, you know, just something I'd rather forget."

"I understand." She had only to consider her painful marriage to Doug.

He placed his arm gently around her shoulders and continued walking north along the beach. "Rosemary and I had been having problems off and on. I don't think she was ever happy living in Portland. While we were in Seattle, everything was fine, or at least I thought it was. But once we moved to Portland and uprooted her, well, things were never the same. She was . . . restless."

"You loved her very much, didn't you?" Lauren asked, hating the question and wrapping her arms around her waist as if to brace herself for the truth. Suddenly, her suede jacket didn't seem to be withstanding the chill of the raw morning.

"Yes, I did. At least in the beginning. But once we were in Portland . . . hell, who knows? I was probably as much to blame as she was. My career, you know. Rosemary didn't know very many people in town and she was alone a lot of the time. That was my fault."

"And you've been blaming yourself ever since."

He frowned, then nodded slowly. "That's the way I see it, I guess. Rosemary was unhappy, and I didn't do my best to help her. That's why I bought this cabin; I thought we could spend some time alone together." His jacket was open and it caught in the sharp morning breeze.

"But it didn't work out?"

He shook his head, and the breeze ruffled his hair. "It only added to the problem," he admitted. "She saw it as just one more way to isolate her from the life she loved."

"Which was?" she asked.

"Rosemary was a very social person. She was born beautiful, an only child of wealthy parents. She had been adored and fawned over all of her life. It was to her credit that she wasn't spoiled, I suppose, but she needed a certain amount of attention as well as a social life, I guess. And I failed to provide her with those particular things that were so necessary."

He rammed his fists into the pockets of his jeans. "At first, while we were in Seattle, she tried to include me in her wide social circle, and I went along with it. But once we moved to Portland, and I buried myself in my work, trying to establish a practice with Wendell Tate, I didn't have time for the parties. On the weekends, all I wanted to do was come here and unwind. Rosemary was bored out of her mind and she told me so. She even went so far as to file for divorce once, just to shake me up, or so she claimed. She never went through with it."

"I'm sorry. . . ."

"Don't be. Maybe things would have worked out better if she'd gone through with the divorce. At least then she might still be alive." He massaged the bridge of his nose as if warding off a headache. "Rosemary was just bored and was trying in her own way to make me wake up to the fact that she was terribly unhappy."

"I take it she didn't work," Lauren said, studying the strained lines of his face before looking away and watching the graceful flight of a marauding sea gull. It was evident to her that Zachary was still a little in love with his wife.

"She tried several things—interior decorating, owning an art gallery, even writing. But nothing ever worked out for her. She blamed it on my lack of interest and support; maybe she was right." He shrugged and let out a long, weary sigh. "I should have seen it coming. . . ."

"What?" Lauren asked.

He stopped to stare at the distant horizon. As the fog lifted, dim silhouettes of small boats and larger ships had become visible in the gray morning. "I came home early one day, and apparently she didn't hear me come into the house. Anyway, she was talking with a friend, discussing the fact that she was pregnant."

Lauren remembered her discussion with Zachary the night before about the possibility of pregnancy. Was it possible that Zachary, caught up in his practice, hadn't wanted the responsibility of a child? "What happened?" she pressed.

"Nothing." His voice was emotionless. "I went into the den and she came in later." His eyes darkened with the memory. "She was carrying a tray of drinks and offered me one. Stupidly, I thought it was to celebrate the pregnancy, but she didn't mention one word of it to me. In fact, she seemed distant, reserved . . . wouldn't let me near her."

"Didn't she want the baby?" Lauren asked, appalled at the image he was painting. Lauren's children were the single most important part of her life.

"I don't know. At least I didn't, not then." He paled a little as the first rays of a frail autumn sun pierced the gray clouds. "Rosemary became moody, and I attributed it to the pregnancy. I thought she was waiting for just the right moment to spring the news on me." His lips twisted cynically as he considered what a fool he'd been. "So I brought Rosemary here."

"To the beach cabin!"

"Right. That was a mistake, not my first by a long shot and unfortunately not my last."

"She wasn't happy."

"That's putting it mildly. She paced around the cabin restlessly, as if she were looking for an excuse, any excuse to leave. She began to drink too much, and I was concerned for her as well as the baby. Finally, I asked her about it."

Zachary remembered the stricken look in Rosemary's round, violet eyes. She had accused him of murderous deeds, and she had lost her battle with hysteria.

"How did you know?" Rosemary had gasped, the blood draining from her lovely face.

"I overheard a telephone conversation last week—"

"You *bastard*!" she'd exploded, pushing her hair away from her forehead in nervous agitation. "Is that how you get your jollies? By eavesdropping, for God's sake?" she'd accused with a sneer.

Zachary shook his head and tried to dispel the vivid image.

"What happened?" Lauren asked, afraid to hear but fascinated nonetheless. What had happened to scar him so badly?

"Rosemary became hysterical and she swore that she was going to get rid of the child," he said.

"An abortion?" Lauren felt sick inside and watched Zachary's dark eyes as he recalled the painful past.

"I'm not about to have this baby," Rosemary had sworn. She'd worked herself into a frenzy. She was drinking from a half-full bottle of wine and staring at Zachary with eyes that glittered with malice. "I've already talked to a doctor."

"I won't let you do it," Zachary had responded. "I have some say-so in this, you know, seeing as I'm the father."

"Ha! You think!" she'd cried, laughing viciously. "Think about it, husband dear. How long has it been since you've been in my bed?" He'd stopped walking toward her as the meaning of her words became clear. "That's right, Zack. The baby isn't yours."

"I don't believe you," he'd replied weakly. But the satisfied smile on her lips convinced him.

"You haven't had time for me, have you? I couldn't possibly be pregnant with your child. It's been over two months since you've been near me . . . not that I'm counting, mind you."

"Then how?" His eyes had grown incredibly dark. *"Who?"*

"Wouldn't you like to know?" she'd taunted, lifting the bottle of wine to her lips and taking a long swallow. His hands had clenched into tight fists of fury, and for the first time in his life he wanted to hurt her. "Well, what do you suppose your partner has been doing while you've been building up the reputation of your firm?"

"Wendell Tate?" he'd said incredulously.

"Who else?"

"You're lying."

Rosemary had smiled, her amethyst eyes dancing. "Sure I am." She tilted the wine bottle to her lips and took another long drink. He could see the movement of her throat as she swallowed. His stomach turned over and he thought for a moment that he was going to be sick.

"I don't believe it."

She shrugged her slim shoulders indifferently. "Suit yourself. You always do anyway."

Zachary stalked across the room, grabbed the wine bottle from her hand and threw it into the fire. The green glass burst into shards that glittered among the blood-red coals. Burgundy wine drizzled down the charred logs, causing the fire to sputter and hiss.

Zachary's fingers tightened around Rosemary's arms. "You're lying," he accused, his voice raspy with the hate blackening his heart.

Her dark, expressive brows arched. "If you don't believe me, ask Wendell."

"Oh, God, Rosemary!" He released her, as if suddenly finding her repulsive.

"Save the wounded hero routine, Zack. It's not as if you've been faithful to me, you know."

His brown eyes impaled hers. "Since I've known you I've never been with another woman," he said, his dark, horrified stare filled with honesty and despair. "I've never wanted anyone else."

"Save it, Zack."

"It's true and you know it."

The facade of mockery and indifference slipped a little as she believed him. "But you haven't wanted me, either. Oh, God, Zachary, all those nights you said you were working late. . . ."

"I was."

"You can't expect me to believe that you haven't had a lover. . . . You certainly haven't been interested in me." She was pale now, and her lower lip quivered. If he'd been more of a man he would have taken her into his arms and comforted her.

"I've been tired, Rosemary, and well, you haven't been interested much yourself." He looked at her pointedly. "I guess we know why."

"I've always loved you, Zack," she protested, tears beginning to slip from her eyes. "You've just never seemed to find the time to be with me. . . . Oh, God, what have I done?" she said, burying her face in her hands.

A little of his anger faded. He placed a hand on her shoulder comfortingly. "Come on, Rosemary, you'd better go to bed—"

"Alone?" she cried. "Won't you come with me?"

He hesitated. "I've got a lot to think about."

"Don't hate me, Zack, please, just don't hate me."

"I don't hate you, Rosemary," he whispered, most of his impotent anger turned now toward himself.

He helped her to the bedroom and tucked her into bed. When she reached out to him, he folded one of her hands in his own and turned away. "I just need a little time to think," he said, not knowing those words would be the last he would ever say to her.

In the past four years he had relived the nightmare of that night a thousand times.

Lauren, ravaged from a year of living without her children, couldn't believe that Zachary's wife would want to destroy her own child. "Why didn't she want the baby?" she asked.

"Because it wasn't mine. She was having an affair with Wendell Tate."

"Your partner?" Lauren closed her eyes in horror at the image. No wonder Zachary was reluctant to talk about it. "Oh, God, Zachary, I'm sorry—"

"It's over," he said. "She thought I was involved with someone else, and that was my fault. As I said, I hadn't been particularly attentive to her needs. Anyway, she was immediately contrite. When we were through talking I put her to bed, thinking that with all the wine she'd been drinking she would fall asleep right away. I checked on her once; her eyes were closed and her breathing was regular, so I went out for a long run along the beach. It was midnight and raining, but I didn't care; I needed to think and work out my frustrations.

"I was just climbing the stairs back to the cabin, and I'd decided that I'd let Rosemary make the decision. If she wanted a divorce, I'd grant it; if she wanted to start over, I'd try. That's when I heard the car. I raced up the remaining stairs and heard her roar out of the driveway.

"First I double-checked the cabin, to make sure that

she was really gone—I had trouble believing that she'd be so reckless—then I called the police. It turned out to be the longest night of my life."

Lauren wrapped her fingers around Zachary's arm, but he didn't seem to notice. "That was the night she died," she whispered.

Zachary nodded, the corners of his mouth whitening with the strain of the memory. "The police found her car and body in Devil's Punchbowl. Have you ever been there, looked down at the water?"

Lauren nodded. The blue-gray waters of the Pacific crashed into the shore and churned furiously in the natural hollow by the cliffs known appropriately as Devil's Punchbowl. She felt sick at the thought of Rosemary's car plunging into the midnight-dark waters churning frothy white.

"According to the only witness, Rosemary had been driving erratically, continually weaving into the oncoming lane of traffic. And then, blinded by the headlights of an approaching semi, she swerved off the road and down the embankment to the sea.

"I heard the news the next morning. That's the last time I was in the cabin. I didn't have the heart to sell it, so I hired a service to keep it up. But after meeting you, I decided to purge all the ghosts from the past and start over." He turned and faced her, his brown eyes searching her face. "You're a strong woman, Lauren, and I feel stronger just for knowing you."

"Don't give me too much credit," she said, pushing aside a windblown lock of coppery hair.

"You're a very special lady."

"Only when I'm around a special man."

He snorted in disbelief. "I thought I wanted to die, you know. A friend took me back to Portland and I had to confront Wendell. It was hell."

"You can't be serious!" Wendell had cried, horrified when Zachary had told him about Rosemary's death and accused him of being the father of her unborn child. "I've never touched your wife, old boy," he'd declared, nervously tugging on the waxed ends of his blond mustache.

Zachary's dark eyes had accused Tate of the lie. "I should want to kill you, I suppose," Zachary had said, and Wendell had taken immediate refuge behind his desk. "But I don't. All I want is the truth, then we'll see what we can do about dissolving the partnership."

The next two weeks had been torture. Rosemary's funeral, phone calls and interviews from the press, and the scandalous rumors were flying. Finally, Wendell had cracked and admitted that he'd been involved with Rosemary.

"That settles it, then," Zachary had said, intent on dissolving the partnership and moving away from the town that had brought him so much pain. Only it didn't work out that way. Three days later, Wendell Tate was found dead from an apparent overdose of sleeping pills. Though there was no suicide note, Zachary had understood—this was Wendell's method of escape. All of Wendell's assets and liabilities were left to his only son, Joshua.

Lauren placed a comforting hand on Zachary's cold cheek, lovingly stroking the stubble on his chin. "You don't have to talk about this."

"I'm okay. It's just that Wendell denied the affair, until he knew that it was useless, then he went home one night, took more pills than his body could handle and didn't wake up."

"And that's how you inherited Joshua as a partner."

"It took a few years, but yes, essentially that's what happened."

"And you blame yourself for what happened to Rosemary and Wendell."

"And the baby," he finished, his jaw set rigidly. "Whether I meant to or not, I caused the deaths of three people."

"So you took in Joshua Tate and made him a full partner of the firm."

"Once he'd passed the bar."

"I don't think you have anything to feel guilty about, counselor," she said, standing on her toes and kissing his cheek. "I think you're wonderful."

He forced a grin. "It's nice to have at least one fan," he teased, linking his arm with hers and spinning her back in the direction of the cabin.

"I'll race ya back," she challenged, hoping to find some way to help him dispel his tortured thoughts of the past.

"You don't have a prayer—" Before he could finish the sentence she had taken off, her bare feet skimming over the cold, wet sand. Zachary was beside her in an instant, his long strides effortlessly diminishing her small head start.

Lauren gritted her teeth and tried to quicken the pace, but just as she did, Zachary's arms reached out for her. She stumbled and they both fell onto the sand.

"Spoilsport," she laughed, tossing her hair away from her face.

"You can't beat me," he announced loftily. "I run seven miles four times a week."

"Like you're the only one in shape. Chauvinist!"

He shook his head and kissed her. "I think that expression went out in the seventies," he said, smiling.

"Still applies." Her arms encircled his neck, and her green eyes sparkled with good humor. Why did she always feel like smiling whenever she was with him? "You know, I'm falling in love with you, counselor, and I don't know if I should."

"Trust your instincts," he said as he pushed her gently onto the sand and stared into her eyes. "I'm one helluva catch."

"What you are is a cocky, miserable, adorable bastard." She laughed and playfully rumpled his hair.

"And you love it." He pulled her to her feet, put a possessive arm around her shoulders and pointed to the weathered cabin perched on the cliff. "Let's go inside," he murmured suggestively, "and we'll finish this discussion in bed . . . with a cold bottle of wine. . ."

THE REST OF THE WEEKEND was perfect. Even the sun peeked through the clouds to brighten the sky and warm the white sand. Lauren knew that she would never be satisfied with another man. She loved Zachary with all her heart. They spent their last few hours alone, before the dying fire, and it was difficult for Lauren to leave the rustic little cabin and return to Portland to face the problems at the bank and the all-consuming task of trying to locate her children.

The clock had just chimed nine when Lauren and Zachary entered her house in Westmoreland. After checking the mail and turning on the coffeemaker, Lauren rewound the tape player and listened to her phone messages. The third one made her heart stand still.

"This is Sherry Engles," a feminine voice said nervously. "I know you don't know me, but . . . well, I might be able to help you find your husband. I knew him a couple of years ago . . . and well, my number is—"

The woman rattled off a long-distance number, and Lauren went white with shock.

"What is it?" Zachary asked, seeing the stricken look on her face and the way her fingers gripped the back of the desk chair near the phone. "Lauren?"

"The woman," Lauren said, her throat suddenly tight. "Her name was Sherry. . . ."

Zachary nodded, waiting for her to continue.

"That was the name. The name of the woman Doug was seeing when he was at Dickinson Investments. I mean, he called me Sherry that night. . . . Oh, God." Her voice faded, and she buried her face in the rough fabric of Zachary's jacket.

Chapter Ten

"YOU'RE SURE THIS Sherry is the same woman?" Zachary asked as Lauren slowly pulled out of his embrace and reached for the phone.

"Positive."

"But you couldn't remember her name a couple of weeks ago."

Lauren picked up the receiver and leaned against the desk for support. "It's the way she said it, what she said, it jogged my memory."

Zachary wrestled the ivory-colored receiver from her tense fingers. "I think I should make the call."

"Why?" she demanded.

"Because of the disappointments you've already faced. Remember how you reacted to Dave Parker's children?" He touched her softly under the chin.

"You can't protect me, you know," she said with a trace of bitterness. "Someday or another I'm going to have to face that woman; it might as well be now, when she has information on the kids."

After a slight pause, he handed her back the phone. "It's your ball game," he said, and paced restlessly to the fireplace.

Lauren's fingers were shaking when she punched out the number.

"Are you sure you don't want me to do this?" Zachary asked, his eyes intent on the drawn lines of her face.

"No . . . I can handle it."

"All right. But I'll be right here if you need me." He folded his arms over his chest, leaned a shoulder against the cold bricks and watched. Lauren turned away from him as she waited for someone to answer. From the area code, Zachary guessed that the woman lived in western Washington. Other than that small piece of information, Sherry Engles was a complete mystery.

The phone rang three times, then four. Lauren's fingers tapped nervously on the receiver. "Come on," she whispered urgently just as the phone was answered.

"Hello?" It was the same feminine voice that had been recorded on the answering machine. Lauren felt her pulse begin to quicken.

"Hello. My name is Lauren Regis. I'd like to speak with Sherry Engles."

There was an uncomfortable pause. "I'm Sherry," the woman admitted finally. "I called you yesterday afternoon."

Lauren's heart began to pound so loudly she could barely hear her own voice. This was the woman who had slept with her husband in the past and now might be able to help her find Alicia and Ryan. Sherry Engles was both friend and foe. "You said you might have some information about my children."

"I . . . I'm not sure. My friend in Portland saw you on that program . . . *Eye Witness* or whatever it was called."

"Eye Contact."

"Right. Anyway, she remembered that I . . . uh, had been seeing a man named Doug Regis . . . a couple of years ago. So she gave me your number."

"I see," Lauren replied stiffly.

"Hey, look," Sherry said apologetically. "I'm real sorry about your kids—I had no idea that Doug was the kind of guy who would run off with them."

Lauren braced herself and forced her voice to remain calm. "Do you know where he is?"

"I'm not sure."

Lauren's heart dropped to the floor. "But you said—"

"I've got a phone number. It's over a year old and I don't even know if it works. Doug and I, we had a fight, and I wasn't interested in moving to Boise. I . . . never called him and I haven't heard from him since."

"Boise?" she repeated, her hopes soaring. Out of the corner of her eye, she saw Zachary stiffen.

"Yeah, that's where he moved."

"With the children?"

"I don't know." Sherry sounded sincere and Lauren believed her. "Like I said, I wanted nothing to do with him. I'm married now, and . . . well, once I met Bill, that's my husband, I wasn't interested in Doug. Anyway, here's the number. . . ."

Lauren's fingers were shaking so badly she could barely take down the information. When she had finished, she glanced at Zachary. His expression was stern and his arms were still folded over his chest.

"Got it?" Obviously, Sherry was interested in ending the strained conversation.

"Yes. Would you mind if I visited you?" Lauren asked on impulse.

Sherry hesitated. Lauren could almost feel the other woman withdrawing. "I don't think that would be such a good idea," Sherry replied. "What happened between me and Doug is all over. Has been for a long time. It's something I'd rather not think about."

Lauren persevered, refusing to let this one vital link

vanish into thin air. "But I have to find my children. You may be the only person who can help me."

"I don't know—"

"What about if my attorney came to visit you?"

"*Your attorney!* Oh, God. I should never have called you." Desperation hung on Sherry's words. "Bill will kill me."

"It's nothing like that," Lauren quickly reassured the woman. "What happened between you and Doug is over, and it doesn't really matter. Not now. I'm not emotionally involved with my ex-husband. But my attorney—his name is Zachary Winters—is helping to track down the kids, and we need all the help we can get. We need *your* help."

"I just don't want to dredge it all up again. Bill . . . well, he never did like me seeing Doug—"

"You have to understand," Lauren interjected. "I don't want to cause any trouble for you; all I want is to find the children. I don't want to disturb your life, and considering the circumstances, I don't like asking you to help me, but I have to. I . . . just don't have any choice. We're talking about my kids, for God's sake."

Sherry let out a long sigh. "Shoot me for a fool," she said, and then added, "Sure, I'll talk to your lawyer, as long as he isn't looking to make any trouble for me."

"He won't be."

"Okay. I live northeast of Seattle, in Woodinville. If he calls me when he gets into town, I'll give him directions."

"Thank you," Lauren said. "I know this isn't easy for you."

When she hung up, Lauren felt like collapsing, but instead she punched out the telephone number that Doug had given Sherry nearly a year earlier.

Zachary quickly crossed the room, took the receiver from her hand and hung up the phone. He'd heard enough of the conversation to know what Lauren was planning.

"What're you doing?" Lauren demanded angrily.

"Trying to save you from making the worst mistake of your life. You can't call Doug and tip him off. Not now." His hand remained steadfastly over the receiver.

All of the pent-up anger and frustration of the past few weeks surfaced rapidly. "They are *my* children, dammit, and I intend to speak with them."

"And say what? That this is Mommy, and I want Daddy to bring you home right now? Think about it, Lauren. Doug will take off all over again, and we'll be back to square one."

"I . . . I have to do this," she said, watching as he lifted his hand from the cradle and scowled at her.

"I want to go on record as being against it."

"Okay. You've got permission to say 'I told you so,'" she snapped.

"Just don't blow everything we've tried to accomplish."

Hastily she punched out the number. The phone rang twice before a recorded message stated that the telephone number had been disconnected and there was no new number.

"No!" Lauren nearly screamed, redialing to make sure she hadn't made a mistake. The recorded message repeated its dismal information.

Zachary's frown eased a bit as he saw the disappointment in her eyes. Quickly, she redialed the phone and waited impatiently for the operator to answer.

"I'm sorry, but I have no listing for a Douglas Regis,

a Doug Regis or a D. Regis," the operator said in response to Lauren's inquiry.

"I know he's there—maybe not in the city, but somewhere close by, maybe in one of the suburbs."

"I've checked my computers—there is no Douglas Regis."

Tears sprang to Lauren's eyes: "Thank you," she whispered, gently replacing the phone and wiping her eyes with the back of her hand. "Damn!" She pounded the old rolltop desk in frustration.

"Lauren—"

"I don't want to hear it, Zachary," she cried passionately. "We were so close, so damned close. . . ." She sniffed but didn't argue when he wrapped his arms around her and kissed the top of her head.

"We still are."

"If only I'd gone on the air a year earlier. If only I'd known Sherry Engles, remembered her name, instead of trying to forget about her affair with Doug!"

"Shh. . . ." His lips touched her hair, his warm breath ruffling the auburn strands. "We'll find them."

She moved from his tender embrace, and her glistening eyes stared into his. Tears ran down her cheeks as she walked across the room. "Will we? Will we?" she demanded before answering her own question. "God, I don't know. A week ago, I thought we'd be able to do it, but now. . . . Oh Lord, what will I do without them?" Her voice cracked, and she crumpled into a weary heap on the couch. Covering her face with her hands, she sobbed quietly.

Zachary walked over to the couch and sat next to her. When his fingers wrapped around her arms, they were tight, the grip painful. "Cut it out, Lauren," he said, giving her a shake. "We'll find them."

Lauren looked into his eyes. "How can you be so sure? Every time I think we're getting close . . . everything seems to fall apart." She was sobbing uncontrollably now, her battle with tears completely forgotten.

"We *are* closer. Don't fall apart on me now," he pleaded. "It's probably going to get worse before it gets better, but I can't find your children without you. You've got to help me. You've got to." He shook her again, quietly insisting that she remain strong. "We can do this, Lauren. We can."

"I'd do anything to find them," she murmured weakly, forcing the tears aside.

"Good. Because what I want you to do is stay here; be strong. I'll call a private investigator in Boise tonight and get the ball rolling in Idaho, then I'll fly to Seattle tomorrow and talk with Sherry Engles." He was stroking her hair, trying to soothe and reassure her by telling her his plans. "I'll take the first flight I can catch out of Seattle to Boise, and depending upon how long it takes to find out if Doug is still in Boise, was there, or whatever, I'll be back."

"I'll come with you."

"No."

"But—"

"I don't want to hear it. You have a job to consider, and you need to stay here and see if any other messages or clues come in."

"That's bull, Zachary. The recording machine—"

"God, Lauren, just listen to me!" he nearly shouted. "I can't take the chance of your falling apart all over again. Okay? Remember the night you thought the kids were in Gresham with Dave Parker? Remember the disappointment? You can't put yourself through that over and over again."

"I can and I will," she declared.

"Every time we come up against a stumbling block, you take it too hard."

"That's because they're *my* children!" She glanced up at the portrait of Alicia and Ryan and felt the tears gathering again.

"And I'm doing my best to find them." He brushed the lingering tears from her eyes, and his face softened slightly. "This time, let me do it my way, okay? That's why you hired me."

She stared at him for a long moment, trying to consider the problem from all angles. "Okay," she finally agreed, forcing herself to gain control of her emotions. "We'll do it your way . . . for now."

He offered an encouraging smile. "I'll find them, you know. Come hell or high water."

God, she wanted to believe him. She wrapped her arms around his chest and lowered her head to his shoulder, feeling the strength his arms offered. This one man she could trust with all her heart. If he said he would find the kids, Lauren knew he would do just that . . . or die trying.

SHERRY ENGLES WAS a short woman with curly brown hair, about six months pregnant and very nervous. It was obvious that she was uncomfortable with the subject of Douglas Regis—she never quite met Zachary's stare; her eyes shifted from one side of the tidy room to the other, continually drifting to the clock over the couch, as if she were fearful that someone would burst into the house and find her talking to the curt lawyer from Portland.

"I wish I could help you more," she said after a two-hour inquisition by Zachary that divulged no other information on Douglas Regis or the whereabouts of

Lauren's children. "But, like I told Doug's ex-wife on the phone the other day, I broke all ties with Doug once I married Bill."

"So Doug never wrote to you—you don't have an address?" Zachary asked for the third time.

Sherry shook her head.

"And he never phoned?"

"Not since he gave me the number."

"Then how can you be sure it was correct?"

Sherry frowned petulantly. "I guess I can't."

"But you kept the number, even though you didn't want to stay in contact with him?" Zachary was clearly dubious, and Sherry swayed uncomfortably in her worn rocker.

"I put the number in the front of the phone book and never bothered to throw last year's book away." She shrugged. "Maybe I should have. Then I wouldn't be involved in the mess."

Zachary left the house not knowing much more than when he went in. For all he knew, Douglas Regis could have given Sherry a phony number, or the woman could have written it down incorrectly. The whole thing could turn out to be just another fiasco. And Lauren would be devastated. Again.

His hands were clenched on the steering wheel of the rented car, and he glowered in frustration at the sluggish traffic as he slowly drove toward Sea-Tac Airport.

Zachary only hoped that the private investigator he'd hired in Boise would come up with something—anything—to help him locate Lauren's children. He honestly didn't know if she could take another disappointment.

"MIND IF I join you?"

Lauren looked up in surprise. She'd decided to eat lunch alone and for this reason had taken a vacant back table in the small restaurant on the first floor of the Northwestern Bank Tower. She wasn't thrilled at the prospect of company.

"So how's it going?" Bob Harding asked as he balanced his tray of food and slid into one of the cane-backed chairs opposite Lauren.

"It's going," she said noncommittally as she stirred her soup and watched the steam rise from the bowl.

"Ouch." Bob winced a little.

Suddenly Lauren realized that Bob thought her comment had been meant as a sarcastic remark. Obviously he was still feeling guilty about being put in charge of the Mason trust. "I wasn't talking about bank business," she said, managing a smile for her friend. "Especially not the Mason trust. That's your problem now." She smiled good-naturedly. "Actually, I don't miss the headache at all. So quit being so sensitive."

"You're one lousy liar, you know." He placed his lunch and a cup of coffee in front of him, then stashed the tray on an unused table.

"So I've been told."

"George West ripped your stripes off by taking the account from you, and it still sticks in your craw. Admit it."

"Okay, my perceptive friend. It still bothers me."

"Don't let it."

"A little hard to do when the entire trust department can't seem to talk about anything else," she pointed out.

"Well, let's forget about the Mason trust for a while." Then, apparently forgetting his own advice, he added sourly, "That Joshua Tate is a royal pain in the neck."

"Not to mention Hammond Mason?"

"Amen."

Lauren smiled ruefully and took a long sip of her iced tea. "Maybe I'm lucky to be out of it."

Bob pursed his lips and pushed his glasses on the

bridge of his nose. "I never liked the way George West handled all that business, you know. It didn't seem fair. Just because you went on television to find your kids and then hired the best man in town to help you locate them . . . well, it just didn't seem reason enough to pull you off the account."

"You seem to forget that Joshua Tate is Zachary Winters's partner."

"How could I?" That kid's as tenacious as a bulldog!"

"Like his mentor?" Lauren asked, arching a brow.

"Yeah. I guess so." Satisfied that Lauren held no apparent grudges, Bob took a bite of his salad. "Speaking of Winters, how're you doing? Any progress in finding Alicia and Ryan?"

Lauren shook her head. "Not much," she admitted. "Zachary's out of town, in Boise, I think, tracking down another lead."

"Another?"

She toyed with her soup spoon and looked up to see the anxiety in Bob's gaze. "We've had quite a few, but they've all turned out to be dead ends."

"I'm sorry," Bob said, frowning.

"Nothing that can be done about it. . . ." She pretended interest in her soup again, and the conversation turned to less disturbing subjects. It was comforting to know that despite all the tension at the bank, she still had a friend in Bob Harding. These days, friends were hard to come by.

ZACHARY RETURNED THURSDAY night. He drove straight from the airport and through the thickening fog to Lauren's house.

When Lauren opened the door, she read the guarded disappointment on his face and her heart twisted painfully.

"You didn't find them," Lauren guessed as she closed the door. The pain in Zachary's eyes couldn't be disguised. He looked as if he hadn't shaved or slept in the three days he'd been gone, and the white shirt that had been fresh and crisp that morning was now rumpled and soiled.

"Not yet," he said wearily, taking her in his arms and stroking her hair softly. She smelled so clean and fresh, looked as enticing as an oasis in a godforsaken desert. "God, I missed you."

Lauren swallowed the lump in her throat and kissed his stubble-roughened cheek. "I missed you, too." She was amazingly calm, though she felt as if all the hope in her heart had turned to ice. She tried to tell herself that all was not lost. At least Zachary had returned. This last separation from him had been difficult, more trying than any separation before. Slowly, her life was beginning to revolve around Zachary, whether she wanted it to or not.

Her arms wrapped around him, and she held the man she loved desperately, clinging to him as if to life itself. What if she never found the children? Could this man be enough? She shuddered at the thought and felt his arms possessively tightening around her waist. Could she ever be content to forget about Alicia and Ryan and start a new life, a new family with Zachary?

Dear Lord, no! If it took the rest of her life, she would go on aching for her dear, lost children. Love Zachary as she might, she could never forget or give up trying to find Alicia and Ryan.

"Tell me about it," she urged, leading him to the couch and trying to hide the disappointment weighing heavily upon her.

Without protest, Zachary slumped onto the couch and let his head fall back. He stared blankly at the ceiling, one arm draped around Lauren's shoulders.

"Doug was in Boise, but he's gone."

Lauren tried to still her pounding heart. At least that was something! For the first time in over a year, Doug had been located. "And you don't know where he went?"

Zachary let out a weary sigh and shook his head. "No. He pulled the same vanishing act that he did here a year ago—no forwarding address or telephone number . . . nothing. Just gone without a trace. Work records didn't help, either."

"When did he leave?"

"About four months ago." Zachary rubbed his jaw. "As far as I can tell, he went from Portland to Boise and got a job with a lumber mill as a laborer on the green chain. I checked with the phone company, the Social Security Administration, the county records and the schools. Nothing. No one seems to know where he's gone. I even talked to some of the workers in the mill, but they said he kept pretty much to himself. They didn't know much about him except that he was living with some woman named Becky and they had a couple of kids."

"They?" Lauren repeated, her lower lip trembling. Another woman was raising her children? Her heart wrenched painfully, and her eyes burned.

"Right. Seems as if Doug let the people he met think that the kids were Becky's."

"Oh, God," she murmured. She had to look away from him for a second to gather her composure. "But . . . but what about the private investigator?" she asked hopefully.

"He's still working on it. . . ." Zachary closed his eyes, sighing. "Sherry Engles wasn't much help, either. She wasn't even sure that the telephone number she'd given me was correct. So I checked. It was, but Doug had discontinued service when he lost his job about four or five months ago."

"But still, we're closer than we were last week," she said, unwilling to accept defeat.

He smiled sadly and turned to gaze into her eyes. "One step at a time, right?" Tenderly, he traced her jaw with his thumb. "I'd just hoped to return with more encouraging news. I really thought that I could come back here and tell you that the kids were found."

"You're not giving up, are you?"

Determination glinted in his dark eyes. "Not on your life, lady." He pulled her gently to him. "I made a promise to you, didn't I?"

"And I intend to keep you to it," she said more bravely than she felt. Her eyes lifted to the portrait of Ryan and Alicia, and she wondered how much they'd grown in the last fourteen months. Would they still remember her? "Soon it will be Alicia's birthday," she thought aloud, swallowing past a painful lump in her throat. "I . . . I was hoping that I would be with her. . . ."

"Lauren, shh. . . ." He kissed her forehead, watching her face and seeing her anguish. "We'll keep trying, and we'll find them."

He followed her gaze to the mantel and stared at the picture for a while. "When is Alicia's birthday?" he asked thoughtfully.

"A week from Friday, the sixth of November—why?"

He frowned slightly. "Because I've got an idea. It might not work, but at this point, I don't think we have much to lose." His weariness seemed to disappear as an idea began to form. Standing, he paced between the couch and fireplace as he thought the concept over. "And it just might work."

"What kind of an idea?" she asked skeptically.

"It's simple, really. All I want you to do is take out

an advertisement in all the major newspapers near Boise—the entire surrounding area. It should be a full-page ad, big enough to catch a person's attention."

"An ad? I don't get it."

"The message should be simple and in large block letters. Something like: 'Happy seventh birthday, Alicia. Your mother loves and misses you and your brother, Ryan, very much. Please call, I need to hear from you and know that you're well.' We'll put your name and number in the paper and see what happens."

"But what if Doug sees it? Won't he pull up stakes again?"

Zachary inclined his head. "Maybe, but at least we'll have a fresh trail to follow. It'll take him a couple of days, maybe over a week to find a new place to live, move, finish with his job and straighten out all the problems of taking Alicia out of school."

"But the last time he walked out in one afternoon."

"True, but the kids weren't in school and he had everything planned out ahead of time. This time we'll force him to be spontaneous. Besides, someone else might read the paper, not Doug. Someone who will be willing to tell us where the kids are."

"I don't know. . . ."

Zachary drew her to her feet, pulled her close to him and hugged her enthusiastically. "As I said, it's a gamble, maybe even a long shot—but it just might pay off!"

"Then, counselor," she said, his optimism affecting her, "let's get to it. You take a shower and change, and I'll put on the coffee. Then we'll figure out our new strategy and the layout for the ad."

His dark eyes glinted, and he placed a kiss on her cheek. "You sure bounce back," he said affectionately.

"Maybe it's because I've got such a good teacher."

His gaze darkened sensually, and one finger touched

the hollow of her throat. "There are so many things I'd like to teach you. . . ."

She angled her head seductively, letting her hair fall over one shoulder, and arched an enigmatic brow. "Anytime you're ready, counselor. . . ."

His hands spanned her waist, and he pulled her body against his, letting his lips linger against the nape of her neck. "No time like the present," he murmured against her warm skin. "No time like the present."

THE NEXT WEEK was torture for Lauren. When Zachary wasn't catching up on other cases at the office, he was in Boise, working with the private investigator. Lauren found her evenings nearly unbearable. Though she tried to concentrate on reading or watching television, her thoughts strayed constantly to Zachary. What was he doing? Whom was he with? Had he made any progress? He called each night, and she hung on to the phone as tightly as if it were a lifeline, a fragile link to the only person she could trust, her only chance at salvation. During working hours, the tension at the bank was nearly tangible as the day for the Mason trust trial got closer. Lauren was pointedly excluded from closed-door meetings, and she'd suffered from more than one unfriendly stare on the day of the trust board meeting.

Only Patrick Evans had seemed to sympathize with her situation. After the board meeting, he'd offered to take her to a nearby restaurant for a cup of coffee. Lauren had felt compelled to accept. Something in Patrick's wise eyes told her that she should listen to whatever it was he had to say.

"So, are you any closer to finding those kids than you were a few weeks ago?" he'd asked once they were settled in the privacy of a leather booth.

"I hope so." She stirred her coffee idly, watching as the cream swirled around her spoon.

"But nothing concrete?"

She shook her head and stared into her cup. "Not really. We did find out that—"

"We?" Patrick inquired, frowning slightly. "By that you mean yourself and Zachary Winters."

"Yes." She watched as Patrick shifted uncomfortably in his seat. "We know that Doug moved to Boise and stayed there for about six months. Now it seems he's vanished again."

"I'm sorry, Lauren," Patrick said sincerely. "I know this hasn't been easy for you, especially with what's been going on at the bank."

"So you're aware of that," she said stiffly.

Patrick shrugged and pulled at the knot of his expensive silk tie. "I know George West and his slightly narrow-minded view of loyalty when it comes to Northwestern Bank."

Lauren looked up sharply. "So what is this—a warning?"

"No." Patrick managed a fatherly smile. "A word of advice, I guess."

"Which is?"

"Watch your step, Lauren. Keep your nose clean. Don't give George any reason to suspect that your loyalties are placed elsewhere."

Patrick's meaning was clear. Obviously George West still thought she was on some spying mission for Joshua Tate. Her green eyes hardened, glittering like cold emeralds. "All I'm trying to do, Patrick, is find my kids. That's not a crime, nor is it a threat to George West or the bank. As for my loyalty to the bank, it's never faltered."

Patrick nodded but avoided her eyes. "I know that and you know it, but George . . . well, he tends to look at things from a different perspective. He's heard talk that you've been seeing Zachary Winters personally as well as professionally."

"So what?"

"Zack's the guy responsible for pushing Joshua Tate through law school at Willamette University and making him a partner of the firm. That fact alone makes George nervous. Very nervous." Patrick took a long swallow of his coffee, his eyes never leaving Lauren's.

"So what are you suggesting—that I tell Zachary he's off the case, per my boss's orders?"

"Of course not, Lauren. I'm the guy that referred you to Winters in the first place."

"But that was before Hammond Mason hired Joshua Tate."

"I know. Nonetheless, I'm just asking you to watch your step."

"I'll keep it in mind," she replied, trying to keep her voice level. She realized that Patrick Evans was trying to help her, even if it was a little backhanded. She liked the silver-haired attorney and respected his judgment. If he was warning her—and that's what it sounded like, whether he admitted it or not—she should be careful. Anything she might do or say could be construed as an act of betrayal.

Patrick rose to leave, but Lauren placed a hand on the sleeve of his gray flannel suit. "Are you suggesting that I quit my job?"

Patrick frowned thoughtfully. "I don't know," he admitted honestly. "But if I were you, I'd keep my options open. This lawsuit has George seeing red."

"Even though he knows he'll win?"

"Well, that's the problem, isn't it? Nothing in law is a sure thing. Oh, sure, the laws are written down in black and white, but they're open to a lot of discussion and interpretation. That's why there are so many cases you can quote to argue your point, be it for or against."

Lauren's blood was boiling at the unfair situation. She felt trapped, damned if she did, damned if she didn't. "I've always been a good employee to Northwestern Bank," she said as Patrick paid the check, "and I've never done anything to jeopardize the bank's reputation. I've said as much to George. If he doesn't believe me, there's not much I can do about it." She squared her shoulders. "Either he trusts me or he doesn't."

"It's not that simple, you see. George has been taking a lot of heat. Several members of the board have been suggesting that he resign."

"But his family owns the majority of the stock in the bank."

"I know. But his sister and brother have been applying a little pressure as well."

"Because of me?" Lauren was incredulous.

"Because of the Mason trust lawsuit and all the media attention it's been receiving over the past couple of weeks. Once the press links your name with that of Zachary Winters, this whole thing will blow up into a three-ring circus. Some members of the board have even gone so far as to suggest a quiet out-of-court settlement in order to save face."

"For whom?"

"The investors and the account holders of the bank." The groove between Patrick's brows deepened. "This lawsuit could cost the bank a lot of money in investor and account holder confidence. No one buys a stock in or leaves his money with a bank he can't trust."

"I see," Lauren said, gritting her teeth. The whole damned thing was so unfair—blown out of proportion.

Patrick held the door open for her, and she slipped her arms through the sleeves of her raincoat. Gray clouds threatened the skies over the city, and the first large drops of rain began to pelt the sidewalk and street.

As they walked back to the bank in strained silence, Lauren made the decision she'd been putting off for nearly three weeks.

Two hours later she was in George West's office, offering her resignation to the president of Northwestern Bank. The old man pursed his lips and shook his head but accepted, nonetheless.

"I'm sorry it had to come to this, Lauren." He sounded sincere.

"So am I," she replied, looking him squarely in the eye.

"Do you have another position?"

"Not yet."

"If you need a letter of recommendation . . ."

"Thank you." She turned and headed for the door, feeling as if a tremendous weight had been lifted from her shoulders.

"Lauren," George called as she reached the door. He stood up as Lauren turned around, and suddenly she realized that he looked tired, and older than his sixty-two years.

"Yes."

"I don't think it will be necessary for you to stay on the usual two weeks; I'll make sure that you're paid an extra month's salary as well as the vacation pay due you."

"Thank you."

"And . . ." He shrugged wearily. "If it means anything to you, I really do hope that you find your children."

"I know that."

She left his office, cleaned out her desk and walked out the front door of Northwestern Bank determined never to look back.

* * *

FRIDAY WAS DIFFICULT. Not only was it Alicia's seventh birthday, and the first day Lauren didn't have to go to work, but it was also the first day that the full-page ads would run in the newspapers surrounding Boise. She stayed home all day, trying to work on her résumé and waiting for the phone to ring. But no one called. Not one person.

In the late afternoon, tired of typing a list of her qualifications, she kicked off her shoes and sank into the cushions of the couch, closing her eyes. What were the chances that Alicia or someone who knew her would see the birthday message? A seven-year-old wouldn't scan the papers, even if Doug hadn't seen the message himself and had carelessly left the paper in the house.

Would someone call? *If* they read that particular section of that particular paper. *If* they knew Alicia. *If* they wanted to get involved. *If* they weren't afraid of Doug.

Too many ifs and not enough answers. She withdrew the pins from her hair and let the thick auburn curls fall free as she remembered Alicia's birth. Seven years ago, Lauren had been draped in the crisp sheets of the maternity ward of St. Mary's Hospital, surrounded by cheerful nurses and holding her new, wrinkled, red-faced, beautiful daughter. She had been on top of the world. And now she didn't even know where that perfect little girl was living, or with whom.

"Someone's got to call," she told herself glumly. She carried her shoes to the bedroom and then made herself a quick cup of hot tea. "Someone will call. They will," she assured herself, glancing at the phone suspiciously as she settled into her favorite chair and picked up the suspense novel she'd started reading long ago. "They've got to."

And if they don't?

She took in a long, shuddering breath and angled her

chin defiantly. *Then we'll try something else.* Closing her eyes against the very real possibility that she might not hear anything for a long time, Lauren made a silent promise to herself. *I'll keep trying until I find them, if it takes me until my dying day.*

Her fingers drummed restlessly on the overstuffed arm of the chair. Where was Zachary? Why hadn't he called? If only she could see him, touch him, be reassured by the determination in his soul-searching dark eyes. Then everything would be all right. . . .

ZACHARY RETURNED ON Sunday. He walked into Lauren's house that cool, clear afternoon carrying a thick sheaf of newspapers under his arm. Once in the kitchen, he spread the pages on the table and let her look at the advertisements he had placed in twelve different papers.

"That's going to cost me a fortune," she thought aloud, pleased nonetheless. Surely someone would read the message and call.

"Won't it be worth it?"

She tore her eyes away from the newspapers and lifted them to meet Zachary's inquisitive stare. "Every cent," she said.

"Even if it doesn't work?"

"Even if it doesn't work. At least I'll know that I tried."

"No calls yet?" he asked, already knowing the answer from the look on her face.

"None."

"It's still too soon," he said comfortingly, but Lauren heard the note of anxiety in his voice. He shifted and forced a smile, hoping to cheer her. "What do you say to a pizza?" he asked impulsively. "My treat."

"I'd have to change."

His gaze traveled down her body, taking in the fact that she was wearing an old checkered blouse and worn jeans. "What're you doing?"

"Nothing. I've just finished."

"Doing what?"

"Stacking the wood that I've been neglecting for over a month."

"I would have done that for you."

"You were busy, remember?" She pointed to the newspapers. "That was more important."

"I guess you're right." He leaned against the wall, a smile on his lips. "Come here."

"What?"

"I said, 'Come here.'"

"What're you doing, counselor?" she asked as she crossed the small kitchen and stood before him.

"It's not what I'm doing now," he said, placing both arms over her shoulders and bending his head so that his forehead touched hers. "It's what I'm planning on doing later. . . ." His voice trailed off seductively, and he played with the top button of her blouse.

Lauren's heart began to flutter erratically as his fingers brushed the skin at the base of her throat. "You're wicked," she said. "You haven't even kissed me 'hello.'"

The next button slipped through the hole. "A mistake I intend to rectify immediately," he responded, letting his lips touch her cheek and the corner of her mouth before capturing her willing lips.

"I love you, lady," he whispered against her ear. The fourth button was freed and her blouse parted, allowing more than a glimpse of the full breasts that fell over the lacy edge of her bra. "It seems like years since I've been here," he murmured as one hand slipped up and gently traced the taut, budding nipple.

"I thought you promised me a pizza," she teased as he finished the tantalizing job of undressing her.

"Later," he replied, lifting her off her feet and heading for the bedroom. "Much later."

THE NEXT MORNING, after a short run through Eastand Westmoreland, Zachary enjoyed breakfast with Lauren and then decided to check in at his office. With very little effort on his part, and maybe because of the current publicity surrounding the Mason trust, the firm of Winters and Tate had acquired several new clients. Zachary's time was once again in demand, and he was determined to make the law practice work.

For years he had suffered over Rosemary's death. Perhaps he had been at fault, giving too much of himself to his practice and not enough to his wife. Then, when Rosemary had died, he'd neglected the business, let it run itself into the ground. This time, he vowed to himself, he would find a way to balance his work against the time he spent with Lauren. It was a new beginning.

That afternoon, Lauren had just finished placing a roast in the oven and was eyeing the kitchen cabinets, contemplating her next project, when the phone rang. She answered it with a sinking heart, expecting to hear Zachary's voice on the other end of the line telling her that he'd have to work longer than expected.

"Hello?"

"Mrs. Regis?" asked an unfamiliar voice with a slight accent.

"Yes."

"This is Father McDougal with Our Lady of Promise. I'm calling from Twin Falls, Idaho. I saw your message in the Boise paper and . . . well, I was a little confused by it. You sound as if you don't know where your children are."

"That's right," she said with a short intake of breath.

"Maybe I can help. I might know where they are."

"What?" Lauren gasped, leaning against the wall for support. "Where?" she asked.

"Here, in Twin Falls. There's an Alicia Regis in Sister Angela's first grade class. Alicia has a younger brother by the name of Ryan. He's about three, I'd guess."

"Oh, thank God," Lauren said, her eyes brimming with tears of relief. At that moment Zachary walked into the house, took one look at Lauren's face and knew that the children had been found. A smile softened his rugged features.

"Can you explain what happened?" Father McDougal asked. "We were told the children's mother was deceased. That's why I called. I didn't think anyone who took out an ad like that would be an impostor."

"Of course not," Lauren replied.

"Then, what exactly happened, Mrs. Regis? Why did your husband lead us to believe that you were dead? Are you willing to tell me about it?"

"Oh, yes, yes." Hurriedly, she told him about the divorce and split custody rights and the painful day Doug had taken the children.

"I see," the priest murmured sympathetically. "You realize that I can't release Alicia to you," he said.

"But she belongs with me," Lauren began to protest.

"Be that as it may, I just can't give her to you without her father's consent. However, if you were to come with a court order, that would be different, I suppose. . . . I'd have to check with an attorney. Quite frankly, Mrs. Regis, we've never had a case like this."

"Of course," she murmured. "Can you give me a telephone number and address where I can reach Doug?"

"I think I can provide that," he said after a slight hesitation. "It's a matter of public record, so to speak, as he's listed in the phone book." Father McDougal gave her a phone number and street address, which Lauren quickly scribbled on a notepad.

"Thank you, Father," she said gratefully.

"Good luck to you, and come and see me when you get to Twin Falls."

"I will," she promised jubilantly. When she hung up the phone, she nearly collapsed. "You've found them," she said, tears of joy streaming down her face. "Doug had them hidden in a private Catholic school! Oh, Zachary, they're alive and well and waiting for me!"

"We can't be too sure about that," Zachary said, tossing his briefcase onto the couch. His triumphant smile had faded slightly.

"What do you mean?"

"There may be another woman involved, one they consider to be their mother. Remember, Doug was living with some woman named Becky."

"It doesn't matter. She has no right . . . they're my children."

"Then all we have to do is find a way to get them back," Zachary told her, adding grimly, "and that might not be any easier than finding them."

Chapter Eleven

THE DRIVE FROM Boise to Twin Falls seemed endless. Lauren gazed out the window at the ominous gray sky and the patches of snow on the sparsely needled pines and juniper stretching endlessly over the flat countryside.

Zachary was driving the rented car, and the fingers of his right hand curled possessively over her, giving her strength to face the ordeal ahead. Conversation lagged, and the Boise radio station began to fade as they closed in on Twin Falls.

Lauren's thoughts centered on Alicia and Ryan and what she would say to them after the long, painful separation. She closed her eyes against the thought that they might not remember her or, even worse, might vaguely remember her but believe Doug's lies. Would they think she'd abandoned them without so much as a goodbye? Perhaps they'd willingly accepted the unknown Becky as a replacement mother. What then?

Lauren hoped that Doug had no idea she was on her way to see him. She and Zachary had decided that it would be best to surprise him. Though she had longed to dial the phone number given her by Father McDougal, Lauren had forced herself to remain patient. The past two days had been difficult for her, knowing where the children were and not being able to go to them; but

Lauren had accepted Zachary's advice and waited, trusting that she would be able to touch and see Alicia and Ryan soon . . . very soon.

By the time they reached Twin Falls, it was nearly four in the afternoon. After taking several wrong turns in the small city, Zachary located the address Father McDougal had given Lauren. The house was similar in design to all of its neighbors' houses and appeared to have been built sometime after the Second World War. The exterior of the house was suffering painfully from neglect. Paint was peeling off the small, screened porch, one of the wooden steps was broken and a rain gutter near one of the corners of the house hung at an awkward angle.

Lauren's stomach knotted in nervous anticipation as Zachary parked the car. "You're sure you want to go in?" he asked, searching her face with dark, omniscient eyes.

Lauren's jaw tightened. "I've spent the last year of my life for just this moment."

Zachary forced an encouraging smile. "Okay. Let's get it over with." He helped her from the car and held her hand as she strode through the creaky front gate, past the slightly overgrown yard, up the three short steps to the front door. She pushed the button for the doorbell, but when she didn't hear the sound of chimes within the small house, she rapped firmly upon the door. As she waited, Lauren's eyes scanned the porch and she noticed a slightly rusted tricycle pushed into the corner. The small three-wheeler had to belong to Ryan!

Two minutes later the door was opened and she was staring into the face of the man who had robbed her of her children, the man she'd once loved. Douglas Regis had aged more than a little in the past year. His curly brown hair, now cut short, was receding from his forehead and beginning to gray near the temples.

"Lauren?" Doug exclaimed, his face growing pale beneath the stubble of his beard. He was wearing only a grimy once-white undershirt and dusty jeans. He opened the screen door for a better look at her. "What're you doing here?"

She didn't smile. "I've come for the kids."

"The kids?" He seemed off balance and glanced from Lauren to Zachary and back again. "They're not here."

"Where are they?" she demanded.

"With friends."

"I want them and I want them now." Lauren's voice was firm, her gaze steady.

"Who're you?" Doug asked, his flinty eyes sliding over to Zachary.

"My lawyer—Zachary Winters," Lauren replied.

"Your *lawyer*!"

Zachary extended his hand and noticed that, though Doug accepted the handshake, his palms were sweating.

Doug turned suspicious eyes back to his ex-wife. "Why did you bring a lawyer?"

"To show you that I mean business."

Doug shrugged. "Big deal." He cocked his head in Zachary's direction. "He's not going to make any difference, you know. Alicia and Ryan are with me now."

"And you intend to keep them?"

"Yep." He crossed his tanned arms over his chest and leaned against the doorjamb, effectively blocking her way into the house.

"I'll fight you, Doug—in court, anywhere; I want my children back." Anger surged through her. "It took me a year to find you, and now that I have, I won't rest until the children are with me again."

"Christ, Lauren, you're serious about this, aren't you?" he said, obviously taken aback.

"Dead serious."

Doug looked disgusted at her strong words. "So, fight me, then. See how long it takes—what happens. I really don't give a damn what you do."

Zachary's jaw tightened and he had to force his fists into his pockets to keep from strangling the bastard. "You're going to lose, Regis," he announced calmly. He rubbed his thumb thoughtfully, almost distractedly, along his lower jaw. "And I'll fix it so that this time you'll be allowed no custody, no visitation rights, nothing. It'll be just as if you never had a kid."

Doug fought a rising tide of panic. The smart-assed lawyer in the suede jacket and smooth cords had to be bluffing. Doug decided to gamble. "No court in the country would take my rights away from me. You're forgetting that this is the time of women's lib and father's rights."

Zachary smiled. "Are you willing to take that chance?" he asked softly.

The bastard looked so calm, so damned sure of himself. Doug felt his insides quiver.

"Wait a minute," Lauren cut in, noticing the ruthless thrust of Zachary's jaw. "There's no need to threaten each other—this isn't doing anyone any good. Especially not the children."

"The kids are fine," Doug said defiantly. "They've adjusted well."

"I don't believe it," she returned.

"Oh, Lauren, don't be so goddamned egocentric. Sure, the kids missed you the first couple of weeks, but after that they were fine. Hell, you know how kids are. They bounce back."

"What did you tell them—about why you took them away?"

"Just the truth, Lauren," Doug said cockily.

"Which was?"

"That I wanted them with me and you wouldn't let me have custody." He managed a smile. "How's that for being straightforward?"

Lauren felt her knees weaken. "Oh, God, Doug, you didn't put them in the middle—make them think that they were the reason we couldn't get along."

Doug shifted his gaze to the distant horizon. "They think you're dead," he whispered after a slight pause.

"What!" Lauren gasped. "Oh, Doug, no. . . ." Instantly, Zachary put his arm around her shoulders. "No . . . God, how could you?"

Zachary's arm tightened.

"You son of a bitch!" he muttered, his dark eyes blazing.

Doug was scared. The cool attorney from Portland wasn't easily fooled. "It's the only way I could handle them," he said hastily. "They were pretty upset and, well it seemed like the only logical thing to do."

"Logical?" Lauren repeated, nearly screaming. "Letting them think that I was dead? That's sick, not logical. For God's sake, Doug."

Doug ignored her despair and continued talking. Fast. "So you see, you just can't show up here—prove me wrong." Though the temperature was only a little above freezing, Doug had begun to sweat; perspiration beaded on his forehead. "It took a little while, but Alicia and Ryan have adjusted. They consider Becky their mother."

"Becky?" Lauren nearly stumbled backward. Zachary's arm caught her and pulled her to him. "You had no right—"

"I had every right. They're my kids, dammit! I got tired of picking them up every other weekend or having to ask your permission just to take them out to McDonald's." He threw a hand up in the air dramatically. "They're all the family I had left . . . until I met Becky."

"Who is?" Zachary demanded.

"The woman I live with. She loves the kids and they adore her. She's all the mother they need!"

Lauren felt as if she were withering deep inside. "No!"

"It's over and done, Lauren. If you take the kids back with you now, you'll only screw them up. They're happy now, here with Becky and me. Don't blow it by showing up and putting them through hell."

"You did that, Doug. A year ago. I won't leave until they come with me," she said, fighting the tears in her eyes as her hands balled into fists of frustration.

Doug shook his head. "Then you're not thinking about the children, Lauren, you're only interested in your own selfish motives. As always. Any mother who would risk upsetting her children is no mother at all."

"What about a father who steals them?" she demanded. "And after that hides the kids and tells them that their mother is dead?" She let out a long, disbelieving breath. "You're more of a bastard than I would ever have guessed," she hissed.

"Why don't you and your . . . 'attorney'—isn't that what you called him?—just leave?" Doug's insolent gaze encompassed both Lauren and Zachary, silently assessing their relationship as more intimate than that of mere client and attorney. The affection they shared for each other might just come in handy. "You're not wanted here."

"I'm not leaving until I see Alicia and Ryan!"

"You're wasting your time. They're not coming home tonight."

"Go get them."

"Not on your life, Lauren, and don't even think about going to the school. Alicia won't be there tomorrow." He started to reach for the door.

"What're you going to do, Doug?" Lauren asked as she sprang from Zachary's embrace and grabbed her ex-husband by the arm. He couldn't deny her the chance to see her children again. She wouldn't let him. "Are you going to run away again?"

Doug poised his hand over the doorknob, and when he faced her, his gray eyes had grown cold. Lauren released his arm.

"I'll do whatever it takes to keep the kids here, with me and Becky." With that, he slammed the screen door and disappeared into the house.

"No!!" Lauren screamed after him, beating on the door with her fists. "Doug . . . please!"

She felt Zachary's hands on her arms but wouldn't stop her pounding. "Lauren, come on, he's not going to let you in."

"But I have to see them," she cried, tears running from her eyes. *"I have to!"*

Zachary cast a worried glance at the door. "It won't do any good. He was too cool and calm. I think he told you the truth when he said that the kids aren't coming home tonight."

"Then where are they? And why aren't they with him? God, Zachary, we came all this way. . . . Oh, please . . . we have to find them. . . ." He gathered her close and held her until she quieted.

"We're not finished," he promised, holding her close as they walked back to the car. "Not by a long shot."

* * *

LAUREN SPENT A restless night in the room she shared with Zachary at The River's Edge, an inn on the outskirts of the city. Their room was attractively decorated in knotty pine, crisp Priscilla curtains and antique furniture, and it had a breathtaking view of the silvery Snake River; but Lauren barely noticed. When she wasn't pacing restlessly on the polished pine floor, she was staring out the bay window, letting her gaze rest blankly on the distant horizon and replaying the terrible argument with Doug over and over again in her tortured mind.

Though Zachary's strong arms had held her tightly throughout the long night, she'd been torn apart by nightmares of Alicia and Ryan being swept away from her by a fierce, unyielding storm. In desperation she'd clung to Zachary and tried to sleep with her head resting on his chest, her arms and legs entwined with his, listening to the steady beat of his heart.

After attempting to eat a light breakfast of fruit and toast in the dining room at The River's Edge, Lauren braced herself for the ordeal to follow. Zachary drove to Our Lady of Promise, the Catholic school located just outside Twin Falls.

Snow had begun to fall from the gray skies and collect on the sloping roof of the school. Zachary parked the car in the school lot, which offered a view of the front entrance to the school. Lauren watched as a small, ungainly parade of cars and trucks deposited students on the front steps of the school. Yellow slickers, brightly colored raincoats with matching umbrellas, hooded ski jackets and boots covered most of the uniforms as well as the faces of the noisy children as they climbed the short flight of brick stairs to the school.

"Did you see Alicia?" Zachary asked once the final bell had sounded and a few trailing students had scurried through the double doors and into the building.

"No." Lauren shook her head, unable to say anything else.

"Neither did I." He let out a frustrated sigh and placed the car keys in his pocket. "There's a chance that Doug made good his threat and Alicia isn't in school today."

"A very good chance, I'd say," Lauren replied listlessly.

"Right. So, let's go talk to your friendly priest."

FATHER MCDOUGAL WAS sitting at his desk when the office secretary announced Lauren and Zachary.

The priest looked up from the notes scattered on his desk and smiled as he extended his hand. His complexion was ruddy, his smile sincere. "You're Alicia's mother?" he asked, nodding his head before Lauren had a chance to reply. "Yes, I can see the resemblance."

"Then you know that I'm dying to see her," Lauren said.

The priest frowned slightly and fidgeted with his pen. "You haven't seen her yet?"

Lauren shook her head and glanced at Zachary before answering. "We tried to, just last night. The children weren't with Doug and he wouldn't tell me where they were. He . . . well, he told me not to bother coming to the school because it would be a waste of my time. Alicia wouldn't be here."

The priest's blue eyes grew troubled and his busy gray eyebrows drew together. "Miss Swanson?" he called, and the tall secretary reappeared. "Are the attendance reports in?"

"Not yet—lots of absenteeism because of the flu, you know," the lanky woman explained.

"What about Sister Angela's first grade class?"

"No."

Father McDougal frowned, took off the wire-rimmed glasses perched on the end of his nose and wiped a hand over his eyes. "Thank you," he said, dismissing the secretary before he looked at Lauren. "Can you prove that you're Alicia's mother?" he asked. "I have to protect the students in the school, and even though I can see a resemblance to Alicia, I'd like something a little more tangible before I let you see her. The way things are these days, one can never be too careful."

Lauren had been anticipating Father McDougal's request. She withdrew an envelope from her purse that contained copies of Alicia's birth certificate, the court papers awarding Lauren Regis custody of her two children and several photographs of Lauren and Doug with their two children. As the priest was examining the documents, Lauren took out her wallet and handed him her driver's license.

"I am Lauren Regis," she said as Father McDougal nodded to himself.

"May I keep these?" he asked, indicating the documents he had just perused.

"Please."

"Good." He offered Lauren an encouraging smile. "Why don't we walk on down to the first grade and see for ourselves if that daughter of yours is here?"

Zachary held Lauren's arm as they walked down the long corridor. She told herself to remain calm, that Doug had probably done what he'd said and kept Alicia out of school for the day. Lauren was so preoccupied that she barely noticed the displays of Thanksgiving artwork tacked to bulletin boards in the hallway.

Father McDougal paused at a door near the front entrance of the school. "This is Sister Angela's class. If you'll just wait here a minute, I'll go in, speak with Sister Angela and bring Alicia back. That way we can avoid any kind of emotional scene that might embarrass Alicia in front of her classmates."

Lauren leaned against the wall and waited. Father McDougal didn't take long. "Alicia didn't come to school today," he said when he returned, closing the classroom door softly behind him and looking at her compassionately.

Lauren nodded disconsolately. "It's not much of a surprise. Doug will do anything to keep her from me."

"Perhaps she'll be in later."

"I doubt it. Doug was pretty adamant," Lauren said with a trembling smile.

Zachary clenched his fists angrily and couldn't restrain a soft oath, which the priest politely ignored. Brian McDougal had heard far worse in his thirty-odd years as the administrator of several parochial schools.

"If there's anything I can do . . ." Father McDougal offered.

"There is, Father," Zachary replied, seizing the opportunity. "If you have any contact with the child, if Alicia returns to school, or you talk to Doug, please call me." Zachary wrote the name and the room number of The River's Edge on one of his business cards. "We'll be in Twin Falls a few more days, and after that you can contact me in Portland."

Father McDougal took the card from Zachary's outstretched hand. "I'll do my best," he promised. Zachary took Lauren's elbow and propelled her out of the building, urging her toward the rental car parked near the school.

"Where are we going?" Lauren asked when he maneuvered the car out of the school parking lot and headed back into town. The thought of facing the small room at the inn was unbearable. *So near and yet so far.* When would she ever see Alicia and Ryan again? "We're going to check on your dear ex-husband," Zachary responded grimly.

"Why?"

"I want a few more answers, that's why. He doesn't seem to appreciate the gravity of the situation, and I think I'll lean on him a little."

"Lean on him?"

"Threaten him with a custody battle that would leave him naked."

"You tried that yesterday," she said, staring at the snow clinging to the parked cars and pine trees near the road.

"Yeah, but now he's had some time to think it over and sweat. . . . Maybe he'll realize that the gamble isn't worth the price he'll have to pay."

The small tract home seemed deserted. Lauren knew instantly that Doug had taken off with the kids again, and her heart sank.

"He's gone," she whispered when she'd looked at the darkened windows and rapped on the locked door. "He took the kids and left—just like before." She had to hike her coat around her neck to protect her from the wind.

"Maybe."

"Doesn't that concern you?" she asked.

"Not yet," Zachary replied cryptically as he walked around and looked through the windows. "I think he'll be back," he said, a gleam of satisfaction in his eyes as he rubbed his hands together and blew on his fingers.

"How can you be so sure?"

"I can't, but the furniture's still in the house, and I could see clothes in a couple of the closets. No, I don't think your ex has skipped town at all. My guess is that he's just waiting until we leave; then, maybe, he'll make some permanent plans for moving."

"Then I've blown the whole thing by coming here," she said miserably. "Just as you predicted."

"Not necessarily." Something in his tone caught her interest, and she looked at him. His eyes were dark but knowing, as if he were a bold and patient predator, certain of his prey.

"What are you up to, counselor?"

Zachary's smile widened. "You should know me well enough to guess that I wouldn't put all my eggs in one basket."

"What does that mean?"

"That I had my private investigator from Boise come here, to Twin Falls, with express instructions to watch Doug and the kids. If Doug left, I'll bet my man is on his tail."

Lauren managed a small, relieved smile. "That doesn't get the kids back."

"Yet."

"Maybe ever."

Zachary placed a finger under her chin. "But it makes sure we don't lose them again."

"Thank God," Lauren murmured.

Zachary glanced at the threatening sky. Snow was beginning to fall in large, crystalline flakes. "Come on, let's go back to the inn, see if there are any messages, and then I'll buy you a cup of coffee . . . or whatever else you might want," he offered, winking suggestively.

"That sounds like a proposition."

"Maybe."

Lauren's lips opened invitingly as Zachary kissed her deeply, wrapping his arms around her and warming the chill in her heart. Lauren snuggled against him and tried to ignore the fact that her fingers were numb. If only she had a portion of Zachary's strength and confidence. "You seem to think of everything," she said.

"Not everything." He grinned. "But I try, and I'll keep trying until we end up with Alicia and Ryan."

THAT NIGHT, AFTER spending a long day waiting for a call from the private investigator, a call that never came through, Zachary and Lauren returned to Doug's small house and were surprised to see a light in the window.

"So our boy's returned," Zachary said with a note of satisfaction. "Let's go see if he's reconsidered."

Lauren placed her hand on the sleeve of his jacket. "Please, Zachary, *if* the children are inside, I want to avoid as much of a scene as I can."

His dark eyes searched her worried face. "I would never do or say anything that might alienate your children from either you or me, Lauren. Someday we're all going to be a family," he promised, kissing her gently on the lips. "Count on it."

"I am," she replied.

"Good, then buck up. This isn't going to be easy."

Zachary strode up the snow-covered path and rapped soundly on the front door. Within seconds a porch lamp made false daylight out of the darkness, illuminating the small screened-in area that offered little protection against the frigid air. By the time the door was opened, Lauren was at Zachary's side, staring at the young woman inside the house through the still locked screen door.

"Yes?" the raven-haired woman asked, eyeing Lauren and Zachary suspiciously.

"I'm looking for Douglas Regis," Zachary said.

"He's not here right now," was the evasive reply.

"When will he be back?"

"Who are you?" the woman demanded.

Lauren stepped closer to the closed screen door. "I'm Doug's ex-wife, Lauren Regis. I've come for my children."

The woman paled and leaned against the door. "I'm sorry, lady, whoever you are, but Doug's wife is dead." Clear blue eyes scanned Lauren's face.

Zachary intervened. "Are you Becky McGrath?"

The woman nodded, eyeing Zachary with distrust and something akin to fear.

"My name is Winters. Zachary Winters. I'm Lauren's attorney and we're prepared to go to court if we have to."

"To take the kids away?"

"To return them to their mother."

"Oh, Lord," Becky mumbled, her chin trembling.

"Look, Becky, I saw Doug yesterday," Lauren told her. "He said the children think I'm dead, but I assumed that you knew the truth."

Becky began to close the door. "I think you'd better go away, both of you."

"I just want to see my children," Lauren cried. "Touch them, see how they've grown. Look!" She reached into her purse and withdrew her wallet, flipping it open to a small picture of the family before she and Doug were divorced. "I'm Lauren Regis, and those children you've been taking care of belong to me!"

"I'm going to call the police if you don't leave," Becky said, her voice trembling.

"Good!" Lauren retorted. "Let's see how Doug talks his way out of this one."

Becky hesitated a moment and then finally unlocked the screen door, allowing Lauren and Zachary to enter. "Doug will probably shoot me for this," she said as she closed the door behind Zachary and turned to face her uninvited guests. “Please sit down.”

“Are the children here?” Lauren inquired, sitting on the edge of a slightly faded recliner near the door.

“No . . . they’re with Doug. He . . . he said that you’d come here and that you’d probably insist you were Alicia and Ryan’s mother,” the young woman admitted sadly.

“I *am* their mother.”

“Doug said that you’d be convincing.”

“That’s because I’ve got the truth on my side. I have proof with me, documents of the court order giving me custody of the children as well as their birth certificates.”

“I’d like to see them.”

“We left them at the school. With Father McDougal. You can call him if you like.”

“Thank you. I will.” Becky disappeared into the kitchen and through the archway separating the two rooms. Soon small pieces of Becky’s side of the conversation could be heard.

As Lauren sat tensely on the edge of her chair, her eyes searched the small house where her children lived. The rooms were small but tidy, in direct contrast to the sorry condition of the exterior of the home. Though the furniture was worn, it was clean and enhanced by the needlework that adorned the rough plaster walls. A colorful afghan was folded neatly over the back of the couch, and a hand-embroidered cloth covered a round table near the picture window. Toys were stacked neatly in a basket near the hallway that led to the back of the house. Barbie dolls and action figures were tossed together with stuffed animals, balls and toy trucks.

Lauren walked over to the basket and pulled out a worn teddy bear that had been Alicia’s favorite when the little girl had been a baby. New button eyes had been sewn onto the favorite stuffed animal. Clearly, Becky McGrath loved Alicia and Ryan. Try as she might, Lauren couldn't fight the tears building behind her eyes.

She was still kneeling at the toy basket, clutching the ratty old teddy, when she heard Becky's returning footsteps. The young woman was carrying a tray of filled coffee cups and trying to force a courageous smile to her pinched features.

"I talked to Father McDougal," she said, her voice barely above a whisper.

"And?"

"And he confirmed your story. Here, please, have a cup of coffee." Becky's hands were shaking as she handed a mug to Zachary.

Lauren returned to the couch and accepted a cup of strong, black coffee.

"I didn't want to believe Father McDougal," Becky continued, running her fingers through her fine black hair. "I . . . well, I love the kids a lot. I've always thought of them as my own."

"I understand," Lauren said sympathetically. Becky's wounds were not unlike her own.

"But Lauren is their natural mother," Zachary pointed out.

"I . . . I know." Becky took a long breath, then sipped her coffee as she sat in a rocker near the bookcase. "Yesterday, when I got home, I knew something was wrong. Doug, he was . . . out of his mind with worry. He said some strangers had come claiming rights to the children, though it wasn't possible, as his wife had died over a year ago. He didn't know what was going on, but insisted that he had to hide the kids, keep Alicia out of school, to see that they, the kids, were safe from danger."

Lauren's throat tightened at the irony of it all. The safest place for her children was with her, where she could protect them. "Where did he take them?"

"I don't know." Tears were running down Becky's face, and she wiped them away with the hem of her sleeve. "I couldn't even guess. He wanted me to come with him, but I couldn't get away from work, and the whole thing . . . it didn't seem right. I thought he was kidding . . . or that the situation wasn't as crazy as he'd said." She stared into her cup and swallowed with difficulty. "I'd like to help you," she said, "but I don't know how."

"Do you think he'll return?"

Becky stiffened slightly. "I don't know. I think so. Most of his stuff is still here. God, I hope he comes back. He's . . . he's been good to me, and to the kids," she added hastily.

"That's hard for me to believe," Lauren said, remembering the bitter, painful scenes during her marriage.

"He loves those kids with all his heart," the woman declared. "He'd never do anything to hurt them."

"Except steal them from me and then lie and tell them that I was dead," Lauren cried.

"He's a good man," Becky insisted, sounding as if she were trying to convince herself. "Last year when Ryan caught a cold that developed into bronchitis, Doug could barely go to work, he was so worried. He took Ryan to the hospital himself, just to make sure that the kid wasn't suffering from pneumonia. Then, for the next three weeks, while Ryan was recovering, Doug held him every night, reading him stories, doing puzzles, anything Ryan wanted to do. I tell you, Doug was worried sick that he might lose him. I . . . I guess that sounds a little selfish to you," Becky added, seeing the look of genuine alarm on Lauren's face.

"I should have been with my child," Lauren murmured, fresh tears stinging her eyes.

Becky was wringing her hands in her lap, her eyes reddened from crying. "I don't know what to do." She shook her head. "There's nothing I can do but talk to Doug—see if he's willing to straighten out this mess between the two of you."

"And if he isn't?"

Becky's eyes widened and she shrugged.

"Then we'll go to court," Zachary announced. "One way or another, I'll see that Alicia and Ryan are back in Portland where they belong. *With their mother!*"

A small cry broke from Becky's throat. "I—I'll try to talk to him," she faltered, her hands moving nervously through her hair. "But I don't know if it'll do any good."

"It had better, Miss McGrath," Zachary responded grimly, determination blazing in his eyes. "If not, I promise you, I'll see Douglas Regis in court, and I'll make sure that he never sets eyes on his kids again!"

"You wouldn't!" Becky cried.

"Don't bet on it." Zachary set his empty cup on the table. "I'm not trying to punish you, Becky, I'm just trying to make Doug see that he's got to let Lauren have the kids, as the courts decided several years ago. And I won't rest until that's accomplished."

Chapter Twelve

LAUREN'S DAYS SEEMED to run together in a haze of job interviews and anxious telephone calls to Father McDougal, Sister Angela and Zachary's private investigator, wherever the man happened to be at the time. It had been over two weeks since Zachary and Lauren had returned to Portland, and though Lauren had tried desperately to get on with her life, her thoughts continued to drift back to Twin Falls and Alicia and Ryan. From her telephone calls to Father McDougal, as well as from information provided by the private investigator, Lauren knew that her children were back in Twin Falls with Doug and were as well as could be expected.

For two days after the discussion with Becky McGrath, Lauren and Zachary had waited in Twin Falls, hoping that Doug would return with the children. He hadn't, and Becky had refused to speak with Lauren or Zachary again. Zachary had left his business card with the worried young woman, and then he'd insisted that both he and Lauren should return to Portland.

During the day, while Zachary was at the office, Lauren busied herself with projects around the house and employment interviews. She had several callbacks and was hoping for a job with a bank located in the heart of downtown Portland, only a few blocks away from Old Town and Zachary's office in the Elliott Building.

Her nights had been spent in passionate embrace with Zachary, and each day she loved him more than she'd ever thought possible. He was strong but kind, stubborn but open-minded. She thought she would be able to live with him forever.

"Marry me," he'd whispered two nights earlier, after a particularly erotic lovemaking session. His body was still glistening with sweat, and the fires of passion lurked in his incredible brown eyes.

"I will."

"Tomorrow," he'd insisted, his warm fingers touching the nape of her neck and causing shivers of anticipation to ripple deliciously down her spine.

She'd smiled to herself and cuddled closer to him, letting the soft hairs of his chest press against her cheek. "I can't, not yet." Even his words of love couldn't melt the ice surrounding her heart. She was still numb with the grief of finding her children, only to lose them again without even a chance to see or talk to Alicia or Ryan.

"Why not tomorrow?" Zachary had persisted, lazily stroking the sensitive skin over her collarbone and staring into the brilliant green depths of her eyes.

Her fingers had played in the soft hair matting his chest. "Don't you think it would be better if we waited until the children are home and have adjusted to the change in their lives?" she'd murmured softly.

"You're hedging."

She'd laughed softly. Nothing was further from the truth. Marrying Zachary was what she wanted more than anything in the world—except, of course, finding her children. "And you're pushing," she'd replied teasingly.

Her wavy auburn hair was fanned out over the pillow

beside him, and Zachary had twined his fingers in the long, fiery strands. "I love you, lady," he'd declared, his voice husky with emotion, and she'd believed him.

Now, she wasn't so sure. In fact, as Lauren stood in Zachary's office, where he sat behind his battered oak desk, she felt as if he'd literally knocked the breath from her body. She'd meant to surprise him, to take him to lunch and tell him her good news—she'd just been hired as a trust administrator for a bank not five blocks south of the Elliott Building. But she forgot everything with the weight of his announcement.

"What—what did you say?" she stammered, still unable to believe what she thought she'd just heard. Her hands gripped the strap of her purse so tightly that the soft leather dug into her palms.

"I said it was all a bluff." Zachary removed his reading glasses and massaged the bridge of his nose. Suddenly he looked older than his thirty-five years. Angrily, as if in self-condemnation, he jerked at the strangling knot of his tie.

"The court battle for the kids? It was a bluff?" Lauren asked incredulously. "Wait a minute, Zachary, I don't know if I understand, or if I want to. Didn't you tell me not two days ago that Doug's attorney in Twin Falls advised him to return Alicia and Ryan to me? What happened?"

Since Lauren and Zachary had returned to Portland from Twin Falls, things had been progressing nicely in her struggle to regain custody of her children, or so Zachary had claimed. Until now, when all of her trust in him had just shattered as easily as fine crystal against stone.

"Doug refused to heed his lawyer's advice. He's going to fight you, Lauren."

She slumped into a nearby leather chair. "Well, I

didn't really expect him to roll over and play dead," she said, holding on to her faltering courage. "If it's a fight he wants, then he's got it."

Zachary tapped his fingers on his desk, and his dark eyes impaled hers. "I don't think so."

"You were the one who threatened him in the first place," she pointed out. "Now you're telling me it's all a bluff?"

"You don't want to drag this through the courts."

"The hell I don't!" she cried, glaring at him. "What's this all about?"

"Your kids."

"The kids that I don't have," she reminded him.

"I don't think you want to put them through the trauma and scandal of a custody suit. Think about what it will do to them."

"What?"

"You saw Doug's house, met Becky. When Doug told you that the children were happy, did you believe him?"

"I . . . I don't know. No, I guess I didn't."

"But you called Sister Angela at the school. What did she report on Alicia?"

Lauren looked away from Zachary's intense stare, the pain in his eyes, and gazed instead through the window at the cars moving slowly across the Broadway Bridge.

"What did Sister Angela say, Lauren?" Zachary repeated.

Lauren glanced back at him and sighed. "That Alicia was a good student, a little shy, but . . ."

"Happy and well adjusted, right?" His brown eyes dared her to deny what the sister had reported. "That's the bottom line, Lauren," he said, more gently, "that the kids are healthy, well adjusted and happy."

"But they don't even know that I'm alive." Her voice cracked.

"Then we'll have to convince Doug to tell them, force him to see that joint custody is the only answer *without* a court battle." He stood and raked his fingers through his hair in frustration. "Look, Lauren, the last thing you want to do is screw up the kids or make them resent you. This has to be handled delicately."

"But you promised," she said unsteadily, her hands opening in a supplicating gesture. "You threatened Doug unmercifully. Now you're going to back down?"

"Those threats weren't idle. We could take him to court, but it would only hurt everyone involved—Alicia, Ryan, Becky, you and me."

Her eyes narrowed with sudden understanding. "That's what this is all about," she said. "It has nothing to do with the kids or their well-being."

"Of course it does."

"No, Zachary. It's what you just said, about you and me an how it will affect our relationship. I think that now that we're talking about marriage and a future together, you finally realized that you don't want to raise another man's kids." He seemed to pale and she plunged on desperately, praying he would stop her, deny her words. "You're still wounded, Zachary, because of the fact that Rosemary was pregnant with another man's child. You can't bear the thought of being around children that aren't yours."

"That's ridiculous!"

"Is it?" She felt the sting of tears but refused to break down in front of him.

"You know I'd do anything to get Alicia and Ryan back to you!"

"Short of the one thing that will guarantee it." She fought the urge to scream at him, to pound his chest with her fists. "You're my attorney; I hired you to find the kids, and you have. Now I'm requesting that you file the necessary papers to take Doug to court."

She noticed a muscle working in his jaw, read the agony in his eyes.

"I can't do it, Lauren."

"Can't?"

"All right then, I won't."

"Why?"

"Because I don't want to tear those kids apart by putting them on the stand. I don't want them to have to see their mother and father go at each other's throats. I don't want to be a part of anything that might make them hate you, Lauren."

"Hate me?" She looked at him incredulously and thought she saw his eyes grow damp.

"Lauren, think! Just think!" His hands clenched in exasperation. "In all probability, Alicia barely remembers you. Doug told her you were dead, and she's worked her way through her grief over the loss of her mother. And Ryan's too young even to remember anything about you!"

"No—"

"You *have* to work this out with Doug," Zachary insisted. "That's the only way to protect the children."

"But he won't—"

"He will! We'll make him!"

"How?" she asked, tears beginning to well in her eyes. Zachary was giving up! The one man she had trusted with her life, her love, her soul and he was giving up! Didn't he understand? This was the man she loved with all of her heart, yet he didn't seem to know just how important the children were to her. She couldn't even think about starting a life with him without Alicia and Ryan.

"It'll take time," Zachary was saying, "but I think we can work with his lawyer and Becky."

"I don't have time, Zachary! Don't you know me well enough to know that I'm dying a little each day that I'm apart from them? Haven't you noticed that these last two weeks have been a torture for me? Dear Lord, if I could, I'd drive to Twin Falls tonight and steal those kids back!"

"And what would that accomplish?"

Tears spilled from her eyes. "I'd have my babies with me again—" Her voice broke on a sob.

"And they'd be more confused, frustrated and guilt-ridden than before. You have to be patient."

"I have been, Zachary. It's been fifteen months. *Fifteen lonely, dammed near unbearable months!* In less than four weeks it will be Christmas. I can't bear the thought of the holidays without my children. I won't have it. I just . . . can't. How can you stand there and ask me to be patient?"

Zachary watched as the woman he had grown to love slowly dissolved in tears before his eyes. "Even if we petitioned the court today, the kids wouldn't be home by Christmas."

Lauren lifted her chin defiantly. "And then you wouldn't have to deal with another man's responsibility. Right?"

"How can you even ask me that?" he cried with a look that cut right through her.

"Because that's the way it is, counselor." With all the courage she could muster, she stood before him and fought against the arguments in her mind, the arguments that told her to trust him. "I think, under the circumstances, that it would be best if we didn't see each other for a while."

Zachary tensed, and his face grew rigid, a mask

devoid of expression. "Think about what you're doing, Lauren. You're throwing away everything we've shared in the past as well as what we could have in the future." She started to back away, but his hands captured her arms in a punishing grip. His face was only inches from hers, and the discipline over his features fell away. Fresh anger twisted his expression cruelly. His near-black eyes drilled into hers, searching for the darkest reaches of her soul. "This argument is just a handy excuse to get out of a relationship you never really wanted in the first place, isn't it?"

"Maybe it was never meant to be."

"That's ducking the real issue, Lauren; a cop-out. People do things because they want to, not because fate deals them bad cards. It's not fate, or kismet or the luck of the draw that brought you here two months ago. You're in charge of your own life, and either you want me or you don't. It's a simple matter of choice."

"Oh, I want you all right," she said bitterly. "But I want the man I knew two months ago—the recluse in the untidy office who agreed to help *me* because he believed in my cause; the man who took my case because he was the best Portland had to offer; the one attorney in town who would be ruthless enough to do *anything* to find Alicia and Ryan and return them to me."

She looked around the clean office. "This man you've become . . ." She shook her head and refused to see the compassion in his eyes. All she could think about was his crisp business suit, the new staff of secretaries in the outer reception area, the tidy room that was dust-free. She'd lost the man she'd met only two months earlier.

"I'm still the same man, Lauren," he said, pulling her to him and holding her close. "The only difference is that I fell in love with you—"

"Don't—please, Zachary." Firmly, she pulled out of his embrace. "There may be a time for us," she whispered. "But it's not now . . . not ever, until I get the kids back." She backed toward the door, and when her hand found the cold metal of the knob, she said, "I think it would be best if I got in touch with another attorney, someone who isn't personally involved."

"Like Tyrone Robbins?" he shot back, his wounded pride taking hold of his tongue.

She felt as if he'd slapped her face. "At least Tyrone didn't play with my emotions," she said, jerking the door open and racing out of the office, past the three secretaries who barely looked up from their word processors, past Amanda Nelson's desk in the outer office, through the doors and nearly into Joshua Tate, returning from lunch. Lauren didn't stop but headed for the elevators, hoping that she could erase Zachary Winters from her life as quickly as possible.

WHEN JOSHUA TATE entered Zachary's office thirty minutes later, he found his partner standing at the window staring at the stark winter's day. Zachary's tie was loosened and hung around his neck like a noose. In one hand was a stiff shot of bourbon; the half-full bottle sat in the middle of the desk. Just like before.

Joshua swore under his breath. "What happened?" he asked as he settled into one of the chairs near Zack's desk.

Zachary didn't bother to turn around, but his eyes narrowed a bit as he studied the murky waters of the Willamette.

"Trouble in paradise?" Josh pressed.

"What's that supposed to mean?"

"That I nearly ran into Lauren Regis as she stormed out of here."

"Hmmph." Zachary took a long swallow of the bourbon, then drained his glass.

Joshua played with the tip of his mustache. "I thought you might like to know that Northwestern Bank settled for two hundred thousand. Just got the call today. I bet that set badly in old George West's craw."

Zachary leaned against the windowsill and studied the younger man. "Quite a coup for you."

Joshua looked puzzled. "I suppose so."

"But you can't find the satisfaction you thought you'd feel?"

"That's a good way to describe it, I guess. Maybe if we'd gone to trial . . ."

"Patrick Evans would have eaten you alive."

Joshua let out a bitter laugh. "Such confidence in your partner. It warms the cockles of my heart."

"What heart?" Zachary tossed out bitterly, and noticed the wounded look in his young partner's eyes. The kid still admired him, despite all the troubles they'd been through together. Zachary sighed and looked into his glass. "I've never lied to you, Josh. I don't want to start now. Settling was a good move." He frowned into his empty glass and reached for the bottle, but Josh's hand stopped him.

"Come on, Zack, I'll buy you a drink . . . a real drink."

Zachary was about to refuse, but Joshua beat him to the punch. "Come on, we owe it to ourselves. At least I do. It's not often we get to knock someone with a reputation like Pat Evans to his knees."

"I don't think you did. George West just panicked."

"Nonetheless, we should celebrate. Really tie one on."

Zachary regarded the eager young man before him. He would have been proud to call Joshua Tate his son.

Oh, sure, Josh still had a few rough edges, and the kid was a cocky son of a bitch, but with a few more years under his belt and a couple of defeats in the courtroom, as well as the bedroom, the kid would come out on top. And you couldn't ask for more than that. Even if Joshua Tate didn't have Zachary's blood in his veins, Zachary still considered the young man like a son, or at least a younger brother. They were bound together and had managed to make the most of it.

Lauren's furious accusations still burned in Zachary's mind, but he knew that she was wrong. He wasn't the kind of man who needed a legacy of sons to carry on his name. Hell, he'd adopt a kid without a second thought. All he really wanted in life was a family with one woman, and that woman now wanted no part of him.

"A drink? Why the hell not?" Zachary asked suddenly to Joshua's surprise. "As long as you're buying."

"Wouldn't have it any other way."

Zachary took off his tie and grabbed his jacket. "Let's go." As the two men passed by Amanda's desk, Zachary called over his shoulder, "Cancel everything this afternoon, Miss Nelson. Mr. Tate and I will be out for the rest of the day."

"But—" Amanda's voice fell on deaf ears as the two men strode out the glass doors of the suite of offices on the eighth floor of the Elliott Building.

NEARLY A WEEK had passed since she'd seen Zachary, and Lauren couldn't get him out of her mind. She'd called several attorneys, met with them and found she couldn't ask a stranger to help her fight the custody battle for her children.

Time was running out. Her new job started right after

the holidays on the second of January, and after that she wouldn't be able to spend much time with an attorney.

She stared at the gray December sky and wondered why she couldn't shake the feeling of doom that had been with her ever since rushing out of Zachary's office last week. He'd called twice, left messages on the recorder, but Lauren hadn't bothered to return them. She needed time alone to think about her future. It looked so bleak without Zachary or the children.

After spending nearly an hour with a Portland lawyer who was more interested in eyeing the clock than listening to her story, Lauren felt hopelessly defeated. She'd missed Zachary's presence in her house, and she dreaded the thought of returning to the empty cottage alone. Too many memories haunted her there. Memories of Zachary with paint splattered over his shirt while attempting to refinish her cabinets in the kitchen; of Zachary studying his notes and trying to think of ways to locate Alicia and Ryan; of Zachary sleeping in her bed, holding her close, making the most beautiful love in the world. And all these memories caught and held in her mind, mixed with the all-consuming loneliness she felt for her children.

Yesterday had been the worst day of her life. The Christmas package she'd mailed to Alicia and Ryan had been returned unopened with a quick note in Doug's familiar scrawl: "Don't try to contact them again. D." The message was simple but infuriating, and it had driven her to the clock-watching attorney's office.

Frustrated and feeling that justice was truly blind, Lauren walked along the sea wall of the park, located on the west bank of the Willamette River. A cool breeze pushed her hair away from her face, and a fine mist settled on her skin. While studying the gray water and watching the Hawthorne Bridge as it opened to let a barge travel upstream, Lauren felt another person's presence beside her.

When she looked up, her eyes clashed with Zachary's enigmatic gaze, and her heart fluttered at the sight of him. He was wearing the same running shorts and gray sweatshirt that he'd worn on the first day she'd barged into his office only two months earlier. Tall and broad-shouldered, with his damp sable-colored hair falling over his eyes, his complexion slightly reddened from exertion and the winter wind, he was as attractive as ever. Lauren felt a lump in her throat at the sight of him. Would she never stop loving this man?

"Lauren," he said, but the smile that touched his lips faded immediately. "I tried to get hold of you this morning."

"I was out . . . business downtown."

She didn't elaborate, but the tightening of his mouth indicated that he understood she was seeing another attorney. It didn't matter. What he had to say was far more important.

"Becky McGrath called this morning," he said, wiping the sweat from his brow.

Lauren's heart nearly stopped beating. Something had happened to one of the children!

"Doug's been in a serious accident in the lumber mill where he worked."

"Oh, no. Is he . . ."

"Becky didn't know exactly what the prognosis was, but she was worried sick. She thinks that he might die and thought you should know about it."

"Oh, God," Lauren whispered. "The children. What about the children?"

"They don't know how serious the accident was. Becky's managed to keep that from them, but she's pretty shook up herself. From what I understand, Doug's already been in the hospital for three days."

"I've got to go to them. They need me," Lauren cried, starting to turn away.

"I'm coming with you," he said softly as he reached for her arm. "I think *you* might need *me*."

She looked up at him, her eyes glistening with tears. "More than you could guess," she whispered, and felt his arms slowly wrap around her. "More than you could possibly guess." The wind ruffled her hair as she held him, clinging desperately to the man she loved. If the last year without the children had been hard, this last week without Zachary had been worse.

"I've always loved you, Lauren. No matter what you might think, I'll always love you *and* your children." The warmth of his breath caressed her hair, and she had to blink rapidly to fight the tears of relief in her eyes.

"I've been a fool," she whispered.

"No, lady, what you've been is a concerned parent. Come on, I'll take you home," he said. "I've made plane reservations, and we leave Portland in less than three hours."

"But wait a minute. You were out here jogging. You couldn't have expected to find me."

"I thought I'd give you about another thirty minutes and then I'd camp out on your door. If you didn't show up in time, I'd change the plane reservations until to-morrow, but I was certain that we'd be going to Twin Falls—together."

"How did you know?" she asked softly.

"Because, lady, I wouldn't have it any other way.'

DOUG'S HOUSE WAS nearly snowbound as Lauren and Zachary climbed the steps to the front porch.

Zachary rapped loudly on the door, and Lauren's heart beat crazily in anticipation. She could hear the sounds of children within the small home and she swallowed back the fear that Alicia and Ryan would reject her.

Becky opened the door. She was older-looking than she had been just a few weeks earlier. "I'm glad you're here," she said without bothering to greet Lauren or Zachary. "Come in, come in."

Lauren stepped into the room, and the two children, who had been playing loudly on the floor of the living room, looked up at the strangers. Tears filled Lauren's eyes as Alicia dropped the doll she'd been holding and studied her mother carefully.

"Mommy?" she asked, her sober blue eyes rounding in recognition. "Daddy said you were dead."

"I told you that was all a big mistake," Becky interjected as a shy smile tugged at the corners of Alicia's mouth.

Lauren bent down on one knee and opened her arms as wide as possible. After only a moment's hesitation, Alicia ran into her mother's arms and hugged her fiercely. "I'm glad you're not dead," she whispered against Lauren's hair.

"Oh, me, too, baby," Lauren said, unable to hide her sobs of happiness. "I've missed you so much. You're such a big girl now and . . ." She held Alicia back and grinned. "You even lost a tooth."

"Two!" Alicia pronounced proudly. "And the top ones are wiggly. See?" She moved the upper baby teeth with a smile of satisfaction.

Lauren hugged her daughter and looked up to Ryan, who was watching her intently.

"Who you?" he demanded firmly.

"I'm Mommy," Lauren said, her voice shaking.

Ryan shook his blond curls and scooted over to

Becky. "Mommy," he pronounced, holding up his chubby arms to Becky. The young woman picked him up and cleared her throat.

"No honey," she said with difficulty. "I'm not your Mommy. Alicia is with your real Mommy."

"No!" Ryan's face pinched together in confusion, and tears gathered in his eyes. "You Mommy," he said brokenly, his arms encircling Becky's neck and holding on for dear life.

"I'm . . . your stepmother," Becky said for want of a better name as she tried to placate the confused child. "You can call me—"

"Mommy," Lauren interjected though her heart was breaking. "He's called you that as long as he can remember. . . . Let's not worry about relationships, not yet." Her worried eyes held Becky's grateful stare in an instant of understanding.

Becky closed her eyes and clung to Ryan. In a few minutes, when the curly-headed boy felt more at ease, Becky placed him back on the floor and Ryan absorbed himself with his toys, only occasionally glancing worriedly at the couch, where Lauren held Alicia.

Zachary stood near the door, getting more than one questioning look from each child. He tried to remain quiet, allowing Lauren a little privacy while he watched the tender reunion. Never would he have suspected that the reuniting of Lauren with her children would touch such a sensitive part of his soul. . . .

"Why doesn't Ryan remember you?" Alicia asked, refusing to let go of Lauren.

"He's too young."

"And dumb!"

"No, honey, I think it's just a little too much for him. Now, tell me, how's Daddy?"

"He got hurt at work. Mom—Becky's real sad about it. So am I."

"Me, too," Lauren said honestly. The last thing she wanted was any more trouble for Doug. The pain she'd suffered at his hands could be forgiven, if not forgotten.

"Maybe your mother and her friend," Becky indicated Zachary, "would like some of those cookies you baked."

"Oh, yeah!" Alicia exclaimed.

"Would you like to serve them?"

"Sure!" Alicia hopped off Lauren's lap and headed for the kitchen.

Ryan was right behind her. "Me, too."

Alicia looked peeved but allowed her younger brother to help. When the children were out of earshot, Becky turned anxious eyes on Zachary and Lauren.

"How is Doug, really?" Lauren asked.

Becky let out a weary sigh and cast a furtive glance over her shoulder, in the direction of the kitchen. "Not good," she admitted. "His accident was very serious. A sharp, heavy piece of machinery broke off and struck Doug in the face. He was unconscious for over twenty-four hours, and for two days the doctors didn't think he would pull through."

"And now?"

"The worst is over, thank the Lord," Becky said, "but the doctors think he'll be blind . . ."

Lauren gasped. "Permanently?"

Becky shrugged. "They're not certain, but the optic nerve was damaged. . . . It doesn't look good."

Lauren shook her head in disbelief. "Is there anything I can do?"

Becky nodded and braced herself. "Yes. Doug's been down, and you can understand why. Anyway, he's afraid that you'll try to take the children away from him—take him to court, see that he never has a chance to be with them again. All he wants right now is partial custody, like before."

Lauren's voice nearly failed her. "And how will I know that he won't take them from me again?"

"For God's sake, the man is blind!" Becky whispered hoarsely before managing to calm herself. "He can't very well take them from you now. And . . . well, you've got my word on it. I . . . I know how much the children mean to you as well as to Doug, and I hope that you can see your way clear to help him!"

"I'll think about it," Lauren said as Alicia walked into the room proudly carrying a tray of chocolate chip cookies.

"I baked them myself," she said.

"I helped," Ryan added.

After Alicia had passed out the cookies, Becky rose. "I'm going to the hospital to visit your dad. You two stay here with your mom and Mr. Winters."

"No!" Ryan cried firmly, running over to Becky and lifting his arms to her.

"It's all right," Alicia said. "It's Mommy."

"No!" Ryan said, and began to cry. Lauren picked him up as Becky walked out the door, but Ryan would have none of it. He held his little hands toward the door and called "Mommy" over and over again, nearly breaking Lauren's heart. Only after two hours did her young son allow Lauren to read to him, and then he watched the door like a hawk, waiting for Becky's return.

THE NEXT MORNING, Lauren went to visit Doug. Zachary was with her, but he stayed in the waiting room while Lauren walked down the stark, polished floor of the corridor to Doug's private room.

"Are you awake?" she asked the bandaged figure lying rigidly on the hospital bed. The room was small, airless and filled with the odors of dying carnations and antiseptic.

"Lauren?" Doug shifted and turned toward her. The entire upper half of his face was covered with gauze, and IV tubes trailed out of both arms.

Lauren closed her eyes against the pitiful sight. This man was the father of her children, the man with whom she'd shared a large, if painful, part of her life. "I'm here."

Doug smiled slightly. "I'm glad. There's something I've been meaning to say to you."

"I'm listening." She took a seat on the edge of a plastic chair near the bed.

"Oh, Lauren, if you could only know how sorry I am for everything I've done."

"Doug, you don't have to—"

"Yes, I do, dammit. All I've done is mess up your life. First when we were married . . . I really never wanted another woman but you . . . you were so smart, always had the right answers. I guess . . . because I was such a failure, I resented you. It made me feel bigger somehow to sleep with other women."

"I don't think we should go into this right now." All the pain in her marriage came vividly to mind. She didn't want to remember the hate and resentment she'd felt. It had been over long ago.

"Yes. *Now.* While I've got the courage. Look, I've been seeing . . . Bad choice of words." He grew silent for a moment and then continued. "I've talked with a psychiatrist. Already had three sessions. Once before the accident and then twice here, in the hospital. Anyway,

I've decided that I've been an A-one, first-class bastard to you, the kids, even Becky. And I want to straighten it all out."

"You returned my Christmas gift to the kids."

Doug sighed and shifted uncomfortably on the bed. "That package was the reason I went to a shrink in the first place. It bothered me. A lot. I felt incredibly guilty. And I want to start again, with you and the kids. I think I can deal with partial custody now."

"Oh, Doug, I don't know—"

"Look, Lauren, this is something I've got to do. I knew it before the accident, and then, when I found out how mortal I was, everything became clear. Maybe it's because I almost died, or maybe it's because I'll never be able to see again. But I've got to get it together. I'm thirty-two years old and I've run out of excuses for my life. I suddenly realized that I couldn't have everything my way, and instead of being mad about it or blaming someone else . . ."

"Like me?"

"Yeah, like you." His fingers moved nervously over the metal rails of the bed. "I decided that I had to be responsible, for what happened to you, our marriage and the children. I'm letting you take the kids back to Portland for good. The only thing I ask is that you let them come and visit me for a month in the summer each year. And when I'm in Portland, I'd like to see them, if you'll let me."

He waited, a pathetic figure draped in white. Lauren couldn't deny him such a small request.

"How will I know that you won't steal them from me again?"

"Oh, God, Lauren, I know this must be hard for you, but I'm asking you to trust me. One more time. I'm petrified of the thought that my children may grow up and not even know me. Becky and I are planning to get married, once I master being blind, and we've been talking about children of our own."

"That's . . . that's wonderful, Doug. I'm happy for you."

"And what about you?"

"I hope that once the kids are settled, I'll be getting married."

"To that Winters guy?"

"Yes."

Doug frowned. "I hope it works for you."

"It will."

She rose to leave and Doug heard the rustle of her skirt. "Lauren?"

"Yes."

"How're the kids, really? Becky . . . well, she tried to hide things from me, make me think things were better than they are, but I need to know the truth. From you."

"I think the children will be fine. Alicia's worried about you, but she's glad that I'm back. Becky explained that I was never dead." Doug winced at the words. "She said that you'd made a horrible mistake. Of course someday Alicia will be old enough to understand the truth." Doug scowled but didn't say anything, so Lauren continued, "I don't know how Alicia will feel about moving back to Portland, but I think she'll adjust."

"And Ryan?"

"He's more difficult. At first he flat-out rejected me. And it hurt, Doug. It hurt like hell. But now he'll let me hold him. He still thinks Becky is his mother."

"My fault," Doug said, self-condemnation evident in his voice.

"What was it you said—something about kids bouncing back?" Lauren asked. "Ryan will be fine."

"I love the kids, Lauren," he said.

"I know," she replied carefully. "And I won't take them away from you forever. I'll let you see them during the summers—or on holidays. . . ."

He sniffed, and his voice was husky. "Thank you. You don't know how much this means to me, after what I did to you; you don't owe me anything."

"Let's just try to do what's best for our children. Goodbye, Doug. And good luck."

"Thanks."

Lauren walked out of the room and hurried back to the waiting room, where the man she loved was pacing impatiently.

"Well?" Zachary asked, his dark eyes searching her face as he folded her into his arms.

"It's going to be all right. Everything is going to be all right!" She hugged him fiercely and promised herself that this time she would never let go.

FOR THE FIRST time in three years, Portland was blessed with a white Christmas. The evergreen trees in the park were laden with piles of pristine white snow, and throughout the neighborhood children made snowmen and sledded on the steeper streets. Laughter and Christmas carols rang through the night.

The lights of the Christmas tree in Lauren's house winked brightly and reflected off the windowpanes. Four stockings hung over the mantel, just below the portrait of Alicia and Ryan. A yule log burned merrily, and the packages under the tree were as brightly colored as the glittering decorations on the sturdy boughs of the Douglas fir standing near Lauren's favorite rocker.

Lauren was pulling the turkey out of the oven when

Zachary came up behind her and slipped his arms around her waist.

"What're you doing?" she asked with a laugh.

"Couldn't resist the view," he replied, nuzzling her ear and holding a ribboned piece of mistletoe over her head. "You're a tantalizing woman, Mrs. Winters."

"I'll take that as a compliment, thank you." She turned and faced him, her arms wrapping lovingly around her husband's neck. Snowflakes still clung to his dark hair. Her own feelings of love were reflected in his eyes, and the smoldering flames of passion sparked as he placed his lips over hers.

"You should," he murmured against her neck once the kiss had ended.

"Should what?"

"Take it as a compliment."

"Consider it done. Oh, by the way, a package arrived from Twin Falls today," Lauren said, watching Zachary's reaction. "Gifts for the kids from Doug and Becky."

"Did you put it under the tree?"

"Of course."

"And how's Doug?"

"Becky wrote a note on the card. He's as well as can be expected, she said. And he got home last week."

"His eyes?"

Lauren shook her head thoughtfully. "It still doesn't sound good."

"This is all going to work out, you know."

"Is that a promise?"

He smiled rakishly. "One you can count on, lady."

She laughed and returned the turkey to the oven. "So where are the kids? Didn't you make some wild promise to take them sledding?"

"Not on Christmas Eve. They're still in the backyard. I think I've had all the fun I can take for one night. Your daughter is deadly with a snowball." His wet sweater attested to his defeat in battle.

"Shame on you for letting a little seven-year-old whip you!"

"Mommy . . ." Ryan's pitiful wail interrupted the kisses Zachary was placing on Lauren's neck.

"Just a minute," she called back, her heart swelling with pride. In just two weeks, both Ryan and Alicia had adjusted beautifully, and though they were still a little wary of Zachary, they were beginning to accept him. Lauren had never been happier. The small, quiet wedding had been perfect, with her two small children in attendance. And the look of love in Zachary's eyes continued to amaze her.

"'Licia put snow down my back," Ryan cried, his eyes filled with tears of frustration.

"You'll just have to learn to defend yourself, young man," Lauren advised, lifting his wet hat and placing a kiss on his forehead.

"You help me, Mom. You put a snowball down her sweatshirt!"

"Not on your life."

Once changed into dry clothes, Ryan disappeared through the back door. Lauren eyed her son lovingly, and her eyes filled with tears as she looked around the small house that had been her home for over three years.

"It's going to be hard to move," she said wistfully.

"But we'll have more room at my place. Room for a dog for Ryan," Zachary replied, thinking of the fluffy half-breed cocker pup that he'd picked up just the day before. Right now the puppy was hidden away in the garage with a large red ribbon that would be placed around his neck early the next morning. Even Lauren didn't know about his surprise for Ryan or the new bicycle he'd bought for Alicia. "I might even spring for a horse for Alicia."

Lauren smiled and wrapped her arms around Zachary's neck. "You'll spoil them rotten, you know."

"Just like I intend to spoil their mother."

"Do I detect a note of bribery in your voice?"

"Maybe. . . . I think it's about time Alicia and Ryan had a younger brother or sister to pick on."

"Two kids aren't enough?" she asked with a laugh.

"Sure. For a start. But I was thinking more along the lines of five or six."

"That's because you're not the one who'd have to go through pregnancy. Not in a million years."

His hands spanned her waist possessively. "Okay, I'll settle for just one more. How about it? Ryan's nearly four already. It's time he had a brother."

"Or a sister?"

"I'm not picky."

The thought of carrying another child, Zachary's child, pleased her. "Whatever you say, counselor. Whatever you say."

A smile spread over Zachary's handsome face. "The sooner, the better. Merry Christmas, darling." He pulled her close and gently kissed her forehead. "Thank you for forcing your way into my life."

"My pleasure," she said with a smile, and tipped her chin, gladly accepting the warmth of his kiss.